SOPHOMORE YEAR
SPRING
A STUPID BOY STORY

G. YOUNGER

Sophomore Year – Spring

A Stupid Boy Story

First edition. November 8, 2018

ISBN-13: 9781731046369

Author: Greg Younger

Chief Editors: BlackIrish and Bud Ugly

Editors: Askepot, Zom, grisbuff and Anon

Proofreaders: Malibu and Jim7

Table of Contents:

More Books by G. Younger

Notes from Author

Interlude

Sandy Range

My brother will be the death of me, I swear.

Devin and I have had to become close because of the loss of our father. Devin's had to be both a big brother and father to me. I sometimes wonder about the father part, since he is only six years older than I was. To keep me out of foster care, he had to agree to take responsibility for me.

At the time, he was overwhelmed. We had the ranch and then the sporting goods business. Add to that a little sister who was grieving. He had to go from hunting or riding horses as his day's focus to running a business. It was a good thing Dad had made sure Devin knew what was going on because he had troubles at the beginning with Dad's company president.

Bill Hutchens felt it would be best to sell off parts of the company. It turned out those were the most profitable parts. Mr. Hutchens made a deal with our biggest competitor with the understanding that he would reap a huge windfall and job after the deal. If Devin hadn't been aware of what was going on in the business, Mr. Hutchens might have gotten away with it.

Mr. Hutchens was let go and Devin had to take over the company. The first thing he did was bring in his best friend Lou and put him in charge of research and development. I think it was just so the two of them could play with all the equipment they made.

Dad had focused on what he thought our core business was. It was all related to outdoor activities you could do locally, like hunting, fishing, camping, and hiking. Devin wanted to expand to include all sporting activities. Dad had been ultraconservative, which meant he had large cash reserves on hand. Devin used most of that money to expand the business.

1

One of the things he wanted to do was start to advertise our new lines of products. One was a youth line. Since Devin considered me a kid—thank you very much—he asked me who I thought would be a good pick to be the face of the line.

Devin had signed a contract with Ford Models and they'd sent over possible candidates. While they were all good-looking, none of them felt right. That was when I saw this cute young guy on TV. It turned out to be David Dawson.

◊◊◊

I first met David in Chicago. Ford was having an event and invited Devin and our board of directors. I was Devin's plus-one. I wanted to meet our potential new youth-line face, David.

I'd never met someone that suddenly gave me butterflies in my stomach. To the point I couldn't put a coherent sentence together. I made a complete fool out of myself when I met him. Then he asked me to dance. I was ready to throw my panties at him and offer to be the mother of his children. I had it bad.

Then my big brother decided to be a big brother. A combination of David being a perfect gentleman and my brother's antics saved me from doing something stupendously crazy. I know it never would have worked, but the good news was that this meeting was the beginning of a friendship.

David also was exactly what we wanted for the face of Range Sports. He was young, athletic, fun-loving, and looked perfectly at home in our gear. Our marketing department loved him. For that matter, Devin loved him.

David and Devin became friends because of their love of sporting equipment. Yes, David was younger than Devin was, but that didn't seem to matter. It also helped that David has a brain. He helped us in London when the models Ford sent didn't seem to work out. He set us up with Adrienne's new modeling agency, and thanks to him she did some modeling for us. David was also Lou's crash test dummy.

They'd built a jet water board that had the two of them giggling like schoolgirls. Devin suggested that David try it out since he was the face of their target market. Lou proposed that they film the whole thing and use it on the website to drive sales. What they got was national TV exposure when David broke it. I've never seen Devin look so cowardly as he did after talking to David's mother. I wish I'd been a fly on the wall for that conversation.

◊◊◊

At Christmas, Devin disappointed me when he went after David's date, Nancy. I don't know what made my brother think he could just take David's girlfriend. It was especially awkward with David's family there. We'd had such a nice Christmas, too. It was the first time since my dad passed that we'd had a house full of people for the holidays. What really pissed me off was that they seemed to accept us into their family, and then my horndog brother goes and ruins it.

I knew something was up by the way David acted. He was normally a happy, outgoing guy, but I could tell something was bothering him. I finally cornered him and he admitted that Devin was hitting on Nancy. David had brought her to see if there was anything between them. I could see the attraction, but she wasn't right for him. She was too old, to begin with. There were some other problems, but it wasn't my place to point them out. David was smart enough to figure it out.

What was sad was that if Devin had been patient, he might have had a shot at Nancy. If I were being honest, Devin and Nancy would have made a good couple. I personally felt he needed someone who could keep him on his toes. His last serious girlfriend had been a gold digger and would have cheated on him. I didn't get that vibe from Nancy at all. Quite frankly, I couldn't imagine David would be attracted to someone who was a gold digger.

I'd taken David to confront Devin about it, with the hope that they could work things out. I could tell that David would grit his teeth and finish the shoot, but I was more worried that their personal relationship would be damaged beyond repair if I didn't get them talking. Devin probably made the biggest mistake of his life. He tried to mollify David with lines like "She must have interpreted my intentions wrong." They both knew that was a lie. David did a masterful job of covering his true feelings, but I knew his friendship with Devin was probably over.

When I talked to Devin about it, he just brushed me off. He knew by then that Nancy had zero interest in him, and for good reason. I think he figured David was too young to understand the betrayal Devin's actions represented. He'd basically admitted to David that he didn't respect him and didn't care if he knew it. I couldn't see David reacting very well to that.

Then Devin pissed me off. He ordered me to make sure David and I remained friends. I would have done that anyway, but when Devin ordered it, I felt dirty. I felt as if Devin didn't respect me either.

That feeling of being used actually helped me. It made me realize that I needed to stop deferring to my brother. Technically, we both owned an equal amount of company shares. While the covenants of the corporation wouldn't allow me to vote at a board meeting until I was 21, it didn't prevent me from giving my proxy to someone else. If Devin didn't wake up, he might find he no longer controlled the company. I admit that would be hard for me to do to my brother, but that didn't mean I wouldn't use it as leverage to have him take me seriously.

G. Younger

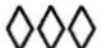

Chapter 1 – Tinsel Town

Thursday January 1

When we got up, Nancy and I walked to the main house so I could say goodbye to everyone. We all had breakfast together and they told me their plans for the day. Devin was taking them all horseback riding in the morning. In the afternoon, the guys would go and watch football bowl games. The girls planned to go to another movie.

I caught a ride with Sandy to the airport, after Nancy gave me a kiss or three. It was a bittersweet ending to the vacation. I liked her a lot, but we were in different places in our lives. We each needed to move on and find someone who was a better fit. Sandy wanted her own goodbye. I was still a little confused as to how exactly this was going to work out. I felt us getting together was a mistake, but you couldn't take it back. I knew we'd always be friends.

When I got to the airport, I went through security and had forty-five minutes to kill, so I called Tami.

"Happy New Year," I greeted her.

"Happy New Year to you, too. Are you headed to the airport?" she asked.

"Already here. My flight hasn't started boarding yet, so I thought I'd call."

"I'm glad you did. I wanted to talk to you about this summer."

"I heard you want to get a place in Chicago."

"Yeah, it's a new program they have set up for promising high school students. Teddy Wesleyan pulled some strings and got me a slot. I have to tell them in the next couple of weeks if I'm doing it. Are you okay with spending the summer in Chicago?"

"I might not be there a lot, but I'd be okay with it. I think you need to convince my mom, though. She's not on board. I'd bet if you let the moms find us a place to live, she might be more inclined to let us do it," I suggested.

"David, I want you to really think about this. We haven't been getting along recently, and then as soon as I get back we'd be sharing an apartment. Are you sure about this?"

"It's not like we'd be getting a one-bedroom and shacking up. I'm sure if we weren't getting along, we could find plenty to do in Chicago to keep us distracted. Plus, like I said, I'll be on the road. I have football camps and other commitments. I would hope, though, that we could work on rebuilding what we once had. It would be sad if we couldn't make it work."

"I miss you, too," she said.

I heard them call my flight. I said goodbye and made my way to the boarding area. I was flying coach, but the good news was the flight was almost empty. The later flights were fully booked. I was happy to be getting out of town before the holiday rush hit. As I was boarded, I got a text from Kendal that said she'd meet me at the hotel. She would get in a couple of hours later than I would.

I boarded and found I had the row to myself. I put on my headphones and played some music. After takeoff, I fell asleep until I felt us start to come down. I guess I needed a nap. I got off the plane and walked to baggage claim. After I collected everything, I went to find a cab. It was sure different from Park City. When I left it was 26°, and the current temperature in LA was 68°. I almost felt like lying out in the sun and working on my tan.

We had rooms at the Beverly Hilton. They'd booked me into a Wilshire Tower Executive Suite, and the room had a splendid view of the city. The flashing light on the hotel phone indicated that I had several messages.

The first message was from Kendal to let me know her flight was delayed. The second voicemail was from Janice Utley, our producer. She gave me the time and place where we were all meeting tomorrow. They made it convenient, as we were meeting in the hotel in one of the corporate meeting rooms. There was a call from Jessup Fields, the director. He wanted to get together with the four leading actors for dinner tonight. Finally, there was a message from Craig Wild. Craig was playing the lead character and he wanted me to go to a party with him and his 'entourage,' as he called them. I think someone had watched too much HBO.

I called Janice and got her assistant. I confirmed receiving her message. I then sent Kendal a text and put the meeting on our calendar. I called Jessup and got his assistant and confirmed dinner. I was told to meet him in the lobby. When I called Craig, a girl answered. It sounded like a party was going on by the loud conversation and music in the background. I heard the phone clatter on the counter and her yell, "That farm boy is on the phone."

"David!" an overexcited guy answered.

I guess he knew who the 'farm boy' was.

"Craig?" I asked.

"No, this is Kent. Craig is, ah, busy right now. He wanted to know if you could come out and party tonight. We're going to Chubby Feldman's place. He always has the best women, so you have to come," Kent told me.

If he was talking about Charles Feldman, then I was there. He'd made some of the biggest-budget movies in Hollywood over the last ten years.

"Can I bring a friend?" I asked.

"Girl or guy?"

"Girl?"

"Is she cute?" Kent asked.

"Yes, she is."

"Is she over 18?"

"Yes. Why the third degree?" I asked.

"Let's just say Craig doesn't have very good impulse control. It's my job to make sure he isn't exposed to underage women."

8

G. Younger

I had to laugh. I was starting to like Kent. I wasn't so sure I liked Craig, but I shouldn't pass judgment until I met him.

"Let me give you some tips before you go. Hire a driver for tonight. If you happen to have a couple of drinks, the last thing we need is you getting arrested. Don't go cheap and just get a cab, because there'll be paparazzi skulking about. You need to have the image of someone successful.

"Don't get drunk or take any drugs at the party. If you want to do that, come over here and we'll take care of you. Now, if you decide to partake in the bountiful supply of women, wear a condom. If they're party hos, they'll be a lot of fun; but, they're a lot of fun with three or four different guys," Kent warned me.

"So, I should stay away from them?" I asked.

"Hell, no! You only live once, and until you've experienced what they have to offer, don't turn up your nose at it. Why do you think I plan on going?" Kent said, laughing.

"I don't know, Kent. I'm just a poor farm boy coming to the big city. Where I come from, you put a ring on it before you ever do anything like that. My mama would be a might disappointed if I were to lose my innocence my first night in LA," I explained in my best farmer drawl.

"I was afraid you heard that. Sorry for the 'farm boy' comment. Craig is someone who grows on you. He actually has a good heart, when he isn't focused solely on Craig. Plus, the poor innocent farm-boy routine is a bunch of crap. I've seen who you've worked with. If you really were some hayseed, Adrienne wouldn't give you the time of day.

"Now it might be a good angle to try on the party hos since they like breaking in young men. On second thought, we might not see you the rest of the week," Kent joked. "Look, I've been around some and I've seen it all. If you need anything, or have any questions, call me."

9

Kent gave me his cell number. I was thinking I got lucky that I didn't get through to Craig. I wondered what a party ho looked like. I had a pretty good imagination. I wasn't surprised that Mr. Happy had some ideas also.

◊◊◊

I'd been awful for the previous couple of weeks I was on vacation, as far as working out went. I went down and used the hotel gym. I lifted and did my *sixty minutes of hell* routine. Afterward, I took a quick shower and swam laps. The water was nice and warm, but once you got out it was a little chilly.

Lori Winnick found me as I walked through the hotel lobby to get back to my room.

"There's our newest Wildcat," she called out to get my attention.

The University of Kentucky's mascot was a Wildcat. She came up and gave me a hug and a kiss on the cheek.

"Let's say I have strong leanings in that direction."

"Keep me in suspense, why don't you. I think you secretly want to go there."

"It could be, but it's way too soon to say for sure."

"What are you doing right now?" she asked.

"I just finished working out and swimming. I was planning on taking a shower and getting ready to go to dinner with Jessup, Craig, Bree and Elizabeth," I answered.

"Good, I want to talk to you," she said, as she took my arm and led me to the elevators.

I let her into my room and she went to the phone and ordered room service. I went into the bedroom and took my shower. I put on nice slacks and a silk t-shirt. When I came out, I found a room-service cart and Lori drinking wine with a young good-looking guy who looked familiar.

In the background, the Oregon and Florida State game was on the TV. I had received a text from the Florida State coaching staff to watch the game. I was sure it was one of

10

their guys who did stuff like that. I was confident it hadn't come from one of the coaches.

"David, I want you to meet Ben Doman. He'll be playing Roman. I just finished a film with him and thought you two might hit it off," Lori said by way of introduction.

I recognized him from the ads for her upcoming film. He stood up and looked to be a couple of inches shorter than I was. I would guess he was four years older than me. I shook his hand, then went to the fridge and got a big water to rehydrate. I also needed to take my after-workout supplements. Ben worked out to keep his looks and wanted to know what all I took and why. Lori soon joined the discussion. She seemed to know more than I did.

We were sitting back down when I heard a key card opening my door. Kendal came strolling in with her bag behind her.

"Honey, I'm home. Oh, hey there. You're Lori Winnick, and you're Ben Doman," she stammered.

"This is Kendal, my agent, who seems to be moving in with me."

"Oh, uh, they lost my reservation."

"Don't worry about it, you can stay with me," I assured her.

Lori and Ben looked at me like I had lost my mind. I guess I wasn't supposed to be nice to my agent.

"What?" I asked them.

"Excuse us, David. I should've known you'd do the decent thing. You just don't see that here in LA all that often," Lori explained.

I caught Kendal up on what was going on tonight. She went to the bedroom to get unpacked and changed.

"You lucky stiff, I've been trying to get an invite to that party for a month. Just be yourself around Chubby, because he hates a suck-up. If he likes you, you could be set for the next five years," Ben coached me. "Be careful with Craig's friends, especially Chaz. He's a drug dealer and bad news. His other friend is Trip. Trip's mom is a big-time actress, and he knows no boundaries. I think Craig thinks of him as sort of a role model. They compete to see who can be the biggest douche. Be careful, because you're his type, if you know what I mean."

"I think Kent's okay," I offered, trying to ignore the comment that I was a *guy's* type.

"Kent's the brains of the group. Pay attention if he tells you something. He's saved Craig's butt so many times it isn't even funny. I honestly have no idea why he hangs around Craig. He could open shop as a publicist and half of Hollywood would hire him. I know I would," Ben shared.

Kendal came out in a little black dress. I think she was pleased that Ben checked her out. We needed to go, so Ben and Lori went to their rooms.

I was able to watch Florida State implode. Their poor quarterback would be seeing his fumble for years to come. I hoped I never made a gaffe like that in such an important game. I still don't know how he fumbled the ball like he did. I would bet big money he was off to the pros. He had a rough year with all the allegations and bonehead moves. I think he was the poster child for what not to do once you were in the limelight.

◊◊◊

When we got to the lobby, Jessup was waiting for us. Everyone else lived in LA, so they would meet us at the restaurant. I'd ordered a driver for the night, so we all went in the limo. On the ride over, I mentioned I planned to go to Chubby's party. Jessup insisted he would go with us. That was yet another clue that this was a big deal. Kendal was a sport and said she'd go back to the hotel. To be honest, I wasn't comfortable having her go with me to a party like Kent described. I would have worried about her all night.

Jessup surprised us when we pulled up to a pizza place. I guess I should have figured it out when he said we were going to Pizzeria Mozza.

"I dressed for something fancy," Kendal worried.

"You look great. We're in LA, and this is the best pizza place in Southern California. You'll fit right in," Jessup assured her.

We were ushered into a private room. Bree Steno, the girl I met at the Nickelodeon kid's thirteenth birthday party, was there. May Zane's dad was a vice president with Range Sports. I think Sandy Range still owed me for going to May's birthday party. Bree was in the vampire show all the cheerleaders watched, and I'd done my audition for this movie with her. I went up to her and gave her a hug.

"I forgot you were so tall," Bree commented.

"No, you're just vertically challenged."

Bree was probably five-eight, so she took the teasing. She grabbed my arm and guided me to Elizabeth Jenks. I recognized her from the movie's website.

"David, I want you to meet Elizabeth. She and I have taken acting classes together. Watch her, she's been asking about you," Bree said with a twinkle in her eye.

Elizabeth blushed and give Bree a dirty look. She then turned to me and put on a hundred-watt smile.

"Ignore her. Nice to meet you," she said as we shook hands.

Bree and Elizabeth introduced me to everyone. They both had agents and publicists there. I introduced them to Kendal. Jessup looked to be watching us closely and had a little smile on his face. I think he was happy to see us hitting it off. It wasn't hard, since they were both very attractive women and fussing over me. A guy could do worse.

Then Craig Wild showed up with his entourage. Both girls pulled me tighter toward them and had momentary looks of concern on their faces. I put my arms around their waists, which seemed to relax them. The concern was soon gone from their eyes and they had big smiles. Jessup caught it and his smile was gone. They both knew how to hide their true feelings well. Craig came over with his crew; one of his guys was looking the girls over like they were on the menu.

"Bree, Elizabeth," he nodded at them.

I noticed neither one of them offered him a hug or even shook his hand. They seemed to press just a little closer to me.

"And you must be David," Craig said and shook my hand. "I'd like you to meet Kent, Chaz and Trip."

Jessup came up and pulled Craig aside. I smiled at Kent.

"Nice to put a face to the voice," I said.

Kent was a good-looking guy. He looked like what I imagined a surfer dude would: tall, tan, and fit with long, sun-kissed blond hair. We heard voices raised; Kent got a worried look and went over to where Craig and Jessup seemed to be having a disagreement.

"Ladies, want to relax before dinner?" Chaz asked as he held out a joint.

Chaz looked to be close to thirty and was a little overweight, with what looked like a week's growth of a beard and dirty hair. The girls both disengaged from me and walked away. I was a little disappointed they left me with this creep.

"How 'bout you?" he asked.

"Sorry, I don't do drugs," I told him.

He just snorted and ignored me.

"Is this your first movie?" asked Trip.

Trip was, well, pretty. He was maybe five-five and rail thin, with very fine features. He had big brown eyes and eyelashes I knew a few models would have killed to have.

If he had a dress on, I might go for him. I mean, not a guy-on-guy thing. Hell! He smiled at me and made me squirm. I had never experienced another guy showing interest in me. Trip took pity on me and turned down the wattage of his smile. He could tell I wasn't interested.

"Ah, yeah, this is my first film."

Kent came over and pulled Trip and Chaz into the discussion Jessup was having with Craig. They started to get mad, but Kent gave them both a look. Craig slouched and nodded. Both Trip and Chaz left the room. I guess Jessup didn't want Craig's entourage hanging around. Kendal came over, took my arm and guided me to the table.

We were all soon seated, and Jessup got everyone's attention.

"I wanted to welcome you all personally. I need to explain the unfortunate incident you just had to witness. I run a tight ship and will not tolerate troublemakers or drug dealers anywhere near my set. We are all here to do a job, not party."

Craig stiffened, and Kent reached over and grabbed his wrist. It looked like Kent was going to be Craig's babysitter. Jessup saw it too, but didn't seem fazed. Bree and Elizabeth seemed to relax some. I caught both of their eyes and gave them a warm smile. I was happy to see they returned it.

"Tonight, we'll break bread and get to know each other," Jessup said.

The door opened and two servers came in carrying appetizers and carafes of red wine. This was clearly not Monical's. They had roasted squash with sage and brown butter, cauliflower fritters with a spicy mint sauce, plus several different bruschettas. I liked the one with chicken livers.

"Let's start with the youngest member of our cast and work up. Introduce yourself to everyone, David," Jessup said turning to me.

"I'm David Dawson and this will be my first movie. Lori Winnick talked me into trying out for the role of

Roman. I guess they liked me because they switched me to the role of Stryker. I live in a small town in the Midwest. I have one brother who's married and is working on a bunch of kids who I love to death. I play football and baseball. I also do some modeling," I finished up, not really sure what Jessup wanted.

Jessup nodded and then pointed at Bree.

"I'm Bree. I've been doing television for the past three years. This will be my first movie and I'm excited to be a part of this. In fact, I've met all of you before. Craig and I did an episode together," she shared.

"Yeah, your boyfriends on the show killed me," Craig said, getting a smile out of everyone.

"Elizabeth and I have taken several acting classes together. David and I met briefly and I also did a photo op with him. At the time, I think he was dating three ladies, and I tried to steal him away from them."

"None of them caught me, so I'm right here," I teased her.

"I see you. Anyway, I'm from Beverly Hills. My dad's an executive at Universal, so I grew up in the business," Bree said.

"I'm Elizabeth. I came to LA six years ago when I was about David's age. I thought I was the kiss of death to a production for the first few years. It seemed like every pilot I did never got picked up. Then I met Jessup and he gave me a couple of roles in his movies. This will be my fifth in four years. Thank you, Jessup, for believing in me when I needed it."

He just nodded to her.

"I guess I'm the old man," Craig started. "I got started early doing commercials. I was actually a Gerber Baby. My parents helped me get into the business. I don't think there's ever been a time I haven't been acting. When I was about David's age, my parents and I had a big split-up and I was emancipated. I went a little wild. I still like to have

16

fun, but I've made a commitment to Jessup that once the filming starts, I'll be good," he said with a weak smile.

"I look forward to getting to know you all and working with you. Despite the rumors, I'm not really a bad guy. I want to apologize to Jessup and the rest of you about earlier. Kent told me I shouldn't bring my rowdy friends. I need to listen to him more often," he said, turning to Kent and smiling at him.

The servers had returned and proceeded to clear the table. Then they started bringing out pizzas. I wasn't back home, that was for sure. California clearly had a different idea of what pizza should be. I personally liked pepperoni, sausage and mushroom. I didn't see anything even remotely close to that. The one pizza I was surprised I liked was the pineapple and jalapeño combination. The sweet and spicy was different. They even had a breakfast pizza with eggs, fried potatoes and caramelized onions. It was okay, and I would have it again. I loved the white truffle pizza. I'd never had truffles before. I also liked the olive tapenade version. It was basically black olives chopped very fine.

Over dinner, the two girls were teasing me about eating like a teenage boy. I had to remind them that I *was* a teenage boy. Craig was a likable guy and he soon was part of the conversation. I noticed the agents and such just sat back and let us get to know each other. By the end of dinner, Jessup seemed pleased. I knew I was starting to like everyone, which was the purpose of the dinner.

Something I teased them all about was playing characters who were basically supposed to be my age. Jessup explained to me that was how it was normally done with young-looking twenty-somethings playing teens. He pointed out the TV show *Glee* was a good example. A few of those actors were in their late twenties, even. I made a comment about hoping the old folks could keep up.

When we were done, I felt good about working with everyone. I told Craig and Kent we would meet them at the party. I'd sent Kent a text earlier letting him know Jessup was going to be my plus-one. Bree and Elizabeth wanted to go. Craig said he would get them in. He suggested they ride with me. Bree's agent offered to give Kendal a ride back to our hotel.

Kendal surprised me. She decided to be responsible. She pulled me aside and had a talk with me about not getting drunk or touching drugs. I kept a straight face when she asked me if I had condoms. I told her I didn't, just to see what she would do. I was shocked when she pulled three out of her purse and gave them to me. When I thought about it, I liked that Kendal was looking out for me in more than a business way. When I got home I would make a point of telling my mom. I knew it would ease her mind when I was on one of these trips.

◊◊◊

We drove up into the hills of LA and soon found ourselves at the gate of what could only be considered an estate. Our driver pulled us in front of a sprawling home. It was over-the-top. Craig waited for us and helped us get past the security who checked people in at the front door. Chubby was waiting in the foyer to greet us.

"Jessup, so good to see you," Chubby called out. "I see you brought your cast with you."

Jessup made the introductions. I was surprised, Chubby wasn't overweight at all. If anything, he was skinny. I guess it was like where you call a guy 'Tiny' but he was a giant. He seemed to be very personable and took the time to talk to each of us. Then another group of guests arrived.

I walked into what I would think would be every teenage boy's wildest fantasy. It looked like the Playboy

Mansion with hot centerfolds running around. I turned to Kent.

"Are they …?"

He got a huge grin and nodded. This wasn't the Playboy Mansion, but all these girls were willing. Bree gave me a hip-check and I turned to see her and Elizabeth pouting. I guess I gave them both an incredulous look because the guys all started laughing.

Before I could go meet the party hos, Bree and Elizabeth wanted to tour the mansion. Jessup encouraged me to go with them. I thought Sandy and Devin Range's home was big. You could have fit three of those into this monstrosity. I did like some of what I saw. The media room was killer. I almost stopped to watch the Ohio State and Alabama game, but the girls had other ideas.

We went upstairs and toured the master suite. It had to be 2,000 square feet. He had a bed I would guess six people could sleep on comfortably. The walk-in closets were bigger than my bedroom and there were two of them. The bathroom had a tub big enough to almost swim in. I tried to figure out how much money I would have to make to get a setup like this. The scary part was we were talking LA money to buy this spread.

We about died of embarrassment when we stuck our heads into one of the guest bedrooms and Craig was engaged with one of the party hos. I would think common sense would tell you to at least shut the door.

"I noticed you guys don't seem to like Craig," I commented as we continued our tour.

"I don't think that's really true. We've just been around people like him and worry what'll happen when he and his friends get started. Craig was right; he did go through a wild-child phase. I'm not sure he's completely gotten through it yet," Elizabeth explained.

19

"Anyone who'd bring their drug dealer is not someone you want to hang out with," Bree said a little more forcefully.

I had to agree. I would never dream of having my drug dealer follow me around. My mom would have my head. I decided to have a little fun.

"Should we go find an empty room?" I asked.

I got raised eyebrows. I took it as a 'no,' but I wasn't done.

"I've heard the rumors. California girls are supposed to be fun."

"Is he serious?" Elizabeth asked Bree.

"You're the one who told me she was horny and he was cute," Bree said.

Bree went up in my estimation. She picked up on me giving them a hard time. Elizabeth's confused look caused me to chuckle. She looked relieved when Bree joined me in laughing. I did get a vibe that both girls had some interest, though. I would file that information away for later.

◊◊◊

We found Kent talking to Jessup in the living room. When we came back, the girls wanted to get a drink, so Jessup took them to find the bar.

"Did you want to meet the entertainment?" Kent asked me, looking over at the party hos.

"Yes, please," I said, bouncing up and down.

Kent ruffled my hair and took me to meet the women. Kent was now my newest best friend. Everyone got back before Kent and I went to have fun. Elizabeth saw what I was up to.

"You're our ride, so you better not disappear," Elizabeth warned me.

"If you have to go, just have the car take you and send him back," I suggested.

Bree kissed my cheek.

"Go have fun," she told me.

Kent took me over to a group of scantily clad goddesses.

"Ladies," he greeted them. "This is my new friend David. He just arrived in town and is a virgin. Does anyone want to take on the responsibility for training him?"

"That would be me," I said, bouncing up and down again.

"It might take more than one of us. He seems to be eager and looks like a big boy," a stunning blond said as she cupped my package.

I describe her as 'a stunning blond,' but they were *all* stunning blonds except for this one gorgeous black woman. We locked eyes and she reached out and took my hand. I followed her to a guest bedroom with a king-size bed.

This goddess slowly undressed me. She worshiped my body with kisses as she took her time and teased my nipples until they almost hurt. I was so aroused I thought about just ripping my pants off and jumping on her!

She kissed her way down my stomach and stuck her tongue into my navel. I gave a little jump and heard her giggle. She then undid my slacks and let them pool around my knees. Mr. Happy was cupped through my silk boxers. They were pulled down, freeing the captive. He was almost purple and definitely drooling.

I heard her hiss, "Nice!"

The next two minutes were the best in my life. Man, I wish I had lasted longer. This girl could teach a master class. She at first gently licked my member to get it wet and then proceeded to swallow it. She did this thing with her throat where I knew I was a goner. It was lucky that I was backed up to the bed because my knees unlocked after I tried to drown her.

I was still dazed when I felt her put a condom on me, coated it with lube and then straddled my waist. I focused on her magnificent naked body. She was athletic, but had thick nipples on large breasts that were swaying as she guided me into her. She took me in one slow stroke and then clamped down on me, making it feel like I was in a vise. I had never been with a woman who had so much muscle control.

This girl was so talented, I wanted to marry her. I reached up, hefted her heavy breasts and began to enjoy them. Her nipples were huge, and I lifted my head so I could wrap my lips around one of them. That brought a moan from her.

She started to get erratic in her thrusts and suddenly threw her head back. I bit her nipple and she screamed.

"YEEESSS!"

She collapsed onto me, breathing hard. I pulled out of her to her disappointed mews. I rolled her over so I could get out from under her, and then rolled her back and grabbed her waist so she was on her knees. Her bottom was nice and round and I couldn't help nipping it. She gave a little jerk and I grinned as I lined myself up and took her from behind.

I proceeded to work her hard. I soon had her chanting, "YES, YES, YES!" as I pounded her. I was glad I'd spent the hours working out because power sex was an athletic event. I released my inner animal and I was happy to see she could keep up. It was as if we were made to do this primitive dance.

I simply manhandled her and put her in several different positions. I was also strumming her button, causing her to climax over and over again. When I finally came, I had her on her back, almost bent in half with her knees around her ears as I pile-drove her. I jerked out, pulled my condom off and offered her Mr. Happy. She eagerly took my full length into her mouth and I unleashed again.

"AAAhhhh!" I bellowed, reaching nirvana.

When I finally caught my breath, I came back to my surroundings. The girl I had just had sex with was curled up and looked to be falling asleep. I slid off the bed and put my clothes back on. I found Jessup, Bree and Elizabeth, and joined them.

"I need some water," I announced.

Elizabeth was off like a shot, and Jessup and Bree both chuckled.

"I think you have a new fan," Bree told me.

Elizabeth came back with a big bottle of water. I almost drained it in one go. I then caught a whiff of myself. I had a strong smell of sweat and sex on me. I also needed to get up early tomorrow, so I suggested we leave. We saw Kent as we walked out, and he told Jessup he'd get Craig home soon so he'd be ready for work in the morning.

We took the girls home and then went back to the hotel. Jessup was on the same floor I was, and he wished me a good night. I went in and found Kendal asleep on the couch, so I took a shower and put on a pair of boxers. I pulled the covers back on the bed, went into the living room and picked up Kendal. She stirred.

"Uhmm, what're you doing?" she asked, still half asleep.

"Putting you to bed," I said as I laid her down.

"'Kay," she said.

I got into the other side of the bed and went to sleep.

◊◊◊

Friday January 2

I woke up to find Kendal sleeping on me. Not next to me, on me. I have no idea how she managed it without waking me. I must have been sleeping the sleep of the truly satisfied. I gently rolled her off me and got up to relieve myself.

I put on my running clothes and headed out. It was perfect weather for a run, and I found my stride lengthening until I had a nice rhythm. I paid attention to where I was going since I wasn't familiar with the area and didn't need to get lost. On the way back, I found a '50s-style diner and popped in. I asked the server if I was okay and she handed me a towel and pointed to a table. I ordered a large steak and half a dozen scrambled eggs. The cook had seasoned the steak with something peppery, giving it a good flavor. I made a mental note to come back here again.

When I got back, Kendal was dressed and wearing a sheepish smile. I just winked at her, went and showered, and got ready for today. We went down and found they had a full breakfast buffet set up in the conference room: greasy bacon and watery eggs that looked old. I was glad I'd eaten earlier. I grabbed a tea and a glass of cranberry juice.

I found Lori and Ben. We were talking when Elizabeth came up with a big smile on her face.

"Lori, Ben, this is Elizabeth," I said by way of introduction.

"How was the party?" Ben asked.

"It was a lot of fun," Elizabeth said. "David, you had a good time, didn't you?"

The little minx was going to get her bottom paddled.

"Yes, yes I did. I think you would've enjoyed it."

Ben was green with envy, and I think Lori knew what the party was probably like because she raised an eyebrow. I blushed; I didn't want to disappoint her and was embarrassed at what she might be thinking.

Karen, the production assistant, got us all to find our seats. They had it organized so we had little table tents with our names on them. I put my tea next to my place card. I was originally seated next to Craig and Bree. I found I was now sitting between Bree and Elizabeth. I bet I could guess who had changed the seating arrangements. The cast was all seated at the main table. Our assistants sat against the walls. I noticed everyone had a thick script. I'd brought my original one with the notes we made in my acting class in the margins.

"We're going to read straight through the script the first time. Then we'll break the scenes up and we'll give you our notes on the scenes. Sometime this week, each of you will go down to the animation studio and get into one of their suits so they can record how you move. We need to get started, so turn to page one, act one, scene one," Jessup said.

We spent the morning and early afternoon reading through the script. It was obvious some of the cast members hadn't read it before. Craig gave me shit about already knowing most of my lines. I didn't know if what he said was good or bad, but I wanted to be prepared and was glad I was. I felt much more comfortable and could tell my acting class had been a great investment.

After lunch, Jessup grabbed Craig, Bree, Elizabeth and me and took us to another conference room along with our agents/assistants. The four of us had quite a few scenes together, so Jessup wanted us to stand up and walk through them. He saw my marked-up script and took it from me to see the notes.

The other three had their scripts to refer to, but I fell into it like I had in acting class. They'd helped me learn most of my lines. I could at least keep the scene going even if I forgot a line. I was really enjoying this. Craig hadn't worked as hard to get ready and it showed. He constantly took notes, and Kent did the same. Kendal took her cues from Kent and made notes on her copy of the script. Jessup would mark out my notes if he didn't agree with how we'd done a scene. I was surprised when he accepted quite a few of my class's suggestions.

When we were finally done, I was exhausted and starved. We had blown right through dinner. To save time, we all went to one of the restaurants in the hotel. After dinner, Jessup pulled me aside.

"If I didn't know better, I'd have thought you were an old hand at this. Good job today. Where did you get all the notes?" he asked.

"That was from my acting class. They were a big help. Thank you for setting that up."

"Let me give you a tip for the next movie you're in. I'd suggest you just learn the lines. How you stand, what emotions you show and how you say your lines will be up to the director on set. I think that you being in an acting class may have been a little over-the-top. What you really needed was a dialogue coach," he said.

"Sorry, I didn't know."

"David, you didn't do anything wrong. We set all this up and provided you a script with way more information than we normally would. Normally you don't see much other than dialog in a script. All the detail is saved for the storyboard. That's where you'll see the details like camera angles and how far the bad guy is from you. I just wasn't aware they had you doing so much extra.

"We may have overdone it with what we sent, but you've never acted before. My fear is you'll come into a scene with preconceived ideas and we'll waste time changing it. I want you to *live* in the scene, and react to the environment and the other actors as the shot unfolds. You just need to have the words already in your mouth, so that you can say your line in a natural way for your character when the moment arrives.

"I know it seemed like several of the more seasoned actors didn't do very well today. They know how we work, and once you're comfortable learning lines and following direction, you'll be fine coming in and doing what they did. I'm confident Craig will learn his lines and deliver a good performance. After seeing you today, I'm much more at ease with you. You're a smart guy. Do you think you can take what you learned and channel it into what we tell you on set?" he asked.

26

"If I know what you want, I'll do everything I can to deliver."

"Dylan tells me you're ready for your fight scenes as well. That part we wanted you to learn in detail because it's critical you have everything down. I'm sending you to the studio in the morning. Dylan and Tish will be there, and we'll get everyone in the sensor suits and have you run through the routines. We want to make sure it looks good before we film them for real," he explained.

◊◊◊

I was ready to go back to my room and just zone out. Kendal found me and explained I had to go to a club tonight with my other main cast members. We were starting the press thing where we'd be seen around town and get interviewed by shows like *Hollywood Central*.

I changed into clubbing clothes. When I came out, Kendal gave me a nod of approval.

"You want to go with us?" I asked.

"No, I'm hanging out with Lori. She told me it was better if you were seen with either Elizabeth or Bree. She suggested you be seen with Bree, because Elizabeth has her eyes set on you. That way you two can get to know each other and just tell the press you're friends."

"Who will Elizabeth be dating?" I asked.

"Craig, of course," she said, and I cringed. "You need to get over that. This is the land of lies. I think Craig is more interested in Trip, to be honest."

"My gaydar must be broken. I never even got a twinge from it. Trip made me nervous as hell, though," I admitted.

"Yes, he is your type," Kendal said, trying to hide a smirk.

"Keep it up, Chuckles, and I'll be letting you sleep on the couch."

I don't think she believed me.

◊◊◊

It was amazing how easy it was to get into a club when you're with three other actors. You didn't even have to stand in line. What you did have to do was make sure you let the paparazzi and gossip people get their pound of flesh. The club got the publicity from you being there, you got exposure for your career and the movie, and the press got their story for the weekend. All I needed to do was start a fight in the club to make everyone even happier.

What really put me off-kilter was the women in the club. Believe it or not, I saw a cute girl kissing her guy, but when she saw Craig, she pushed her boyfriend away and was all over Craig. These women were hot, too. I was impressed Craig was able to resist some of them. The need for security—private security—was obvious. More than once I had to step in front of an overaggressive guy trying to hit on Elizabeth or Bree. If we did this again, I wanted to make sure we were safe.

We ended up hitting five clubs before I'd had enough. I explained to them that the next ass-hat who spilled their drink on me, or squeezed one of the girls' butt, would get his head handed to him.

They got worried looks because they could tell I was serious.

◊◊◊

Chapter 2 – Leaving LA

Saturday January 3

I woke up to find Kendal lying on me again, but this time she was naked. She hadn't been home when I'd returned, and I had gone to bed. I took one smell of her breath and knew she'd been drinking last night. It dawned on me that she and I would end up sleeping together if I didn't find her a hotel room, and soon. I rolled her off me and was able to see what I had been missing. Was I stupid to pass this up? No. She was my agent and friend. I needed her to be only that. I didn't want sex to change how I felt about her.

I got up and ran again. I ended up in the same diner and ordered the same breakfast. The waitress brought me a clean bar towel and sat down with me. That got my curiosity going. She had the morning's paper and pointed to a photo of me with Bree.

"Is this you?" she asked.

"Yes," I admitted.

She handed me her head shot with her info.

"I hear you're currently working on a movie. Can you give this to their casting director?" she asked hopefully.

I had a funny feeling this wouldn't be the last request of this type I would receive. I would have to decide how I would handle it in the future when someone approached me. I thought the best approach was to just return the photo to her. But then I worried she would do something to my breakfast, so I decided I'd just give it to Kendal. If she threw it away, I could live with that.

"I'm a complete newbie in this business. I'm not sure who I would need to give this to. Would it be okay if I gave it to my agent?" I asked.

She seemed satisfied. When in doubt, just be honest.

◊◊◊

I went to the front desk and found a room for Kendal. After then taking my supplements and a shower, I got dressed and went down to the lobby. Karen Least, the production assistant, had waited for me with Ben and a couple of the other actors. They had one of the hotel's minibuses take us to the studio.

We arrived at the studio and they showed us to a large soundstage. It was set up for them to record our movements via a special suit. The sensor suits were basically black spandex which covered your whole body. The suit had sensors at each joint. When I moved, it recorded where I was. From that they could computer-generate a likeness of me. It was helpful for stunts that were considered too dangerous.

At one point in the movie, my character has a confrontation with Ben's character and some of his buddies. I'm happy I'm not one of Ben's buddies because if there was a sequel, they wouldn't be in it. It took the techs about thirty minutes just to get me in the suit and make sure everything was working right.

I was happy to see Tish and Dylan there to supervise the fight scene. When everyone was suited up, we walked through the fight scene at half speed. Ben was graceful in his movements. My guess would be that he had dance training in his background.

One of the extras wasn't getting his steps down. Basically, a fight scene is an intricate dance. The man having problems must have been six-ten and weighed over 350 pounds. He looked like a giant offensive tackle in the NFL. At one point he was supposed to use this huge ax to try and cleave me in half. Dylan and Tish were working with him while I worked with the other members of the cast to make sure we all knew our steps.

Jessup suddenly showed up.

"Is everybody ready?" he asked.

"No, we're still working with our barbarian. We may need to delay this," Dylan suggested.

"Why don't we just run it and see what we have. David, you can ad-lib some if need be, can't you?" he asked me.

"Yes, sir," I said.

"Jessup, I'm worried about safety here. While these practice blades won't cut anyone, you sure can break some bones. I'm not comfortable moving forward yet," Dylan told the director.

"This is costing us money. I need to get this done now. Do you think you can give it a try?" he asked the big guy.

Of course, he said he could.

We were all soon in place and they started yelling out status.

"Sensors ready?"

"All sensors are a go!"

"Film rolling!"

"Scene one, take one!"

"Action!" Jessup ordered.

I exploded from my imaginary hiding spot and instantly cut two of the actors down. Ben barely escaped and rolled back behind the barbarian. He was supposed to swing his ax around his head and then come straight down where I was. I was supposed to roll to the right and hamstring him, bringing him to his knees.

Instead, our barbarian made a blood-curdling scream and tried to cut me in half. If I hadn't been ready, he would have either broken my arm or ribs. As I rolled, I swung my sword to hamstring him. He had on a special guard so I knew I hadn't hurt him. He didn't act like I'd touched him as he turned and tried to cut me in half again. I dodged a wild series of swings from him and started to back up. He clipped me pretty good on my left shoulder. I was dazed for a moment and then looked up to see him charge me. He had a weird look in his eyes and I had a déjà vu moment: it reminded me of Tommy Cox when he lost control during football practice.

In a split second I realized I was in serious trouble, and Cassidy's training kicked in. I did a front kick to his nuts and spun out of the way as he barreled past me. I put my sword tip down and tripped him. By now Dylan and Tish had realized this was no longer a game. They pushed me out of the way and faced him as he came back to get me. It was all over in the blink of an eye. Dylan had him in a bear hug and Tish slapped his face hard to get his attention.

Ben and Jessup ran up to me.

"Are you alright?" Ben asked.

I pointed to my arm and saw the material was ripped. I was still on such an adrenalin rush I didn't feel it yet. I could tell I would have a hell of a bruise.

"I might want to get some ice on this," I told them.

I was pretty sure I'd been dinged up much worse playing football.

"Can you continue?" Jessup asked.

Ben looked scandalized, but I could tell Jessup needed to get this done now.

The continuity gal and Jessup talked to Ben and me about how to proceed from here. Basically, I was to begin right after the barbarian had crashed past me. While they figured things out, the CGI guys affixed a new sensor on my shoulder. They got me into position and went through their pre-shot callouts. When Jessup called 'action,' Ben and I did our bit. Where the previous fight was brute force as I tried to just survive, this was poetry in motion.

The fight scene was intended to have big sweeping cuts and both of us basically freestyle running through an obstacle course. In the end, I defeated the evil Roman. Cue the music. When they called 'cut,' Ben and I laughed like two kids playing at *Star Wars*.

Today wasn't about perfection, it was about getting our movements recorded so they could play with it and get ideas for better visual fight scenes.

While we did our fight scene, they had quietly gotten my attacker out of the studio. He'd told them I looked like a candy-assed kid who needed toughening up. He thought he was doing me a favor by not holding back. A little warning would have helped.

◊◊◊

My afternoon was spent in makeup and then costume. They shaved my head and painted on different tattoo patterns. When Jessup and Janice were happy with the look, they continued the patterns down my neck and then all over my torso. They took photos of what I was supposed to look like for when they'd do it for the actual shoot. They explained they would use henna tattoos to keep a consistent look. It felt weird not having hair. I sent Lily one of the shots with me stripped to the waist with my full makeup on. Janice had encouraged me to 'leak' a photo and then pull it down in a few days.

I also got permission to send a photo to Adrienne so she could share it with Dakora. They needed some idea of what I would look like so they could pick out what I would wear for their photo shoot.

◊◊◊

The four of us got dressed up and went out to dinner. Craig's publicist made sure we had plenty of press waiting for us. The *Hollywood Central* guy wanted to know what had happened to my hair. I sent him the link of what my character was going to look like. I warned him off camera it would be taken down Monday. Mission accomplished. I was also in Jade's clothes. I sent a text to Tiffany to make sure they taped *Hollywood Central* on Monday. That way Ford could show Jade I wore their clothes in LA.

At dinner, Elizabeth made it clear she wanted to spend the night with me. I was glad I'd gotten Kendal a room.

I admit I was disappointed. The sexual chemistry just didn't seem to click, as far as I was concerned. Unfortunately, she thought differently. The fact that I didn't get off in the first few minutes seemed to be a vast improvement for her. Don't get me wrong, even bad sex is better than dating your right hand. Slot A fit attachment B just fine. Elizabeth just wasn't an active participant. It was like having sex with a blow-up doll.

We tried it three times to make sure. It might have had something to do with her hot body and me being horny, but when all was said and done, I was glad it was over.

◊◊◊

Sunday January 4

I got up and ran again. We were flying back home today. I felt much more confident I could pull this off. I went to my regular joint, if that's what you can call it after only three days. My waitress wasn't there, but I enjoyed my breakfast.

I got back to the room and jumped into the shower. Elizabeth joined me, and I'm embarrassed to say I used her body to get some relief.

Kendal and I caught a ride to the airport. I had upgraded us to first class because I was in no mood to fly coach for such a long flight. It was a good thing I did because the plane was full.

The flight back gave me a chance to think about what I had coming up for the next few weeks. School started tomorrow. I was scheduled to be in Canada a few times over the next two months. There was one stretch where I'd be gone for eight or nine days. I had made the necessary arrangements with the school. They weren't complaining about me being gone so much.

The bad news was that I was probably wouldn't be able to play seven-on-seven football this year. I decided to work on baseball instead, based on my schedule. Moose had arranged for me to use the batting cages over at State. I wanted to get a batting coach to help me prepare. I was going to ask Mike's dad if he'd help me with my pitching.

I took a power nap and felt great when we got to Chicago. Kendal had had her brother drive her to the airport, so I took her home. When I finally got home, it looked like we were getting new neighbors. The house next to us had finally sold. Mom had listed it and she told me the new buyers had kids about my age.

I went inside to find Duke throwing a fit in the laundry room. Mom and Dad had told Angie that I'd take care of Kyle's new dog. I was completely fine with that because I had been begging for a dog for years. Mom had just put him in his crate, so we left him to his theatrics. We needed to get him crate-trained as soon as possible.

Mom made me unpack my clothes in the laundry room, saying she'd do laundry tomorrow. I went up to my apartment to check my email. Lily had it set up so that all my tweets and Facebook stuff went to her. Somehow everyone had figured out my private email address. I had one for public use, which Lily monitored, and one for work for Ford and Adrienne. Kendal monitored the work one for me. The girls forwarded anything they thought I needed to see. I had to keep reminding Lily that pictures of scantily clad girls were okay to forward on to me. Then I had a private address for my friends and family. I found several hundred new emails in my private inbox. I would have to get a new private email address, or this would drive me crazy.

I sent a text to Lily and gave her my login and password to my emails. She would sort through them for me. I really needed to start paying her. I put that on my to-do list—AGAIN!

It felt good to sleep in my own bed.

◊◊◊

Monday January 5

Having a puppy may not have been a great idea. I got up to go run and went down to the laundry room to let Duke out. He was happy to see me as he bounded out of the crate and made enough of a racket to wake Mom and Dad. I was proud of him, as he hadn't peed in his crate. He saved it for as soon as he was free and peed in front of the back door. He squatted to do something worse when I scooped him up and put him outside in the snow. Mom was not happy.

She made me come back in and clean up after 'my' dog. I thought he was Kyle's dog. When I was done, I went outside to run and Duke was nowhere to be found. How could a clumsy 12-week-old puppy up and vanish in under three minutes? Fortunately, he wasn't very stealthy. I heard him yipping at something. He was behind the garage, where the garbage cans were kept. I heard a hiss that sounded like a bobcat. I ran around the corner to witness Duke getting popped in the nose by the biggest cat I think I've ever seen.

I expected to see my pup back off, but he was now determined to take the big kitty on. What followed was chaos. The cat decided this pup wasn't worth playing with and tried to squeeze behind the trash cans. Duke literally seized the moment and latched onto the cat's tail.

Ever have puppy teeth embedded in your hand? It's like having little needles dig into your flesh. Duke played tug-o'-war with the cat's tail and got a reaction! There were soon garbage cans, full of trash, knocked over, as the cat pulled Duke in between the garage and the cans.

I think I finally understood the phrase 'catch a tiger by the tail.' The cat had nowhere to go but over the garbage cans. He tried to leap to get away, but Duke had a death grip and wouldn't let go. He was shaking his head like a crazed windshield wiper.

Like the 'stupid boy' I was, I decided to help save the kitty. The cat latched onto my arm and began to climb its way out of its predicament. Of course, my soon-to-be dead-to-me puppy decided at that moment to let the cat go so he could bark at it. This freed the rabid beast to climb up my arm and latch itself onto my head.

Holy crap!

This damn cat would not let go! I felt it dig its claws into my bald head. I never realized that hair might be a form of protection. I finally ripped the Tasmanian Devil off my head and tried to keep it from reattaching itself to me as it flailed in my hands. Then the bastard decided to take my thumb off. I was in the process of helping Duke end the cat's miserable life when I heard a scream.

Apparently, 'Precious' was the new neighbor's cat. Three blond kids who looked alike and were about my age were watching me extract my thumb from Precious's jaws. I tossed the cat from hell to one of the guys. Duke thought it was loads of fun that we were playing keep-away with his newest chew toy. I scooped him up and he wiggled all over. This was the most fun he'd had had since he'd arrived here.

"Get her off! Get her off!" one of the brothers begged.

The girl had a huge smile on her face as the two brothers got clawed to death by their family pet.

"Want me to go get my gun?" I reasonably offered.

The girl gave me a dirty look, but the brothers seemed to think it over before they finally subdued the cat. They left Duke and me to clean up his second mess of the day. He romped around in the snow while I picked up trash.

I walked into the kitchen as I bled all over myself, carrying a victorious puppy. Mom took pity on me and checked my wounds. The only bad one was my thumb. The beast had punched a hole in the web of skin between my thumb and hand. It stung a lot when Mom doctored it up. Needless to say, I didn't get my run in.

◊◊◊

I pulled up to school and saw the local TV station setting up. This seemed to draw a crowd of onlookers. I got out of my Jeep and grabbed my book bag, and as I made my way to the front door I recognized their entertainment reporter. Jessup had told me they would send out press releases over the weekend and I should expect something. I just didn't expect it first thing in the morning.

Peggy saw me and waved. I went over and I kissed her good morning.

"Are they here for you?" she asked.

"I think so. The director told me they were doing a press release over the weekend."

She checked out my bald head.

"Did you try to shave it yourself?"

"No, the new neighbors have this cat from hell. She scratched me this morning."

She ran her hand over my head and smiled. I just arched an eyebrow and I heard the reporter call my name. Peggy kissed my cheek and I went over to do the interview. It was your typical fluff piece, used as filler on the nightly news. When I was done, I had a bad feeling this was just the beginning.

I walked Peggy to her locker. Our schedules weren't in sync, so I wouldn't see her the rest of the day. She had somehow drawn the short straw and had second lunch. I would have to introduce her to the freshman cheerleaders and Yuri.

"When are you done today?" she asked.

38

quick

"I have *sixty minutes of hell* right after school and then I plan on going to the dojo and working out with Cassidy. Why don't you come over for dinner?" I suggested.

"I'll ask Mom if it's okay. If she says no, it'll be after dinner," she said.

I hurried off to my locker to dump my book bag and coat. I had math first period. The first day of the semester was always such a waste of time. All you did was get your books and a syllabus. I spaced out and didn't really pay attention during my morning classes.

I came out of my daydream for lunch. I was happy to see my friends were all there. Cassidy had saved me a seat between Tracy and Pam. It looked like the new couples were all there. Alan was with Stacy Clute, Wolf with April, Jim with Piper, and Jeff sat next to Cassidy.

Tracy reached under the table and took my hand to hold. I glanced over and saw she had bags under her eyes. I just squeezed her hand and let her hold it. Something was up, but I didn't think we needed to talk about it in front of everyone. I looked up and saw that Gina was looking for a place to eat lunch. I called her over to join us. She looked at Alan and he gave her a smile.

"Tell us about your vacation," Pam said.

"I went to Park City, Utah, to work for Range Sports. My family came with me, and we spent an extra week snowboarding. It was nice to have everyone in the family together. Then I went to LA and started working on my movie."

"I saw you went out with Bree," Piper jumped in.

"Who's Bree?" Alan asked.

Piper explained she was the star of the vampire show that all the girls liked. Alan had no idea who she was, so I pulled out my iPad and showed him her picture from the *Star Academy* website. The rest of lunch was spent talking about the movie.

After lunch was PE. I had signed up for ballroom dancing. I was surprised when most everyone from lunch was in the class. Tracy had come out of the locker room with Pam, and she walked up to me and grabbed my hand again. I'd given her a curious look and saw her start to tear up. I led her over to the edge of the bleachers so we could have some privacy.

"What's wrong, baby?" I asked her.

She just put me into a bear hug and started to cry. I held her and felt her shaking. I had begun to get concerned when Pam came over. She looked as concerned as I felt.

"Take care of her. I'll call her mom," she told me.

Everyone was curious as to what had happened. The PE teacher let me take Tracy to her office so we could have some privacy.

"What's wrong?" I asked again, once she had calmed down.

"I tried to hurt myself over Christmas."

"How come?" I asked.

"I don't know. I just felt it would be better if I did," she confessed. "I need you to be my friend right now. I don't know what I'd do without you," she started, and then began to cry again.

I guess I wasn't surprised when both Tom and Mary showed up. I was surprised when Dr. Hebert walked in. Mary and Dr. Hebert took Tracy and left. Tom sat down with me.

"David, I want to apologize. We didn't want to burden you with Tracy's problems while you were working," Tom started. "She had an incident at the start of Christmas break. She's been having some issues, but we thought she was ready to come to school. I guess she wasn't."

"She told me she tried to hurt herself."

He had a haunted look in his eyes. It was clear this had been weighing on him.

"Yes, she took sleeping pills," he said, and then just kind of stared off into space.

"Are you okay?" I finally asked.

"No, not really. I need to ask you a favor. You seem to be one of the few people she really listens to. Can you try and be her friend?"

I liked Tracy, but I was worried I'd get in over my head. It seemed her problems were getting worse, and I didn't know if I wanted to get in any deeper with her. This was too much responsibility for someone who was supposed to be just her friend. Then I saw the look in Tom's eye. It looked like he was grasping for straws here. At that moment, I didn't know how to tell him no.

"Of course. Tracy and I will always be friends," I assured him.

"Thank you. Not many guys would put up with everything she's put you through. I know I haven't helped with that, either. Just ... thank you," Tom said.

"Is this related to what happened to her?"

I was referring to what Bill Rogers had put her through. It caused her to have to see a therapist since the fall of last year.

"Tracy's been depressed. We'd hoped she was getting better. Her self-esteem was better, she was more engaged, and she was having more good days than bad," Tom said as he looked at the floor.

"What happened? I never had a clue she was having problems this serious," I said, concerned.

"None of us did. She hid it well. Dr. Hebert said she admitted to having insomnia and some other symptoms," Tom said without looking at me.

"Dr. Hebert said there's never usually a single reason someone might try and hurt themselves," Tom continued. "The hard part is we may never know what really happened. Part of the problem with depression is it also affects concentration; it makes it hard to learn. We got her

41

grades and they've suffered. Who knows what the tipping point was, but she took the pills. She was lucky Mary went to check on her. She spent the majority of the holiday getting better. The last few days she seemed to start to come out of it.

"Dr. Hebert encouraged us to let her come back to school. She seemed eager to see you, and the doctor felt that being around her friends would be positive," Tom said, and then seemed to gather himself. "I need to go check on her. I'll call you if we need you and I promise to keep you in the loop."

I wondered if Tracy's mental illness would ever get any better. It scared me to think she might hurt herself, or worse. I was a little pissed no one had told me sooner. I would have come home to be with my friend if I'd known how serious it was. Tom left me to my thoughts.

◊◊◊

My last period was study hall. I grabbed Jeff and we went to my house so I could let Duke out. He did his business but didn't want to go back into his crate. I wasn't going to leave him loose; there was no telling what he would get into. Instead, we grabbed his leash and a blanket for the back seat of the Jeep and I grabbed my baseball glove. Jeff and I could play some catch before it was time to work out.

We swung by Jeff's house so he could get his glove. We snuck Duke into the school and changed to work out. He was being surprisingly good. He hated the leash but was okay if I carried him. He would become a big dog, so I needed to stop hauling him around before he figured this was how we did things. We went into the gym where we found Pam, Mona, Kim and Sammie sitting in the bleachers, talking. They saw me with Duke and fell in love with him at first sight. I had an epiphany that Duke might be an even better chick-magnet than Kyle. They volunteered to watch him.

Jeff and I were doing some long tosses to warm up when Coach Hope came into the gym with my new neighbors.

"David, Jeff, come over here," he called to us.

We jogged over and they all saw the puppy. Coach Hope looked at me.

"Whose dog is that?" he asked.

"He's mine," I said. "He's a service dog."

I thought I had pulled a fast one.

"Yeah, right," Coach Hope said, and then turned to the new kids. "This is Britanie, Brock and Bryan Callahan. They just moved here from Sayreville, New Jersey. Brock and Bryan play football and baseball, and Brit plays basketball. This is David, one of our captains from last year's football team, and Jeff, one of our starters. Can you guys introduce them around and help them work out this afternoon?"

"Sure, Coach," Jeff said.

Coach Hope ignored Duke and went to his office.

"Are you twins?" Jeff asked the guys.

"Actually, triplets," Brock said.

"How's Precious doing?" I asked.

"I think she'll survive," Brock said, then explained what I was talking about to Jeff. "She's Brit's cat. I was rooting for your dog to take her out."

"You just shut up, or I'll drop her on you when you're sleeping tonight," Britanie threatened.

Jeff wanted details, so the triplets filled him on the excitement this morning. People started to arrive for our workout. Jeff took the triplets around and introduced them to everyone. I caught up with everyone I hadn't seen yet today. Yuri told me he was still working on getting a girlfriend. Cassidy came in and put us to work doing our forms.

After she was done with the workout, the Callahan triplets looked like something Duke would drag into the house. I personally felt good. It looked like I'd soon be back into the routine of working out.

Jeff said he wanted to go with Cassidy and me to the dojo. When we arrived, I went looking for Mr. Yamamura, the owner and main trainer. Jeff was put in charge of Duke. I think my dog liked having so many babysitters.

Mr. Yamamura insisted he supervise Cassidy as she trained me. It was his dojo and hence it was his rules.

Cassidy was teaching the basics of joint manipulation. She demonstrated what at first looked hard, but turned out to be really easy, in theory, until Cassidy used the countermoves on me. All I needed to do was bend a joint into an unnatural position. She demonstrated and put me into an arm bar. She basically tossed me on the ground, and once she was on top of me slid to the side. She then grabbed my arm as she placed pressure on my face with her foot. She made a believer out of me when she pulled back and my elbow felt like it was going to pop.

Cassidy demonstrated how you could gain an advantage using the joints of the shoulder, elbow, hip and knee. Jeff flinched when he heard me squeal like a little girl. I offered to allow him a turn. He was such a wuss.

"A commonly overlooked technique is attacking the small joints," Mr. Yamamura told us. "You can easily neutralize an attacker by breaking his fingers. It can cause a lot of pain and will affect his chances and usually even his desire for attacking you."

Cassidy was all smiles. I started to shake my head.

"No, you don't. I need my fingers," I told her.

It didn't stop Mr. Yamamura from demonstrating on me. I soon found out he could make me do about anything once he had my thumb. He let me practice on Cassidy. I tried to keep the grin off my face when I got a little payback.

At the break, I went to get a towel out of my bag. I had to pull my glove out and Mr. Yamamura saw it.

"You play baseball?" he asked me.

"Yes, sir. I play shortstop and pitch," I said, and then nodded at Jeff. "He plays right field for us."

"I used to coach pitching when I was younger. In Japan baseball is taken almost as seriously as martial arts. My brothers and I played in high school. Our team made it to the semifinals of Kōshien," he shared.

"What's that?" Jeff asked.

"Twice a year there's a big baseball tournament, played nationwide. The finals are played in Hanshin Kōshien Stadium. I played pro ball for six years and then went into coaching after I retired. When I came to America, my brother bought a dojo and I switched to martial arts. I love teaching. You Americans could learn a few things."

"What do you mean?" I asked.

"In America, you rely on power. You use big sweeping motions with your whole body to whip the ball as hard as possible to the plate. Everyone seems to have the same pitching motion, as if you're trying to standardize or mimic a particular pitching form. In Japan, there is much more deception."

We went back to the mats to train. Mr. Yamamura seemed to understand what Cassidy was teaching me. He had a few pointers on how to make the same moves but with minimal effort. His approach was the same as Cassidy's, just smoother. She was all quickness and explosiveness. He was much smoother and more deceptive. With his approach, you suddenly realized you were in trouble, and by then it was too late. Of course, Cassidy liked it and had to have a practice dummy. I wondered what a boyfriend was for if not to take the punishment.

◊◊◊

Peggy had come over for dinner and I found she and Dad were cooking. It brought a smile to my face as I remembered Greg and I had done the same thing with Dad. I let Duke go into the house so he could say hi to everyone. I went up to my apartment, took a shower, and came back to find dinner ready. Dad and Peggy had made blackened chicken breasts, baked sweet potatoes, and a big salad.

During dinner, I told Mom and Dad about Tracy and what Tom had told me. Mom stated she'd sold a house today. Dad shared what was going on at work. One of his staff had driven a big salt truck across one of the fairways. The fear was he had possibly dropped salt on the grass. They placed stakes around it and were keeping an eye on it for any problems.

Peggy caught us up on her holiday. It sounded like her parents were doing better. She told me her parents had taken her to a New Year's Eve party and my buddy Mitch had been there. She said he'd kissed her at the stroke of midnight. Mom shot me a look to see how I'd take the news. When I thought about what I'd been doing at midnight, Mitch's kiss didn't seem like a big deal. I decided I didn't need to share what Nancy and I had been up to.

I was happy I could hear she had kissed Mitch and not completely freak out. I think part of it was I trusted Peggy. I knew she'd tell me if I had anything to worry about.

After dinner, I told Mom and Dad that Peggy and I were going up to my place to study. Mom made me take Duke and his crate to my apartment. We needed to get a bigger one for when he started to grow. Peggy put him on his leash and took him for a tour of the backyard while I moved all his stuff. Mom told me he would *not* wake her up in the morning.

I was filling up his water bottle when Peggy came up the steps carrying him. I had gotten him what looked like a big gerbil bottle. Sandy had told me they had them in the barn and the pups knew they could get a drink out of one. This saved putting down a bowl that he would just step in or tip over.

"He said he couldn't do the steps," she explained as she handed him to me.

He promptly licked me in the mouth. Peggy was grossed out even more than I was. She sent me to the bathroom and told me to use mouthwash if I expected her to kiss me. My apartment was child-proofed for Kyle and Mac. I put up the baby gate at the top of the stairs; I didn't need Duke falling down them. I put him down and went to brush my teeth. When I came out I found he had conned Peggy into letting him up on the couch so she could rub his ears.

"Don't be teaching him to get up there. You realize he's going to be a horse? You won't want him on your lap, once he grows," I warned her.

I picked him up and put him in his crate. He was tired and sacked out. Peggy thought we needed to sack out ourselves. I'd missed her. I teased her that she was getting chubby because she hadn't been running since cross-country was over. She told me to shut up, that there was just more of her to love.

◊◊◊

Friday January 9

Duke and Precious had come to an uneasy truce. Precious only popped him when he got too rowdy, but she tolerated the pup. It seemed like Precious waited for him when I would let him out in the morning. I was worried the first few days, but they had started to learn each other's boundaries.

I'd started to run with Duke. He was pretty good for around the block once at a slow warm-up pace. I would then open the back door and let him terrorize my mom and dad. He had learned to go up the stairs, and Dad said Mom would reach down and help him up on the bed. I could hardly wait until he could get up on their bed by himself.

I hadn't heard them complain, so we fell into a routine. Duke would get his morning loving while I ran. I would then take my shower and come down for breakfast. We'd gotten Duke a crate for the laundry room. This way whoever got home first could let him out. Mom was coming home a couple of times a day to help potty train him.

I would pick him up and take him to work out with me. Mom wanted him to eventually go with her to the hospital for her cancer patients, so I needed to get him socialized with groups of people. He had yet to meet someone he didn't like and there were plenty of volunteers to take care of him.

Tracy had finally come back to school. Between Pam and me, we kept an eye on her. I picked her up after Peggy in the morning. Pam took her home after school. I was surprised when Peggy invited her on our date. We weren't doing anything out of the ordinary, so I was okay with it. We were grabbing a bite to eat and then would go to a movie. I was just surprised Peggy would be so thoughtful. Tom told me it was important she remain engaged in social settings.

Tracy had at first refused because she didn't want to be a third wheel. I finally convinced her by asking Yuri to be her date. I explained to Tracy that Yuri needed a practice date before his first real date. I explained to Yuri that if he got out of line with Tracy, I would end him. All in all, I thought it would work out for everyone.

◊◊◊

I picked up Peggy and Tracy first. Yuri's mom wanted to meet everyone. They lived in an apartment building on the way to State. Yuri had told me that his mom was a professor.

I knocked and could hear Yuri yell, "I got it!"

The door opened and his mom came into the living room. She came right up to me and smiled.

"Ah, David, I'm Nadia. Yuri talks about you all the time," she said, and Yuri blushed. "I hear you've arranged a practice date. May I ask how this is supposed to work?"

"First let me introduce the girl I had to bribe to go out with Yuri. This is Tracy," I said, and Tracy did a little curtsy. "This is Peggy, my date for the evening."

She did the same, which brought a smile to Nadia.

"What do you have to do to have Tracy take my son out?"

"That depends on him. The more inappropriately he behaves, the more I have to give. So far, it's only costing me dinner and a movie. I'm sure, though, by the end of the night I might have to buy her a car."

His mom gave Yuri a stern look. He gave her his 'little angel' look and had us all laughing. We all knew better. Well, I knew he'd be on his best behavior. I told him what Greg had told me about this date, how it could affect his reputation. If he treated Tracy right, she'd let the girls' network know he could be a gentleman, and he would have future dates with … who knows?

Peggy and Tracy wanted to go to the Chinese place next to the park. I was excited to see they had sushi now. Sushi was Japanese, but they invited a special chef in on the weekends to make it. I ordered a California Roll as an appetizer to introduce sushi to everyone. I figured it was a safe choice. When it came, I taught them how to prepare their wasabi and soy sauce. Peggy wasn't a fan, but Yuri and Tracy loved it. With that in mind, I ordered a platter of different sushi for three. Peggy ordered a traditional meal.

Over dinner, we started to teach Yuri about dating.

"You need to learn how to compliment your date," Tracy told him.

"Like what?" Yuri asked.

"Peggy, compliment David," Tracy suggested.

"Seriously? You know how he gets," she complained.

"If he gets out of hand, we can always tell his mother."

I put up my hands in defeat. They all knew how my mom was. I wasn't willing to cross her without good cause.

"Good call," she said with a smirk. "Okay, let's see. When I'm around you, I always feel like your focus is only on me. You make me feel special, and at the same time, safe. You're my best friend and closest confidant. When we're alone, you take your time and look out for my needs. I think you're a special guy."

"Good. Now David, it's your turn," Tracy instructed.

"You're hot!"

Yuri about fell out of his chair after he saw the looks both Tracy and Peggy gave me. I was sure my mom would be hearing about this, but I figured it was worth it.

"He's right, you're both hot," Yuri agreed.

The girls gave up and we just had fun the rest of dinner. Yuri surprised me in his taste for sushi. He liked the stronger, fishier-tasting fish, like mackerel. Tracy liked the different rolls. One had cream cheese in it, which she really liked. I enjoyed the yellowfin tuna they had as a special. Yuri's eyes about popped out of his head when he saw how much the bill was. Filling up two teenage boys on sushi could be expensive. He was relieved when I told him he could get the movie and I'd pay for dinner.

I was proud of Yuri when he refused to see *Selma*, a picture about Martin Luther King's march from Selma to Montgomery, Alabama, which led to the Voting Rights Act of 1965. He explained if he was going to spend good money on a *practice* date, he wanted to enjoy the movie. Yuri told us if it was a 'real' date, he'd let the girl pick. I had a big smile on my face when we got to see *Taken 3*. For an old guy, Liam Neeson kicked butt.

Before the movie, both Tracy and Peggy held my hands. Yuri just shook his head at me.

"You know, if you'd sprung for popcorn, you might be getting some loving, too," I teased him.

"Don't bother. Your making me watch this action crap ruined those ideas," Tracy complained.

I tickled her. Tracy jumped.

"Okay, okay, I really wanted to see this, too," she confessed.

"So, girls torture us with a chick flick for what reason?" Yuri asked.

"Don't knock it, it puts them in the mood," I suggested.

He thought about it for a moment, and then looked at me and nodded like I'd given him sage advice. The real reason guys agreed to go to a chick flick was because they were wusses. They didn't want to potentially upset their date by being honest about what they wanted to see. I might go to a romantic comedy, but would refuse to go to a movie which compared itself to *The Notebook*. I didn't need a teary-eyed girl on my hands.

Tami had tricked me into seeing it on DVD. I wasn't sure who the bigger girl was after watching it. I still contend I have allergies, and that's why my eyes watered. I wouldn't fall into that trap again.

After the movie, we took Yuri home. Tracy wanted to go to my place to see my new puppy. He wasn't much fun because it was past his bedtime. I put him back into his crate and he seemed happy. Peggy and Tracy led me to the bedroom where we made out a little bit.

I woke up to hear my mom talking.

"I found them. They're asleep in David's bed. No, they're fully clothed. Okay, I'll make sure she's home first thing in the morning," Mom said. I heard her dial another number and a similar conversation took place.

We'd forgotten to call the girls' parents to let them know where they were. I would hear about it tomorrow. When Mom left, I woke up the girls and told them what happened. I got undressed, they both joined me under the covers, and we went back to sleep.

Chapter 3 – Making a Movie

Saturday January 10

I woke the girls early. I planned to get doughnuts as a peace offering. I took a shower and then the girls each took a turn. I had to chuckle when I realized they both had clothes here. I wasn't laughing so much when Peggy showed Tracy where my good t-shirts were. Tracy picked out one that I really liked, and they both were shocked when I made her put it back. I found one that I knew she'd like. Alan had gotten it for me. It said, '**Fuck You!** *You Fucking Fuck!*' I wasn't brave enough to wear it. I could just hear Kendal complain if a picture of me in that t-shirt got out. Tracy thought it was funny as hell.

We went to the bakery and I let the girls pick out a half-dozen doughnuts each. I knew if I sent a full dozen home, the moms would be all over me about getting them fat. Greg and Angie were coming over with Kyle and Mac today, so I got two dozen for my house. I figured Angie and Greg would take a dozen home with them. I made sure there were plenty of chocolate doughnuts. When Angie was pregnant with Kyle, she craved chocolate.

Tracy made us go in with her. Tom and Mary were drinking coffee. I handed Mary the doughnuts.

"I see you finally decided to bring my daughter home," Tom said.

"I figured if she was going to have to do the walk of shame, I should be here for the fun," I shot back.

"You're not helping," Tracy complained.

"I need to get this one home before they send out a search party," I said as I nodded towards Peggy.

"Why don't you bring your mom and dad over for brunch next Sunday?" Mary asked.

"I think they'd like to come," I said.

"Peggy, you and your family are invited, too," Mary said.

"I'll have my mom call you. I need to get going," she said as she grabbed my hand and pulled me to the door.

When we got to Peggy's, she made the call that I should just drop her off. I wasn't one of her dad's favorites. She gave me a kiss and told me she'd see me in school on Monday. She and her family were going to her grandparents' for the weekend.

I had brought Duke with me. I didn't think it was such a good idea to let him loose on Mom and Dad this morning. He had curled up on the floor in the back of the Jeep. I'd grabbed his blanket from his crate and put it back there; he seemed to know what it was for.

I got home in time to see Greg and Angie pull up. I got Duke out and the doughnuts.

"What did you do?" Angie accused me.

"Peggy and Tracy fell asleep last night and Mom had to field angry-parent calls."

"Did you get me chocolate ones?"

"Of course, I did."

We'd all gone in and I'd put the doughnuts on the table. Mom and Dad already had coffee, so I poured cups for Greg and Angie. I got glasses of milk for myself, Kyle and Mac, and made bacon and eggs. I tried to stay on my high-protein diet, but I admit I had a doughnut or three. I'd gotten Boston creams, so that was never a question, because they were the best doughnuts ever made.

Mom got busy being a grandma, so she left me alone. Dad gave me a look that said I wasn't going to skate free. I made a point to make extra bacon for Greg and Mom, otherwise they'd steal mine. I figured I better get it over with.

"Mom, I'm sorry you had to talk to Peggy's and Tracy's parents last night. I was really planning on taking them home before their curfews."

"They were okay when I talked to them. Just be more careful in the future," Mom said.

Greg, Angie and Dad's heads snapped around. Who was this woman and what had she done with my mother? Greg started to say something, but I threw a doughnut at his head. Mom gave me a dirty look, then turned on Greg.

"David's been acting more like an adult lately. I figured that until he does something stupid, which we all know he will, I'll treat him like one," Mom said.

Oh, crap! She planned to give me enough rope to hang myself. Dad began to chuckle when he saw me go white as a ghost.

"Dead man walking," Angie mumbled as she patted my hand.

I hurried up and ate before I could give Mom a reason to jump on me. Kyle and Mac were on the floor while they played with Duke. I had to remind Duke they were just babies when Mac tried to rip the hair off his back. He yelped, so I figured they'd work it out. Angie and Greg were on the floor to keep an eye on the three of them.

◊◊◊

I had reserved three of the batting cages and two of the indoor mounds at State. I'd invited everyone from the baseball team to come out if they wanted. When I got there, Wolf, Jim and Jeff were batting. Justin and Bert were pitching to Mike and Tim. Bill, Trevor and Jake awaited their turns to bat.

I was surprised to see Coach Fog helping the guys at the batting cage. Rusty Fog was a pitcher from St. John's, and Coach Fog was his dad. I'd knocked out Rusty when he beaned Wolf last spring. Coach Fog was an assistant coach at State. I nodded to him as I went over to watch the pitchers.

I'd asked Mr. Yamamura to come coach me and he'd agreed to help. I talked Bill into helping me stretch and do some long tosses. Right on time, Mr. Yamamura showed up.

"Thank you for coming," I said and then introduced him to everyone.

"My first name is Shigehito. My American friends call me Shiggy. When we're outside the dojo, I would appreciate if you'd either call me Shiggy or Coach."

"Yes, sir. I like the name Shiggy."

"To start, I'd like you to just pitch," Shiggy told me.

"I haven't pitched since spring, so I'll be a little rusty."

He was fine with it. The other guys stopped pitching so they could see Shiggy work with me. Tim volunteered to catch. I was taking it easy so I could focus on my technique. After about twenty pitches, he had me stop.

"In America, you're taught to use your whole body when pitching. The pitching motion is one fluid motion. American pitchers are generally taller than Japanese pitchers, which helps you whip the ball. Where you rely on power, we rely on deception and the lower body. Your legs are powerful muscles. In both countries, success depends on a consistent and repeatable release point.

"Let me show you an example of a Japanese pitching motion," Shiggy said.

He moved slowly back into his balance point and then dropped his hands while coming forward. He had begun his windup, or pitching motion, and it seemed to be drastically different because the Japanese trained with an emphasis to set up the lower half of your body to create power. He showed me how the standard US delivery featured a smooth tempo throughout. The entire body was involved to generate power. Many Japanese windups featured a change of tempo, with a deliberate initial phase and sometimes a pause in order to focus on loading their lower half.

"In the US everything is about power, how hard you can throw or how many home runs you can hit. In high school ball, you're not going to throw hundred-mile-an-hour fastballs. If you try, you'll hurt yourself. I can teach you to throw harder, but safer, by using your legs to do the majority of the work.

"I can also show you how to incorporate deception into your pitching. If everyone throws the baseball with the same motion, it's easy for the hitter," Shiggy continued. "Hitters are usually sitting on the same tempo and rhythm. Pitchers need to change their timing to put the hitters off balance. Pitchers in Japan are encouraged to find pitching motions which create troublesome elements in the timing and appearance of their deliveries to the batter. You'll see them slowly rock back to their balance points before exploding to the plate.

"The glove is also used for distraction. So, too, is making a concerted effort to bring the ball behind the back to hide it from opponents. I often teach that it's good to keep the ball hidden behind your body. The goal is to make batters guess where the ball is for as long as possible."

The new throwing motion felt awkward. What I did find was my arm didn't seem tired when I was done. Japanese pitchers tended to throw a lot more pitches than we did here in the States. I think part of it was because they weren't putting as much pressure on their arms while pitching.

When I was done, I was also surprised to find Bert was getting training from Shiggy. If he could learn some control, it would really help his game. I went over to the batting cage. Coach Fog just wanted to watch my swing today. When I was done, Bert went into the cage.

Mike and Justin also talked with Shiggy. Neither one of them wanted to change their pitching motion, so he helped them improve what they were comfortable with throwing. When they were done, they both seemed happy.

Coach Fog and Shiggy agreed to work with us after school Monday through Thursday and Saturday. Everyone committed to being here. I was glad that we'd be starting at seven each evening. That gave me time to work out at school and then head to the dojo with Cassidy. I also committed to lifting before school. I'd just have to get up earlier to run.

◇◇◇

I got home in time to watch the Duke vs. North Carolina basketball game. Then we watched the Patriots beat the Ravens 35–31. Dad and Greg had kicked back while Mom and Angie caught up in the kitchen. I made myself a salad with poached chicken and boiled eggs for lunch. Kyle, Mac and Duke went down for naps. I spent the afternoon hanging out with my family.

My coding team showed up after the basketball game. Alan had some bad news: he'd found existing software which did ninety-five percent of what we wanted. It incorporated both video and the playbook. One of the cool additional features it had was you could pull out video of an individual player. Gina showed me how you could put together a highlight video we could send to recruiters.

We put together a plan so we could use the software next year. I would talk to Coach Hope about using it. Lily came up with the idea of loading all the video from last year for all our upcoming opponents. Gina and Alan would work with the coaching staff to do that. This was the one piece where someone with football knowledge needed to be involved. The data going in would determine how much value we could get out of it.

Jeff suggested the managers learn to do the input of videos, once the basics were set up.

◇◇◇

Tracy sent me a text to let me know Mona planned to have a party tonight. I decided it sounded like I'd have more fun there than just sitting at home. Cassidy hadn't needed me to double-date with her since she started to date

Jeff. They'd been going out with Alan and Stacy. I hadn't had a chance to be with Pam since I got back, so I sent her a text to see if she wanted to go with me. She sent me a text saying I wasn't allowed to bring a date. I got a little worried.

I flipped through the paper and saw Granny's had an ad for a prime rib special tonight. I pointed it out to Mom and it was decided we'd all go there for dinner. When it got close to time, I was surprised when Sun showed up at our front door.

"Is it Girl Scout cookie time?" I teased her.

"I wish. I could use a Thin Mint. I'm here to babysit."

"Come in and I'll introduce you to the baby," I said, and led her to Duke's crate. "Now don't feed him people food, and you need to let him out every couple of hours. Also, don't let him on the couch. I don't need a lapdog when he's eighty pounds or more."

Angie strolled in.

"Are you done being a comedian?" she asked me.

"What? Duke's my baby," I told her.

"Do I get paid extra for putting up with David?" Sun asked.

I took Duke outside before they could abuse me any longer. Since the weather had turned cold, Duke had learned to do his business and come right back in. I swear I looked away for just a second but turned back just in time to see a blur dash for the back of the garage. Then I heard two cats start fighting. I ran around the corner to see Precious trying to kill an orange tabby. Duke was dancing around and looking to see how he could help his buddy.

"Stop them!" Brit cried.

"There's *no way* I'm sticking my hand anywhere near that," I informed her.

I was proud to see Duke was smart enough to not get involved. Brit started to cry, so I was trying to decide if I should help when my dumbass dog decided to jump into the middle of things. I think he learned his lesson when both cats turned on him. This time I was smart enough to grab the cats by the napes of their necks. When Duke was free of their clutches, he hid behind me.

"You're hurting her!" wailed Brit.

Neither cat liked being held, but they calmed down. I handed Precious to her.

"Did the bad man hurt you?" she asked.

I swear Precious gave me a dirty look. I set the orange tabby down and he made a run for it. Duke pranced around like he had done something. I sent him towards the back door and let him in, then I went and changed clothes.

◊◊◊

When we got to Granny's, the place was packed. Granny loved me, so Dad sent me up to get us a table. She saw me and had a big smile.

"David! It's so good to see you," she said as she gave me a hug. She saw who all was with me. "I can seat your family right now if you don't mind sitting with someone else."

She only had tables for four available, so we wouldn't be sitting together, but I knew she'd put me with someone who was fun, so I agreed.

She took my arm and we went to each table to talk to everyone. I felt like a rock star. She had one of the waitresses taking pictures for anyone who wanted one. She made me out as a big deal, and it was fun. She wanted a picture with just the two of us. When she was done, she sat me down at a table of twelve- and thirteen-year-old girls.

I recognized one as April Lacier's little sister, Jill. It was Jill's thirteenth birthday. Jill made one of the girls switch seats with her so she could sit next to me. She was still drop-dead gorgeous and major jailbait. I decided to beat her to the punch on flirting.

60

"So, are you finally old enough that we can go out?" I asked.

It was amazing how a table full of teen girls could go from constant chatter to dead silence in a split second. They all looked at Jill to see what she would say. Jill got a little pink, and for once, was stumped. I tried to keep a smile off my face. I thought I might have made a small miscalculation when she attacked me. She had me in a headlock and was trying to pry my lips apart so she could shove her tongue down my throat. Luckily Angie came over and pulled her off me.

"He's not old enough for you," Angie suggested.

Her comment got all the girls to giggle. I just nodded in agreement. Jill would eat me up and spit me out. I would hate to think what she'd be like when she turned eighteen! I would need to put that birthday into my calendar for future reference. I would have to be careful my senior year because she'd be a freshman. With her looks, she'd be breaking plenty of hearts.

After the initial awkwardness, the girls and I got on great. They reminded me of my freshman cheerleaders. I treated them like they were little sisters and we had a good time. Granny told my dad dinner was on her tonight. Dad wanted to try some other restaurants and see if I could get us free meals. Mom told him not to get his hopes up.

◊◊◊

Cheerleaders *know* how to throw a party. I parked out back and found the keg on the patio. I wondered at what temperature a keg would actually freeze. The good news was the beer was cold, and it seemed like this time they'd spent a little extra and had gotten something not completely terrible. I drank one and then poured myself another before going in.

I found Mona at the back door with two empty pitchers. She thrust them into my hands and I was sent back to fill them. I came back in to find she had drunk my beer. She refilled it from a pitcher and then went to play hostess. I found the bedroom where you could dump your coat and then went to see what kind of trouble I could get into.

I was surprised to see my new neighbor talking to Gina.

"David!" Gina called and then gave me a hug.

"You know this cat-killer?" Brit whined.

"David would never kill a cat," Gina defended me.

"You haven't met Brit's cat from hell. It was trying to kill another cat tonight."

"She was just defending her territory," Brit said with a huff.

Gina gave me a patient look. A song I liked came on and I headed for the dance floor. I was surprised when Brit was right there and started to dance with me. I hadn't really noticed her until now. She was tall, maybe five-ten. She looked to have a Nordic heritage. The Vikings had invaded England, back in the day. You would expect that with a name like Callahan, she'd be a redhead. She instead had blond hair and was well endowed. I did a mental check and kicked myself for not checking her out more closely. My only excuse was that she'd been yelling at me almost every time we had met. During the song, I realized how pretty she was when she smiled.

Gina cut in and I danced with her next. Something clicked a couple of songs later when I remembered Pam's comment from when I called her and realized I had danced with four single girls. Somewhere, someone had coordinated this. I thought I'd found my culprit when I saw Tracy talking to Pam and then Pam was next. I was happy it was a slow song. I suspected Tracy knew what the playlist was.

"How's my surfer girl doing?" I asked.

"Good. Did you hook up with my sister's slutty friend?"

"No, but I learned what party hos are," I shared.

"Oh, I forgot to warn you about them. Did you have a good time?"

"Hell, yes! I wish we had party hos here."

"We do. We call them cheerleaders," she said, which cracked me up.

"So, are you my party ho for the night?" I teased her.

"I can be, but Tracy says you have to pick from the single girls tonight. You're not allowed to pick until you've danced with them all."

"What if I just throw you over my shoulder and haul you off to a bedroom?"

"I'd be happy, but Tracy's on a mission tonight. Do me a favor and pick Sammie. She's the only core varsity cheerleader you haven't been with, and now that Jeff and she are no longer going out, she wants to sample you."

"Why don't I take all five of you to a bedroom and we'll see if I can survive my party hos?"

"I think the five of us would be too much for you, but I can see if they're willing," she teased me.

"I'd better not. I'm trying to cut back," I said, acting noble. "Why don't we see if we can make a weekend out of it at Tracy's cabin?"

"You, my friend, are full of good ideas. We could get all the cheerleaders there and have a real party weekend," she said.

"Speaking of a real party girl, how's your sister?"

"She's hooked up with a frat guy. I give it two more weeks until she's bored with him. You really need to stay away from her. She's getting to be a little too wild for even you," she advised.

She was probably right. When the song ended, Kim was my next partner. I ended up dancing with fourteen girls before Tracy let me off the dance floor. By then I'd sweat through my shirt and needed another beer. Mona was being a great hostess and I had an ice-cold beer in a jiffy.

Tracy came up to me to talk.

"So, who's it going to be?" she asked.

"Does Peggy know about this?" I asked.

"Yes, she's fine with it. Normal rules apply. No making a fool of yourself and wear a condom. Before you ask, that means no six-somes."

"When did you become all responsible?" I asked.

"When Tami left me in charge of you until she comes back."

I laughed out loud. I'd be afraid to leave Tracy in charge of Duke, let alone a human being. Don't get me wrong, I cared about Tracy a lot. She just wasn't stable enough to trust with anything that mattered.

"Let me be clear on this: this is the same Tami who threatened to kill you and neuter me when we got together last spring?"

"Yeah, she and I talk about once a week. She misses you quite a lot and regrets going out with Simon. I think she still loves you," Tracy shared.

If only Tracy knew what a damper she had just thrown on the evening. I wasn't sure I wanted to sleep with someone new tonight. If Tami was going to wait for me, I could do the same for her. Tracy caught my mood. One consequence from having been so close was we could still read each other.

"Don't go all moody on me. Tami said you needed to go have fun and get it out of your system. She warned me you might not want to."

I thought about it for a moment and decided they were right. I wasn't happy they tried to manipulate me, but I wanted to get laid. I needed to sow my wild oats now before I made a commitment. I just nodded to Tracy and went to find Mona. I needed another beer before I picked my girl for the night. I found a worried Gina instead.

"I, ah, didn't understand what dancing with you meant," she began.

"What? How am I going to compare all three sisters if I don't spend time with the youngest?" I complained.

"You've been with both of my sisters?" she asked as her eyebrows disappeared into her bangs.

"I'd never kiss and tell, but you'd be breaking up a matched set," I teased her.

"Oh, bite me! You big slut."

I stuck my tongue out at her and found Mona, the beer goddess. She fixed me up and I went hunting for Sammie. She was surrounded by Pam, Kim and Brit. I walked up and smiled at her. She blushed and did a little bunny hop to show she was happy. I grabbed Sammie's hand and pulled her upstairs.

When we got to the bedroom, I closed the door and turned around to find her hopping around, trying to get her boot off.

"Want some help?" I asked.

She smiled at me, sat down on the bed and put her foot up. I put it on my stomach and untied it and took it off. I did the other one. She scooted back and undid her jeans. I grasped the cuffs under her heel and pulled them off. She sat up and took off her sweater, leaving her in just her socks, panties and a t-shirt. I took off her socks and then began to massage her feet.

Sammie just laid back and enjoyed it. I worked her feet, finding all her tender spots. Once I found them, I worked to make her feel better. Women love a good foot massage. I made a point not to rush. I saved the sexy spots on her feet until the end. When I finally began to massage the spot Greg had shown me, she began to moan. I heard giggles outside the door. Sammie started to get vocal.

"Oh God. OH God! OH GOD!" she said as she had her first orgasm.

The door swung open and Mona marched in as Kim, Pam and Brit peeked in.

"That's my good comforter. Move over, bitch," Mona commanded, and she pulled it off her bed.

She winked at me as they left.

"Carry on," she said as she closed the door.

I heard Mona order all of the voyeurs to leave us alone. I pulled Sammie's t-shirt over her head and then kissed her.

"Lie on your stomach," I ordered.

This time I started at her scalp and worked my way down her neck, shoulders, back and butt. Sammie was putty in my hands by now. She was ready: I could smell her arousal and there was a huge wet spot on her panties. I gently rolled her onto her back and started to work on her front. I paid special attention to her firm teenage breasts. She had another little orgasm as I chewed on one of her nipples.

It was time to make her mine. I decided I'd better be a considerate guest and went to the bathroom and grabbed a big towel to put under Sammie's butt. I wanted her to be able to remember tonight when she was ninety. I peeled her soaked panties down. I savored the smell of her arousal and then began to slowly build her to a huge orgasm as I teased her shaved little sex. Sammie never knew what hit her as I brought her off the first time. I made a point to bring her off three more times; each time I'd gotten more aggressive.

Then I slid two thick fingers into her and hunted for her G-spot. I went to work to see if I could get her to squirt. I started off slow, then sped up and used a stronger touch to bring her closer to another orgasm.

"Oh, God! I'm going to pee!"

I just grinned and pulled my face out of her crotch so I could watch the fireworks. It was good that Mona had saved her comforter and I had gotten the towel because Sammie sprayed all over the place. I had not gotten far enough back, because she even got my face!

Sammie was out of it with a glazed look and a dopey grin on her face. I think I'd accomplished my goal for the night. I went and got a washcloth and cleaned up.

Sammie came to her senses. She got out of bed and stripped me. I put on a condom. She pushed me onto the bed and straddled my waist. She lined me up and sank down on me. Being a cheerleader, she was flexible and strong. What followed was some of my favorite sex. I love a girl who enjoys a good time. There was none of the gentle loving stuff; this was about giving each other fantastic orgasms.

I reached up and grasped a breast in each hand as I pumped into her depths. I was getting close and could tell Sammie was already there. She slumped onto my chest, so I grasped her firm little butt-cheeks and held her in place as I powered into her until I could no longer hold back. I felt the familiar throb as I reached my climax.

I rolled her off me, disposed of the condom and cleaned up. I caught a glance of myself in the mirror and then stepped back to take a harder look. Looking back at me was a happy boy. I took a moment because wanted to remember how I looked.

As always, I got hard again quickly when I found my hot little cheerleader on all fours waving her cute butt at me. It put me in a particular mood. I quickly put on another condom and knee-walked up behind her. I gripped those perfect butt-cheeks and then drove myself into the center of her core. I looked down as I pulled out and admired her spectacular little tushy. Looking down my hard abs, I had her sex split open by Mr. Happy. This was another memory I wanted to burn into my brain.

"The girls warned me," Sammie began as she looked at me over her shoulder. "They said I'd be hooked if I ever slept with you. I couldn't imagine what they meant until now."

I grinned at her and then snapped my hips forward to bury the last bit. I found I could get deeper from behind, and the moan Sammie let out made me think I'd hit an area that had never been touched before. I reached up, grasped her hair, pulled her head back and twisted her head so I could lean forward and kiss her. I began to plumb her depths with long, deep strokes as our tongues danced with each other.

Sammie's arms gave out and I rolled us on our sides so we could spoon. I pulled the hair from her neck and kissed and sucked on it. I tried to be careful and not leave any hickeys. I slowly pumped into her from behind. Sammie's mouth was slack and her eyes were closed, so I took advantage of her momentary distraction to change my position. I lifted her right leg up and over my shoulder while moving to straddle her left leg, all without disengaging. I had watched some Internet porn and wanted to try this new position. Doing it sideways was fun!

In this new position, I had some options. I had clear access to reach down and toy with her nubbin. When I first touched it, Sammie moaned and hunched over. I had switched to short, powerful strokes. I made short, staccato thrusts into her velvet vise. In a rush it became too much for both of us. We both exploded.

"AAAIIIIEEEEE!" I bellowed.

Sammie clamped down hard and I could feel the telltale pulse as her tunnel gripped me. She let her leg fall off my shoulder and I spooned her. I left myself buried in her and just held her tight. I waited until I could feel myself going soft before I pulled out.

I must have drifted off to sleep. I woke up to Sammie playing with Mr. Happy.

"Do you have one more in you?" she asked.

"For you? Of course, I do."

She grabbed another condom and put it on me. I just rolled over on top of her and we did the basic missionary position. There was nothing urgent about it. I could tell my feelings for Sammie had changed. I just wanted to make love to her now. She captured my lips and we kissed. After what seemed like forever, I finally came. I'm not sure if Sammie came again, but I don't think that was the point by then.

We finally finished a little after midnight. I helped Sammie put her t-shirt back on and then she fell asleep. I picked the comforter up off the floor and pulled it over her. I took a quick shower to remove the smell of sweat and sex. Mona had this minty shampoo I was going to have to find.

I came out and Brit found me right away. I looked at Pam and she just shrugged.

"I think I need to go home," I said.

"Can you give me a ride?" Brit asked.

"Am I going to be safe?"

"I promise to be good," she said with a smile.

She kept her word until I had pulled to a stop and turned off my Jeep. Then she grabbed me and kissed me hard. I was too tired to fight it, but I was also too tired to do anything about it either. She thanked me for the ride and ran to her house.

Her brothers were staring at me through their window as I went into my apartment. That didn't look good.

◊◊◊

Friday January 16

Tracy had another breakdown midweek. Her depression didn't seem to be getting any better. Tom talked to me and told me that he, Mary, and Doctor Hebert were talking about Tracy dropping out of school for a semester to get some extensive treatment. He never came out and said it, but I suspected they were worried she might do something stupid. I'd gone over to see her Thursday night, but she was asleep. I never got a chance to talk to her.

One unexpected result from last Saturday night was Brit's new bodyguards, aka her brothers. She was a little put out that they'd become so protective. I, on the other hand, was fine with it. Brit seemed like a nice girl, but there was no way I would date the girl next door—literally!

On the school front, I was amazed at how helpful they were being. Each teacher had taken the time to sit down with me and tutor me on my assignments for when I'd be gone. Kendal told me there would be a tutor on site and time set aside for my studies. This was one of the reasons teenagers weren't used as much for movies. I was told a typical day could be twelve or more hours. They didn't want to take breaks so the talent could go study their lessons.

I was let out of school at noon so I could travel to Canada. The production staff had made allowances for me. They'd pulled all the studio scenes that included me from the storyboard and scheduled them for the next two weeks. On this trip, we would shoot on sound stages in Vancouver. There was a part of the movie where we would shoot outdoors. The plan was for this to take place in a few weeks in the Northwest Territories at a place called 'Yellowknife, the Gateway to the North.'

◊◊◊

Kendal picked me up from school. We swung by my place to let Duke out and grab my clothes for the next couple of weeks. Mom had originally said she'd go with me, but her real estate business had picked up and she decided to make money while she could. We were quickly on the road to the airport.

"Now that I have you captive, I want to tell you what's going on in your career," Kendal teased me.

"I hope this *isn't* my career," I shot back, meaning I wanted to do more than act or model.

"We got our first check for the movie. Let's just say I get to ride in first class with you now," she said as an indication of the amount of money involved.

I would quickly find that movie stars could make a lot of money. Even my role as a supporting actor would earn me more than I had to this point in my career. The even better news was the possibility of residuals. I could make money for years to come if this turned out to be a hit. Craig and Lori were reported to be making ridiculous money on this movie.

Bree was in the next tier as she parlayed her vampire TV exposure. She'd made a conscious decision to try her hand at a movie. There had been a big scandal on the set of her TV series. She and one of the leads had a messy breakup in their personal life. Just a week after, he had brought the girl he had cheated on her with onto the set. Bree had told the producers either the new girlfriend was barred from the set or she'd walk. While she never said, I thought her next step would be to move on from the show. The chemistry she'd formerly had with the male lead was now dead.

I was on the next tier, as far as compensation goes. The reason was twofold. The first was my modeling. They realized that having my head shaved could affect my marketability for other projects. The good news was, this wasn't five years ago. Some guys wore a buzz cut now. I liked that I didn't have to use all the stupid hair products anymore.

The second reason was I was athletic enough to do a lot of the work that would normally be done by a stunt double. They had a few scenes in the movie where even I wouldn't want to do it, because it was too dangerous. Jessup had been over-the-top with his praise of Ben and me for our sword work at the studio. He thought he'd need to use CGI (computer generated images) for some of the fight scenes. They might have to do some of that for my fight with the barbarian; I wasn't really up to trusting him with a giant ax, even if it were fake.

The next tier was Ben and Elizabeth. After them, it was mainly peripheral players that got paid a daily rate. The drop-off in income was dramatic, but it was all relative. The daily rate group could make as much in a day as someone might in a week at a real job, and if you had lines it earned you even more.

"Adrienne called and said she has the Dakora photo shoot confirmed. You'll be going to New York and staying in their new-talent apartment," she said with a smirk.

I knew that meant I would stay with Kara. Knowing Adrienne, we would have a good time as we explored New York on our downtime.

"Sandy Range called and confirmed they either want you for spring break or after school in New Orleans. Devin won't be able to make it. Sandy's going to take over doing the shoots with you."

I was relieved. I still had a problem with Devin hitting on Nancy. Nancy had called me when she got back to Kentucky and told me Devin had called her several times. She'd hinted that she might let him come visit her. That had really cemented my feeling that Nancy and I were done as more than just friends. It was for the best. The funny part was, I thought Devin and Nancy would make a great couple. I just didn't like how they'd gotten together.

"I have one final thing I need to tell you," Kendal said.

I could tell by her body language that I might not like what she was about to say.

"Eve Holliday has decided to go a different direction with her music videos. She has a new boyfriend and thinks they need to move the focus off you."

I was happy to hear that. After I'd seen Eve the last time, I really didn't think we were friends anymore. She had moved on to doing her music. I could understand it. What bothered me was how she had switched from being a friend, and even more, to being cold and distant. It had all started with the bullshit breakup song.

Kendal and I talked about our trip and how everything was going for her. I enjoyed the time we spent to catch up with her on nonbusiness-related topics. She was someone I could count on.

◊◊◊

When we landed in Vancouver, it was in the mid-40s. The Pacific Ocean kept the temperature warmer in the winter than you'd expect for a city so far north. When we left Chicago, it was in the 20s. Kendal and I found our bags and a cab in short order. The production company had rented several floors of a hotel across the street from the studio we'd be using. We ended up in adjoining rooms with a door between them. I opened mine so she could come in whenever she needed to.

In my room, I found a schedule for tomorrow and the updated script with diagrams of how the blocking was going to go. I was thankful someone had highlighted my script and marked where changes had been made. It would save me time and allow me to focus on what was changed. I started to learn my new lines and found that Kendal was a tremendous help. She ordered us dinner in my room and then spent several hours working with me on my lines for tomorrow.

"David, don't get uptight about the script. This isn't like a play where if you mess up you have to just keep going. They'll be doing takes like they do in your commercials," Kendal assured me.

"I know, but I'm the rookie here. I don't want them to regret hiring me."

"If they can make former wrestlers look like seasoned actors, I'm sure you'll be fine," she said with a chuckle.

I just glared at her and we got back to work.

◊◊◊

Saturday January 17

I got up early and went down to the fitness center. I had peeked outside and it was raining. I had no desire to run in that type of weather. I walked in to find Ben and Kent working out. Ben was supposed to be my biggest nemesis in the movie. Kent was in Craig's entourage and the only member of that entourage with any common sense.

"You ready for this?" Ben asked.

"I had some jitters last night, but I think I'm ready to go," I said as I got onto the treadmill.

"I bet you were obsessing about the script changes," Kent teased me.

"Yeah, I want to make a good impression."

"Let me give you a tip. When you get there today, they'll have made more changes. Craig used to worry about it when he first started. They'll work with you to make sure you learn your lines. If you have anything too taxing, they may have you use a teleprompter. The writers know you're new. They're not going to have you do a five-minute speech that can't be cut on your first day," Kent assured me.

I felt better after I worked out. Kendal had waited for me when I got back, so I hurried up and showered so we'd get across the street on time. I had one of the more elaborate makeup jobs, and they wanted to tattoo me this morning. They planned to use a nonpermanent product which would last several weeks. They also needed to shave my head again. The good news was once I had my tattoos, I was good to go for the next two weeks unless they had to do touch-ups. Then it was just normal makeup.

The process wasn't so bad. They had a paste-like product that stained my skin. The problem was it took what seemed like forever to do all my tattoos. When I was done, I was pretty scary looking. When I had to wait for wardrobe, I wandered around to see the setup, and people did double takes when I walked by.

When I was finally ready, they didn't waste any time. They had me on set and doing my first scene. Jessup knew I'd be nervous, so he threw me into the fire, so to speak, to get me started. I was glad I did my lines just fine for the first take, but Craig, not so much. I soon learned that multiple takes was the norm. Catalog modeling, where you do the same poses repeatedly, turned out to be great training. The trick was to keep focused and your energy up. I found it was the same with acting. You had to have the same energy level on take one as you did on take thirty-one.

Jessup was happy with my first day.

"Good job. Just stay focused and you'll do well. We had a short day today. Be ready for a regular day tomorrow," he told me.

I grimaced. I'd arrived on the set at eight this morning. It was six now. I guess a 'short day' was ten hours.

◊◊◊

I was starved. Kendal had raided the buffet for me, but Jessup had me in back-to-back scenes all day. I was able to grab a bite between takes, so I did get something to eat. Kendal made arrangements with a lot of us for dinner. We picked a place not too far from the hotel so we could all walk.

Everyone was in high spirits. I was focused on getting some food, so I didn't notice her at first. She put her hand on my chest to get my attention. When I looked down, my breath caught. There's just something about certain women that get an instant reaction out of you. An example would be Lisa Felton: while not the best-looking girl in school, she caught every guy's notice. She was sexy as hell.

When I looked down into incredibly green eyes, everything around me went away. Here I stood in the

75

middle of a crowd of actors, many of whom were stunning, and this girl had me mesmerized. Her eyes looked familiar. She had incredibly long eyelashes, which were obviously not the result of makeup because she had none on. The next thing I noticed was her smile. She simply lit up the room when she smiled at me.

Her giggle was music to my ears. She grabbed my hand and led me to our table. As we walked to the table, I got a chance to check out her body. She was five-five, had long brown hair and was very fit. She had the legs and butt of an athlete. How I missed her breasts I have no idea. Those poor things were being held hostage by her evil blouse and they needed to be set free. They were at least a D cup. I had no idea as to who was sitting with us. It was just the two of us in a sea of conversation.

"Hi, I'm Halle, Trip's sister," this goddess told me.

Trip was part of Craig's group. If he wasn't gay, he was surely bisexual. I suspected he and Craig were more than just friends. I remembered when I first met him he made me nervous by how he'd looked at me.

"David; nice to meet you," I finally got out. "Where have you been all my life?"

"Waiting for you, silly," she said with a smile.

"I'm so sorry," I said.

"Why's that?"

"If I'd known, I would never have been so rude as to make you wait."

"Kent warned me about you," she said.

"Why would you need to be warned?" I asked in confusion.

"He said if we ever met, we'd be drawn together like magnets. Even with your scary tats, I couldn't take my eyes off you. Then you ignored me," she pouted.

"My best friend calls me a 'stupid boy.' Now I know you're around, so be assured I will not be ignoring you."

I found out later everyone was highly amused by the two of us because we totally ignored everyone else. To be honest, I'd never had a girl affect me the way Halle did. It was like Adrienne, but with Lisa's something extra. There was just something about how she moved that captured my full attention. I normally am at complete ease around beautiful women. Halle was my kryptonite. Around her, I was a tongue-tied teenager who couldn't stop blushing.

The sad part was Halle knew it. She could lead me around by my nose like I was a puppy. Thankfully, she didn't take advantage of it. Somehow, we ended up in front of my hotel room, and she kissed my cheek goodnight. Kendal had waited for me with tomorrow's packet.

"Did you see her?" I asked as I bounced up and down on my bed and almost knocked Kendal to the floor.

"Yes, everyone saw the two of you," Kendal said with a pained expression. "You do realize she's only thirteen?"

What?!?

"Are you bullshitting me?" I asked.

"Nope. She's jailbait."

"Are you sure? She has to be like, uh, eighteen!"

"No, Trip's sister is only thirteen," Kendal said to ruin my day. "She does have the hots for you, though."

"A lot of good that does me!"

I think I need to fire Kendal. She had way too much fun with this. She handed me my homework and we prepared for tomorrow. I had a hard time concentrating because I'd just gone from imagining Halle in bed with me to figuring out how to fend her off.

◊◊◊

Chapter 4 – Little Happy Dance

Sunday January 18

They didn't need me until noon today, so I worked out and then went to church. When I got back to the hotel, Halle was in the lobby and had obviously waited for me.

"Hey, want to take me to lunch?"

"I think you might be too young to be hanging out with me," I said, as I tried to put the brakes on our potential relationship.

"I think I might be your age or older," she shot back.

I told her how old I was and she smirked and said she was the same age.

"Do you only date older women like Elizabeth and Bree?" she asked.

"I think my agent is going to die. She told me you were thirteen."

She had a good laugh at me and shook her chest at me.

"Do you think a thirteen-year-old would have these?" she teased, then got serious. "Trip tells everyone I'm too young. I bet he told Kendal I was thirteen. He's just being a big brother. Plus, I don't need everyone hitting on me. I'm not that kind of girl."

She smiled at me when my face dropped.

"You big dork, did you think I was going to jump into bed with you? Kent told me you were a lot of fun," she said, then her expression changed. "Wait a minute; are you the guy they were talking about in LA? Are you the guy who went with them to Chubby Feldman's party?"

I guess I gave it away.

"You are! No wonder Trip said I couldn't hang out with you, and Kent said you were a lot of fun. I think you might be a bad influence on me."

"I hope so," I teased her.

"Not so fast, Buster. I'm a good girl," she said, as if she was superior.

78

"Still want to grab lunch?"

She thought about it for a moment.

"Kent would have warned me if I needed to worry about you."

We found a quick taco place and stuffed our faces. I could eat a few tacos. I think Halle was impressed with how many I consumed. I couldn't hang out with her for long because I had to go to the set.

◊◊◊

Today went better. Craig was more prepared and we were able to complete the scenes with fewer takes. I found out Halle was in the film when we did a scene with Lori and most of the cast. Lori addressed the student body. Trip was also in the scene. He was eyeballing me and his sister. She gave him a little-sister look and rolled her eyes.

At one point the script had me get separated from my team as we investigated a network of tunnels. I was sent over to another set where they had created a maze of tunnels. It was a pretty slick system. They could reconfigure a tunnel in no time. The walls would just snap into place. I had to be careful not to bump into a wall too hard or it would come undone. I found this out as I did a scene where I had to run from one hiding place to another and went a little too fast. The set guy had been nice about it, but I felt bad. Every mistake like that cost time and money, as Jessup constantly reminded us.

I really enjoyed this part of the movie. I was able to run, dodge, and use my new sword-fighting skills. Some of it was shot with a blue screen behind me, and I had to imagine where the monster I was fighting was. That was hard to do. One of the mistakes I made early on was not looking where the monster was supposed to be. It was difficult to focus your eyes when there was nothing to focus on. I even looked at the camera a couple of times. It was just human nature to look at what was there.

I'd find out about it later when they viewed their dailies. Dailies are the raw footage sent to the producer to review at the end of the day. The director can check the playback on set but doesn't have time to spot minor errors. They'd have to reshoot some of the scenes I'd done today. Thankfully, Jessup took the news well and I learned a valuable lesson.

◊◊◊

We didn't get done until almost midnight. I walked back to the hotel, exhausted. I really had no idea how the crew and Jessup did it. They'd still been working when I'd left. Kendal and I agreed to work on tomorrow's script in the morning.

◊◊◊

Wednesday January 21

I had to laugh. Kendal figured out they had someone who would help me learn my lines. Agents rarely were on a set and even more rarely did this type of work. The only reason she was here was my age. My dad had talked to Tom last spring and they'd agreed I was not to work without someone to look after me, at least until I turned eighteen.

Kendal was fine with what we'd been doing because she wanted to learn as much as she could. Jessup and his staff were very accommodating and allowed her access an agent normally wouldn't have. I appreciated the allowances they made for me. That was until Halle offered to read with me. It seemed no one thought I would get any work done if she helped me learn my lines. I thought about throwing a hissy fit, but Jessup gave me a look that told me not to push it.

Trip started to treat me better when he found I hadn't pushed his sister to sleep with me. Don't get me wrong, I wanted to sleep with her. Hell, she could get me aroused at fifty paces with just a glance. The good news was the feelings were mutual. We would probably have been going at it like crazed bunnies if I didn't work twelve to eighteen hours a day.

The other thing that hadn't happened was my schoolwork. It just seemed I was either on set or preparing to be on set all day long, and I just didn't seem to find time for school. But I refused to skip my workouts in the morning. I found that if I worked out, it helped me keep my energy all day and I just felt better.

I was finding a lot of actors are health nuts. Their bodies are what make them a living. There had begun to be a good crowd in the hotel gym each morning. I introduced them to *thirty minutes of hell*. The thing was, actresses are not your normal everyday girls. When they showed up in leotards and bounced around to work out with me, it was about to drive me to distraction. In other words, I was horny as hell.

◊◊◊

Today was a lot of fun. Well, not so much fun for me, but the other cast members seemed to enjoy my antics. We filmed a scene on board a spaceship. Craig was in the captain's chair, and Bree and Elizabeth were seated in front of him. I was off to the side in front of a panel of knobs and buttons and a small screen.

"Okay. We're going to run through the scene until we all have our lines and blocking right. Then we're going to do this in one take," Jessup told us.

It was a scene where we were ambushed and the ship took heavy damage. Jessup had explained they would simulate some smoke and a few sparks on set and then, during post-production, special effects would be added to make the scene more realistic. We were told to act like we

81

were worried. Craig was supposed to be the calming leader and keep us alive.

We finally had run through our lines several times without any errors. Jessup seemed nervous and looked at all of us.

"Okay, no matter what, don't stop. We'll only get one take. Are you all ready?" he asked.

We all said 'yes.'

"Places everyone! Quiet on the set! Cameras ready?"

"Ready!"

"Sound ready?"

"Ready!"

"Scene 85. Take 1! Action!"

"Dropping out of jump," Elizabeth said.

"Scan for hostiles," Craig ordered.

"No contacts, sir," Bree said.

"Stryker, warm up the weapons to be safe," Craig ordered.

"Sir, yes, sir," I responded.

That was when all hell broke loose. I had no idea our spaceship was on hydraulics. I was shaken from my seat and rolled to the back of the set where I slammed into the wall.

"What the hell!" I yelled.

"Get to your station, Mister!" Craig screamed.

That was not part of the script. I'd messed up big time, but quickly recovered and scampered back to my seat. The whole time the ship rocked in unpredictable directions. I had a death grip on the console in front of me.

"Report!" Craig ordered.

"Three contacts closing fast," Bree said.

"Main engine damaged. 85% efficiency," Elizabeth reported.

"Plotting firing solutions," I said.

"Fire at will," Craig reported.

I smashed a button.

"One hostile eliminated. Incoming missiles!" Bree yelled.

There was a tremendous crash and the bulkhead right above me suddenly had a huge dent. At the same time, sparks and flames shot out of my console and it started billowing smoke. The set shuddered and then pitched and I went flying again. It was good that everything was padded, or I could have gotten hurt.

Bree jumped up with a fire extinguisher and put out my console. I staggered up and grabbed the back of Craig's chair to steady myself.

"Weapons switched to my station," Craig said.

There was another loud crash as if we were struck again. Somehow, I managed to hang on and not crash across the set again.

"Aw, shit!" I cried.

Again, not part of the script.

"Engines are down, thrusters only," Elizabeth reported.

"Firing!" Craig yelled.

"Hostiles eliminated!" Bree reported.

I did a goofy little happy dance as the stage quit tipping around.

"Cut!" Jessup shouted. "What the hell was that little dance, David?"

"Sorry, I just kind of got into it," I said sheepishly.

Jessup had us gather around so we could see playback of the scene. I looked at the remains of the set and understood why they only wanted to do it once. When the video started, I watched in amazement. It really looked like we were on a spaceship. When the shaking and rocking started, everyone laughed at the surprised expression on my face.

"You didn't tell him, did you?" Bree asked.

"No, and I think we got what we wanted. Look at the terror in his eyes when the console blew," Jessup said with glee.

When I did my happy dance, they all looked at me with big grins.

"Dude, you are so screwed," Craig crowed.

"Why?" I asked in confusion.

They all laughed at me.

"You're screwed because they'll use your dance in their marketing. You'll be plastered all over TV doing the 'Stryker Dance,'" Bree shared.

Shit!

"And what was with all the cussing?" Jessup said with a stern look on his face.

I just shrugged and his face broke out into a grin.

"Relax, David," he said. "We can edit it. I, uh, think"

"Since we just went from PG-13 to an R rating, we may have to up the heat in the sexy scenes," Elizabeth said with a smile.

She and I had a make-out scene. I could see her evil mind at work. I just had a lopsided grin.

We had several more scenes to shoot on the damaged set. We needed to get the ship back to the academy.

◊◊◊

We were done by five and Jessup let us go early. Halle found me in the dressing area in just my boxers. I heard a sharp intake of breath.

"What are you doing back here?" I asked

"I came back to see if you'd take me to dinner," she said with a big grin.

"If your brother catches you, we're both dead."

"Let me worry about my brother. Are you taking me to dinner or not?"

"Sure, I'll meet you out front."

She dashed off just as Craig and Trip came out of the shower.

"What was my sister doing back here?" Trip asked.

"She wanted to ask me to take her to dinner."

He just shrugged and went back to talking to Craig. I hurried up and got dressed. As I walked to the front, one of the production assistants did my dance. I just shook my head and went to find Halle. I found her; she rushed up and kissed me. It was just a quick kiss, but it held so much promise. I was a little dazed as she grabbed my hand and led me out to the town car that awaited us. I heard someone yell my name, and I turned to see a photographer take our picture.

Halle must have decided to make her claim on me because she grabbed the back of my head and gave me a scorching kiss. I reacted naturally and pulled her into my arms. I felt her firm breasts mash into me and suddenly wanted to skip dinner. We broke our kiss and smiled at each other as our foreheads touched. I was brought out of my lust by the sound of a rapid-fire camera going off.

The paparazzi wanted to know where we were going. I was surprised when Halle told him. When we got into the car, I asked her about it.

"You forget I grew up in the business. My mom taught us how to get our names out there. Being on the arm of an up-and-coming star will do both of our careers a world of good," she explained.

"Are you only going out with me to get a mention on the Internet?" I asked.

"No, that's just a side benefit. I'm going out with you because I like you and want to get to know you better. Speaking of which, kiss me," she ordered.

I didn't have to be told twice. Her soft lips found mine and I wasn't sure who moaned, but we both enjoyed it. I had decided to continue to be a gentleman until she grasped Mr. Happy. I knew for a fact that I was the one who moaned when that happened. I couldn't help myself, I wrapped my hands onto her shirt-puppies and didn't let go until the driver cleared his throat to let us know we were at the restaurant. I tipped him very well for his discretion during our make-out session.

When we walked in, I could tell we weren't dressed for this place. I wore jeans, a t-shirt and my letterman's jacket. Halle was in jeans and a sweater. Everyone else was in at least a sport coat. The maître d' looked at my tattoos and it looked like his first inclination was to throw us out. That was until Halle explained who we were. She then explained I looked like that because of the movie we were making. I was shocked as his attitude changed. Halle just winked at me as we were led into the center of the restaurant and seated where everyone could see us.

As we walked in to be seated, it looked like the other diners had mixed emotions. Some looked like they were offended that two teenagers dressed the way we were could be allowed to invade their space. Others looked on with curiosity as we were being paraded to a prime location. Then I caught a few who looked at either myself or Halle with lust, much more so with Halle. The women who checked me out had to think I was some sort of bad boy.

During dinner, I focused on Halle. She told me about growing up with a famous mother and the battles with paparazzi. Her mother wanted to protect her and Trip from the public eye, but it was a losing battle. They finally decided to just embrace it and use them. The high school she went to had several teens that were in the business, so she didn't get bothered much. The downside was she didn't get asked out. The boys at her school knew to date her was to invite the public into their life. Other boys just wanted to be able to say they scored with her, and a handful wanted the fame.

"You're telling me you have never been kissed?" I asked.

"Not exactly, but I've never been kissed by someone who was doing it without an agenda. I had a long talk with Kent and my brother about you this week. They both agreed you hadn't shown any of the mercenary tendencies I try to avoid. Kent said he genuinely likes you. My brother says you're hot," she said with a blush.

"How does that work for you two? Have you ever both wanted the same guy?" I asked.

"If you gave off even a hint of interest in the same sex, my brother would have bedded you by now," she said to my discomfort. "My brother and I have different taste in men. That was the case until he met you. He somehow knows if a guy has any leanings. Trip is very successful at seducing men. I have zero interest in a guy like that. I let my brother have first shot so he can weed them out. He said you had a terrified look on your face when he checked you out."

"Yes, I was a little nervous. Something told me I was being stalked by a guy. I've never had that happen to me before," I confessed.

"Don't worry, you're safe from Trip. Now that he knows I'm interested, he'd never make a move on you. I think if you got to know him, you and he would be good friends. He's a great guy, even if he is my overprotective brother."

"I like Kent a lot. If he and your brother are friends, I suspect I'd like your brother."

"I'll tell him you said that," she teased me.

"Careful. I would hate to dump you so early in the game," I shot back.

We had a wonderful meal. I had a huge rib eye and Halle ate a vegetarian dish. Everything had gone great up to the point some ass-hat sent a drink over to her. The waiter dropped it off and we both got a confused look on our faces because we weren't old enough to order alcohol.

"We didn't order this," I said.

"The gentleman over there sent it to the young lady," the waiter offered, pointing to a man seated alone by the windows.

"Please take it away," Halle said.

The guy got up and walked toward our table.

"Get security over here, or I'll kick this guy's ass right here in the middle of your restaurant," I told the waiter.

The waiter took one look at my face and blanched. He hurried off to get help. The guy looked like he was in the junior mafia. He was at least thirty. When he got to our table, I stood up and stepped between him and Halle.

"I don't know what your game is, sending alcohol to a high school girl, but I would suggest you not approach my date."

I think he didn't realize how big I was. He looked up, saw the look on my face and my tattoos, and flinched. Several restaurant employees showed up.

"If the lady wants to talk to me, she can," he postured.

Halle stood and touched my arm. I allowed her to walk in front of me.

"Sir, are you some kind of pedophile?" she asked, loud enough that several guests gasped. He looked around and saw he'd made an ass out of himself. "I didn't ask for your unwanted advances. I'm here with my date. Please allow us to enjoy our meal without you trying to embarrass us."

The guy glared at her. Halle grabbed my hand and led me out of the restaurant.

"Don't we have to pay?" I asked.

"Not when they do something like that," she told me.

I guess she was right because no one tried to stop us. I think some of it had to do with the swarm of paparazzi that waited for us as we walked out. While the doorman found us a cab, we chatted with *Hollywood Central*. Let me rephrase that: Halle chatted with *Hollywood Central*. She announced to the world I was her new boyfriend. I wondered what Peggy would say about that when I got home. The sad part was I knew she'd be fine with it.

◊◊◊

When we got back to the hotel, Halle invited me up to her room. I needed to get ready for tomorrow, so we called it an early night. We were getting to know each other, and the more I knew, the more I liked. I started to like the idea of being Halle's boyfriend.

◊◊◊

Friday January 23

My phone had blown up yesterday because the *Hollywood Central* footage had aired. I got messages, emails, and phone calls from everyone from Adrienne, who wanted to know if this meant we were over, to Tami, who sought details on my new girlfriend. Mom and Uncle John even called to give me a hard time. Uncle John was a little jealous because Halle was so hot, but Mom took the cake when she wanted to know when the wedding was.

I was in the makeup chair when Halle found me.

"There's my boyfriend," she announced as she jumped onto my lap and gave me a big kiss.

The makeup guy gave us a few minutes.

"So, why are you so happy?" I asked.

"Mom called this morning and they're playing us up big in LA. The movie's getting a lot of buzz, and with the *Hollywood Central* interview, my agent also called. There've been some inquiries about a few acting gigs."

"That's great news."

"I think I have even better news. One of the production assistants overheard Jessup. He's ahead of schedule, so he's letting us off early today and we get tomorrow off. I think this calls for a party," she said.

"Man, I could really use a break. I have two weeks of homework and reading to do," I complained.

She wiggled her butt in my lap and rubbed her glorious breasts into my chest.

"I was thinking I need to show my boyfriend some appreciation. Maybe I could convince him to come out and play with me tonight."

Did I mention I was horny?

"If we must," I pouted.

"Cheer up. I'll help you with your homework tomorrow," she assured me.

Why did this not sound like a good idea?

◊◊◊

Halle's rumor turned out to be true. We *were* ahead of schedule, and Jessup gave us Saturday off. Our producer, Janice Utley, had flown back to LA to give the studio an update. They were happy with the dailies and felt the film was on track and on budget. At four o'clock we were set free.

Kendal stopped me when I got back to the hotel.

"I talked to your mom," she started the conversation. "You need to call her."

That was never something I wanted to hear. It sounded like Kendal had tattled on me.

"Why do I need to talk to Mom?"

"She's concerned you're not keeping up with your schoolwork. She said the deal was you wouldn't let it slide. I've gone through your class assignments and reading, and they really didn't go too hard on you," Kendal shared.

We spent the next thirty minutes reviewing what I had on my plate. She'd planned out what I needed to do to catch up. The unfortunate outcome was I would be required to spend most of tomorrow working on it. Kendal said I could go out tonight and have some fun. Kent had called her and told her the plans. They arranged for everyone to go to a dance club to blow off some steam. Kendal had met a guy who worked on the movie, so she had a date.

Kent told her she had to help me pick out clothes for tonight. I guess jeans, a t-shirt and a letterman's jacket

90

wouldn't cut it. Their publicists had already put out the word as to where we were all going tonight. Kendal hired a car for Halle and me. Kent had told her we needed to be seen together, not as part of the group. I started to think Kent had helped Kendal quite a bit with how to handle things. If Tom's firm ever opened an LA office, they could do worse than to hire Kent to run it.

◊◊◊

Halle met me in the lobby of the hotel. She sported a dress that showed a lot of leg and cleavage. I was all smiles when she saw me. Halle had mischief in her eyes as she approached.

"Are you ready to take me out, Handsome?"

"We may need security, with you dressed like this."

"I take it you like it?"

"You would be correct in your assumption. You make that dress look fabulous. Of course, you could be wearing a paper sack and make it look good."

Her eyes lit up as she pulled me down to kiss her. I had instructed Kendal to have security for us tonight. I didn't want a repeat of the last time we went out. Not that I wasn't confident I could protect her, I just didn't want to get arrested in the middle of shooting a movie.

I was surprised, though, when Chuck was our security. He looked like he was in the Secret Service, with his dark suit and sunglasses. I ruined his persona when I ran up and hugged him.

"Halle, this is Chuck. He'll be keeping the perverts away from us tonight," I said as an introduction.

It was lucky for Chuck that he had on sunglasses or his eyes might have fallen out. After he saw Halle's dress, I could tell he thought he might need backup.

"It's nice to meet you, Chuck."

"Ma'am."

He hadn't ever sounded this formal when he worked with me before, even when we were around Adrienne. Halle had obviously worked with security before. When we were in route to the restaurant, she detailed our plans for tonight and any potential trouble spots we might encounter. I made it clear Halle was his main focus tonight. I could tell Kendal had told him something different, but he wouldn't argue with me in front of her. We told him about the problem we'd had when we went to dinner last time.

When we got to the restaurant, there were several paparazzi. Halle was on her game and was a little temptress for the photographers. I was the lucky recipient of the looks she gave out. Everything had gone well until Halle suddenly froze. Chuck could tell something was wrong and he rushed up. Halle leaned over to him and whispered something in his ear. I followed his gaze and saw the guy from the restaurant on Wednesday.

Halle didn't miss a beat as she smiled and played up to the cameras. She then led me into the restaurant.

"Can you believe the guy is stalking us?" she asked.

I didn't think it was us. I was pretty sure it was her.

"Don't worry, Chuck will take care of it," I assured her.

We walked into the lobby of a hotel. I gave Halle a curious look. She just pulled me to the elevators. Was I getting lucky before dinner? No such luck. We entered the elevator and found it was a nonstop that would take us to the top floor. I stepped out to see the skyline of Vancouver. She'd picked an upscale revolving restaurant. The windows must have been twenty feet high and made for a spectacular view from the forty-second floor.

Halle looked at me and must have seen the wonder in my eyes. She gave my hand a squeeze to remind me I was with her.

"This is perfect," I told her.

It was, too. The sun was just setting, and it turned the sky orange and reflected off the windows of the high-rises. If I hadn't been with Halle, I would have just stared out the window all night. Everything really was perfect. I got to try a new dish called cioppino. It was a fish stew made with tiger prawns, mussels, clams, salmon, sablefish, and scallops in a tomato-white wine-fennel broth.

I found I was falling for this girl. She was so different from anyone else I'd ever gone out with. She had a quiet confidence and sophistication. I kept waiting to wake up from this dream. In many ways, she reminded me of the things I found attractive in women. I loved women like Tami and Kara who knew what they wanted and went after it. I think in many ways that was what attracted me to Nancy. I didn't need a woman who made me the center of her universe. Halle would be a famous movie star in her own right. She had taken her first tentative steps out from her mother's limelight.

I found it refreshing that she was moneyed, but handled it with grace, unlike Teddy Wesleyan, who felt everyone was on the make. She just accepted she had money. She reminded me of Missy Stone. Her interaction with Chuck showed me a lot. She hadn't been condescending or bossy. You could tell a lot about a girl by how she treated others who gave service to her.

Something I appreciated about Halle was her sense of style. From modeling, I had come to appreciate well-done makeup. Halle had on just the right amount for her age and the occasion. As well, I noticed she dressed like a young woman. So many girls think if they're going to dress up, they have to look like an adult. I think it's why prom dresses usually look awful. Could Halle pass for older? You bet, but she didn't look like a soccer mom going to a New Year's Eve party, either. She looked like a young woman who was on the cusp of being an adult. She was a young woman who was outgoing, fun, vibrant and sexy.

The final thing I'd liked about her was that she was very bright and perceptive. You wouldn't get any bullshit past her. I liked that she challenged me, but wasn't argumentative. She made me think. Our dinner conversation was varied and interesting. As I commented before, dinner was perfect. Yeah, I was rambling or babbling.

After dinner, we went to the club. When we pulled up, we could see there was a line to get in. Chuck jumped out and checked our surroundings. When he was satisfied everyone was okay, he opened the door and let us out. The doorman saw us and motioned us in. When we entered, we could feel the bass from the music, like a physical wave had hit us. We checked our coats and a hostess escorted us to the section of the club reserved for our group.

Halle held my hand as I talked to everyone and called them by name. That seemed to impress her. When we finally sat down, she leaned in to talk to me over the pulse of the music.

"I'm fascinated," she told me.

"With what?"

"How did you learn everyone's name? How did you know what to say to each of them?" she asked.

"I've gotten to know them. Plus, these are the people who make me look good. I want them to like me so they look out for me," I explained.

"But you even knew the caterers."

"I'm trying to stay on a high-protein diet. Did you know Tia is also a dietitian? She makes sure I have a good balance of foods to meet my needs. When she found out what Kendal was giving me during slow times on the set, she started putting together healthy snacks for me. If you asked her, she'd do the same for you," I explained.

"Here I just thought you'd made some weird demands in your contract, and that was why you were getting steak

94

while we all ate peanut butter and jelly sandwiches," she confessed.

I blushed.

"Sorry, I had no idea people thought that. No, I didn't ask for M&Ms with all the green ones taken out," I teased her.

"What are those pills and shakes she brings you?"

"Protein shakes and my supplements," I explained. "I thought everyone talked to her and told them their dietary needs. I really feel like I've taken advantage of her now."

"No, I'm sure if she was put out by it she wouldn't have been so friendly with you. I think I need to stay close to you so some of this extra stuff trickles down to me."

"They all know you're my girlfriend," I teased her.

"Good, I don't want any of them thinking they can steal you away."

"Don't worry about it. Craig taught me about the private massages with the happy endings. I find it amusing they send a new girl each time."

"What?!?"

I couldn't help myself; I started laughing. She grabbed my hand and made me dance with her. I hoped all her punishments are as severe. Watching her athletic hips sway and her shirt-puppies jiggle and shimmy as she moved was pure torture—that I'd willingly volunteer to undergo any time, any place.

Halle begged off after the fifth dance. I'd have to work on her stamina. I went over and grabbed Tia and made her dance with me. I think she quite enjoyed the attention. I made a point to dance with any of the support people who wanted to dance with me. I was proud of Halle when she danced with Julio, our makeup artist. Now that boy had some moves!

It wasn't just the production crew who was dancing. I quickly found my fellow actors had some serious dance skills. I tried some of my best stuff, but Ben and Craig had moves that put me to shame. I wanted to have them teach me their moves. The girls in my dance class would be jealous. Bree and Elizabeth were no slouches either.

I was glad everyone deferred to Halle for all the slow songs. She was quick to find me and we would come together into an embrace. That was true for all except for one slow dance. Lori found me.

"You're making me look good," she told me.

"How so?"

"I'm getting credited with discovering you," she said with a smirk. "I saw the outtakes of the spaceship scene. You were very believable."

"If you mean it looked like I shit my pants, you'd be right. They didn't tell me the place was going to move and fire was going to shoot into my face," I complained.

She thought I was pretty funny. She then told me she had to leave to go finish working on the sequel to *Disparate*. They had some work to do to get it ready for an end-of-March release. She was excited because even though her character had died in the first movie, they'd worked her into the second one.

◊◊◊

When the evening was over, I walked Halle to her room. I gave her a nice kiss goodnight that held a lot of promise. Apparently, I'd done the right thing by the look she gave me. I respected the fact that she wasn't ready for more.

◊◊◊

Saturday January 24

Kendal woke me up and made me study. She ordered room service and wouldn't let me leave the room until I was caught up. In English, we were reading Shakespeare's *The Merchant of Venice*. I'd spent half my time looking up words like 'argosies,' 'seigniors,' and 'ague.' The rest of the time I tried to figure out the meaning behind many of the lines.

Then I cheated: I pulled out my iPad and found a site which explained each section of the play. I found out why we were reading Shakespeare: he used language in ways that made you think. There could be several meanings to what was said. I had to force myself to put it down so I could finish up my other classes.

I was a little put out when Kendal checked my work and I discovered she had the teacher's answer sheets. I thought she worked for me.

Saturday January 31

I was beat when Kendal and I finally headed to the airport to go home. It had been a trying two weeks. I had learned how hard they actually worked on a film. Towards the end, everyone had gotten a little touchy, but Jessup was good at what he did. He seemed to know what we all felt and always had the right words to say to keep us going. I felt sorry for most of the cast because they still had several weeks of work to do.

Craig had confided in me the outdoor work would be very trying. He explained why natural light was much harder to film in and only gave a limited time to get the scenes shot. You couldn't have shadows from a morning shoot be different in the next scene shot in the afternoon. They tried to fix most of the shadows with lighting, but for long shots it was impossible. He advised me to really work on my lines because they wouldn't want to do as many shots of a scene if they didn't have to.

Craig, and by extension Trip, and I had become friends. Trip came to realize Halle and I were taking things slowly, and his overprotective big-brother nature went away. I found I really liked him and thought he and Craig made a good couple. It was a little sad Trip had to be very careful in public around Craig. Craig's career could take a serious hit if it was known he was bi. While people were more tolerant now, you just didn't get the leading male roles with the stigma of liking men.

I would miss Halle. It simply came down to us living in two different worlds. The two weeks were great and I was glad for the time. I vowed to myself if we ever could be in the same town for an extended period of time, and we were not committed to anyone else, I would make a serious play for her. We both knew the score, and I was glad she was smart enough to not allow our relationship to get too physical. If we had, it would have been very hard to say goodbye. We would see what the future held.

Chapter 5 – Dakora

Monday February 2

Peggy and I walked up to the front of the school. Pam saw me and hurried over. She didn't look happy.

"Tracy withdrew from school," she blurted out.

"Okay. I take it she's in treatment," I said.

"Her parents took her Friday. She's in a depression treatment center."

"What can we do to help?" Peggy asked.

"I don't know. I wish there was something," Pam said.

"Have you talked to her or her parents?" I asked.

"I talked to Mary for a minute. They were a little busy, so I said I'd call after school today," Pam said.

I gave her a hug. I could feel her relax, knowing we were there to help her. She gave Peggy a funny smile, but Peggy ignored it. We both knew Pam was attracted to me, but she respected Peggy. I tried not to think about what the three of us had together. Peggy helped to not make it weird by giving Pam a hug as well. Peggy was very perceptive of other people's feelings. That was one of the things I liked about her.

We agreed that if any of us got word about Tracy, we would contact each other. I hoped the intensive treatment would finally allow Tracy to have a normal life. I could only imagine what all she must have gone through to get to this point.

◊◊◊

Lunch was a hot mess. Everyone wanted to hear about the movie. More importantly to the girls, they wanted to know about Halle. The guys wanted to see my tattoos. My last day on the set they had reapplied the tattoo staining paste so that the tattoos would be fresh for the photo shoot with Dakora this weekend. I looked a little jarring if you just saw me on the street.

Halfway through lunch, everyone was clamoring to ask questions. I finally called a halt to the madness. We had people standing three-deep around our table. I jumped up on a bench and Coach Hope came to stand beside me.

"Settle down!" Coach Hope called.

"This is the last time I'm doing this," I started as the crowd quieted down. "The tattoos aren't permanent. It takes them about 90 minutes to put them on me and then I have to sit and let them stain my skin. They'll be visible for three to four weeks before they fade."

"Are there more than what we can see?" someone asked.

"Yes, they're also on my torso and arms," I said and pulled off my t-shirt.

"That is so cool," Ed blurted out.

I did a slow spin and then put my shirt back on. The next fifteen minutes were spent answering their questions. There was something different about the way everyone was treating me. Uncle John had warned me, but I was just the same old David. I was relieved when the bell rang. Coach told everyone to go to class.

◊◊◊

In PE we were learning the box step. I was glad we didn't have to change clothes for ballroom dancing. We just had to make sure we had on tennis shoes so we wouldn't mark up the gym floor. I was bored as I danced with Donna, one of the girls in the class.

"I learned some new moves from the actors I hung out with in Vancouver," I whispered to her.

"Anything good?"

"Oh, yeah."

We had no idea where our teacher went each day. Donna looked around and then ran over to the sound system. She stopped the song.

"David's going to show us some new moves he learned," she announced and then put on some dance music from this century.

Craig, Ben, Bree and Elizabeth had shown me their best moves. Halle upped the ante and put a whole new meaning to sexy. Then there were the choreographers. Those girls put us all to shame. Once I learned that everyone was talented, I would bug them to teach me new moves each day between takes.

Donna had taken dance since she could walk, so I always liked dancing with her. I grabbed her, pulled her onto the dance floor, and started showing her moves. I just did my thing for a song or two and then started showing them all how to do the moves. Our teacher came in at the end of class to see us all shaking, jumping and shimmying to the beat of the music. She joined us and danced with us for the last song before the bell.

I was in a much better mood after class.

◊◊◊

When I got home, Tami's mom was sitting at the table while Mom and Dad made dinner. I went to her and gave her a hug. I was a terrible boy and hadn't been to visit her for several months. I had promised her way back when Tami went to Wesleyan that I would come and visit her. When Tami went off to the UK, it had become hard for me to see her. I was happy she was here, though.

I took Duke out. I was teaching him how to play fetch to wear him out. He thought the game was to have me throw the ball and for me to go get it while he followed me. Then Duke would rush up and snatch it just before I could pick it up, and then would make me chase him. When we were done, Duke was dragging. I let him in the back door to get a drink while I went up and showered and came back down.

Mom hit me with the four words that put fear into every guy.

"We need to talk."

Dad was finishing up dinner when Mrs. Glade and Mom had me sit down. Mrs. Glade took the lead.

"I want to know your honest opinion about living in Chicago this summer," she said.

I thought about it for a moment.

"I don't think it's a great idea. I know you're not happy about it. It's not like I don't think we can take care of ourselves, but we're only going to be seventeen," I said, then argued the other side. "It would help Tami, though. I know she'll make a great doctor. If this would help her, I'd do anything to be there to support her. Plus, I miss her. I think it would do a lot to bring us closer together."

"Do you want to do it or not?" Mom asked.

"If this stays just between us, then not," I admitted. "I'd rather have her come home for the summer. She's been away too much since she went to Wesleyan. We all miss her. I think she thinks just because she can, she does. She forgets about everyone she's left behind."

Mrs. Glade's eye's misted over. I wondered how Mom would take it if I was gone for nearly two straight years. I was sure she missed Tami more than I did.

"Okay, if neither of you can make a decision, I will," Mom started. "David, you can't move to Chicago for the summer."

Mrs. Glade looked relieved. Mom was going to take the bullet on this one. I gave her a fake pout and Dad whacked me in the back of my head. I just stuck my tongue out at him. I knew what it cost Mom to do this. Tami and she had always been very close and my best friend might not take this very well. I loved my mom for being the

102

responsible one. Plus, I wasn't ready to grow up and leave home. I'm glad I didn't have to say that out loud.

◊◊◊

After dinner, Peggy came over to study. I was surprised when Pam knocked on my door. She looked stressed.

"I didn't know who to talk to, but I need to talk," she babbled.

Peggy hugged her and Pam started to cry. I silently thanked Peggy, and when Peggy gave me the eye to get out, I was more than willing to go to my bedroom to let them talk. Then I got a text I wished I hadn't. It was Tami who wanted to talk. This must be bugging her, because it was already late in the UK. I jumped onto video chat.

"What did they do to you?" she demanded when she saw my tattoos.

"I got drunk and Jeff and Alan talked me into getting it done. I have to say Mom isn't happy."

"Is this why we're not getting an apartment in Chicago for the summer?" she asked.

I knew better than to lie to her. She could read me like a book, so I didn't bother.

"No, it's my fault. Your mom and mine cornered me tonight to get my true feelings about the summer. I confessed I was only doing it for you. I think your mom misses you, so mine told me I couldn't go. Don't be mad at them. They love you."

She got a tight look on her face and then nodded.

"Okay, I agree," she said, then she smiled. "I think you're starting to grow up. You'd have never let them know how you really felt before. You keep it up and we may have to see if we're ready to date when I get home."

"Don't say it if you don't mean it," I warned her.

She knew I would jump at the opportunity, but if it ever began, it would be forever. I'd never give her up again.

"I know. I feel the same way. Thanks for telling me. I need to go. I'll talk to you later."

"Tami, I love you," I said.

"I love you, too," she said and then logged off.

Twenty minutes later Peggy came and got me. She gave me the generic version of what had transpired. Pam's best friend Tracy was being treated and couldn't have any visitors except for family for the time being. Mary told her Tracy had settled in and looked forward to the treatment.

The cheerleaders had decided to elect Mona as Head Cheerleader. That had upset Pam quite a bit. Pam also had begun to realize she didn't have any close friends except for Tracy. Peggy pointed out we thought of her as a friend. She said Pam seemed much happier after that.

Peggy then reminded me we hadn't nearly made up for not seeing each other for two weeks. I agreed she had a point.

◊◊◊

Friday February 6

"Gina Tasman to the office," the speaker called.

I was waiting for her when she walked in. Kara had arranged for her to come with me to New York for the weekend. It was supposed to be a surprise.

"Can I help you?" the office lady asked.

"I'm Gina," she told her.

"Ah, yes, Miss Tasman, you're to go with Mr. Dawson," she said, pointing me out.

"Let's go," I said and took her to her locker.

"What's going on?" she asked.

"Get your coat and your purse. Your mom told me to take you home."

104

She started to get nervous, so I winked at her. I was surprised when she just followed me out to my Jeep.

"What's going on?" she asked again as we drove to her house.

"I'll let your mom explain," I said.

She knew if I went quiet, there was no making me talk, so she decided to ignore me. We pulled up to her house and she jumped out to be met at the back door by her mom with her suitcase. I heard her squeal as her mom told her what was going on. Gina hugged her mom and then ran to the Jeep. I grabbed her suitcase and put it into the back. I waved at her mom and we drove to my house.

We met Kendal there and I put Gina's bag into Kendal's car. Mom was home, so I went in and hugged her, then grabbed my suitcase and garment bag and we were off to the airport. I let Gina ride up front with Kendal and put my earbuds in. I knew Gina and Kendal could both talk. I pulled out my reading and homework. I wanted to get it done on the ride to the airport so I wouldn't have to do homework in New York.

Whenever I would glance up, Gina was about to jump out of her skin, she was that excited. Kendal enjoyed her enthusiasm, or so I thought. I really should have listened to what was going on; I would later find out they had compared notes on me. I would find this out shortly after takeoff when Gina would innocently ask me what party hos were. I heard Kendal break up laughing in the seat right behind us. The conversation got more embarrassing the longer it went. I was never so happy to get off a plane as I was when we finally landed in New York. I vowed Kendal and Gina would sit next to each other on the flight back.

◊◊◊

Chuck was waiting for us when we made it to baggage claim, as he was my security for the weekend. I really appreciated he was my designated guy. I hadn't seen him since the night he was with me when Halle had spotted the stalker from the restaurant. During the rest of our stay, the production company provided security, so I was interested to find out what happened. He waited until we were in the car to tell me.

"The guy Halle pointed out was not a normal fan. He had bad intentions. The Vancouver police arrested him and turned up some interesting things in his van. Let's just say Halle was lucky he didn't get his hands on her," Chuck told me.

"What's this all about?" Kendal asked.

Chuck gave me a glance that told me he'd tell me everything later.

"Halle had a stalker in Vancouver and we took care of it," Chuck told her.

I was glad Chuck took care of it. The guy had given me the creeps.

◊◊◊

When we arrived at the condo, Tyler met us at the new talents' apartment. Currently, Kara and three other models were staying there. They had configured it so eight people could live there comfortably. Tyler showed Chuck, Gina and Kendal where they would sleep. While they settled in, she took me up to their place. I was staying in their guest bedroom.

"How's business?" I asked.

"We just signed a big deal from one of your leads from England. Remember Olivia and Courtney from your modeling camp?"

"Oh yeah, they both were local. Have you seen them?"

"They're two of the girls living in the apartment with Kara. We signed them when their Ford contracts expired. The two of them are going to do the shoot for the English company. They're also excited to see you. One other girl you might remember, Abby Ferrell, also lives with Kara."

"What happened to her sister Andi?" I asked.

Abby and Andi were twins that I had worked with in Miami.

"Andi's in Atlanta doing a shoot. She's normally here, you just missed her."

"What are the plans for the weekend?" I asked, getting down to business.

"You'll be working with Dakora all day Saturday and on Sunday till about four o'clock. Tonight, Adrienne wants to take everyone out on the town. Kara and the other girls wanted to take you dancing tonight. They know you have to work, so it won't be anything too stressful.

"Tomorrow Kara's taking Gina sightseeing while you're at the photo shoot. Then tomorrow night, you and Adrienne are having dinner with some key people," Tyler said.

"Could you be any more mysterious? What do you mean by key people?"

"I'll let Adrienne tell you. I wouldn't want to ruin the surprise."

I just shrugged. They'd tell me when they were ready.

I was shocked, shocked I tell you, that they made Adrienne cool her heels in the bar when our table wasn't ready. What was this world coming to? The girls and Adrienne thought my outrage was funny. I contended if a celebrity of Adrianne's magnitude couldn't get us a table, then what good was it.

That was when someone came up behind me and put their hands over my eyes.

"Guess who?" a sexy voice whispered in my ear.

"Hannah?" I asked.

"When are you going to give it up?" Adrienne moaned.

"Hey, a guy can dream," I shot back.

I was let go and found a pissed-off Halle.

107

"Oh, hey, baby," I said a little sheepishly.

"Who's Hannah?" she demanded.

"Just a girl I met once. I asked her to Prom last year and she turned me down repeatedly," I confessed.

"Okay, show me a picture of Hannah. I need to know who my competition is," Halle ordered.

I quickly grabbed my cell phone and went to the folder where I had my Hannah Minacci pictures. They were from when she surprised me on my flight to New York. The first one was her sitting next to me, vamping for the camera as I tried to sleep. Then she kissed me. I showed Halle how she could start the slideshow. It even had music.

Everyone chuckled when Marvin Gaye started singing *Let's Get It On*. I was swaying to the music as Halle looked at me incredulously.

"I don't suppose you have any pictures of me?" she accused me.

I took my phone back and opened her folder. I hit the slideshow and Bruno Mars sang *Just The Way You Are*. Halle teared up and then put me into a death grip as she kissed me.

"Aawwwww," Gina said in a singsong voice.

"What brings you to New York?" I asked.

"Kendal told me where you were going to be this weekend. She got me in touch with Tyler so I could surprise you. Surprise!"

I found out the restaurant was just waiting for Halle to get here to seat us. I was relieved they weren't treating Adrienne badly. Yes, my sarcasm meter really did go that high.

◊◊◊

When we arrived at the nightclub, we were escorted to the VIP section. They were smart in that they had rooms with floor-to-ceiling windows overlooking the dance floor. The rooms were climate-controlled, so if the club got hot you could take a break and cool off. The other feature I loved was you could turn down the music so you could hear yourself talk. All the girls went with Chuck to the dance floor and left Halle and me alone.

"How goes the movie?" I asked.

"Good, Jessup's ahead of schedule. I do have one piece of news for you, though," she said, getting a mischievous look on her face. "Remember when you were having everyone teach you how to dance?"

"Yes."

"The cameras were running and they put together a short of you dancing. It's *very* funny," she told me.

I just closed my eyes and took a deep breath. I could just imagine me doing some of the goofier moves. They had blackmail material on me for years to come.

"What's it going to cost me to keep it from going public?" I asked.

"Not a chance in hell, Buddy. The marketing people love it. Dancing Stryker will be used in the ad campaign."

She giggled when she saw the look of horror on my face. She patted my hand.

"Don't worry, you may look like a special-needs dancer, but it comes off as funny. Everyone who's seen it has about peed their pants. It makes you more human and approachable. When my mom saw it, she said you're going to be a star someday."

This just got worse the more she talked. What's that prayer? Just deal with what you have control of? This was out of my control. I could either choose to get upset, or embrace it. I decided to embrace it. I grabbed her hand, took her out on the dance floor, and showed her some of my goofier moves. I had Halle in stitches. I pulled out the Carlton dance from a show I'd seen in reruns, *The Fresh Prince of Bel Air*. They had a character named Carlton who thought he could dance. I had his hopping from foot to foot and the weird arm-swing down pat. All I needed was the

Tom Jones song to be playing. Halle threatened to quit dancing with me if I kept it up.

We had a great time. Halle and I were becoming good friends. I don't think either of us felt there was a future there, at least not right now. She and Adrienne hit it off as well. I wouldn't be surprised if Adrienne signed her to do some modeling. It seemed like they were thick as thieves whenever I was out dancing with one of my other friends.

At the end of the night I grabbed a cab so the others could continue to have fun. I dropped Halle off at the Gramercy Park Hotel. She had an early flight back to Vancouver. I was impressed she'd fly across the country just to spend a few hours with me.

◊◊◊

Saturday February 7

I got up early and went down to the apartment to collect Kendal. I found Olivia and Courtney trying to wake up.

"Where can I get a good bagel?" I asked them.

"There's a place just around the corner that makes them fresh. How about we grab some clothes and you buy us breakfast?" Courtney offered.

"That sounds good to me."

They hurried off to change as Kendal came out. Her hair was still damp. I wasn't surprised when Gina and Kara joined us. Olivia taught Gina the finer points of eating a bagel. They still thought Kendal was a barbarian when she loaded hers up with cream cheese. They'd taught me you only did a schmear when you put the cream cheese on. Their smoked salmon was mouthwatering. New York knows how to do bagels.

We met Tyler, Chuck and Adrienne in the lobby and took a car to the shoot. On the ride over Chuck gave me a hard time about going out without him. I think he just wanted a bagel. Kendal had brought one for him, and when she produced it he stopped whining.

Dakora was in the garment district and we were going to do the shoot there. They had a place off the design area set up for us. Tyler and Adrienne met with their management while Kendal and I went to find makeup and wardrobe.

Ever been somewhere where you get a bad vibe? I had one, almost immediately. There were four other male models there for the shoot. I'd seen them in previous ads for Dakora when I researched the brand for the shoot. What I noticed was they all seemed uncomfortable. There was just something about their body language that was off-putting.

I'll give Dakora credit. Their clothes were hip and trendy. Any guy with some fashion sense would want to be seen in their clothes. It was mainly geared to younger, upwardly mobile playboys. Their claim to fame was their sport jackets and suits because they weren't afraid of color. I had on a lime-green suit which surprisingly looked good. Of course, I would never be caught dead in it, but I could see a confident man could pull it off and actually stand out.

I came out of wardrobe and Kendal put her hand over her mouth. Tyler rolled her eyes and Adrienne gave me a big grin.

"What do you think?" I asked them with mock seriousness.

"You look very metrosexual," Adrienne said as she straightened my collar.

Tyler caught my look.

"It's a good thing. You look handsome," she reassured me.

It felt like a compliment my mom would have made when she didn't know what else to say. I looked at Kendal and she wouldn't meet my eye. My shoulders slumped in defeat as I walked to the set. I could hear them all giggle at my expense. I found I didn't have the worst outfit on: one of the guys had on pink.

During the shoot, I figured out what was wrong; two things, actually. The first was the other models were worried I would take their gigs from them. I had no control over that, so I didn't worry about it. It was what it was. Models lost jobs all the time.

The second was a little more elusive. It was an attitude which seemed to go through the whole company. It was the big-city-elitist-looking-down-on-the-world-with-contempt attitude. They were all very careful to be politically correct, but you just felt they thought I was a hayseed from the backwoods. I think if I'd pointed it out to them, they would have been horrified anyone would label them as such. The more I was in contact with *any* of their people, the more I disliked them.

The shoot turned into seven hours of grueling, repetitive work. The photographer wasn't very good, in my opinion. He used a set formula for how he worked and wouldn't take any suggestions. Not that I ventured any suggestions, but when Adrienne makes a suggestion, I would listen. She's a smart businesswoman who's done thousands of shoots. She knows what sells and what gets more out of the talent than just about anyone I know.

I was a little surprised when he ordered her off his set. I fully understand the photographer was in charge. I just thought he looked petty and foolish by doing it. The other side of it was if you pissed her off, she was one of the few people who could run you out of town.

When we were done, Adrienne had left Tyler and Kendal to review the photos. I went and showered and came out to find the wardrobe gal packing up my clothes from today.

"Is that for me?" I asked.

"Yeah, they said you were going to wear them. Did you want to change into one of them?" she asked.

I took the worst ones and put them back on the rack. She looked concerned.

"I don't live in New York. People back home would make fun of me if I wore these," I explained.

She looked around to see if anyone was listening.

"I'd suggest you take them. No one said you have to wear them," she almost pleaded.

"Do you know anyone who'd wear them?" I asked.

I hated to take something and then toss it. These were $500-and-up jackets, after all.

"Yes, I'm sure I do."

"Put them in a different travel bag and I'll leave them with the doorman at the place I'm staying."

I gave her the info and then picked out something to wear. For all the over-the-top clothes they had, they had just as many that were really good. Creative people needed to push boundaries to get better. Some things worked, and others didn't. This was why Dakora was becoming the twenty-something's Armani. If you wanted to impress, you wore Dakora.

◊◊◊

When I got back to the condo, Adrienne was sitting in the living room having a glass of wine with Greg and Angie. I was a little shocked they were here, and also that they were dressed like they were going to a business meeting. Greg had on a suit and tie, and Angie looked very professional in a blazer and slacks. Angie gave me a hug and kiss and Greg just smiled at my confusion.

"I bet you're wondering why we're here," Angie said.

"A little, but I'm glad to see you."

"Come sit down and I'll let Adrienne tell you," she said as she led me into the living room.

"I talked to Angie when we were in Utah for the Range Sports shoot. She told me about you working with her to set up a nonprofit to help teen moms. I get hit up for charitable causes all the time. One of my friends mentioned she wanted to put together a coalition of like-minded groups to assist pregnant women who might need help.

"One of the ideas they came up with was an ad campaign. Tonight, we're meeting to talk about organizing it and hopefully convince some people to volunteer their time and talent," Adrienne said, looking at me meaningfully.

I think they thought I would just agree on the spot. If I hadn't just spent a day from hell, I might have.

"Do you have any food? I'm literally starving."

The three of them looked at each other, trying to figure out what to do. Then Angie just shook her head.

"Don't even try. We better feed him. If we don't, he gets a one-track mind and won't let it go."

"What do you mean?" Adrienne asked.

"If you ever want to distract him, all you have to do is mention something he loves, like food," Angie clued her in.

"Yeah, you should see him if you tell him there's a batting cage he can use," Greg teased me.

"We have one in the basement. A couple of the Mets and Yankees live here," she informed me.

"What? You have a batting cage? Can we go use it?" I asked.

They all laughed at me. Tyler must have been eavesdropping because she brought out a cheese and cracker platter. I don't think she was used to having a teenage boy visit. It looked like a half a serving, not something you would share with five people.

◊◊◊

We ended up at the Waldorf Astoria. It was very elegant. The Silver Corridor is something you must see. Greg, Angie and I acted like tourists as we walked through the hotel on our way to dinner in the Empire Room. I was glad I had Dakora on because everyone was dressed to the

114

nines. I spotted Hannah Minacci. I decided on a different tack to try and win her over. Begging hadn't worked last time.

I pulled out my cell phone and sent Angie a text, even though she was standing next to me.

'Who's on Greg's Free Pass list?'

Her phone dinged and she dug it out of her clutch. She gave me a dirty look when she saw it was from me. About that time Hannah walked up. Angie looked up and sucked in her breath. Angie and Greg had a list of people they could bed without getting permission. It had started out as a joke. They put people on their list that they would never get to sleep with. Greg had gotten a little irritated when I unknowingly started to work through his list. Angie decided to up the ante by putting me in all three of her slots. Greg knew it would never happen, but if it did, he couldn't complain.

The big one on his list was Hannah Minacci. He'd been green with envy when I sent him pictures of her kissing me. Standing in front of us was Greg's, and my, dream girl. Angie was suddenly nervous.

"Hey, Hannah," I said nonchalantly and then looked back down at my phone.

Out of the corner of my eye I could see Adrienne arch her eyebrows—she'd figured out what I was doing. There are two things you can count on with very attractive women. The first is they do not get hit on as much as you'd think. Guys just voluntarily eliminate themselves, because they figure the girl's out of their league. The second is they're used to everyone treating them as if they're the most important person in the room. If you want one of these girls to notice you, make a point to ignore them.

I sent Greg a text.

'Now or never!'

He checked his text and flinched. I was proud of him, though, for starting to talk to her as I slightly turned and played with my phone. In reality, I was sending text messages to my friends, letting them know Greg was hitting on Hannah Minacci. Alan called bullshit, so I had to sneak a picture.

"Hi, I'm Greg, David's brother, and this is Angie, my wife," he said as an introduction.

I wasn't impressed with his game. It's not a good idea to introduce your wife if you want to hit on someone.

"So, how've you been, David?" Hannah asked.

Angie had to nudge me. I looked up as if I hadn't heard her.

"What?" I asked.

"Hannah was talking to you," Angie chastised me. "He can be such a 'stupid boy' sometimes. I think he's gotten worse since he became a movie star."

I could have kissed Angie at that moment. Hannah tilted her head in interest.

"What's this about a movie?" she asked.

"Lori Winnick recommended me for a part. She's starring in a new sci-fi thriller," I said, shamelessly name-dropping. "You know how it is. If modeling wasn't enough, then doing a movie causes everyone to go nuts about you. You should see the list of A-Listers who want to go to Prom with me. I might have to be contrary and take one of the girls I'm dating this year."

"Oh," was all Hannah said.

I think Adrienne choked on something. I about ruined my act by shooting her a dirty look. I recovered and saw Deb Thomas, the vice president of talent development for Ford's Chicago office. I put a big smile on and waved her over.

"Hey, Deb, I think you know Adrienne and Hannah," I said, knowing full well she did. "This is my brother and his wife, Greg and Angie."

"I hear good things about your movie. Are you and Halle really dating?" she asked.

116

Hannah wasn't sure who she was, so I showed her a picture of Halle.

"We're friends. She wanted some publicity, so we went out a few times," I said, working it like a seasoned fly fisherman putting the bait right in front of the big fish.

Hannah seemed to be thinking about it. My only problem was, Hannah didn't need me, but that didn't mean I wasn't going to give it my best shot. She finally looked over at Adrienne and the jig was up. Hannah blushed.

"Did he just do that to me?" she asked incredulously.

"Yep, that's my boy," Adrienne crowed.

"Hey, you both owe me a Prom date!"

"In your dreams, Buster," Hannah said with a big grin, while Adrienne stuck her tongue out at me.

I could tell I was wearing them down. It might not be this year, but I would get one of them to go to a prom with me.

◊◊◊

Greg and Angie did their tour of the room. I asked Adrienne if she wanted to join me. She talked Hannah into meeting people with us. You'd be amazed at the number of people who are willing to talk to you if you have a supermodel on each arm. Then, to top it off, if you ask them for money for your nonprofit, they would whip out their checkbooks and give you lots of it. I figured out pretty quickly that if Adrienne or Hannah asked, the checks were bigger. I would need to get them both to the next fundraiser I was involved with.

They were also very good at convincing the *talent* to donate their time. I personally wasn't given a choice, but I think I'd get over it. I was already scheduled to meet with Hannah and Adrienne after I finished up at Dakora tomorrow.

◊◊◊

Greg and Angie were exhausted when we got back. Angie had talked to the other directors of the nonprofits to get ideas. They all seemed to have the same problem: not enough funding. They hated the constant battle of trying to do good things while having to spend a large part of their time working to get the money to get them done. They were thrilled about some of the ideas they had learned tonight. I could tell Angie was excited.

I went downstairs to the apartment. Tyler had given each of us a key, so I snuck into bed with Kara. I hadn't seen my friend for a while and I missed her.

"You smell like perfume," Kara accused me after she'd given me a kiss. "Go take a shower."

I crawled out of bed and did as ordered. I think it was all a ruse to get me naked because she attacked me in the shower. I liked how she thought. She used me in several pleasurable ways. I really wished (again) that Kara wasn't working full time. I would have loved to be her boyfriend, but not part-time. She finally was able to slay the beast.

"Are you sure you can't get it up again?" she asked.

"Give me a minute," I answered.

"While you're reviving, I need to talk to you."

Not her too!

"I'm worried about Gina. What happened between her and Alan?"

"Neither of them really said. I think they just decided it had run its course. I haven't heard either one say anything bad about the other. If there was anything earth-shattering, Alan would have told me," I shared.

"Does she seem happy?"

"I think she was a little unsure of how we'd all treat her. At lunch, Alan made a point of making sure she was welcome at our tables. She doesn't call me a slut as much as she used to, but I don't know if it's because she's worried about what I think, or if it's just a function of me being gone so much."

118

"So, you measure people's happiness by them calling you a slut?"

"Pretty much," I said, showing her that Mr. Happy had come out of his coma.

"You *are* a slut," she said, and then squealed as I jumped on her.

Chapter 6 – Only the Lonely

Sunday February 8

I bounced out of bed early and started making a racket to wake up all the girls. They apparently had been out showing Gina the town last night, based on the drunken noises they'd made at two in the morning.

"David, shut up!" Olivia complained.

"If you get up, I'll buy you breakfast," I offered.

"I think I just threw up in my mouth," Gina complained.

"We can then go to my shoot," I said as the models all threw stuff at me. "We're shooting accessories."

That was code for underwear. I heard a bunch of grumbling, but they were soon up getting their showers. Kara had to explain it to Gina, but then Gina ran into the bathroom, to the amusement of her sister. I went upstairs and crawled in bed with Greg and Angie. I was entertained when she snuggled up to me. Greg cracked an eye open.

"What are you doing with my wife?" he grumbled.

"I thought I'd wake her up so she could go to breakfast with me and then I'd take her to my photo shoot. There'll be five good-looking guys in their boxers."

That got her to sit up.

"I think the breakfast thing sounds okay, but I don't think she'd want to see something like that," Greg pondered.

"Think again," Angie told him.

She went and took her shower. Greg gave me a hug and then joined his wife in the shower. I made sure Chuck was up so he wouldn't complain about missing breakfast. When we got downstairs Tyler talked to the doorman about getting us a minibus. You'd be amazed at what a New York doorman can get you if he was properly motivated. In his case the motivation was cash.

We went to the place around the corner. Bagels seemed to settle the girls' stomachs. I had steak and eggs. Greg and Chuck went for the waffles. I was a little jealous because they looked good. Angie joined me in getting steak and eggs. She had decided she wasn't going to put on as much extra weight this time. My understanding was that a woman's body would do pretty much what it wanted during pregnancy, so I just bit my lip. She might be able to keep a few pounds off, but her goal was to be healthy. I noticed she made Greg give her some of his waffle.

The girls had been bad last night. They had flirted shamelessly with a group of guys. Gina had suggested they give them fake names and numbers. That had just emboldened the bunch. Not that they needed any encouragement, but Kara had warned them that they were there with her little sister. All in all, it sounded like tame fun.

◊◊◊

When we got to Dakora, you could feel the models were more relaxed, due to the management team not being there today. It was just the photographer and his people in makeup, wardrobe and lighting. I introduced the girls to all the models.

The photographer even seemed to be more relaxed. He made a point to talk to Adrienne and apologized. Tyler filled me in later, saying he'd been ordered to do the shoot a certain way. He was even gracious to my guests. I normally try not to bring anyone to work. I had to think, but I don't believe Greg or Angie had been to a shoot like this. They'd participated in the one that turned into a snowball fight at the Range Ranch, but they had never seen the entire process for a studio shoot.

It very quickly became apparent who the pros were in our group because they were all chatting with each other. Meanwhile, Angie and Gina watched every move we made.

Thankfully Kendal noticed and talked to them. While we're used to stripping down in front of a group of people and letting them take pictures of us, it's not the same as being ogled like you were part of the Chippendales.

When we finished, I talked the photographer into taking a group shot of all my friends. I wanted to have a picture to show Craig when I went back, to show him what an entourage *should* look like. When I explained what it was for, the photographer and models were on board. I had to laugh when the female models all stripped down to their underwear. Kara even got Gina to go along with it, and I about fell down when Greg and Angie joined us for some shots in their underwear. It seemed like the only ones not doing that were Kendal, Tyler and Adrienne. I did get them in some of the shots, though.

Tyler loaded up everyone and headed for the Gramercy Tavern for lunch. Chuck, Adrienne and I went to the next shoot.

◊◊◊

Tattoos suck. The makeup gal had to cover them all up and then put a wig on me. It was nice to see the normal me again in the mirror. They had me in jeans and a football jersey. I came out to see them shooting Adrienne and Hannah together. They both had baby bumps.

I could tell the mood was a little tense due to the serious subject matter. They both looked like they'd been crying. When they wrapped up this portion of the shoot, I stepped out and hugged them both. They gave me strained smiles, so I waggled my eyebrows and 'woofed' at them.

Who could blame me? Seeing Hannah and Adrienne pregnant was sexy as hell. I had impure thoughts while I imagined them carrying our babies. If Adrienne hadn't broken my focus, I might have seen how far I could get. I was glad Hannah gave me a warm smile.

The idea for this shoot was for me to stand with my back turned, as if I'd abandoned my pregnant partner. I had to endure two hours of that. It went against everything I believed in, so I wasn't surprised when I was emotionally wiped out by the time the shoot was over. What made it worse was the raw emotion both Adrienne and Hannah brought to it.

When we were done and looked at the pictures, there wasn't a dry eye in the house. The girls gave me a funny look when they saw me smile.

"What's up with you?" Hannah asked.

"I'm just proud to say I was part of this—something this good. You were both magnificent. I'm humbled by your talent. Ladies, any time, any place. If you *ever* need me to work with you, just let me know; I'd be honored to be there."

"You keep it up and I *will* be going to Prom with you," Hannah teased.

I got serious.

"Hannah, I wasn't just saying that. I mean it. No strings attached. Just call. And I hope you do."

Hannah gave me a funny smile and hurried back to change. I looked at Adrienne to help explain what I'd done to cause her reaction. She just shook her head and went to find Hannah.

◊◊◊

On our flight back, I sat with Gina, against my better judgment.

"Your sister's worried about you. How are you doing?" I asked.

"I have good days and then bad. It's gotten easier as time goes by."

"What happened?" I asked.

Gina thought about it for a moment, and from her look I thought she was going to tell me it was none of my business. I had pointedly not taken sides, even though Alan was one of my best friends since grade school. Gina had become a good friend in her own right. I think they both appreciated I never asked or pushed them to get information.

"I really don't know. I think a lot of it was we were each other's first. Neither one of us knew what a real relationship was. I'm pretty sure we still don't. Over the last few months, we came to understand we weren't each other's soul mate. Alan and I like each other a lot, just not enough to go out anymore."

She reached over and took my hand.

"Thank you for not making me uncomfortable. I know Alan's your best friend. It would've been easy to make me feel bad. I think Alan took his cue from you, and we're still friends," she said and then squeezed my hand. "Kara's going to be calling you."

"Why's that?"

"You're supposed to find someone to go out with me."

"Why me?" I asked.

"She knows you'll make sure I go out with a nice guy, but don't make him too nice."

"What are you looking for in your next guy?"

"No dumb jocks. I want someone who's cute and who can carry on a conversation."

"I can't ask you out?" I asked, to measure her reaction.

"No, I need you as a friend."

I could understand that. I didn't want to lose her as a friend, either. I was also attracted to her sister. I didn't need to cause problems there. Then it hit me: Mike. He wasn't currently dating anyone. He was consistently in the top ten when the class rankings came out, as far as grades went. Mike never seemed to be one to love 'em and leave 'em. The kicker was I knew they liked each other, and as more than just friends. I'd caught each of them checking out the other.

"I have just the guy for you. Do you trust me?" I asked.

"No," she said, and she pulled her hand out of mine and crossed her arms.

I just gave her an evil grin. She'd be dating Mike by the time lunch was over tomorrow.

When I finally got home, I found Peggy waiting for me in my apartment. She had Duke curled up next to her with his head in her lap. I just ignored them as I went and unpacked. I came out and kissed her on the cheek. She turned off the show she was watching and gave me a serious look.

"We need to talk."

I could tell by her body language and the tone of her voice I wasn't going to like this. I sat down in the chair across from her.

"Okay, what do you need to tell me?"

She looked down and I knew we were over. Peggy had gotten word she had a partial scholarship offer from Arizona State. I knew Mitch had already been accepted there. He didn't plan on going out for sports, but he wanted to get as far from home as he could. I also remembered they had spent some time together over the holidays.

"Mitch," I blurted out to let her off the hook.

She nodded and started to cry.

"Hey, no tears," I warned her. "What've we said all along? We're just dating because we both knew this day was coming. It's just come sooner than we expected. Does he make you happy?"

She nodded.

"Then I'm happy for you," I said, then asked, "Can we still be friends?"

"Yes! Yes, please. I would hate this if you weren't my friend," Peggy said, and then got up and put me in a fierce hug. "I'll always love you. Don't ever doubt that."

"Can I kick his ass if he doesn't treat you right?"

"I'll be sure to tell him that," Peggy said, then kissed me on her way out of my apartment.

Then she was gone. I was lost in my own thoughts when Duke nudged my hand. The thing about a dog was their love was unconditional. It was either that, or he needed to go out. I elected to believe it was love, but I let him out anyways. Better safe than sorry with a puppy.

◊◊◊

Monday February 9

By lunch, word of Peggy and me no longer dating was all anyone wanted to talk about. I had grabbed Yuri when he saw Peggy and Mitch holding hands. My little Russian tough guy had to be convinced I was okay with it. I appreciated that he would be willing to deal with that. Peggy nodded to me to say thanks. Luckily, Mitch was none the wiser.

I walked into lunch late because I'd had to fend off Lisa Felton. She'd gotten it in her head I should take her to the Valentine's Dance on Saturday.

"What was the reason you couldn't go out with me last spring?" Lisa asked as she slowly moved towards me.

She herded me into a corner like I was a frightened colt.

"My friends told me I couldn't," I admitted.

There was no way would tell her they all thought she was a prostitute.

"Where are all those friends now?"

"They're in college," I admitted, another factoid she felt was important.

"This year, what was your excuse?" she asked as I took an involuntary step back.

"Ummm, I was dating Peggy."

"Why else?" she goaded me.

"You dated Brad Hope," I said as I felt my back touch the wall.

She gave me a smirk. She finally had cornered the guy she had chased since freshman year.

"Let's call Brad a really bad idea on my part. Since then I've gone out with a few guys on dates. None of them got past second base. I've always known you were the guy for me. Word is you don't like to share your toys, so I didn't want to give you the wrong idea. Plus, I'm trying to restore my reputation. I think you're just the guy to help me with that."

I raised my eyebrows. How could I, the biggest male slut at Lincoln High—at least, according to Gina—help her reputation? She saw my expression and almost lost the smoldering look she'd been using on me.

"I call bullshit," I shot back.

She knew this tactic hadn't worked. She went a different direction, one I had no real defense against.

"Okay, I could really care less about my reputation. People are going to believe what they want, and no matter how much I deny it, they'll never change their minds. There's one thing neither of us can deny, though: you think I'm hot. I see the way you look at me. There's no denying you want me."

I bit my bottom lip. She had me there. If I thought I could get away with it, I might just throw her against the wall and have my way with her. It wasn't just me, either. I think every guy at Lincoln High had fantasies about Lisa Felton. There was something about her that woke your inner animal. Right now, Mr. Happy was trying to wrest control of the body from the big brain.

She gave me a little pout and caressed my arm. She knew what effect she had on me when goose bumps appeared on my arm and I shivered. I jerked my arm back and cracked my funny bone on the wall. That was enough for the big brain to retain control.

"Lisa, we both know that when we get together it's going to be something special. We might actually miss a week of school," I said, and she gave me a doubtful look. "I think you're not looking for a torrid weekend."

"No, that's not what I want," she confessed.

"If that's the case, do you really want to be the rebound girl?"

I was surprised it sounded logical. I had pulled the argument out of my butt as a Hail Mary attempt. It stopped her for a moment so she could think about it. Then her eyes snapped up and stared me down. She got a big grin.

"Have you ever heard the term 'sexual healing'?"

Mr. Happy, the sneaky bastard, caused me to lean down and kiss Lisa. Lisa hit me like a runaway linebacker who Bert forgot to block and slammed me against the wall. I may have blacked out a little because I had no idea Coach Hope had watched our byplay until he physically pulled us apart. He had an amused look on his face.

"About the time I think you might be acceptable to date my daughter you do something like this. Go wash your face," he ordered me. "You have lipstick all over it."

"You, young lady, need to go to lunch, and I better not see you anywhere near Mr. Dawson. If I do, you both will be getting detention," Coach Hope added for good measure.

I ended up doing something I'd only done once before: I found the handicap stall and beat Mr. Happy into submission. There was no way I could walk around the rest of the day with him standing tall. When I finally got to lunch, I found it was vegetarian day. I wasn't happy when all the sack lunches were gone, so I grabbed three apples and two bananas. I then went to the vat of peanut butter and scooped out a healthy serving onto my plate. I just prayed Maryanne Webber hadn't licked the spoon.

I found Mike and Gina and pointed at them. They followed me to an empty table—well, it had three freshmen sitting at it, but they decided to leave. I wasn't normally a bully. I made a mental note to make it up to them later.

"Gina tells me you did a photo shoot with Hannah Minacci and Adrienne," Mike ventured.

I pulled out my iPad and put in the password, then handed it to Mike so he could see the pictures from the weekend. While he flipped through the pictures, I cut up my fruit and dipped it into the peanut butter. Gina gave me a funny look but kept her peace. When Mike was done, Jeff darted over and stole my iPad. I figured it would keep everyone else busy so I could talk to these two.

"I've decided it's time," I said.

Mike was always a good straight man.

"Time for what?"

"It's time that the two of you go out," I said, and they both gave me a look. "No whining. Gina, you think Mike's cute. I've heard you comment on his butt more than once."

Poor Mike went beet red.

"And I've heard Mike say you're okay," I said with a straight face.

Gina went from shocked to pissed in under a second. She glared at the two of us.

"I never said that," Mike complained. "I've always said she was good-looking. You were the one who said she was just so-so."

Gina turned on me, as I held my hands up.

"I had to say that. You were dating my best friend."

I don't think she bought it, but she had bigger matters to worry about. I would need to watch my back for the next few days.

"Anyways, it doesn't matter what I think. What matters is Mike has it bad for you. Do a guy a favor and take him to the Valentine's Dance," I said to change the subject.

I kicked Mike under the table. He got the hint.

"Gina, will you go to the dance with me?"

She gave me a hard look and then turned to Mike and smiled. My work was done. I went to find the freshmen, invited them to our table, and showed them pictures from my weekend. Cassidy pointed over at Mike and Gina smiling at each other and gave me a kiss on the cheek.

◊◊◊

When I was done with practice at State, I went straight to Tom and Mary Dole's house, since I hadn't gotten much news about Tracy. I figured they would tell me face-to-face, and feed me. When Mary opened the door, her face lit up.

"Have you eaten?" she asked.

If Mary was cooking, it wouldn't have mattered. I would have had a second dinner with them. Luckily, I hadn't. I called Mom to let her know I would eat at the Doles'. Mary made fried chicken with all the fixings. During dinner, we just caught up on what was going on each other's lives.

Tom said he'd received the first cut of my ads for the single-mother campaign. He showed me the shots they planned to use for the first wave of advertising. Adrienne and Hannah both had come alive with their raw emotion.

"How could you? Sorry," Mary said, getting caught up in the image which had me turn my back on them.

"I think if either of them was carrying David's baby, it would have been a whole different shoot," Tom said, coming to my defense.

Mary just nodded. We went to the living room and I brought up what I came over for.

"I want to see Tracy."

Tom and Mary looked at each other. Finally, Mary nodded.

"Right now, only family can see her. Let me call Dr. Hebert and see if we can get you in."

"Can she leave the facility?" I asked.

"Why do you ask?" Mary questioned.

"Saturday is Valentine's Day. I thought maybe I could spend the afternoon with her and then take her to dinner."

I could tell they weren't sure.

"Tell you what, talk to Dr. Hebert. See what she thinks. I'll abide by whatever she decides. I just miss my friend."

◊◊◊

When I got home, Duke was a wild child. He and I were sent to my apartment for being too rowdy in the house. I'd planned on going to the Dole's so I hadn't taken him with me today. I didn't realize how much the girls wore him out while I did *sixty minutes of hell*. I would have to bring him tomorrow.

Just before I went to bed, I received a text from Tami. I jumped onto video chat.

"Tell me everything," she ordered.

I looked at the clock and figured it had to be in the middle of the night in the UK. Tami must have been worked up to want to talk about it when she should be asleep, so I told her everything. We spent the next two hours and talked about everything from Peggy dating Mitch, to Lisa Felton, to Halle, to my Valentine plans with Tracy. Tami, to her credit, just listened, and every once in a while, asked a question to clarify something. She never made a judgment or suggestion until the very end.

"I want you to think about something. In the last few weeks, you've been close to Nancy, Halle, Peggy, Kara, Pam, Tracy, Sammie and now Lisa. Now I know you haven't slept with all of them, and in the cases of Nancy and Peggy, it's run its course. When do you think you'll be ready to be with just one woman in your life? Oh, and

131

something else to think about is your need to get close to them so quickly. Can you just be friends with *any* of these girls?"

That brought me up short. In a little over three months, Tami would come home for the summer. Tami could see I got her message. She gave me a look that told me she loved me regardless of whether I was all over the map with women. The clear message was to get my act together if I expected her to start dating me.

"I love you," Tami said and then logged off before I could answer.

That was a calculated shot. I had to remind myself I was still in my mid-teens. Was I really ready to make a lifetime commitment, even if it was to Tami? I finally had to agree with my mom. It might be too soon for me to date Tami.

◇◇◇

Wednesday February 11

My days were full; I had almost no free time. In the morning I would get up and run a little with Duke. He was growing like a weed and full of energy, so he needed the exercise and was a good running partner. He wasn't confident enough to go off sniffing things, so he followed his pack leader. I wanted him to learn to stay with me because I didn't want to worry about a leash all the time.

Dad surprised me. He'd taken on the task of training Duke in the evenings. Duke was learning to sit, stay and come. Dad also taught him things like to lie down in the other room when we ate. Duke had figured out that Kyle and Mac were sources of people food. Dad was waging a losing battle on that front.

I would run with Duke for several blocks and then take him back to the house where he would go terrorize my parents. Mom had put a footstool at the end of the bed, and he figured out how to navigate it to get some morning loving. I would then finish my run.

I would have breakfast and then go to school where I'd lift weights. Then it was off to my classes. Jeff and I would skip out of last-period study hall and come to my place. We'd let Duke out of his crate and then take him to the gym where there was always someone willing to watch him while we worked out with Cassidy. We would then go to the dojo and Cassidy would kick my butt.

I would take Jeff and Cassidy home and then eat dinner. After dinner, I would pick up Jeff, Wolf and Jim and meet everyone at State to work on baseball. Next, it was back to home where I would study and then go to bed.

The workouts and practicing the fundamentals of baseball had started to pay dividends. My hand speed and control of the bat had made a big jump from my freshman year. I'd learned to place the ball by trying to hit down each baseline, up the middle, and bunt.

I was surprised when word seemed to get around that we worked out at State each evening. It seemed like someone from State's coaching staff would show up with a few of their players each evening. They taught us drills and techniques which we could all see would make us better players.

Some of the most fun I had was learning from Shiggy. Since I'd started working with him, my fastball speed had jumped from 78 to 82 mph. I now used my strong leg muscles to give me extra pop on the ball. I found I had more control as well. Part of it was just a natural growth in talent, but a big part came from Shiggy's coaching.

Last year I had four pitches: the four-seam fastball, the two-seam fastball, the forkball and the changeup. Shiggy had added a slider and curveball. I about killed Wolf the first time I threw my curve in live batting practice. It forgot to curve. It's a good thing we're good friends, or he might have taken it the wrong way. Plus, I could outrun him. Jim was also good enough to let me hide behind him until Wolf finally calmed down.

What was my point of talking about my schedule? I didn't have time to find a replacement for Peggy. She really had gone out of her way to accommodate my schedule. She made a point to come to my house and have dinner with us. Half the time, she and Dad or Mom made the meal. She'd be waiting for me when I got back from baseball, spoiling my dog. We would study and spend some quality time together. Then she'd go home.

I had no idea how good she'd been to me until she wasn't there anymore. I missed her, but when I saw her with Mitch, I found I wasn't jealous, which surprised me. I had to think long and hard about that one since I knew I would have gone nuts just a few months ago. I finally figured out Peggy had done a good job of preparing me. She was never the jealous type. She'd always insisted that we just dated. I found I honestly felt like we were more friends than lovers.

Two things hit me. First, I was lonely. I know, it had only been a few days, but I missed my time with Peggy. I was used to our talks every day. I missed the scent her cinnamon shampoo left in her hair. I longed for someone to just touch me and make me feel cared for. I missed the intimacy we had. Why did I need the intimacy so badly?

The second was something I wanted to work through, and that was what Tami had asked me. Was I ready to settle down? I didn't know.

If all this was just about sex, I could find that with just a few phone calls. Hell, Lisa Felton was chasing me. Deep down I knew it would be a mistake, but I had a sinking feeling she might catch me this time. Tami told me I needed to get it out of my system before she got back from the UK. Could there be a better way to do that than with Lisa?

All of this swirled around in my head as I went to lunch. I don't know why, but when I saw Lisa looking for a seat, I walked up behind her.

"Let's find a table of our own," I suggested.

That apparently startled her because she about dumped her tray. She checked to see if I was teasing her or if I was serious. She must have decided I was serious because she found a small table off to the side.

"What do I owe the pleasure of eating with you today?" she asked.

"I thought if we were going to go out, we should get to know each other better," I said.

"Look, David, I'm not really in the mood to play any games today. If you're just leading me on, please tell me. I really don't think I can get my hopes up anymore."

I took a deep breath. The last thing I wanted to do was to hurt her feelings. Was I ready for the backlash this would cause? Hell, just having lunch with her would get me a bunch of shit from my friends. Actually, dating her would be much worse. The thing was, though, I could survive it. I was a stronger person than I was a year ago. Not to sound conceited, but if I said it was okay, then my friends would accept her. That was one of the benefits of being a leader, or an 'Alpha Male,' as my uncle would have said.

"Here's the deal: I would like to date you. I don't know if we'd ever become more than that, but I wouldn't rule it out. How about I take you out Friday night? We do the dinner and dancing routine and see how it goes. I'll warn you, though, I have plans for Saturday. Before you ask, I don't plan on going to the Valentine's Dance. I have a friend who's sick and I want to spend the day with her."

"Tracy?" Lisa asked.

"Yes."

"What about your other friends? What about the actress?" she asked.

"Lisa, I never said I was going to be exclusive with you," I said, and she stiffened. Even to me, I sounded like a dork. "I didn't mean to be so harsh, but for now we'd just be dating. Could we get to the point where we're exclusive? I don't want to give you any false hope, but maybe."

"You're either the biggest dick or the most confident guy I know," she complained.

"If you need to test the biggest dick theory, I might have some suggestions," I teased her.

"I might enjoy that," she said with a smile, and then got serious. "Seriously, though, I appreciate you letting me know where I stand. Most boys would have just taken me out and then dumped me. I can't really see you doing that. Before I agree, I have one more concern: what're your friends going to think of us going out?"

"They aren't going to be happy. I can talk to them and they'll grudgingly accept it, but I doubt it'll keep them from making comments that might be hurtful. You need to decide if you want to go through what's coming or not. I wouldn't think any less of you if you decided not to."

"To know me is to love me," Lisa said with a big smile.

I could almost feel the earth tilt on its axis when Lisa crawled onto my lap and kissed me. I wasn't aware that everyone in the lunchroom had watched us. Lisa and I both noticed the whole room go quiet. Lisa looked me in the eyes and started giggling.

"Oh, shit. I think we may have just become the top targets for gossip around here," Lisa almost whispered.

"Then let's give them something to talk about. Take my hand and we'll walk out of here with our heads held high," I suggested.

We did just that. The lunchroom was quiet until we hit the door and then pandemonium erupted. Lisa and I laughed as we walked to our next classes.

◇◇◇

I expected some backlash, but I didn't expect it so soon. Waiting for Jeff and me when we went home to let Duke out was Peggy.

"What do you think you're doing?" she started.

Jeff, wise man that he was, fled to my apartment. He'd let Duke out while I dealt with this. I raised my eyebrows and looked at her. This, of course, didn't unnerve her at all. She knew me too well.

"Don't even go there," she warned me. "I want to know why I hear you're going out with Lisa Felton only a few days after we broke up."

I think even she realized how dumb it sounded.

"I think you just said it. You broke up with me."

I would leave the rest unsaid, like that she no longer had a say in who I decided to date. I figured it would just get me chewed on even more. Tami had taken the time to teach me little things like that the hard way. No one ever said I wasn't trainable.

"I don't care. It doesn't give you the right to go out with her."

"I'm sorry if I'm about to say something really stupid, but how does our breaking up—you know, where you said you no longer wanted to date me, then you started to date someone I happen to loathe—how does that not take the *right* to say who I date away from you?" I asked.

"I'm glad you realized you were asking a stupid question. I was afraid I was going to have to explain it to you," she said as a jab at me, so I gave her a dirty look in return. "I have the *right* because you still love and respect me as a friend."

I thought about it for a moment, but it only made my head hurt, so I gave up. It had to be a girl thing. This was what every guy thinks if he can't figure something like this out.

"Let's assume I understand why you get to pick out who I date," I said to set the hypothetical premise. "Why can't I date Lisa Felton?"

Peggy gave me a smug look. I suddenly didn't feel like I was on firm ground, for some reason.

"Lisa's related to you. Your mom's maiden name is Felton," Peggy informed me.

"I call bullshit!" I snapped back.

"Oh, really? You might want to verify it before you act like you live in the backwoods and knock up your cousin."

That brought me up short. Peggy gave me a peck on the cheek, got into her car and left. Jeff had heard the last part of the exchange and had a silly grin on his face.

"Now I know why you want to go to Kentucky," he said as he took off running.

Duke thought it was great fun when Jeff ended up in a snow drift!

◊◊◊

Before I went to the gym and did *sixty minutes of hell*, I called Kendal.

"Do you work for me?" I asked.

"Yes, why do you ask?"

"I just want to make sure you don't work for my mom or dad. I want to be sure you answer to me!"

"That's an interesting question. Technically I work for your dad, since he signed your contract papers. Why do you need to know? Are you thinking of getting emancipated?"

"No, I just need you to do something and don't want my mom to know."

"This is interesting. Tell you what: I give my word I'll not tell your mom as long as what you're asking me to do isn't immoral or illegal."

"Define immoral for me," I asked for clarification sake.

"Just spit it out. If you don't trust me by now, then you never will."

"I need you to find out if Lisa Felton and I are related, before Friday."

"Oh, Dear Lord! Did you knock her up? You know I saw what you did to poor Hannah and Adrienne."

"Bite me! Chop, chop, get to work," I ordered.

"Keep it up and I'll call your mom," she threatened, and then hung up on me.

I think she was working on it.

◊◊◊

I got home from the dojo to find cars in my driveway. Peggy and Kendal had beaten me home, and I had to park on the street. Of course, Duke spotted Precious, and the two of them were rolling in the snow. Duke had gotten to be all legs and clumsy. Poor Precious, the evil cat from all nine levels of hell, had the upper hand. I had to pick her up by the nape of the neck to get her to let my puppy go. I was amazed when he just shook it off and led me to the back door.

Duke barked to announce our presence.

"Oh, good, David's here," Mom said cheerfully. "Let's go to the office."

I made a point to ignore Kendal. I had serious doubts if she would be my agent after this betrayal. It was so hard to get good help these days. Even Dad followed us into the office. I wondered what was going on when Mom dialed the phone and put it on speaker.

"Hey, Mom, did you find your genealogy chart?" my mom asked my grandmother.

"I did. Now tell me again. What was the girl's name?"

"Lisa Felton. She's David's age and has a brother Billy, who's a couple of years younger," I said.

"Yep, here they are. Your great-grandfather had two boys, Claude and Jedidiah. So, you are related to Lisa."

139

"Thanks, Mom," my mom said and then hung up.

Everyone looked at me.

"If you decide to start dating your cousins, make sure you're serious about it," Dad advised. "I'd hate to start trouble within the family."

Of all the people in the room, I had not expected my dad to take a shot at me. I think my mom was as shocked, because she turned and looked at him with her mouth open, and then burst out laughing.

Then I remembered a conversation I'd had with my mom. Grandpa Felton wasn't her biological father. Her biological father had had a drinking problem and had died. Grandpa Felton was Mom's stepfather. I looked in her eyes, and she saw I'd figured it out. She just shrugged. They all left the office except Peggy. She grabbed my hand and we sat down.

"Look, it was just a shot in the dark. I needed to think before I talked to you," she explained.

"Lay it on me," I said.

"You're one of the good ones. Everyone knows you're a slut, but a lovable slut. You don't go out to ruin a girl's reputation or do anything mean-spirited. You're like that uncle we all have who's not quite right, but we love him. If you didn't have a really good heart, I would never have dated you."

"Okay," I said, waiting for the other shoe to drop. There had to be a 'but' in there somewhere.

"Lisa Felton has a reputation, whether she deserves it or not," she said as she held up her hands so I wouldn't interrupt her. "David, I want you to think about something. Why would I come to you and try to stop you from dating her? I know you've dated other girls. I might not know all of them, but have I ever come to you and warned you off? I think you know I wouldn't be here if I didn't have strong feelings about this."

140

Peggy was almost in tears. I think even I knew dating Lisa was wrong. I'd heard all the rumors. I didn't believe them all, but where there was smoke there was usually fire. Was it a cop-out?

Peggy knew if I went quiet I needed to think it through. She respected me and let me decide. I think my knee-jerk reaction was I wanted to date Lisa. I knew I could stand up to everyone and get away with it. The question was, just because I could, should I?

Part of being a leader was to act like one. Lisa Felton had an animal magnetism that drew me to her. Would I honestly take the relationship past just sex? That was the real question. Don't for one minute think I wouldn't do something just for sex—I was a teenage boy, after all, with hormones coursing through my body. Hell, I got a hard-on several times a day. Lisa Felton was one of the causes of the swelling.

What I needed to think about was if I dated Lisa Felton, would it in some way hurt the people around me? According to Peggy, it would. Last year Cindy, Beth, Suzanne and Eve all agreed it would. Even Tami had made not-so-veiled threats to me if I dated her. If all the women I cared about felt so strongly about me not dating her, shouldn't I listen?

Then again there was the whole teenage-boy-wanting-hot-monkey-sex thing.

I think Peggy could read my mind. It could have also been the bulge in my pants that would grow and then go down.

"David, if this was just about sex, I would say you should go for it, but I just think you're better than this. I know you work very hard not to tarnish your public image. I think you also care what your friends think. I'd hate for either to be hurt because you needed to get laid. I'd also be shocked if you couldn't arrange to get laid by a number of friends with just a phone call."

I picked up my phone and dialed a number. Peggy heard her phone ring and looked at it. I grinned at her and she got a serious look on her face.

"Do you really want to sleep with me?" she asked.

I couldn't read her expression. Did I want to sleep with her? The honest answer was no, not if she was going to save her virtue until she was married. If she wanted to just have no-strings-attached sex, then yes.

"That depends on you," I said.

I started to feel guilty because I knew Peggy had just started a relationship with Mitch. Even though I thought Mitch was a jerk, I thought enough of Peggy to not put her into that position.

"I'm sorry. I should have never asked. I hope this hasn't hurt our friendship," I said.

"And there you go making me love you even more. I'm not stupid. I was surprised you never pushed me to go beyond where I put our boundaries. I also know you wanted more, but you put my feelings before yours. I'm sure if you'd wanted to, you could have convinced me. That's something I'll always appreciate about you. Just so you know, you asking made me very happy."

"Okay, I'll call Lisa and tell her we aren't going out," I said.

Even though I had gone along with what Peggy wanted, I didn't feel like I'd caved. I'd thought it through and agreed with her. Something else I'd been holding off on was Pam. I thought the two of us could date until the end of the year and be happy. When Tami came home, I would play it by ear. If the spark was still there, then it was an easy decision. Tami had always been the one.

◊◊◊

Peggy stayed for dinner. Kendal saw the way I looked at her and suddenly had to be somewhere else. After dinner, I went up to my apartment with Duke to study. I wasn't

142

able to concentrate because I had to have a talk with Lisa. I finally gave up and called her.

"This is a surprise. Can't wait until Friday to talk to me?" Lisa answered.

Obviously, she'd looked at her phone.

"Yeah, about that …" I started.

"Seriously?! What do I have to do to get you to take me out?" Lisa ranted. "Don't tell me, your friends think it's a bad idea."

"Did you know we're related?" I asked.

"Technically, yes, but what does that have to do with it?"

"I just thought I'd throw it out there."

"David, just man up. Tell me we're never getting together and I don't need to chase after you ever again. Don't keep making me hope. Please, just tell me," Lisa said as she started to cry.

I felt like the biggest dick. I really did like Lisa as a person and this just wasn't fair to her. She'd never done anything to me to deserve this.

"Lisa, you're right. I haven't been fair to you, and for that I'm deeply sorry. I'll understand if you never want to talk to me again, I really will. Just know I consider you a friend. If you ever need anything, I mean it, anything, call me. You're right, though. We'll never get together, or be more than just friends," I confessed.

She hung up on me. I guess I deserved that.

Chapter 7 – Confession is Good for the Soul

Friday February 13

Ever do something you knew was wrong, but you couldn't stop yourself? I knew it wasn't right. I knew there was a special place in Hell for me, but I didn't care. I knew when I was doing it I would regret it in the morning. Everyone told me not to. I'm so weak. What did I do?

They say confession is good for the soul. Let me tell you what happened.

◊◊◊

Friday the thirteenth. My Grandpa Dawson died on Friday the thirteenth. My mom wasn't normally a superstitious woman, but she always warned me to be extra careful whenever that day came up. For me, it was a doubly weird day. I was without a date on a Friday night. Better yet, tomorrow was Valentine's Day and I was visiting a sick friend.

Who would have guessed it? Not me. I had a date planned for Friday night, but I'd broken it off. Lisa Felton had skipped school the last two days. I felt awful for how I'd made her feel. It wasn't like me to hurt someone. I talked to Tami, and she told me it would have been worse if I'd gone out with Lisa only to dump her. The unsaid part of it was Lisa and I would have slept together. I've always said sex changed things. By her reaction when I broke our date it was clear she had deeper feelings for me than she wanted to admit.

So here I sat on a Friday night with my trusted puppy to keep my company. He thought it was great I would sit home and watch a DVD while I rubbed his ears. I'd gotten last year's *Transformers* movie from a Red Box. It was one of the worst movies I'd ever seen. Mark Wahlberg's character was a joke. Normally I like him in movies, but

144

they had him say crap I couldn't believe he let them film. They'd turned him into a cartoon character.

I'd gotten to the part of the movie where they suddenly had dinosaur transformers. Oh my, that was when I realized I was about ten years too old to watch this. It had to be written for six-year-olds. I was relieved when I heard someone knock at my door. It couldn't be any of my friends. They all somehow knew the code to get in.

I ran downstairs and found Lisa Felton, who looked pissed. Suddenly the movie looked a little better. My buddy Duke decided he needed to go out.

"Come on in. I need to round up my pup. There are sodas in the fridge," I told her as she pushed past me.

I admit I let Duke explore the county before I went back up. He ran up ahead of me and I came upstairs to find a happy boy in Lisa's lap, kissing her. Puppy kisses will put anyone into a good mood. Lisa smiled and rubbed his tummy. I think Duke had another fan.

I picked up Duke and put him in his crate and then turned to face the music.

"I've been thinking about us for the last two days. I can see now we're never getting together. My problem is I can't get you out of my head. I need closure," Lisa told me.

"Whatever you need, I'll help," I said.

I understand why girls think guys are stupid. Well, not stupid, just clueless. As soon as I said it, I knew I couldn't unsay it. 'Whatever you need' caused Lisa to get a smile on her face. She stood up and dropped her coat from her shoulders. I just looked at her from my recliner and tried to figure out what she was up to.

I took a good look at her and there were klaxon warning sirens going off in my head. She had worn her naughty Catholic schoolgirl uniform, the one with the white button-up blouse that was so sheer you could see her dark nipples sticking up through it. Her plaid skirt barely covered her hidden treasures. She had on white stockings that came up to mid-thigh. This was the X-rated version of the Catholic schoolgirl fantasy.

She went to my stereo and looked at my playlists on my phone. She picked my 'sexy' playlist. I heard her choke, trying not to laugh at me as she turned it on. I guess she liked it because she began to sway to the track that began to play. When she turned around, I noticed she'd unbuttoned her blouse to her navel.

Over the years I had fantasized about this very moment: Lisa Felton, as she seduced me and had her way with me. Lisa was the bad girl you could do things with you would never dream of doing with the girl you were dating. She was a small girl who probably didn't weigh more than a hundred pounds. You just knew the sex with her would be life-changing. She would ruin you for other women. Every fantasy, every desire, would be fulfilled during a night of raunchy, no-holds-barred sex.

Of course, there's always that question about girls like this is: can they even hold a candle to the fantasy? Let's face it, you imagine mind-blowing sex that most women would have no idea about, let alone a teenage girl. You imagine a girl who would get ahold of you and drain you of all your bodily fluids. The funny thing was, Lisa Felton exceeded my fantasies.

The little vixen crooked her finger at me.

"Come dance with me," she almost whispered.

I leaped out of my chair. She pulled me into her arms and she tilted her head back so I could kiss, lick and suck her neck. While I kissed her, she worked on getting me naked. I stood there in just my socks. I know, not the sexiest image. Then she grabbed Mr. Happy and used him to lead the body to the bed. He was now firmly in control. The big brain had shut down when he saw what she wore for me. Lisa had me sit on the edge of the bed as she took off her shirt. She hiked up her skirt a half-inch, allowing me to confirm she hadn't worn any panties.

She climbed up on my lap and looked me in the eyes. I drowned in the deep waters of her soul as she tilted her head and kissed me. I had always said Tracy was the best kisser of any of the girls I had ever been with. Lisa was just as good. I would have to probably kiss them both at the same time for several hours to decide who was better. Oh God! I would never get that fantasy out of my head.

I just let it happen. I found my hands had found their way to her backside. I gave her small butt a massage while Lisa ground herself against my quivering rod. She seemed content to slide up and down my shaft as I kneaded her butt-cheeks. Her hands caressed the back of my head to hold me in place. My peter rapidly became slick with her juices.

She finally broke our kiss as I felt her shudder in my hands, and my groin got soaked as she went over the edge. She was breathing hard and had a gleam in her eyes that told me she was ready to rock my world. She pushed me back and slid down between my spread legs. She grasped my member and examined it.

I don't know how to describe it. It was as if she worshiped Mr. Happy. I was sure he would want to start his own religion sometime soon. She took her time and got to know every inch of my manhood. I was a quivering mess by the time she took the crown into her mouth. I reached for the back of her neck to help feed her my length, but she swatted my hand away. She made it clear this was her show as she started to take me into her mouth.

How I didn't climax right then and there, I have no idea. I think I was still in shock that I was in bed with Lisa *Frickin'* Felton. Every guy at Lincoln High would give his left nut to change places with me right then. The best part was she sucked me with a vengeance. She no longer played around and toyed with me. She was full-on head-bob, tickle, stroke, and tongue tricks, all geared to make me explode. There was no thought of slowing things down.

She demanded my first offering of the night and she worked hard to get it. Mr. Happy was a satisfied boy, and he felt she deserved her reward.

"Ggghhhaaaa!" I bellowed.

I pumped into her mouth. When I shook my head back and forth, and tried not to pass out, Lisa did the sexiest (and also one of the grossest) thing I had ever seen. She showed me my load on her tongue. Then she leaned over me and drooled it all down over my sex, making me a slick, slimy mess. I wasn't sure if I would barf or not, but damn!

I just lay there as she crawled up over me and then tried to stuff Mr. Happy into herself. She was so tight I didn't think I'd get in, but suddenly she had me buried in her depths. She bounced up and down like she was on a pogo stick. I got a little light-headed from the pleasure. Her box felt like someone had wrapped Mr. Happy in a giant rubber band. She went at it until her legs started to shake.

Now it was my turn. I jerked out of her and put her on her stomach. She raised her butt and I straddled her thighs. I slid home and found I was able to get all of me into her. She squealed and squirmed under me as she had another big orgasm. I just continued to pound her from behind.

When I got close, I turned her over into the missionary position. I wanted to be able to look her in the eyes as I finished. I felt myself go over the edge and found my release. Lisa grabbed my butt-cheeks and used her fingernails to pull me as deep as I could go.

"Holy cow!" she muttered as I collapsed on her.

We laid there in a daze as we tried to get our bearings back. I needed some water, so I went to the living room and got a couple of bottles out of the fridge. I sucked down half a bottle. Lisa kept up with me, and when we finished our water she gave me a searing look.

"I need you to do one more thing. I need you to take my backside," she commanded me.

Mr. Happy had thought about calling it a night. When he heard what she wanted, he caught his second—or was it his third?—wind.

"There's some lube in the nightstand," I said.

"I thought I was going to have to talk you into this."

"Tonight's your night," I told her.

"How do you want me?" she asked.

"On all fours," I suggested.

I opened the lube and covered myself. I then got behind her. Her sex was red and swollen, and juices were leaking out of her and running down her thigh. I almost stopped right then. I had just had wild unprotected sex with Lisa Felton.

"I hate to be 'that guy,' but are you protected?"

"Yes, I'm protected," she assured me.

Now she wanted me to put my member into her tiny bottom. I lubed her up and then manned up. I put a condom on. Bad things can lurk in a colon. I then pressed into her rosebud. When I took her, she screamed, which caused me to stop and start to pull out.

"Don't you dare! You finish it!" she ordered.

I let her get used to my rod and waited until she started to move. I tried to be as gentle as possible. If I thought her velvet tunnel was tight, her backside was unbelievable. What I couldn't believe was she was getting off on it. I basically held still as she rocked back and forth to get me all the way in. When she had finally taken it all, she stopped.

"Do me," she demanded.

I grabbed her hips and did just that. Normally I can go for a long time after I've climaxed twice. Not tonight. The visual was enough to put me into erotic overload. I was gentleman enough to wait until she finally found her release, but it was a close thing, I can tell you.

I lay there and tried to make sense out of what just happened. Lisa had taken me around the sexual world tonight, and it was even better than I could have ever imagined. Lisa got up and went to the bathroom to clean up. When she came out, it looked like she'd been crying. I sat up.

"What's wrong?" I asked.

"We could have had *this*," she said, as she broke into sobs and ran out of the bedroom.

I lay stunned in my bed. It took me a while to fully grasp what I had done. I'd had sex with Lisa Felton. I'd had *unprotected* sex with Lisa Felton. How stupid could I be, and on so many levels? It was just wrong, but I would do it again.

I was right. Sex changed things.

◊◊◊

Saturday February 14

I was still beating myself up as I ran in the morning. I've always found a long run helps me think things through. The good news was I now knew how good Lisa was in bed. Sadly, that was also the bad news. Last night had been one of the best nights of sex I'd ever had. I hoped I had gotten her out of my system. Who was I kidding? I'd do her right now if she wanted. God, I loathed myself for being so weak.

◊◊◊

I hadn't realized we had a mental health facility over by State. I guess it made sense; it could be used for teaching purposes. It looked like an upscale nursing home from the outside.

When I went into the facility, I was directed to a common room. Tracy was seated with a number of other people. She saw me and smiled. In contrast to her smile, she had dark circles under her eyes. I was worried about her. She patted the couch and I sat next to her.

"David! I almost didn't believe Dr. Hebert gave me permission to spend the day with you. *Meow* that you are here, I want you to meet my friends," Tracy said.

Did she just say 'meow' or 'now?' I gave a little involuntary chuckle.

"What's wrong with you? Are you making fun of me *meow* I'm officially mentally ill? I'll have you know *meow* that I'm on medication, I feel better *meow*. Dr. Hebert said I should be cautious *meow* my treatment is starting to take hold so I don't backslide. *Meow* I know you wouldn't want that, *meow* would you?"

I burst out laughing. She was saying 'meow!'

"All right *meow*, David, stop it! You're awful, making fun of me. *Meow* I know your mother raised you better than that!"

"You stop! What's with all the 'meow'?" I asked.

Tracy and the other residents broke up laughing. It was obviously a joke they played on me.

"We saw the movie *Super Troopers* last night. In the movie, they played a game to see how many 'meows' they can get into a conversation. How did I do?" she asked.

"Ten," one of them answered, which caused Tracy to high-five me.

"I beat Janice," she explained.

She then had me meet everyone. It seemed everyone was in good spirits. I think it was because Tracy was in such a good mood. Tracy was determined to get out of this place. Today was the first day they'd given her a day pass. We went to the front desk to get her signed out and then we were soon in my Jeep.

"Where to?" I asked.

"I need things. Let's go to my house," she suggested.

I called Tom and let him know where we were going. I also called Pam and told her. I'd told them I would play it by ear. Dr. Hebert said if she stayed in a good mood it was okay for her to see a few people, but not to overwhelm her.

151

She also warned me Tracy's mood could change quickly. If it did, I would have to take her back. Tracy's safety was the most important thing.

Tracy gave her dad a hug at the door. She then went to the kitchen where Mary was making lunch. Tom and I went to his office.

"How's she doing today?" Tom asked.

"Good. They have a new game they're playing at the facility, the Meow Game. Instead of saying 'now,' they say 'meow.' You and Mary will have to let her play it. You just act like you're not hearing it. They get points for each 'meow.'"

Tom just shook his head.

"I'll keep Mary in the dark. I think it'll be more fun if she figures it out for herself."

"You may be right," I said, then changed the subject. "She looks worn out. Is she getting any better?"

"I don't know. I had no idea she was that bad. I feel like I've failed her in some way," he confided.

"Tom, I know you're not very religious, but have you thought about praying? I don't talk much about my faith, but I find in times like this, it helps me."

"What do you mean?"

"I have found a little prayer is useful in situations like this. Don't worry about what you can't control. I believe you need to focus on what you can do. In this case, I think all we can do is let Tracy know we love her unconditionally and will be there whenever she needs us. This battle she's facing is up to her. We must rely on Tracy, and Dr. Hebert, to get her well again. I'm afraid this may be a lifelong battle."

"I hear what you're saying, but I still worry we're not doing enough," Tom complained.

"Just ask her, Tom. Just ask Tracy if there's anything you can do to help. If she says she doesn't need anything, accept it. Make sure she knows the offer's there. The wrong thing to do is to push yourself on her. She'll let you know what she needs."

"When did you learn all this?" he asked.

"My mom is a cancer survivor who now works with cancer patients. She and I talk a lot about what she does. If you won't go to church, you might want to come over to our house for dinner. I know you know our family has some very honest discussions. It might do you and Mary some good to be able to talk about this over with my mom. I just warn you, she won't pull any punches. Also, realize she doesn't intend to hurt you, she's just brutally honest."

Tracy came and got me and took me up to her room. She wanted to put on some makeup before Pam came over for lunch.

"Your dad's worried about you," I started out.

"I know, but I don't know what to tell him. It's not like I can snap my fingers and make myself better. If I could, I would have a long time ago."

"How about you tell him to love you and if you need his help you'll tell him."

"Do you think it would help?" she asked.

"I think so. He just needs to know you still love him."

She looked at me in the mirror and smiled.

"Thanks."

"You're putting too much on," I suggested.

She turned around to look at me. I don't think she ever thought she would get makeup advice from a guy. I smiled at her.

"May I?"

"This I have to see. Go ahead, Macho Man."

I got a cleaning towelette and wiped off her makeup. I then found face cream and put on a thin layer. I had learned to do this from Adrienne. I'd had my makeup done many times. This was the first time I had applied any myself. My goal was to make Tracy look like she didn't have any makeup on. The focus was to cover the dark circles under her eyes, so I used a concealer. Then I applied a little eyeliner to define her eyes; I wanted the eye to be drawn to them. Next was a muted lipstick. When I was done, I turned her around to the mirror.

"You better not let word of your talent get out," she teased me.

"I know. Who'd think I could do something like that? I already get enough shit about being a model."

She kicked me out so she could change clothes. I went downstairs and saw Pam.

"Go on up. She's changing," I told her.

Pam went to Tracy's room and I went to find Mary. She was about to make apple tarts. I was glad she waited and let me make them with her direction. I missed cooking with Mary. She gave me a hard time because my knife skills had slipped. One of the keys to cooking was to cut things the same size. This way everything cooked at the same rate. No one wanted undercooked or overcooked items in their dish.

When Tracy and Pam came downstairs, Tracy whispered that Pam said she looked great. Lunch was nice and everyone seemed to enjoy themselves. After lunch, we went to the living room where we relaxed and had dessert. Pam kept her visit short and went home. This was all part of the script Dr. Hebert had written for us.

Tracy grabbed my hand and took me up to her room. She wanted me to just hold her. We didn't say anything, but she had me in a death grip. I think she just needed what I so desperately needed, intimacy.

I think I finally realized it didn't have anything to do with Peggy and me breaking up. Peggy and I had never been in love. If we had, I wouldn't have taken the news she was going to date Mitch so well. In a way, it was like what Eve and I had. Once I knew she would leave, the relationship lost some of its intensity.

Bottom line, I was lonely. I could tell that Lisa Felton felt the same way. She was looking for the guy who made her feel special. If it was just the two of us, I would like to be that guy. What I needed to decide was if she was really the one. The short answer was no. I wanted to move on and just be happy we had the one night together.

Tracy finally let me go, and I could tell her mood had changed. It was hard to put my finger on what was different, but she just wasn't as engaged. She suggested I take her back. We said our goodbyes to her parents. When we got back, she thanked me for the day. We made vague promises to do it again.

I tried to figure out why she pulled back. Was it something I'd done? There was something in the back of my mind that said I was responsible for Tracy's mood change. It seemed to happen when I started thinking about other girls as I held her. Could she pick up on me not being there while I held her? Surely that couldn't be it, could it? If it was, then I needed to remember who I was with. Tracy deserved my full attention.

◊◊◊

I don't really know what I was thinking, but I found myself on the Wesleyan campus. I hadn't talked to Missy or Harper since the Christmas Dance. It was Valentine's Day. Surely, they had dates for tonight. Truth be told, I wanted to see Harper, so I called her.

"Hey, it's David," I said.

"Hey, stranger, I was just thinking about you. What's up?" she asked.

"I was in the neighborhood and thought if you weren't busy I would take you out," I suggested.

"Hang on a second," she said.

I heard a muffled conversation.

"Missy wants to know why you didn't call her," Harper said.

"You're killing me," I said, and I heard laughter.

I was on speaker phone.

"Okay, here's the deal: there are four of us going out tonight. It's the annual 'guys are jerks for not asking us out' extravaganza. If you want, you can escort us," Harper offered.

"And take the heat for all four? Okay, I feel like taking some abuse," I shot back.

"Do you have any decent clothes with you?"

"Of course."

I had put my favorite Dakora outfit in the Jeep in case Tracy wanted to dress up. Everyone was in Missy's room. Lisa, Missy's twin sister, kissed me as soon as I walked in. I could tell by the way she kissed.

"Lisa, are you going out with us?" I asked.

"How did you know?" she pouted.

"Missy's a better kisser," I teased her.

That seemed to make her sister happy. Then a girl stood up and it was Jennie Wesleyan. This could be a long night.

"Ass," she called me.

"Bitch."

For some reason that made her happy and she laid a serious kiss on me. I was a little dazed when Missy got her turn. I gave her a confused look.

"Lisa?" I asked.

They both broke out laughing. I had made a mistake. The girls were happy because they could fool me. Harper just smiled at me. I guess I wasn't getting a kiss. They all left so I could change.

◊◊◊

They wanted to go to a French restaurant. The last one I had gone to had small portions and unreasonable prices. I was surprised when Harper told them she would ride with me to the restaurant. The clear message was she and I were together tonight. We got a chance to talk on the ride to the restaurant.

"What's going on?" she asked me.

"I just didn't want to be alone tonight."

"Why me? You must have several girls who would have gone out with you tonight."

"I wasn't looking to go out with just any girl. I wanted to go out with someone I cared about."

"You want to ditch these girls and go talk?" she asked.

"Could we?"

She called Missy and told her I needed to talk. She directed me to an Italian place. The hostess said it would be an hour wait since it was Valentine's Day. I slipped her a large bill and suggested if there were any openings to keep us in mind. We were seated a few minutes later.

"Get the lasagna. It's what they're noted for," Harper suggested.

When the waiter came, that was what I ordered. I was glad I did because it was very good. Towards the end of the meal, Harper wanted to know what was really up.

"Okay, here's the deal. I like you, more than just a little bit. If it wasn't for the distance, I'd want you as my girlfriend. I thought about it last summer, but it was too soon after both of us breaking up. This fall I had football. Then modeling and the movie were taking up my time. I know all those things were excuses. If we wanted to, we could have worked through those obstacles. I guess I'm doing a terrible job of asking if you want to be more than just friends with me," I finished with a rush.

Something I liked about Harper was she was her own woman. She wasn't clingy or needing my constant attention. I wasn't looking for high-maintenance. I couldn't, with my schedule the way it was. Harper also was very direct. I guess the best way to describe her was she wasn't a game-player.

Something else about Harper was I knew I was attracted to her within moments of meeting her. At the time she was dating a childhood friend. I flirted with her shamelessly, even though I knew I couldn't have her.

"What about Tami? She comes home in three months," Harper pointed out.

"Here's the thing: I've been waiting for Tami my whole life. She tells me I'm the one, but I need to grow up. Then she started dating other guys. To be honest, I'm not sure if there is a Tami-and-me as more than friends. If Tami came to me and said she loved me and wanted us to date, I'd have to give it a chance."

"I guess I knew that. I just don't know if I'm willing to date you and then give you up."

"Harper, I'm not asking you to. I want you to be my girlfriend. I want to be exclusive. I can't worry about Tami. Only she knows if we have a future," I said, and then paused. "You know what? Part of Tami and my problems have centered around my bending to her will on everything. It's always been her choice if we date, or if I can talk to her. I can't continue like that."

I looked Harper in the eye.

"Will you be my girlfriend?"

◊◊◊

Chapter 8 – Stryker

Thursday February 19

I was on my way to the airport with Kendal. We were going to be gone for a four-day weekend to finish up the on-site work for the movie. Our destination was the Northwest Territories. We would be staying in the small town of Yellowknife. It was called 'The Gateway to the North.' I was excited to finish my portion of the movie. There would be some big chase and fight scenes that would allow me to use my newly acquired gun skills.

Craig had called me earlier in the week and told me he was trapped in the sticks. I didn't feel sorry for the city boy. Yellowknife sounded like the kind of place I'd feel at home. Well, except for the weather. It was located just 250 miles from the Arctic Circle. Craig complained he was sure he would freeze certain body parts off. I called Sandy Range and she sent up a supply of thermal wear to Craig and the rest of the production group. I packed accordingly.

Craig told me the only fun they'd found was a local bar where they did karaoke. I explained singing was not in the cards for me. I didn't even sing in the shower. He told me I could lip sync. They wanted to go out one night and have a contest to see who the best was. Craig told me to bring my 'A game' because he planned to kick my butt. I wish he hadn't done that. It made me get my dance-class girls and the theater group to help me. We'd see who kicked whose butt.

◊◊◊

It ended up I stayed Saturday night with Harper and then all day Sunday. We didn't sleep with each other, but we did do a lot of talking. I didn't know as much as I thought I knew about Harper. Harper was from old money. I knew her last name was Mass, but didn't know it was *that*

Mass. The Mass family owned about a quarter of the land that was currently downtown Chicago. Her grandfather had been governor of Illinois. As a side note, he was one of the few who didn't end up in jail.

Harper's father owned Mass Investments. Their business was wealth management and construction. If you had a lot of money and wanted to keep it, you wanted them. His passion, though, was building. One of his current projects was to convert several blocks of Lincoln Park, a neighborhood in Chicago, into high-end houses. He'd designed them to look like they were part of the neighborhood by using reclaimed brick and building styles similar to those already there.

Her mother was State's Attorney for Cook County, where Chicago was located. Her office had over 900 attorneys and was the second-largest prosecutor's office in the country, behind only the Los Angeles County District Attorney's Office in terms of the number of lawyers.

I was more than a little surprised her father had had me investigated. Harper showed me the file. They'd done it when she told them she was going to San Francisco with me. I was shocked to see they had information I didn't about what happened the night Lily almost died. She had been dosed with a drug called 'GHB,' or 'liquid Ecstasy.'

I found an article about GHB and it said it was tasteless. One of the quotes scared me. It was from a girl who lost twelve hours of her life. When she came to, she said, "My heart is palpitating and my hand-eye coordination doesn't work and it feels like if I stop concentrating on breathing I'll stop breathing. Am I dying?"

It made me wonder if this ever happened to Tracy. It wouldn't surprise me if Bill was behind Lily being drugged.

After I read the report, I filled Harper in on the details the report had missed and updated her on everything recent.

She, in turn, told me all about herself. Harper always had gone to private schools. She begged her parents to let her go to Wesleyan for high school. They wanted to keep her closer to home, but she wanted the education Wesleyan provided. She talked Ray into coming with her so she'd have a friend there.

When Ray came out of the closet, it had shaken her, but she supported him. She just wished he'd told her before they'd started to date. His drug problems weren't getting any better. He'd been kicked out of Wesleyan and the subsequent boarding school. He was now at Lane Academy, a school for troubled boys.

I found out Tami and Harper had something in common: they were both extremely smart and motivated. I knew Harper was smart. She more than held her own with me. She told me she was an outcast back home because she felt the kids were so immature. When she came to Wesleyan she fit in better and had made some great friends.

Once we had the background covered, we talked about our friends, specifically Missy, Lisa, Jennie and Tami. I didn't realize the first three were halfway in love with me. I thought Jennie hated me by the way she acted towards me. Harper explained she was just acting out because she was frustrated I wouldn't even consider her more than just a friend.

I explained to Harper what a self-centered person Jennie really was, and what she, Mark, and her mother had pulled on me. Harper had never heard about any of it and understood why I wasn't interested. I also told her about Teddy Wesleyan and his attitude towards money. I was surprised Harper was pissed when I finished telling her.

I was emotionally exhausted by the time I went home on Sunday. The only other person, besides my family, who I had let in like this was Tami. By the end of the weekend, I knew Harper was the right one for me. The good news was she felt the same way. We both knew that trying to

161

maintain a long-distance relationship would be hard, but we decided to give it chance.

I don't really know how to describe it, but I felt like the missing something I had been longing for had been found. The corny line about another person completing me now made sense. The only thing was, there was something in the back of my mind telling me it should have been Tami.

◊◊◊

When I got back to school on Monday, I ran into Lisa Felton. I was surprised when I didn't feel the attraction I normally had when I was around her. She just gave me a sad look and we didn't speak. I thought for now this was the best approach. I didn't want it getting out that we'd slept together, and was sure she felt the same way.

While I was gone visiting Harper, Mom and Dad had talked to Tom and Mary. Mom shared with them what they needed to know to be supportive of Tracy as she recovered. Mom told me she found it funny that Dr. Hebert had told them the same things Mom had, but for some reason it didn't sink in until Mom explained it.

On the school front, I had a 'B' going in English Lit. Dad had reminded me I promised I wouldn't let my grades suffer. I called Suzanne and hired her to be my tutor again. We tackled Shakespeare. So much of it could have multiple meanings. Suzanne confessed that money was tight and she missed teaching dumb jocks. It was a good thing I liked her. What I didn't like was she made me reread everything with her notes on what to look for. Something I liked about Suzanne was she didn't just give me the answers. She helped me really understand whatever the topic was, so I had no choice but to take my Shakespeare books with me to Yellowknife.

◊◊◊

We flew into Calgary and then had to switch to Air Canada to get to Yellowknife. We boarded a smaller plane that only had twelve rows of seats, two to a side. It was all economy seating. I caught myself before I became an ass. It would be very easy to get used to flying first class. Kendal reassured me I'd be okay sitting with the common folk. I reminded her she could be replaced. She didn't believe me for one second.

The flight took two hours and ten minutes. When we landed, it was three in the afternoon and a balmy 5 degrees out. Of course, in Canada they use Celsius, so they'd say it was minus 15; that better describes how it felt. I was glad I'd brought my Range Sports thermals. Kendal almost turned around to go back home, but I'd gotten thermals for her also. It was cold enough you actually felt it in your lungs when you breathed in the cold, dry air.

There was a minibus waiting to take us to the hotel. Yellowknife was the largest town in the Northwest Territories, with a population just under 20,000. I was surprised to see they had several taller buildings of ten-plus stories.

At the hotel, one of the production staff met us. They wanted me to go to a meeting concerning tomorrow's shoot. I had three scenes to do before I left. The first was supposed to be at an outpost. The school, in the story, had organized a training exercise at a remote location we were supposed to be protecting. The major rival to Craig's character, Royal, was in charge of our two four-man teams. Royal was in charge of Bree, Elizabeth and me.

The plot said the other guy was an arrogant ass and left Royal and Stryker—me—to defend the outpost while they all went into town to party. While they're gone, we'd be attacked. I'd spent a lot of time working to get ready for this part of the movie. I wasn't surprised Jessup would want to talk about it. I found the conference room where we were supposed to meet and was the last to arrive.

"Ah, good, you made it. Everybody, let's get started," Jessup said, taking command of the room.

Craig had saved me a seat next to him. We said our hellos and got comfortable.

Jessup had rented a warehouse so we could practice tonight. We were prepping at the warehouse instead of doing it on location because of the cold. Jessup had scouted the locations last fall before the temperature dropped. It was predicted a cold front would blow in from the Arctic Circle, so the temperature was supposed to drop all day. They wanted to get as much of the outside work done early as they possibly could.

From reading the script, I knew he was talking about me. The Stryker character was a hard-charging guy who gets up close and personal in a fight. Craig's character, Royal, was the guy who had your back. The outpost was surrounded. Stryker would be outside, doing his thing, while Royal picked them off with booby traps and rifle action.

Jessup explained that Stryker's wardrobe wasn't really designed for the predicted -25 degrees Fahrenheit. The plan was to rush me out, have me do my part of the scene, and then bring me back in and warm me back up. The only problem was I was extra-sensitive to the cold ever since I was buried alive in the basement after the avalanche. I was worried I might have problems doing what was needed.

Jessup had his storyboard out for tomorrow and had video of the location. He and the special-effects people went through each step of what would happen. Craig and I felt a little pressure because the reality was if you blew up a shed, and the shot went wrong, then it took time to put everything back the way it was before you could blow it up again.

Something else they were worried about was when to use stunt doubles. The more they could avoid using them, the more usable footage they'd have that wouldn't need to be touched up. The problem was that even though the special-effects guys were the best in the business, when you blew stuff up sometimes it didn't go as planned.

Another problem was, as a teenager, I thought I was indestructible. Craig sat back as I told them I could do it and didn't look concerned. I felt like Superman. After the meeting, Craig took me aside.

"Huge props on volunteering to do the stunts. It all sounds like a piece of cake in a nice, warm hotel conference room. Let me ask you something. When they bounce you off the trampoline and you fly twenty feet into a foam mattress, it sounds like fun. I can see it in your eyes. I was you once. Just for sanity's sake, ask yourself what happens to a foam mattress when it's minus twenty-five degrees? Does it turn into a giant ice cube, and it's like landing on concrete?" Craig asked.

"I hate you," I told him.

"No, you love me. Make some crazy stuntman figure out if it's going to break all his bones. You just look pretty as I blow you up."

Of course, I didn't want to believe him, so I went and talked to my stunt double. After him telling me about all his injuries and surgeries, I decided I'd better not try some of the more dangerous things Jessup had planned. I might even let Craig blow the stunt guy up. I had a feeling Craig wanted to blow me up too much for my comfort.

To be honest, Craig and I were becoming friends. He treated me like a little brother and looked out for me. That was unless he could torment me—as I said, he treated me like a little brother. I found out he was behind the whole dancing-Stryker nonsense. I was so going to take him down at the lip-sync contest.

◊◊◊

We didn't get done practicing for tomorrow until nearly midnight. Kendal bailed on me around ten o'clock. With the time difference of two hours, I was ready to collapse by the time we were done. I had to be up at five the next morning to catch our ride to the location. It was nearly an hour drive, and Jessup had arranged for me to get my tattoos redone on the trip.

I was just about bouncing off the walls when I got to my room. I had a ton of nervous energy and knew I needed to go to sleep. It was a restless night.

◊◊◊

Friday February 20

Kendal had to wake me up because I'd slept through my wake-up call. I rushed down to find I was the last one on the bus. I was five minutes into the trip and the makeup guy had my shirt off. They shaved me and put the tattoo stuff on me. The only problem was someone told me it was minus eighteen degrees outside and it felt like it wasn't much warmer on the bus. I could feel the cold seeping into my bones. I was miserable and tired. If Kendal hadn't had a big thermos of hot tea with her, I would have been cranky, too.

One of the cool things about it still being dark was that you could see the Northern Lights. Suzanne had told me the lights were caused by charged particles hitting the atmosphere. It was something I would want on a bucket list, things to see or do before you die. I found a seat close to the front so I could watch as we finished our trip. I got out my iPad and recorded the lights so I could send it to my friends. By now, the bus's heater had decided to work and I was feeling better. When we pulled in, I was ready to go.

When we arrived, Craig showed me where the food was. We were able to get a hot breakfast while the poor production crew had to set up. I went to wardrobe and they got me ready. I was in what amounted to black body armor. I wasn't happy that I didn't have any headgear. They wanted me to be recognizable. The actors who were going to be the bad guys were all bundled up in white snowsuit-like outfits that looked toasty-warm.

Just before I went out, I had to sit down with one of the special-effects guys.

"I understand you know how to handle a gun," he stated.

"Yes, sir."

"This works the same as what you've been practicing with. There are blank rounds loaded in these guns. Even though they're blanks, that doesn't make them toys. You can seriously hurt someone if you're too close when you fire your gun. Please don't point them at anyone who hasn't been approved."

I gave him a reassuring smile, then checked to see if a round was in the chamber and verified the rounds were blanks. The special-effects man was happy to see me being cautious.

"I'm serious, David. If I see you messing around, I'll call off the shoot."

"I'll be careful," I promised him.

The day was a lot of fun. I got to shoot guns and run around. It was a lot like paintball, except everything was fake. It was like watching a magic show and knowing the trick. I was also an amazing shot. I would just point and fire and people died. It was a little unnerving to see fake blood gush out of gunshot wounds I was supposed to have caused.

If anyone thought I was a good shot, Craig could shoot the eye out of a fly at 500 yards. If it hadn't been so cold out, I think we'd have really had a good time. I learned some things I never wanted to know. Did you know sweat would freeze to your head and eyebrows?

You know what else sucked? The continuity girl. She thought that once ice had formed on my eyebrows, it looked stupid in the next shot if there was no ice there. I kind of could see her point, but I was willing to ignore it. Jessup was no help with my suggestion. Thank goodness, the makeup people figured out a solution before I turned my guns on the evil woman who saw everything.

At our lunch break, they had a cold-water bath for me to soak in. It helped thaw me out enough that I could stand to get into a hot shower. I was glad I had my Range Sports thermals underneath my costume. Kendal was smart enough to bring an extra set for me to change into at lunchtime. The wardrobe people took my morning gear and washed it so I could wear it home after the shoot.

Something the intense cold did was dry you out. There was almost zero humidity in this cold air. I needed plenty of fluids, especially since I seemed to be running all day.

After lunch, the rest of the cast showed up. We needed to do a few shots with them before the special-effects guys did their major fireworks. The good news was the majority of the cast only had to do a handful of scenes. They'd shot everything I wasn't in earlier in the week. I couldn't believe all the whining about how cold it was. I wanted to shoot Ben before we were done. I was glad I was mainly working with Craig today. He hadn't bitched once all day.

Finally, at the end of the day, Craig was supposed to set off some landmines, which were supposed to send me flying as if I'd gotten blown up. I snuck out to see where I was supposed to land and confirmed the pads were very firm. I told Jessup there was no way I was doing it. I think he was a little relieved.

I left the comfort of the trailer to watch the scene. The stuntman had guide wires to help direct his flight. I watch in amazement as he shot like a rocket to the landing area. He landed awkwardly and didn't move after the scene. The medical staff was checking him out when I decided to go back in. I went right up to Craig and hugged him.

"Thanks for talking me out of that. I think they killed him," I said.

"Are you serious?"

"No shit. I think he's really hurt."

Everyone ran out to see except Kendal, who stayed to make sure I was alright. I was done for the day, so I went and changed. When everyone came back in, they assured me he'd be okay. They did think he broke his arm and possibly a few ribs.

◊◊◊

On the bus ride back, Craig talked smack about how I'd go down tonight at our lip-sync battle. He told me Bree had a killer set that would blow me out of the water. I wasn't worried. My classmates had put together two songs for me I knew would kick butt. Kendal thought I was crazy even to think about doing it.

Kent organized dinner for everyone. It was good to see Craig's right-hand man again. We went to a local bar and when we got there it was packed with everyone who worked on the movie. I was surprised to see Jessup and Janice, the producer, both there. It was obvious some of the cast and crew had been drinking before we arrived.

I was happy to see Halle come in and sit next to me. I talked to her and Kent while I ate. When they had cleared the table, Craig jumped up.

"You ready, Dawson?" he challenged me.

"Bring it on!"

Craig went up to the stage and found the mic.

"We have a special treat tonight. We're going to have a lip-sync-off!" he said to cheers from the crowd.

Several people had pushed up to the stage to get a front-row view.

"To kick things off, we have our favorite dancing machine, joining us from Hicksville, USA, David Dawson."

"I'm going to need a little help with this. I need everyone to gather around. Don't be shy," I said to get everyone closer to the stage.

"Shake it, baby!" one of the girls yelled.

"For my first number, I thought I'd release my inner rocker. I'm going to do a little something from AC/DC called *You Shook Me All Night Long!*"

Jessup just shook his head when I tore my shirt off halfway through. I made sure to throw it to Halle so I could get it back. She acted like she'd won some big prize as the girls screamed. I could see the doubt creeping into Craig's eyes as I finished.

Halle tossed me back my shirt and I put it back on, to the complaints of some of the patrons.

"Now I thought I'd change it up to something a little more recent. I need Halle, Bree and Elizabeth to join me on stage," I called out.

Once they were on stage, I covered the mic and told them what I wanted them to do.

"For my second number I would like to do something from Jessie J, Ariana Grande and Nicki Minaj called *Bang Bang!*"

I got the crowd to clap and the girls to start shaking their hips to the beat of the music. Then I started my dance routine as the lip-sync portion started. When the 'Bang Bangs' started, the girls had gotten into it. When the rap section with Nicki began, I had the headshake going. By the end I had the crowd shaking it. When the song ended, I tossed the mic to Craig and strutted off stage.

"Not so fast, David, come back up here," Craig called.

I strolled back up to people laughing and clapping.

"We need to let you in on a little secret. This was all a practical joke. We got a little help from our friends to film

170

this," he said and then pointed out the cameras around the room.

I was so going to get even with him. If there hadn't been cameras, I might have hurt Craig. I guess it was 'haze the new kid.' Jessup and Janice had big smiles on their faces. There was no chance everyone wasn't going to see this. I just decided to own it. I grabbed the mic from Craig.

"I have one more, if you want to see it," I offered.

The girls had dusted off Carly Rae Jepsen's song *Call Me Maybe* as a backup. My dance class had put together a line dance for this song last year for baseball. I taught everyone how to do it and then started the song. Of course, my shirt came off for this song, too. You have to do the lawnmower scene shirtless. I had Bree, Elizabeth and Craig on stage helping me. It only made sense Janice would want the four of us on stage to promote the movie. I noticed Halle had disappeared, but she came back later.

I think everyone had been under a lot of pressure and they needed to cut loose. I ended up having a great time with everyone. The only awkward moment was when I told Halle I had a girlfriend. I think we both knew we were just friends.

Kendal finally made me go back to the hotel because we had to be up early to be on location at zero dark thirty.

◊◊◊

Saturday February 21

The day started out better since I didn't have to get tattooed. I was able to keep warm and mostly sleep on the bus ride. We'd be shooting the scene where we took the town and saved all our classmates who'd left us at the outpost.

We started out at the outpost and did a final scene where Craig patched me up. At the very end, I would ad-lib something like, 'It's really cold out. I need some protective gear.'

Jessup finally agreed I could cover up my tattoos. They added to the scene where we jump on overpowered snowmobiles. I was able to take a coat and headgear from a downed rebel. I was thankful they let me because we rode all over the countryside during the morning.

For the afternoon, we moved to a new location where they had a small town built. I was amazed most of the buildings were just fronts. They hadn't bothered to build sides or roofs. I asked Jessup about it.

"We'll add the rest of the building's structure in post-production. We'll also be adding smoke and other details to make the town look more lived-in. We need the fronts for place markers so everything looks seamless," he explained.

By the end of the day, Jessup was happy. On the ride back, he cornered Kendal and me on the bus.

"I wanted to tell you that you're doing a great job, but I have a problem: your stuntman's hurt and won't be able to work tomorrow. There are a couple of shots I can get with other stunt people, but there are two I need you to do."

"I have to answer to his mother, so you better tell me what you want him to do," Kendal said.

"We're doing the cliff-face scene where he has to swing across a frozen waterfall. The other is him rappelling down the cliff face."

"I've never done anything like that before. I'm not sure how safe it would be," I reasoned.

"I understand your concern. Think about it and let me know tomorrow," he suggested.

I was glad Kendal didn't look sold either. I'd watched what happened yesterday and was a little gun-shy.

◊◊◊

When I got back to the hotel, I checked my emails. I had one from Bo Harrington, my quarterback coach from freshman year, so I gave him a call.

"I wanted to touch base with you and see if you wanted to hire me this summer?" he asked.

"Of course, I do. Have you heard from the Elite Quarterback Camp to see if there's a slot for me this year?"

"That was something else I was going to ask you. They do have a slot reserved for you. The question they have is who do you want to coach you. I can send you over a list, or make a recommendation."

"Is Bud Mason coaching again?" I asked.

"Yes, and he requested you as someone he wants to coach. You want me to set it up?"

"I liked Bud and learned a lot from him. Do you think it's a good idea to use him? Or try someone different?"

"Good question. Normally I'd look for someone who teaches your style of ball. Coach Mason, though, has years of pro experience. I think we can agree he made you better. There's no one I'd say is better or you could learn more from. I say go for it," Bo suggested.

"Yeah, set it up."

"I have a favor to ask of you, and I'll understand if you say no. Alabama wants you to come to their camp this year. They said they also needed a quarterback coach. Nothing improper was said or offered, but I want to be that coach."

"Hmmm, let me think about it for a moment. We're talking about one of my top five programs I want to go to. It would give me several days to explore their campus. I think I could be talked into it."

"I hate to ask, but what are your top five right now?"

"Alabama, Ohio State, Florida State, Notre Dame and USC," I shared.

Of course, the list was dependent on me checking out the campus and football program. I also wanted a chance to play sooner rather than later. If they all picked up stud quarterbacks between now and when I went, it might change my mind. I wasn't afraid of competition, but I wanted to know they were confident in my abilities.

"Not a bad list. You want me to put the word out you're interested in them?"

"I was hoping you'd help me with recruiting like you did last year."

"I'd be willing to help out. Anyone else you'd be interested in me jump-starting your recruitment with?" Bo asked.

"I think I'm good with Kentucky. Florida has a new coaching staff; I think I want to see what happens there. I like Texas A&M; Missouri has some potential; Cal and Stanford out west. I also like the idea of staying closer to home, so in the Big 10 Michigan State and Wisconsin stand out. The one program I might be talked into is Michigan with their new coach."

"What about Oregon? Your skills would fit with their offense," Bo suggested.

"Sure. They always have a good team. My concern is will their style of offense make me ready for the pros?"

"Maybe not, but winning cures a lot of doubts. Let me get working on this and I'll send you over a contract. If you want, we can lock in the next two years and I'll throw in specialty training as part of the package."

"Like what?" I asked.

"I'd send you to a training facility where you would improve your speed, flexibility, strength and agility. I send my college guys who want to improve their draft status there so they do better at the combine."

"Send it all over to Kendal. She handles all my contracts. Talking to you makes me want to go out and hit somebody."

"I always tried to avoid getting hit," Bo said.

◊◊◊

Kent set up another group outing that Kendal and I went to. Tonight was a different pub that allowed me in to eat. The legal drinking age in the Northwest Territories was

19. I think Halle and I were the only ones not old enough. My plan for the evening was to have a nice steak and then go to bed. I had another long day in front of me.

I was talking to Halle and Kendal when we heard voices raised in anger. I was surprised when it was Ben and a couple of locals. Kent and Craig jumped up to try and calm things down.

"Do you think they need help?" I asked.

"Just stay out of it. Ben's been chasing this girl all week and I think he just met her boyfriend," Halle informed us.

"You need to tell Ben your rules," Kendal suggested.

"What rules are those?" Halle asked me.

At that moment, Ben punched one of the locals. His buddies looked like they didn't want to get involved, and the boyfriend looked like the fight was out of him.

"My brother taught me these rules," I said, turning back to Halle. "One of them is to never date a girl who's in a relationship with another guy."

"Or girl," Kendal offered helpfully.

"Oh, yeah. That must be why I can't hook up with Adrienne," I said and smacked my forehead.

"It's also why you can't take Hannah Minacci to Prom," Kendal supplied.

Halle watched us try to figure out if we were pulling her leg or not. It never hurts your reputation to be able to name-drop a couple of supermodels as potential dates. It all goes back to what Greg had told me about women wanting a guy other girls want. Kendal was being a great wingman. The only problem was I had a girlfriend.

"You never told me you were interested in Adrienne," Halle accused.

"Oh, he has video and naked pictures," Kendal said, not helping this time.

"Come on, Gizmo Boy, I know you have it on your phone," Halle demanded.

175

"First of all, there are *alleged* nude fashion photos," I said in my haughtiest voice. "Said photos were taken without permission, and if I allegedly had any, one very pissed-off fashion model would have me by my balls."

I pulled up the video of when I first met Adrienne and kissed her. I heard things heating up with Ben and his new friends. I was impressed; Ben could take a punch.

"That looked like it hurt. Do I you think they need help?" I asked.

"You stay right here. I'll tell you if you need to help them," Kendal told me.

Halle had just gotten to the part where I kissed Adrienne.

"Oh, my!" she said, as she put her hand over her mouth.

Kendal rolled her eyes at me as I broke out into a big grin. It never got old seeing a girl's expression when they saw our video. When it ended, she handed me back my phone.

"Show me the nude photos," Halle ordered.

"Alleged nude photos," I corrected her.

I looked around to make sure no one was looking and brought the photo up from the Miami shoot. A model had taken pictures of Adrienne and me as we were getting our spray tans. I hung onto the phone to show her. There was no way I was going to let this photo get out.

"Oh, my!" Halle said again.

Adrienne was spectacular *in* clothes. Out of them, you got an idea of how truly remarkable she really was. There was a reason she was at the top of her game even at the age of 27. She could continue making money in our business for the rest of her life. She was just one of those rare talents.

I noticed several of the locals and now most of our production crew were squared off. Kent pulled a guy off Craig and got punched for his troubles. I'd only seen something like this in a movie or on a TV show. They had a real brawl going. I looked at Kendal and Halle and they both shook their heads.

Things changed suddenly. Some idiot tossed a beer and it landed on both Halle and Kendal. The poor guy had no idea what hit him as both girls jumped up and started swinging. I figured I better pull them off before one of them broke a nail. I had one under each arm when Mr. Brave took a swing at me. I was able to duck and weave out of the way. I sat the girls down behind me.

"Can I punch him?" I asked.

"Take him down, but don't hurt him too much," Kendal said.

The dumbass decided he could take me. He had to be only five-nine and a buck fifty. I didn't want it to get out of hand, so I used one of Cassidy's moves and took him down. I put him in an arm bar I'd learned at the dojo and he was suddenly very cooperative. Meanwhile Ben was in the process of getting the shit kicked out of him.

"Hold him like this," I told Halle, and she took over subduing our beer-tosser.

I ran over to Ben's guy and tossed him. This was one of the things I had learned for the movie. I was checking Ben out when the guy tried to tackle me. Some assholes just didn't learn. Jeff and Alan had accused me of being the Hulk because I was stronger than I looked. I picked the guy up and sent him straight down on the floor. Ben winced as all the air was expelled from the guy's lungs.

I think everyone else was just posturing and hanging onto their guy. When they saw Ben's guy get body-slammed, they all stopped. Kendal rushed up and grabbed my collar and pulled me out of the Pub.

"Let's go. I don't need to bail you out of jail tonight," she told me as everyone started to make a hasty retreat.

When we got back to the hotel, others showed up and wanted to talk to me about what had happened. Halle had

had the sense to grab Kendal's and my coats. She arrived with Ben, Kent and Craig. Ben put me into a bear hug.

"Thanks, man. I was in a little bit of trouble there," he told me.

"Why didn't you use the stuff they taught you for the movie?" I asked him.

He looked at me funny and then it dawned on him. We had all been taught some moves for the action scenes. He used some of them in our sword fight.

"I guess I just forgot."

"How strong are you?" Craig asked.

"Strong enough to break you in half if you keep hazing me," I said as I gave him a menacing look.

Everyone cracked up when it dawned on him he might want to be more careful with his pranks.

Kendal pulled me to the elevators because I needed to get some sleep. When I got to my room, I was still keyed up, so I got my Shakespeare out to read. It didn't take long for that to put me into a coma. I would have to remember that particular sleep aid.

◊◊◊

Sunday February 22

The script for the day called for me to climb down the face of a cliff to get into a complex. When I got to the location, I had to admit that it was obvious why they'd picked it. It was perfect. The concept was we were on a frozen world. Looking out over the valley below the cliff, you could see a frozen landscape for miles.

The cliff we were shooting at was only about thirty feet high, but it was high enough that if something went wrong I could kill myself. One of the fears I had was of heights, so when I looked over the edge, I felt my stomach tighten. The stunt coordinator took a moment to explain everything to me.

"We know you're not a climber, so we're going to rig it so it looks like you are. What we'll do is put you into a harness and attached it to a cable. A winch will lower you safely. You just need to lean back and walk down the wall."

When it finally came time for my portion of the shoot, I was okay. They only had to lower me about ten feet. The stunt people could do the rest.

The other shot they needed me to do was to take a couple of running steps, then swing away from the wall and jump over a frozen waterfall. They'd positioned a camera on a crane to capture the wide angle. They had other camera guys on cables, like me, to catch it from both sides.

I was scared to death of this one because I had to let go of the cable and run across the face of the cliff at almost a ninety-degree angle. I then had to kick out and let my momentum swing me out away from the cliff face. It sounded straightforward, but I wasn't sure I wanted to do it.

Jessup had to give me a pep talk, and the stunt coordinator had to have one of his guys do it so I could watch before I let them dangle me over the edge. They had the wire attached just above my waist to keep me from tilting too much. The harness they had me in, under my wardrobe, felt stable.

I leaned out and trusted they knew what they were doing, took three big steps and then pushed off. It was obvious I hadn't gotten enough speed as I looped out away from the cliff face and went sailing towards the frozen waterfall. I ended up about half as far as I needed to go. I figured out as I was flying through the air that if I didn't look down, this was actually fun.

I think I shocked everyone when I just bounced off the waterfall and turned, and when I swung back I ran back towards where I started and kicked off to fly through the air again. This time when I reached my starting point, I twisted around, took several long strides, and then kicked off hard.

One thing I forgot was that I had no brakes. My eyes got big as I sped out and around the frozen waterfall because the cliff face was rushing up to me. My instinct was to reach and grab onto the wall, but I knew that would mean slamming into it. I instead used my legs, leaned out, and ran a few steps before grabbing for a handhold.

I was relieved I was done, or so I thought. Jessup ended up wanting me to do it six more times. By the time we were done, I no longer had the lump in my throat. I was having fun. When they finally let me off the cliff face the stunt crew were all waiting for me.

"You keep that up and we're all out of a job," one of them commented.

"After I felt secure, like I wasn't going to go crashing to the bottom, I was okay. It was as if I was flying. It reminded me of doing a zip line. The only difference was you don't have any brakes."

"First time I ever did it, I crashed into the wall and about knocked myself silly. I forgot to tell you about landing. You figured it out, though. As long as you use your legs you're okay."

"Thanks for that," I said with a big grin.

Jessup was happy all the hard shots were done. All that was left were the dialog scenes that needed to be done outside. We got the majority of them done in the afternoon. I had just a handful to do tomorrow morning and then I was scheduled to fly back.

◊◊◊

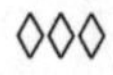

Chapter 9 – It's a Wrap

Friday February 27

On-site production of *Star Academy* had wrapped up Thursday. All that I had left to do was voice-over work. I was flying out today to get that done. Jessup and Janice had talked, and they liked the fight scene between Ben and me. They said they might have us go back into the studio and add to it.

On the home front, Harper and I hadn't been able to get together since we started dating. She'd been making all kinds of suggestions which quite frankly were uncalled for. By the end of two weeks with no female companionship, Mr. Happy was even checking out Lisa Felton. Harper had decided me being gone again this weekend was not acceptable. She had booked a flight, through Kendal, to join me in LA.

Of course, I told my parents what we were doing. I was a little surprised when my mom called Harper's mom and they discussed it. I didn't find any of this out until Harper called me. She was a little pissed I hadn't given her a heads-up. The fallout was my mom and Harper's were going with us to LA. Of course, Mom had met Harper and liked her, but she wanted to get to know Mrs. Mass.

When we got to the airport, we met Harper and her mom at the gate area. Harper looked excited and nervous at the same time.

"David, Mrs. Dawson, and you must be Kendal," Harper greeted everyone. "This is my mom, Beverly."

"My friends call me Bev," she supplied.

The moms seemed to hit it off. We only had two first class tickets, so I gave them to Bev and Mom. Kendall had the three of us seated together. I noticed she kept the center seat for herself. Harper took her aside and I realized Kendal was just giving us a hard time. I let her have her fun with Harper. After some intense negotiations, they switched

181

tickets. We all had to go to the counter to make the adjustments.

When we finally were seated and safely in the air, I leaned over to Harper.

"Wanna join the mile-high club?" I asked.

"Who says I'm not already a member?" she said, and then giggled when she saw my reaction.

"You two better cool it. Knowing boy wonder, he'd get you caught," Kendal warned us.

"It's like we have three mothers with us," I teased Kendal.

I was not expecting Harper to whack me. Kendal gave me a knowing look. I wondered if that was part of the negotiations for the seat.

"So, you didn't answer my question," I said to Harper.

She squeezed my hand and gave me a chaste kiss.

"I think I might be worth the wait."

I knew she was.

◊◊◊

I had a message from Jessup when I arrived at the hotel. He and Janice, our producer, wanted to take me to dinner. I called him and we agreed I could bring everyone with me. We were invited to BOA, a high-end steak house.

The ladies used the occasion to dress up, so I pulled out one of my new Dakora suits. I figured since I was in LA, I could pull off the green one they'd given me. I'd brought it because I couldn't think of too many other places I could wear it. Personally, I wasn't thrilled with the suit, but Adrienne pushed me to broaden my horizons and embrace my inner model. I think she was full of it, but I knew what she meant. I needed to wear the clothes to help promote the ad campaigns.

One thing I didn't do was shave my head. I hoped I didn't have to get it shaved again this weekend. I wanted my hair to grow back out. I was tired of looking like I could scare small children. The only positive I found was the emo girls and girls looking for a bad boy found me sexy. For some reason, Harper wasn't a big fan of my look.

When we met Jessup and Janice, they were in high spirits. The studio executives loved what they were seeing. Janice pulled out her laptop and showed us some of the things they'd worked on. One of the scenes was of me skipping across the cliff face.

"Did you let my baby do that?" Mom said indignantly.

I had to agree. Once the CGI guys did their magic, it looked like I was a hundred feet off the ground. Jessup looked up, concerned. I don't think he'd ever faced someone like my mom.

"Mrs. Dawson, I can assure you David was in no danger doing the scene," he started to explain.

I figured I should help him out. Jessup helping Craig and the rest of the cast to pull practical jokes on me may have colored my help.

"Mom, they told me I was safe. At first, I was worried because my stuntman had to be taken to the hospital the day before. Jessup assured me I needed to do it or it would alter the shots and hold up production."

"What happened to your stuntman?" Harper asked, starting to be concerned.

"They slammed him into the ground. It was a little scary," I said, and then gave a dramatic pause. "Wasn't he hooked to the same kind of wire I was on?"

Janice raised her eyebrows and watched Jessup squirm.

"I had full confidence in David," he said weakly.

"Mom, I was fine. It was a blast. You saw how I flew through the air. They did forget to tell me how to stop, though. The first time through I thought I was going to end up like the stuntman did. I was so glad we were done with it and without any problems or injuries, but Jessup's a professional and only wanted what was best for the movie.

He made me do it six more times," I said with my best 'little angel' look on my face.

"Let me see if I understand this. A professional was injured doing stunt work the day before. You decided to dangle my son from a cliff and send him flying through the air. Did you have any of the other actors do something like this?" Mom asked.

Janice and Jessup looked at each other. While they were trying to decide how to respond, Mom turned to me.

"So, you had fun?" Mom asked.

I just nodded my head yes.

"Except this time, I didn't have to go to the hospital."

"What do you mean, this time?" Mrs. Mass asked.

Kendal had seen us do this before and started laughing. I think Mom took ten years off Jessup's life. I showed them the video of when I tested the Range Sports Jet Water Board. After they saw the jet water board video, me flying through the air on a frozen cliff looked tame by comparison.

Over appetizers, Janice broached the subject I was sure this meeting was all about.

"As I told you earlier, the executives are very happy with your work and the potential the film has. They're tentatively floating the idea of shooting two more pictures. What do you think about that?"

"This was fun and all, but I don't know when I'd have time to do it. I need to focus these next two years on sports if I plan to get a scholarship to play football. I can't take time off to do two movies," I told them.

Kendal had talked to Kent during the week. He had sources that said insiders at the studio were projecting big numbers for our film. There was talk of moving the release date to Christmas. He warned her the studio might approach us about the next two movies. They hoped to play on Kendal and my inexperience and lock us into a two-movie deal now, before the first one was released.

The gamble was if the movie was a flop and I hadn't signed, I could be hurt financially. If it turned out the movie was a huge hit, I'd be better off working with the other three lead characters and negotiating as a group. Kendal and Tom had talked to the agents for both Bree and Elizabeth, and they'd agreed to the second strategy.

Kendal, and especially me, had to play hard-to-get. It was easy for me since what I had just said was true. They would have to make it worth my while not to focus on football. I couldn't just ignore it, either. The two-movie deal could potentially pay me more than I would ever make playing professional football. There was also no guarantee I would ever make it to the pros. Too many extremely talented players had been hurt or just didn't pan out.

"What if you were to make enough money you didn't need a scholarship to go to college?" Janice asked.

"I'd have to really think about it. I'd need to talk to my family before making a commitment of any kind. Can you give me an idea of what kind of money we're talking about?" I asked.

Janice looked a little uncomfortable. She gave me an approximation, which was twice what Kent had told us to expect. Kendal gave me a funny look that told me I needed to hold off. I had forgotten Harper and Mrs. Mass were in the room.

"I think you might be valuing David's contribution too low," Mrs. Mass offered. "I have a feeling he's tested very well with your focus groups. I understand you also have footage of him that will be used to market the film. I haven't seen his contract, but I suspect you'll need to compensate him for the extra work-product. I suggest you negotiate in good faith and pay him a bonus so as to avoid any unpleasantness."

Both Kendal and I turned to stare at her. She obviously had done her homework. Janice and Jessup looked at each other. I don't think they had expected us to be prepared. I sure as hell hadn't. Then she gave them her best winning smile.

"Of course, what do I know? I'm just the mother of David's girlfriend," she said.

I was glad to see we'd slowed them down for now. The rest of the evening was enjoyable. Janice and Jessup were gracious hosts. BOA had aged beef that was some of the best I'd ever had. We all shared a variety of side dishes. When the check came, I glanced at the bill. It was more than many people made in a week. Even though it wasn't cheap, I felt for a special occasion I would go back for sure. The meal really was outstanding.

When we got back to the hotel, Mrs. Mass wanted to talk to us. I invited everyone to my suite.

"I'm sorry if I overstepped my bounds at the restaurant. What I do for a living is read people. I was getting the vibe they were going to take advantage of you."

"David had been warned before the meeting. He was playing his part tonight," Kendal told her. "I have to say, though, you helped our cause tonight."

Mrs. Mass gave me a hard look and I just stared back at her. Then she smiled.

"How old are you?" she asked.

"The same age as your daughter," I said with a big smile.

"You were serious about playing football, though," she said.

"That part was true."

She watched me closely. I never wanted to play poker with this woman. It was as if she could read my mind. It was unnerving, but I was sure it served her well in her job as a District Attorney.

"Mom ..." Harper warned her.

Mrs. Mass seemed to shake it off and just smiled at me. I knew at that moment I would never lie to this woman. First of all, I didn't make a habit of lying. Secondly, it would be futile. She dealt with professional liars on a daily basis.

◊◊◊

Everyone left after they'd made plans to go shopping tomorrow. Mom bragged that since I was rich now, she wouldn't feel bad about using the debit card I gave her. The problem I had was figuring out if she was joking or not.

Both she and Dad were working full time, but sometimes they used the cards I got them. I should clarify that: they didn't use the card unless they told me they were doing so. They'd used it to order airline tickets to Utah and for some Christmas shopping. Dad had tried to start paying me back for the money they'd borrowed while Mom was sick. I finally convinced him he needed to look at a weekly grocery bill and average it out over the years since I was born. When I added in clothes and the rest of my upkeep, he thought I owed him money.

Twenty minutes after everyone had left I heard a soft knock at my door. I was happy to see it was Harper.

I pulled her into my arms and gently kissed her.

"What's your mom going to think about this?" I asked Harper.

"Why? Do you plan on telling her?" she asked.

"You're kidding, right? All your mom would have to do is look at us and she'd be able to tell we'd been up to all kinds of fun. She's a little scary," I said, letting my fears show through.

"What's a little statutory rape between friends?"

She looked down as the lump in my pants disappeared.

"Oh, baby. I'd never let my mom put you in jail," she assured me.

"I don't know if we should do anything if she's just down the hall."

"And my roommate," Harper finished.

I started shoving her towards the door.

187

"Go, before she worries," I said while trying to hustle her out the door.

"You know, big bad Stryker would never be such a wuss," Harper said as she tickled me.

"Big bad Stryker isn't here."

"I bet if you shaved your head and took your shirt off he would be. I want to be ravaged by the bad boy of the galaxy," she said as she cupped my package. She wasn't playing fair. The little boy in me wanted to be the bad boy of the galaxy and ravage Harper. Mr. Happy made a serious play for control to the body. It didn't take much to convince me to go shave my head. I was doing this for Harper, after all.

I went into the bathroom and looked in the mirror. I was a little sad as I shaved my head. I'd brought dark blue silk pajama bottoms with me. Angie said I looked good in them, so I hoped Harper would think the same. I got out a skin cream to give my skin a slight sheen. In essence, I oiled up to highlight my muscle definition. I was going to give Harper the Stryker experience.

I strode back into the bedroom with confidence. Remembering the scene I'd done to get the part, I pulled out a chair and put it in the middle of the room.

"Sit," I ordered her.

Harper flushed when I commanded her; she was in no way submissive. I could never see her agreeing to allow me to tie her up, or to order her around. I turned my back on her for a moment to get into character. I had a slight smile on my face and watched as Harper reacted to the feral look I gave her as I turned to take her in. Harper's eyes widened when she realized I was fully into my role now. I walked up to her, making her eye-level with my groin. She began to get a little nervous. I just smirked at her as I played up the rogue.

"You look like you're going to devour me," Harper said, and she licked her lips.

I reached out and caressed her cheek, drawing her eyes to mine.

"The chase is about feeling what your prey is feeling," I said, remembering the lines.

"Okay," Harper responded with a nervous flutter of her hand.

I slowly circled her, as if stalking her. She watched as I gracefully moved.

"It's all about the timing, when you make your move. Not when you're ready, but when they are. The anticipation builds. When they know what's coming. Every nerve-ending is tingling and ready for it. It's the moment when they're most alive, with the expectation that the hunter has them in his sights," I told her.

"Are you trying to seduce me, David?" Harper asked.

I kept a straight face. Bree had said those same words to me at the audition.

"No," I said as I grasped her hair. "That part is already done."

I pulled her up out of the chair and she came willingly into my arms. I looked her in the eye for a moment, then leaned down and kissed her with a fierceness that communicated my desire to possess her. Harper ran her hands up my back and grasped me at the base of the neck. I picked her up and she wrapped her legs around my hips. I walked us into the bedroom and laid her on her back as I covered her. She had me wrapped up and was not letting go.

All the times I'd been with Harper came flooding back to me. This was what was missing. I was with someone I loved. Not just as a friend. I know I had a habit of falling hard for every girl who went out with me. With Harper, it felt different. It felt like we were both on the same page. I thought about just making love to her, but she'd asked for the Stryker experience. I wanted to make her happy, and vowed right then to give it my all.

I leaned back and broke our kiss. I looked deep into her eyes.

"Strip," I ordered.

She gave me a shy look and bit her lower lip. She giggled when I pinched her nipple and I jumped up so she could get her clothes off. I went to the bathroom, got one of the big towels, and put it under Harper's butt. I winked at her.

"Spread your legs, woman," I ordered.

I grasped her thighs and slid my hands up until they were just under her knees. I then pushed her legs wide and back so I had unhindered access to her center. I rolled my tongue over her nubbin a couple of times and felt Harper stiffen and then grunt. I knew this meant she'd had a little orgasm. I was going to build her up to something she had never experienced before.

Now that I'd gotten her to climax once, I wanted to up the ante, so I buried two fingers in her and hunted for her G-spot. I knew I'd found it when she grabbed both of my ears and started guiding my tongue.

"Make me your woman!" she cried out, almost making me laugh.

I pulled my face up so I could watch her. Her eyes were closed as she made a funny face and grunted her arousal. What I wouldn't give to have my phone close to take a picture of her at that very moment. She was just on the edge of orgasm and began to tense up. Then she came hard.

"Yes, Yes, YES!" she cried as she began to shudder.

As she began to recover, I put on a condom. Her eyes snapped open as she felt me slot myself and slowly sink to the bottom.

"Do me hard, Stryker!" she called.

I had other plans. I wanted to see how hard I could make her climax. She was huffing and grunting which meant that she was close. Her legs came up off the bed and wrapped around my waist. She used her heels to drive me harder into her. When she slammed her heels into my butt and held me there, I knew this was it. I reached between us and stimulated her.

"eeeeEEEEEEEEEEK!" she screamed, and then it suddenly stopped and she collapsed.

The look she gave me had me a little worried. I had seen Harper get in this state, and it usually meant she was ready for some serious fun.

"Stryker, you stud. Get back in me and we shall see what you're made of," she challenged me.

"I plan on breaking you," I said with a big smile.

"Never!" she exclaimed.

"Okay, let's go," I said, jumping back onto the bed.

This time I flipped her over and took her from behind. I loved to see my hard flat stomach slap into the round orbs of her bottom. I reached up, grabbed her hair, and held her in place as I pounded her. I loved the sound as I drove into her. I started to sweat and could feel the burn in my stomach as I worked her over.

Harper started to give me the telltale signs of an impending orgasm. This time I felt her clamp down with her internal muscles. I was right there with her. As I approached my peak, I reached under her, grabbed both her nipples and twisted them. It was too much for her.

"JEEEEZZZZuzzz," she yelled as she collapsed under me.

I was surprised I was a little unsteady on my feet on my way to the bathroom to clean up and dispose of the condom.

When I got back into bed, Harper was wasted. I grabbed a couple of pillows and climbed into bed. I pulled her to me and then wrapped my arms around her. She put her head on my chest and drifted off. It didn't take me long to join her in a happy slumber.

◊◊◊

Monday March 2

When I went to school this morning, there was an extra bounce in my step. I had a girl whom I loved, my movie obligations were done for now, and best of all was baseball tryouts started today. I was excited about this season. We were finally going to get to play varsity ball.

I noticed they'd broken ground on the new field house. They planned on having it done by the start of the coming school year, next August. I could hardly wait to be able to use it. Dad was also excited. He, Tom, Coach Hope and Mrs. Sullivan had worked hard to make this a reality. I was proud of them.

I found Jeff and Alan had waited for me in front of the school.

"Are you done?" asked Alan.

"I did some voice work this weekend. I also added some fight scenes on Sunday. They told me I was done until they're going to launch the movie. Then I might have to do promotional work," I said to fill them in.

"Did I see Harper with you on Facebook?" Jeff asked.

"She came out for the weekend," I said with a big smile.

Our Friday night Stryker experience had not gone unnoticed by our mothers. Saturday had involved some very direct discussions. I think Mrs. Mass was surprised when I didn't try to cover it up or sugarcoat it. She appreciated my honesty. Harper was a different story. She didn't want her mom to know we'd had sex. She was more than a little surprised that her mother knew she'd been sexually active with both Ray and me.

When I came back from working on Saturday, Harper and her mom had come to grips with her having me as a boyfriend and everything that entailed. I think part of it was due to them shopping all day with my mom. The other part was due to Craig scoring us invites to another Chubby Feldman party. This one was much tamer. Unlike last time, I actually got to see all of the house and grounds.

At the party, Craig, Bree, Elizabeth and I all got a chance to talk about possible future movie deals for the *Star Academy* series. I filled them in on Janice's initial offer to me. Elizabeth had also been made an offer and hers was much less. To me, that wasn't surprising. One of the big studios had been hacked, and it came to light that women made less than their male counterparts. We were split, at first, on how to proceed. The girls wanted us to negotiate the same pay for everyone. Craig, after he heard what Elizabeth was offered, thought he'd be better off going it alone.

I hadn't decided what I should do, so I went looking for Kent. The other three were still arguing when I brought him back. He listened to all four of us. My biggest concern was I didn't want to take the time to make two more movies. The other three didn't understand my point of view, because this was their full-time job. Kent made a suggestion which surprised me: he proposed we try and get the studio to shoot the next two films at the same time.

I was glad Kent also insisted on all four of us negotiating together. I had read the books and knew that the four of us were the core group. We also agreed that Kent, through Craig's agent, would lead the negotiations. We all liked and trusted Kent to do what was best for our team. I think the girls were relieved that they would make more money.

Alan and Jeff filled me in on their weekend. They had double-dated Saturday night. It sounded like they'd had a good time.

◊◊◊

Moose gathered us all around to give us his opening speech of the season.

"Okay, settle down. I'm Moose. Just so we're clear, I answer to Coach or Moose. Either one is fine. Coach Diamond is going to work with the outfielders. Coach Herndon will work with the pitchers and catchers. The rest of the infield will be with me. The JV team will go with Coaches Haskins and Hope.

"I also want to clear something up for you freshmen and first-year players. You will not be playing varsity ball. I don't believe in throwing anyone onto the varsity squad before they have at least a year of high school ball under their belt. This is nonnegotiable. The first one of you that has his momma or daddy call me about it will be running until they either drop or quit; I don't really care which.

"There will be two teams this year, varsity and JV. Normally I try to put only first-year players on JV. If you are cut from varsity I will consider. Did you hear that? I will *consider* letting you try out for JV. I use the JV team to give first-year players a chance to learn. If I feel that you could develop, I'll let you play JV ball. I know that sounds harsh, but it has worked for twenty-six years. Are there any questions before we get started?"

I remembered how pissed I'd been when I heard that speech last year. I still thought that if you had the talent, you should be able to play varsity ball. Just because you hadn't played under him yet didn't mean you should have to play junior varsity. The Callahan twins raised their hands. I had a hard time telling which was which. Moose pointed at them.

"We played varsity last year at our old high school. Do we get a chance at playing varsity here?"

"No," was Moose's one-word answer.

I needed to talk to them before they pissed him off. When we broke up I trotted over to the twins.

194

"Sorry about that, but you'll never change his mind," I told them.

"But he said that he didn't believe in letting anyone play varsity unless they had a year of high school ball under their belts. We both started last year," one of them complained.

"I understand what you're saying. All I know is Moose is old-school. I tried to get him to let me play last year. I felt I was better than their starting shortstop. Moose almost kicked me off the team for challenging him," I said, and then looked around to make sure no one was listening in. "If you repeat this, I'll deny it. Once I knew that I wasn't going to make varsity, I decided to just have fun. Looking back, I had a lot more fun playing JV ball than the varsity squad did. I suggest you do the same. Just have fun and play ball."

"That's easy for you to say. You get to play varsity," the other one said.

"I don't have any guarantees I'll play varsity ball," I said.

They both laughed at me and then went to where the JV was going to work out. I smiled when I thought of what Coach Hope had in store for them. I was sure he'd run their asses off before long.

"Tim, David, get your butts over here!" Moose bellowed.

Shit, we'd only been at practice for like ten minutes and Tim and I were getting yelled at.

"We're going to change things up this year. I want you to take them to the track and run steps. You know how to do that, don't you?" he asked.

I nodded, and Tim looked at me and sighed. I thought we'd gotten away from having to do this now that we were trying out for varsity. We got everybody and jogged over to the track. Coach Haskins smiled as we came up and joined the JV.

"Okay, Dawson and Foresee. Get them started," Coach Hope ordered us.

We escorted the team to the starting line. Tim and I broke them into groups of five. Tim took the first group out and they ran one hundred yards and then began walking the next one hundred. I sent the next group when the first was halfway done. I kept them spaced out until I joined the last group. By now, they knew what to do. The next step was two hundred yards running and one hundred walking. The final step was a four-hundred-yard run and walk one hundred. When we completed the first set of steps, Coach Hope told us to go again.

I winked at him because I knew none of us would quit this year. Coach Hope used the running to weed out players. We had all had Cassidy abuse us since the first of the year. Running steps was nothing compared to her workouts. He gave up after we'd completed our fourth set.

We all laughed and played grab-ass when we went back to Moose. He had an evil glint in his eye and we all quit smiling when we saw Cassidy waiting for us. She'd finished doing her after-school workout program. How she was able to do back-to-back *sixty minutes of hell* was beyond me. When we were done, Moose sent us to the showers. I had to chuckle as we passed the JV. Coach Hope was running them through his version of *sixty minutes of hell*.

◊◊◊

After our shower, I took Jeff and Cassidy home with me for dinner. We had agreed to go to the dojo three times a week. Tonight was taco night. Jeff and I high-fived each other because we could polish off some tacos.

Before I ate, I had to deal with a problem. Duke was a complete spaz. I hadn't taken him today because I was going to practice and wasn't sure who would watch him. Normally Pam or one of the other cheerleaders played with him and wore him out. I was going to have to figure out how to take him to baseball practice. I sure hoped Moose would be on board with it.

After dinner, we went to the dojo. Cassidy was not respecting I had kicked butt in Yellowknife in the bar fight.

"I'm a badass now!" I told her, to see what kind of reaction I'd get.

She looked at Jeff, who was wisely staying out of it. She tilted her head and then came to a decision. I had started this as a joke to tweak Cassidy. I'd told her at lunch about my bar fight. She was mad at me for using what she'd taught me in a fight. I tried to explain Ben was getting his butt handed to him. She made some smart comment that pissed me off. So tonight I thought it was a good idea to act like a tough guy.

"Okay, badass, let's see what you've got," she challenged me.

Shiggy stuck his head out of his office and hurried out about the time I tried to toss little Cassidy. Somehow, she went from being tossed to having wrapped her thighs around my neck, and she face-planted me into the mat. I had started to black out from the chokehold she had me in when Shiggy made her let me go.

I staggered up and faced her. There are times when it's not a good idea to be a teenager and think you're indestructible. My mouth was going before my brain could slow it up.

"You got lucky," I said.

"David, shut the hell up," Jeff advised me.

Shiggy shrugged and motioned for us to begin. Cassidy did a flurry of attacks and then stopped. I got a smug look on my face. I'd been able to counter all her moves. Then she pointed down. The heel of her right foot was almost touching my ball-sack. I was glad Cassidy was my friend and hadn't finished her move. I would have been singing soprano.

"Still think you're a badass?" Cassidy asked.

"No, I am yours to mold," I said and bowed to her.

One of the classes they had at the dojo was kickboxing. That meant they had both heavy and speed bags. The speed bag was six feet off the floor.

"Tonight we're going to work on a hook kick. We'll use the speed bag so we can do it full force," she taught me. "Now get into your stance so I can show you basically what I want you to learn."

I turned to the side so my left leg was forward and bounced on the balls of my feet.

"What I'm going to teach you can either be done with your trailing leg or your front leg," Cassidy said.

She then bounced up and used her front leg to catch me with her foot right behind my knee. I could see how she would cause me to get off balance.

"Notice how I did it with my front leg. I could do it with my back leg, but if you pop me in the chest I'd be off balance," she said and demonstrated, then showed me how to counter her move. "Think of this as an option play. You can either hook behind the knee or kick hard into the thigh. The third option is to go upstairs."

She did a little boxer bounce and then I felt her tap my thigh, then her foot shot up and she touched my chin. If she'd done this at full speed I would either be out cold or wondering what truck hit me. Shiggy decided to make his presence known.

"Very good, but use the flat of your foot. It'll give you more range. If you're serious about taking them out, use your heel and aim for the temple."

Cassidy had Jeff get a pad and hold it at knee level and then had him crouch down under the speed bag. Cassidy did it at full speed. It sounded like she hit both at the same time. *Smack, BAM!* It sounded like a heavyweight had just crushed the speed bag.

I tried it at three-quarter speed to get the technique down. Cassidy and Shiggy watched me, so they both coached me up. The first time I tried it at full speed I was off-balance and landed on Jeff.

"Sorry, man," I apologized.

He just shoved me off him and we laughed. One thing was obvious: I wasn't getting the power Cassidy had put into her kick. At least, not until Shiggy told me to kick to a point beyond the bag, and the lightbulb clicked on. It was the same as in football: I hit them as if they were further upfield so I drove through them. When I did it right, it sounded like a gun had gone off. *BaPow!*

Cassidy made me do it five times in a row before she called it a night.

Chapter 10 – Baseball Bag Boy

Tuesday March 3

Duke tested my patience as we ran this morning. I noticed over the last couple of weeks he'd seemed to forget what he'd been taught. He tested his boundaries more. Uncle John had warned me he'd do this, so I was prepared. Instead of giving him his full leash to check out every neighbor's yard, I shortened it and brought him to heel. He didn't like it at all. I laughed aloud when he stopped and flopped on the ground and tried to push his collar off with his feet.

"What do you think you're doing?" I asked him.

Then I thought about what I wanted Duke to do and gave him a command.

"Sit!"

He still tried to get away, so I picked him up and put him on all fours. I then pushed his butt down and raised the leash to get him to sit. Uncle John told me when he threw a fit to break his concentration and then make him mind. Once he did mind, then I was to reward him. He loved to have his ears rubbed, so that was his reward.

"Good boy. Heel!" I commanded, and we began again.

Uncle John also instructed me that I needed to go so far and then turn around and head in the other direction. This would teach Duke to pay attention to me. Pam and Mona had helped with his training as well. He had learned some valuable commands like sit, heel, no bite, and down. They'd also taught him to fetch. I was happy it no longer involved me chasing the ball. He thought it was a great game, and I was glad they'd him worn out when they would bring him back.

While I taught him the basics, Mom had committed to take him to formal training classes so he could be used as a service dog. If she planned to take him into the hospital, she needed to be able to control him. Dad still worked with him also. Not that he was normally a bad dog, he was just young and full of energy. Uncle John said he would act like a teenager. I think he just took a jab at me.

◊◊◊

Pam, Kim, Mona and Sammie had me cornered at lunch. They had requested I eat with them alone. I was such a 'stupid boy.'

"What do you mean you can't take one of us out Friday?" Sammie asked.

"I have a girlfriend, Harper. I think you've even met her couple of times," I said.

"What does you having a girlfriend have to do with you going out with us?" Mona asked.

"Seriously, David. When you went out with Peggy it never stopped you," Pam added.

They had me there. I could see where the difference between dating and a girlfriend could cause some confusion.

"Peggy and I were dating. We were not committed to each other. Harper's my girlfriend."

"Would it be easier if we all just come over Friday night and have our way with you?" Kim helpfully suggested.

They'd teased me since I made the announcement Monday. If I hadn't known they were teasing, I would have crawled up a wall. I got a big smile on my face thinking about all four of them being naked in my apartment. I was about to call their bluff until I noticed the little smiles that came across their faces. They'd be willing to go through with it. I groaned when I realized they were evil girls trying to break me.

"You four stay away from me," I ordered. "I might be able to resist you one-on-one, but when you gang up on me, I want to do bad things. You have to stop!"

Gina selected that moment to come over to our table.

"I need to talk to David," she said.

Thank God. I got up to go with her when they all burst out laughing. I glanced down and it was obvious what had caused their merriment. Mr. Happy had tried to burst through my jeans. I'll never understand women. Gina took an involuntary step back. I just glared at her and then she joined in. I was about to storm off, but Gina grabbed my hand and led me outside.

"I take it they're still testing your willpower."

"They upped the ante. They suggested we all get together on Friday."

"Slut," she accused me.

"Hey, I used to resemble that remark. Not anymore. I'm now in a committed relationship."

"You poor 'stupid boy,' we all know you won't last," she said and then squeezed my hand. "You just aren't made to be a one-woman man. I think it'd be sad to see you trapped like that."

The sad part was I knew Gina meant every word of it. I didn't feel trapped being with Harper. I liked the idea of us being exclusive. I decided I wanted to change the conversation.

"Okay, I need to work on this a little bit. Now tell me why you rescued me."

"I wanted to let you know Kara's coming home for the day on Friday. She wanted to know if she could spend the night with you," Gina said with a straight face.

Oh Dear God! How could they do this to me? Wait a minute, was she teasing me?

"I call bullshit!" I exclaimed, and then she started laughing. "Do you all think this is funny?"

"Oh, yes. This is the most fun we've had in a while. Wait till we send Lisa Felton after you."

I knew that wasn't happening. She still hadn't talked to me.

"So, you wanted to get me alone so you could torment me?" I asked.

She just squeezed my hand and smiled at me. I saw Mike tossing a baseball to Tim out of the corner of my eye. He'd seen us come out. I decided to get a little payback on Gina. She walked me to my thinking tree and began to sit down, but I pulled her back up and pressed her up against the tree.

"You win," I said, looking deep into her eyes. "I'm weak and have all the base urges a horny teenage boy has."

I started to lean in to kiss her. I heard her suck in her breath and her eyes went wide. At the last moment, I turned my head and went for her earlobe. I sucked it between my lips and heard her moan. I felt a tapping on my shoulder and turned to see Mike giving me a curious look. I winked at him. He knew me well enough to know I was just teasing Gina. I blew a raspberry on the side of Gina's neck. She gave me a hard shove and squealed. She was surprised to see her boyfriend standing next to us with his hands on his hips. I decided to help.

"It's not what it looks like," I said in a panicked voice, raising my hands and taking a step back.

Gina blushed. Mike and I couldn't help it, we laughed. You could see the changes on her face from the look of being caught, to confusion, and finally 'all boys must die.' Mike and I both took a step back when we saw the last one.

"You're supposed to be my boyfriend! Do not encourage this one," Gina said as she pointed at me. "And you!"

She huffed and stormed off. I looked at Mike and shrugged.

"You might want to go after her," I suggested.

"Are you sure?" Mike asked.

"I know it makes no sense, but it's worse if you don't," I assured him. "And find out why she needed to talk to me.

I snatched his glove out of his hand and he trotted off to find Gina. I put Mike's glove on and Tim tossed me the ball.

"What was that all about?"

"If I understood girls, I'd be rich."

"I thought you *were* rich," Tim teased.

"Don't you get started. I have pictures of you," I threatened.

"What? What pictures?" Tim asked with more than a little touch of concern.

I just gave him an evil grin. He about wiped it off when he threw a high hard one at my head. It was a good thing I was an athlete, or I might not have caught it. I threw one at his nuts. Who knows how these games get started? Someday, someone would get hurt. By the end of lunch, we had a crowd watching us as Tim and I tried to kill each other. We laughed our heads off and threw taunts as well as the baseball. I think we were lucky the bell rang, or one of us would have eventually killed the other.

◊◊◊

At tryouts, the coaching staff concluded they weren't going to weed us out through conditioning, so they went old-school and had us run baseball drills. Moose had the infielders break up into groups of four. I (at shortstop) teamed up with Jake (at third), Mike (at second) and Wolf (at first).

Moose would call out where the base runners were and then smash a grounder to see us handle the ball and then throw to the correct base. The four of us had practiced together at State. I guess Moose saw that after only hitting about ten balls.

"Get in here," Moose ordered us. When we were close enough where only we could hear him, he gave us our assignments. "I've seen enough. I heard you were working out together, and it shows. I need to have some versatility on my roster. Jake, I want you to go practice center field. Wolf, you go work on playing right field. Mike and David, I want you to go with the pitchers."

"I guess this means we made the team," Mike told me as we jogged over to his dad.

"Sounds like it," I answered. "What do you think your dad's going to think of my new pitching style?"

"I think if you can get batters out, my dad'll be fine with it. He called Shiggy to find out what you and Bert were doing. Dad told me Shiggy has also talked to Moose. He's getting his background checks done and will be helping coach this year. Moose wants to develop a deeper rotation so we can go further in tournaments."

I could count on Mike to get the inside information since he lived with one of the coaches. We found Coach Herndon.

"Mike, go warm David up. I want to see him pitch," Coach told us.

Mike and I warmed up and did some long toss to loosen up my arm. When I took the mound, I threw Mike all my pitches at three-quarter speed. I hadn't pitched in six days, so I felt fresh.

"It all looks good. Throw me the four-seam fastball at full speed."

I uncorked it, and it felt good as I used my lower body to power the ball into Mike's glove. I heard the satisfying pop that told me I'd done it right. Mike had a big grin on his face as he popped up behind the plate and jogged the ball out to me.

"Want to have some fun?" he asked conspiratorially.

"Of course, need you ask?"

"No, but this might piss my dad off," Mike warned me.

"He likes us. How mad could he get?"

Mike thought about it for a moment. Then he clued me in to his plan. I wasn't convinced, but I owed Mike for dealing with Gina earlier today.

"Coach, I need your help," Mike told his dad as we jogged over to where he was evaluating pitchers.

"What's up, Mike?" his dad answered.

"David says that he can strike anyone out with his new Kung Fu pitching style. I told him he couldn't strike my dad out," Mike said.

Oh, he was good. He'd just used the 'My Dad' routine. He had his dad eating out of his hand. Coach Herndon puffed up at his son's confidence in him.

"David, have you been talking smack again?"

"Sir, it's not smack if I can back it up," I challenged him.

He gave me the look every parent gets when they decide they'd make an example of you. I knew Mike's dad had played minor-league ball. He'd faced much better pitching than I could bring.

"Is that so?" he shot back.

I just nodded and tried not to smile. I had a flashback to a conversation my mom had with her mom. I had made some smartass comment, and grandma looked at my mom and told her paybacks were hell. The point she made was karma was a bitch, and your children would get even with you someday. I wondered if my little monsters would be this bad.

"We'll test this theory of yours. At the end of practice, I'll send up three batters for you to face as everyone watches. If any of them gets a hit, you have to be the batboy for the first game."

That got the team's attention. I started to wonder who Mike was setting up.

"But I want the best. Mike tells me you used to be able to hit at one point, until you got old," I said, throwing down the gauntlet.

My mouth had quickly written checks my butt couldn't pay for. Even Mike looked shocked.

"Okay, tough guy! If you strike out three batters, you'll get a shot at me. If you strike me out, too, I'll be your bag boy this season. If you lose, you do it for the team. You'd better think about how tough you think you are. Are you sure you want to do this?"

I looked around and everyone had a gleam in their eye. They all wanted a piece of me. If I could pull this off, I'd be 'King of the Hill' for the rest of the year.

"Hell, yes! Bring it on!" I said to the cheers of the team.

The cheering got the attention of Moose. He jogged over to see what the commotion was. While Coach Herndon explained, Tim and Mike pulled me aside.

"Dude, what did you just do?" Mike asked.

"This was *your* plan," I shot back.

He just sputtered.

"Okay, Cap, you got us into this, we'll help you win this challenge," Tim assured me.

I felt better knowing that Tim, my normal catcher, would help me out. It would be easier with him behind the plate.

I wasn't surprised that Moose was all for this little exhibition. He, too, wanted to knock me off my pedestal. Towards the end of practice, he sent Tim and me to the bullpen to get ready. He brought both the JV and varsity together to have his after-practice talk since tomorrow would be the first round of cuts. He told them how it worked. There would be a list on his door in the morning, and if you were on the list, you should show up for practice.

He told the rest of our team my challenge. He asked for volunteers to bat against me. To a man, they all raised their hands. I noticed Mike even volunteered. I might have to bean him if he was selected.

"Looks like they all want a shot at you," Tim said casually.

"Looks that way."

"How do you want to do this?"

"What do you mean?"

"You want to put them in the dirt?" he said with an evil grin.

"Nah, I'll just dazzle them with my bullshit."

"I'd put 'em in the dirt," he suggested.

I just shook my head. I just might before we were done.

The coaches got together and decided who should bat against me. I was surprised when none of the guys I'd worked out with at State were chosen. I guess they didn't want me to have any knowledge of who I'd be up against. I also think they didn't want my buddies to help me. It turned out Coach Haskins had some ideas. He selected Bryan and Brock Callahan. He also picked Nick Rake, one of my freshman lunch-mates from the first semester.

"Here are the rules: all the batter has to do is get the ball in play," Moose announced.

He let me throw a few warm-up tosses, so I could get a feel of the mound. Coach Herndon had the three batters together in a huddle and was telling them what to look for. Coach Haskins had volunteered to call balls and strikes.

The first batter up was Nick. He didn't look happy. I understood why when he squared around to bunt. Coach Herndon thought he could get a quick win with this strategy. I took Tim's advice. I threw a high hard one right at Nick's chin. I damn near clipped him. I'd let my anger get the better of me. I liked Nick.

Moose would have none of this.

"Dawson, these are your teammates!" he yelled at me. Then he turned on Nick. "You will swing away. No bunting!"

When Nick got back into the batter's box, his body language said he was afraid. A fastball thrown at your head will do that to you. I think Tim saw it, too. He called for my new curveball. Shiggy had taught me how to throw a big sweeping curve. My starting target was the batter's head. I snapped it off and saw Nick's knees buckle as he tried to get out of the way. The ball slapped into Tim's mitt without him having to move it.

"Steeriiike One!" Coach Haskins called out.

Nick didn't stand a chance. I threw two more curveballs and on the third one he finally stood his ground and took a cut at it. I think he was glad when he was done.

Up next was Bryan. He'd played varsity ball on his high school team in New Jersey. I wouldn't get him out just by throwing curve balls. What I did know was Coach Haskins. His philosophy was to see a pitch first, then battle. His idea of a good at bat was to foul the ball off five times. He wanted to have the opposing pitcher throw as many pitches as possible to tire him out. I'd seen him talking to the Callahan twins earlier. I would bet he told them to take the first pitch.

The twins were big boys. I also bet they would love for me to challenge them with a fastball right down the center. I'd use my knowledge against them.

My first pitch was a four-seam fastball. Bryan hesitated, but it looked too good to pass up. The four-seam tends to rise up when thrown correctly. The combination of the rise and Bryan's hesitation had him miss badly.

Bryan got a determined look on his face. He wouldn't miss again. Tim called for my forkball. In warmups, it had worked well. It was a fastball that seemed to drop right off the table. When I threw it, Bryan had it zeroed in. He made a mighty cut as the ball disappeared on him. He slammed his bat on the ground in disgust. I could hear Tim jawing at him to get him more worked up.

Tim wanted me to throw another four-seam fastball past him. I wasn't confident that was a good idea, but he was my catcher. I put a little extra on it and I heard the crack of the bat. SHIT!

Bryan had put a thundering shot on the ball down the first base line. I watched as it slowly curved foul. I was a little disappointed in my teammates as they groaned when it landed. They all laughed when I pointed at my eyes and then at them to let them know I was watching how they acted.

To this point, I had only thrown strikes. Tim called for my two-seam fastball, low and away. The two-seam has a different movement than the four-seam. It tends to tail, or sink, either left or right. With all of the movement, it was a harder pitch to learn to control. I planned to throw it so it tailed down to the left and way out of the zone. Poor Bryan lunged at it and missed. I was happy to see a few of my teammates cheered for me.

The team was more into it now. It looked like it was split down JV and varsity lines. I stalked around the mound like I was getting pumped up to uncork a huge fastball. Brock dug in and smiled at me. It reminded me of the smile Precious gave Duke right before she pounced on him. I reared back and threw a changeup. Brock might have had a chance to hit it once he corkscrewed around again. Tim was having loads of fun as he teased him about it.

I had him guessing. Tim signed for the changeup again. If I were Brock, I would expect the fastball this time. I made him look silly a second time.

My next pitch froze him. I threw him the curveball, but it was just out of the strike zone. I got him out on the two-seamer, low and away. He walked out and shook my hand.

"Hell of a job. You had me guessing. I'm glad you're on our team," Brock said.

Now was money time. I don't think Coach Herndon thought he'd be batting. Everyone laughed when I had Mike run out to the mound with a bag.

"I just wanted you to see what you'll be carrying all year," I tweaked him.

Tim trotted out to talk strategy.

"You haven't done your full Japanese ninja act yet, and you haven't shown your slider," he advised.

"How about this: I throw the two-seam low and away. Let's see if he'll chase it. As soon as he holds up, we throw the slider to catch the corner."

We agreed and Tim went back and took his place behind the plate. The whole team was now in my corner. It was one thing to root for your teammates, it was another to root for a coach. Coach Herndon took the ribbing well.

On my first pitch, I did everything Shiggy had taught me. I had an exaggerated motion where I brought the ball and glove over my head and down to my chest. I slowly rocked back, and when I found my center, I used my back leg to explode forward. I brought the ball back behind my shoulder as long as I could before torquing a hummer towards the outside corner, except it wasn't outside.

Luckily, Coach Herndon had taken the first pitch. I was surprised when it was called a strike. I thought it was a little low. Right down the middle, but low. I knew if I made that mistake again he would take full advantage.

I had one more trick up my sleeve. Shiggy had shown me how to flip my glove during a pitch. The movement of the glove was intended to distract the batter, especially if they weren't used to seeing it. Tim called for the same pitch. Coach Herndon was able to hold up as the pitch ended up outside.

The next pitch, the slider, completely fooled him. I had a huge grin on my face when Coach Haskins called it a strike.

"Didn't know I had that one, did you?"

"Nope. But you're still going down," he challenged as he dug in.

To his credit, Coach Herndon had a good eye. I threw back-to-back four-seam fastballs eye-level for balls. I couldn't entice him to swing at them. I now had a full count. Normally I'd try to just dig down and bring the heat.

I had a feeling that wouldn't work with Coach Herndon. Tim came out to the mound so that we were on the same page.

"Just throw it by him," Tim said.

"No, he'll be guessing fastball. Let's get him with the curve," I suggested.

"Are you sure?"

"Either that or the forkball, but I think the speed difference for the curve would be better."

"Okay, curve it is," Tim said and went back to his place behind the plate.

The pitch was perfect. Coach had guessed fastball. How he got a piece of it I have no idea. But luck was on my side. Tim snagged the foul tip and hung onto it. The team acted like we'd won the World Series. There was a happy look on all the coaches' faces, even Coach Herndon. It had been a great team-building activity.

◊◊◊

Friday March 6

The final cuts had been made and I wasn't surprised to make the team. I'd made Coach Herndon carry my bags for only a day. I figured I'd better not push it. Moose agreed with me and allowed me to stop running. It was funny how that worked out.

Something that changed was Bryan and Brock now got rides from me. They shared the back seat with Duke on the way home. They were bummed Moose hadn't bent on his rules and they had to play JV ball. Jeff claimed shotgun.

Tonight, I dropped everyone off and grabbed my bags. My plan was to head up to Wesleyan to see Harper. We had a late dinner planned. This was the last weekend before baseball started, so I wanted to go to Harper instead of her having to come see me.

I was running a little late, so I called Harper on my hands-free phone. It was one of the little features of the

Jeep I was still learning to use. Mom had ridden with me to the grocery store and about took my head off when she found out I wasn't using it. To be perfectly honest, I'm a guy—I hadn't even realized the Jeep had the feature. Knowing would have meant reading the manual. I thought I just had a fancy radio.

She'd driven me to the Sullivan car dealership and embarrassed the hell out of me (I know, imagine that). Mom went in and found a cute girl to come out and show me a few features and how they worked. For example, it was Bluetooth-capable and it responded to voice commands. I could play my songs that were on my phone through the car speakers. She even showed me how to download my favorite songs to the Jeep. I could make calls by just saying the person's name. She gave me a cradle for my phone and pointed out an app I had that was a turn-by-turn GPS.

I pulled up to Harper's dorm and she came right out. I almost felt like one of those jerk guys who just pulls up and honks the horn. She gave me a sheepish look that told me something was up. My first clue was she was in jeans. I'd thought we were going to a nice place to eat.

"Change of plans," she began as she tried to judge my reaction. "We're going to a party."

"That's fine, as long as you feed me."

"I have it covered. We're picking up the pizzas."

"What's this party all about?" I asked.

"I'm friends, still friends, with a lot of Ray's theater group. I let it slip I was dating you and they wanted to meet you. I promised you'd go," she said in a rush.

I think I might have made some facial expression as to how excited I was to talk to theater kids about making my movie. Not that I had anything against theater people; some of my newest friends were in the business. I'd thought tonight was about Harper.

"We can leave early if you aren't having a good time," she quickly suggested.

"No, I just had other expectations for tonight, like spending time with you. I'm also overdressed."

"You could change in the bathroom at the pizza place," Harper said way too cheerfully.

I guess this was part of being in a relationship. Sometimes your better half changed plans on you. Of course, I would think part of a good relationship would include communication. One quick phone call would have done wonders for my mood, because as it was I felt manipulated. When we pulled up in front of the pizza place, I turned off the car and turned to Harper.

"Before I ruin our evening, I need to get something off my chest. I really am not a control freak. I can usually roll with the punches. I want to be clear I'm not upset about the change of plans. What's causing me a problem is it feels like it's a setup."

"I didn't think you'd want to go," she told me.

"Harper, I want to be with *you*. If it means going to a theater party, I'm there. You don't have to trick me into going."

"Oh."

"All I ask is you trust me enough to tell me what you want. The worst that could happen is I might say 'no.' You have to believe me: I'll at least listen to you, and then tell you why not, if I don't agree. If we can't at least talk to each other, and be honest, I can't do this."

"Wow, someone did a number on you," she said. Then it dawned on her. "Tami."

I just got out of the Jeep and grabbed my bag. I couldn't go there right now. I was surprised at how raw my emotions suddenly were, and I needed a few moments to collect myself. When I went into the restroom to change, I realized it wasn't just Harper who'd rubbed me the wrong way. It was all the girls this week. I wanted to file that away and think about it later. What I had to decide right now was whether I would let this go for now and just enjoy the night or not. I didn't see an upside to being upset. Harper and I had the rest of the weekend to talk about this.

I came out of the restroom to find Harper at the counter with a stack of pizza boxes. I handed her my bag, picked up all the pizzas, and carried them to the Jeep. We drove in silence to the party. When we got there, she stopped me from getting out of the Jeep.

"Are we okay?" she asked.

"Yeah, let's go meet your friends and have a good time," I said, forcing a smile on my face.

I don't think she believed me, but what was she going to say at that point? We'd stopped at an apartment complex. It was obvious which unit was having the party. We walked into the small living room that must have had fifty people in it. We had to push our way to the kitchen. The counters were covered in empty and half-empty beer cups.

As soon as Harper made room enough for me to put down the pizzas, a sea of people decimated them. I could tell by the smell, people were getting high. I was more than a little irritated I didn't even get a slice.

I then looked around and Harper was gone. I like a girlfriend who doesn't feel like they have to hang out with you every minute, but this sucked. I didn't know anyone here except Harper. I thought she'd brought me here to meet her friends.

I made my way back through the living room and out the front door. I went and sat in my Jeep. That turned out to be one of the smartest things I'd done recently.

I was contemplating just leaving to get something to eat when the police arrived in force. I was able to have a front-row seat as the drama unfolded. The police were much more organized than our hometown force. I sent Harper a text to tell her the police were about to raid the party. I watched as they knocked and then several rushed in. I would later learn those officers went to the sinks and bathrooms to prevent the destruction of evidence. They also had officers at all the windows, so there was no sneaking out that way.

These guys had done this before. They would take one person out at a time and search them, determine if they'd been partaking in anything, and verify their age. Of course, they were all high school kids who'd been drinking and getting high. I was surprised when I recognized a couple of girls from Tami's old floor. This was when I decided I might inquire if some of the offenders might be let go.

I walked up and a female officer stopped me.

"How may I help you, sir?" she asked.

"I'm here to pick up some of my friends. They were at a party where they felt there was a bad element. Would it be possible to take them home?" I asked.

"And which ones would those be, sir?"

"To begin with, those two," I said pointing them out. "I'm sure there are a few more here."

About that time Jennie Wesleyan came out, and she looked scared. Harper was brought out a moment later.

"I take it you know those two also?" she asked.

"Yep, one is Jennie Wesleyan. The same family the school's named after. The other is Harper Mass. Her mother is the State's Attorney for Cook County."

Turns out the police in this town do not release minor girls to minor boys.

I liked our police a whole lot better. It might have had something to do with them knowing me all my life. That, and I helped them score free food at football games, and gave them half a keg of beer last year. Oh, and my brother went to school with some of them. My family wasn't rich, but our name was well known, partly from my football successes. I guess these police didn't know who they were dealing with.

The night went downhill from there. I called Beverly
Mass to tell her where her daughter was. I met Harper's dad
at the police station. It was not one of my top choices as to
where to meet the father of the girl I was dating. I was
happy to see Jerald and Abigail Wesleyan. They let Jack
Mass know I wasn't a mass murderer. I was sure we'd all
laugh about this someday.

◊◊◊

The only good thing that came out of tonight was
Abigail invited me to stay at their house. Jack also decided
to stay, since it was close to two in the morning. I was
starved.

"Abigail, do you mind if I make something to eat?" I
asked when we all arrived.

"Help yourself, David. I'm not sure there's anything in
the refrigerator."

The convicts had all been sent to their dorm rooms, so
it was just the four of us. They all followed me into the
kitchen. The refrigerator didn't have any bread or anything,
so I checked the freezer. I found some ground beef I could
cook up. I looked in the pantry and they had mac and
cheese. I had the makings for a late-night meal.

I began cooking when the inquisition began. I smiled
to myself. This group was a bunch of amateurs. Either my
mom or Bev Mass would have eaten them up.

"Why weren't you arrested with everyone else?" Jack
asked.

I'd learned to keep it simple. Sticking to the truth was
also a very good idea. Spilling your guts was not always
helpful, as I'd learned the hard way.

"Harper told me she needed to drop off some pizzas at
the party."

Abigail gave me a curious look. She might be a
problem. When Jack and Jerold weren't looking at me, I

slightly shook my head. She gave me a look that said we'd talk later.

"I still don't see why you weren't with her," Jack pressed.

"She went there to talk to some of her friends. Once the pizzas were delivered, I went back to my Jeep."

"So you were inside the party," Jack pounced.

Crap! I just ignored him as I plated everyone some of my mac-and-cheese-with-hamburger creation. I sat down and focused on eating. Abigail decided to bail me out.

"This is actually pretty good," she said.

"Who knew?" Jerold commented.

OMG! Have these people never had this before? It looked like Jack wanted to continue the interrogation.

"Okay, guys. Why don't you go to bed and we'll pick this up in the morning? David, will you help me clean up?" Abigail asked.

We put everything in the dishwasher and started it. I wiped down the counters and stove. Abigail waited until we were done before she led me into their office. She called Bev and put her on speaker phone. I was surprised when she and a couple of her people were on the other end of the line.

I spent the next ten minutes being interrogated by a professional. She broke me like a twig in winter. I told her everything I knew. I think five minutes of the conversation was taken up with both moms explaining to me what a big baby I was. It turns out women are allowed to change your plans, and I was to suck it up and go with the flow.

I was worn out and finally called a halt to it.

"Bev, I'm about to fall asleep on you," I said.

"Sorry, David, I want to thank you for everything you did tonight. The girls were lucky you were there and you were brave enough to go talk to the police and then call us. Most boys would have just left. This could have been very messy if we hadn't been able to get involved early in the process."

I had no idea what she was talking about and was sure I didn't want to know. If good looks and charm weren't enough to get by on, what were we coming to? The good news was they let me go to bed.

Chapter 11 – Season Starts

I woke up to two teenage girls bouncing on my bed.

"Get up!" Harper ordered me.

My eyes cracked open to see Harper and Jennie smiling at me. I glanced over at the clock. It was only ten. I had barely gotten eight hours of sleep. They were killing me. I crawled out of bed and heard both the girls squeal.

"See, told you," Harper said.

I turned back and they both stared at my crotch. You would think they'd never before seen a naked boy with a piss hard-on. I needed to take care of my condition and take a shower. I came out with a towel wrapped around my waist to find both girls lounging on my bed.

"He has a towel on," Jennie complained.

I ripped it off and jumped onto the bed in between them. I put Harper into a lip-lock and we reminded each other why we were dating. Harper rolled me over on my back and started to kiss my neck. I was a little surprised when Jennie kissed me, and not in a friendly way, but one of passion. Gina was right, I was a slut. I let Jennie have her way with me.

I lost track of Harper until she engulfed Mr. Happy. Jennie took advantage of me being distracted—by Harper giving me a blowjob—to get naked. Several questions popped into my mind, but I figured Harper would put a stop to it if she had a problem with where this was going.

Jennie, never the shy one, straddled my face and presented her fat bald beaver. I grabbed her butt to get her where I wanted her and began to use my tongue and lips to give her pleasure. I think someone was as horny as I was: Jennie was soaking wet. I decided to step up my game, so I grasped Jennie's hips so she couldn't get away. I used my tongue like a metronome and rhythmically brushed across her button until she was screaming. She finally jerked loose from my grip and crumpled beside me as she tried to catch her breath.

Harper had found my condoms and put one on me. She'd gotten off the bed to get undressed. You snooze, you lose, so I got on my knees beside Jennie. She was curled up on her side and faced away from me. I grabbed her top leg and lifted it up as I straddled her other leg. Her womanhood opened up to me as I pushed into her folds and then hesitated. I looked over at Harper to ask permission. She smiled at me, crawled up behind me, and pressed her tits into my back. She looked up and pulled my head down so we could kiss.

Jennie didn't wait. She scooted towards me, so I began to penetrate her. Harper reached down, grabbed my hips, and then shoved me into Jennie. Harper got up tight to me and acted like I was her strap-on. She had a firm grip on me as she controlled my movements while I had sex with Jennie.

I kept my hands busy, using one to toy with Jennie's breasts and the other one to reach behind me and play with Harper's butt. I let my hand work further down until I had access to her sex and began to pleasure Harper.

Harper let go of my hips and grabbed my shoulders for support. Jennie was gasping for breath as she got closer to her orgasm. I could feel I was getting close as well. I let go of Jennie's breast and reached down to strum her nubbin. Harper started the chain reaction. I felt her sex clamp down on my finger and then she bit my back as she moaned. I jerked hard to get away from being bitten, which caused my hips to snap forward and bury myself a little deeper into Jennie. That set her off. Feeling Jennie's tight little tunnel spasm up and down my length was all the additional stimulation I needed to climax fast and hard.

I ended up facing Jennie with myself buried in her and with Harper plastered to my back. I gently pulled my finger out of Harper's sex while I looked into Jennie's eyes.

"Ass."

"Bitch," I shot back.

I then leaned forward and kissed her.

"Brunch is probably ready," Jennie said.

"Oh, shit," Harper said, and she got out of bed and ran to the shower.

"You have another condom?" Jennie asked.

I pointed to my bag. She got another one while I took off the used one. She soon had the protection in place and turned to show me she wanted me to take her doggie style. I'd just gotten a good pace going when Harper came out.

"Greedy bitch! Take him to the shower and you two get cleaned up. Our parents are downstairs," Harper said, being all bossy.

I grabbed Jennie by the waist, picked her up and took her to the shower while continuing to do her. Harper wasn't amused, but I think Jennie appreciated the effort. I didn't try to make it last. This was just fun and we needed to hurry. I pushed her against the wall and just pounded her from behind. She started to scream again, so I clamped my palm over her mouth and let her express herself into that. I was more than a little worried that if she made too much noise we'd have parents showing up.

After we were done, we hurried up and made sure we were both clean. I bounced out and pointed out Mr. Happy to Harper to show he was still willing.

"You're a freak. Get dressed before one of our dads comes up to see what's taking so long."

Jennie scampered out, leaving Harper and me alone for a moment. I gave her a curious look.

"This was my way of saying 'sorry,'" she explained.

She didn't give me time to think about it. She pulled me behind her to go face the parents.

◊◊◊

We came downstairs and Jack, Harper's dad, gave me a hard look.

"I don't think your dad likes me," I whispered to her.

"I don't think my dad likes any of my boyfriends," she told me.

"I thought he liked Ray," I said.

"He did, until Ray turned out to be gay and taking drugs," Bev said as she walked up behind us.

She'd apparently arrived this morning.

"I guess that might be a problem," I answered.

Abigail had ordered in food. We all sat down and had brunch. Over the meal, Bev filled us in with what had happened last night.

"The 911 call to the police said there were gangbangers having a wild party. They described a big guy with tattoos in a leather jacket carrying in boxes of drugs," Bev said.

Everyone turned to look at me. I sometimes forgot the tattoos from my movie were still visible. This might explain why the police weren't willing to release drunken teenage girls to me. I was relieved it wasn't because my good looks and charm had failed me.

"Anyway, they thought they had a major drug party going on. Since this would have been their first one, they wanted to do it by the book. Turns out theater majors tend to smoke all their dope, so they didn't find much."

"That, and David warned us the cops were on the way," Harper offered.

They all turned to look at me, again. I just gave them a blank stare.

"I take it you don't have a smart comment about that?" Bev asked.

"No, ma'am," I said, as I'd been trained by a mother of my own as to when to respond and when not.

"Anyway, where was I?" Bev asked.

"You were at the part where they didn't find any drugs because David had tipped off the perpetrators that the police were about to raid their party," Harper supplied.

Where was my mom when I needed her? Harper got everyone to look at me again. I think she was a little pissed I hadn't gotten to enjoy jail time with her. I noticed Jennie was smart enough to stay out of it. Jack was still eyeing me.

"Oh, yes. That was helpful, Harper," her mom said as she gave Harper a look and then glanced at her dad.

Harper blanched a little bit as she realized the peril I was in.

"The police pulled everyone in and didn't find the gangbangers they were looking for. One officer reported a polite boy who'd tried to spring some of the girls. The officer stated an arrest was determined inappropriate because even though he had tattoos and a leather jacket, he didn't appear to be in a gang."

Again with the looks!

"They told me this morning that no charges were being filed. I talked to the DA, and he said he had better things to do than deal with a party full of kids. He'd be interested in apprehending the fictional gang that's roaming his streets. I told him I might have an idea where he could start," Bev said.

This time they all laughed at me when they looked my way. It's a good thing I was used to this kind of abuse.

◊◊◊

During the afternoon, the girls decided to go shopping. Jerald, Jack and I settled in to watch Kentucky demolish another opponent in basketball. I watched as they poured it on and the lead just kept building.

"What do you think that does to the rest of the field?" I asked.

"You mean for the NCAA tournament?" Jack asked.

"Yeah, do you think it scares them, or do you think it'll make them prepare even harder?"

"Why do you ask?" Jerold asked.

"I'm thinking in terms of football. If we outclass a team, should we hold back or crush them? Would we have an advantage over our future opponents if they saw game film of us destroying the opposition? The other side is, would it mean they would prepare even harder if they saw it?"

They both looked at each other.

"What makes you think you're good enough to dominate your opponents like that?" Jack asked.

"David is currently the number one quarterback in the sophomore class," Jerald said to my surprise; I had no idea he knew. "His high school team almost ran the table last year, with sophomores. Next year's team will only lose three varsity players. The core group will be intact for the next two years. I predict by the time David graduates from Lincoln High, he will be a two-time and maybe a three-time State Champion." That surprised me even more.

"I thought you were just a model and did a movie," Jack said.

"He's also a straight-'A' student, and Wesleyan would welcome him with open arms," Jerald said as he made his pitch.

"So, should we crush them or not?" I asked.

"It all depends if you're looking at the short term, or the long term," Jack started. "I had to learn this early on in business. If I wanted to keep doing business with people, I couldn't crush them, or they wouldn't do deals with me down the road.

"This applies to sports as well. Back in the early 90s, the Detroit Pistons put together back-to-back championship seasons. They had a reputation they would do anything to win. They reveled in the nickname 'Bad Boys.' I personally believe their poor behavior tarnishes the whole city of

Detroit to this day. At the time, though, teams feared them, and they won many a game just on reputation alone. Half the country celebrated when they lost. I mean, who can forget them walking off the court with time on the clock when the Bulls put them down?"

It was before I was born, so I kept my mouth shut.

"The last couple of years the Detroit Lions have started being better. People are quicker to judge them as being bad for football because of their unsportsmanlike play. I think it's in part due to the Pistons," Jack surmised.

"I agree. You shouldn't embarrass the other team. I do think, though, you should play to the best of your ability. When you dominate, you need to be careful as to how you're perceived. Don't give them any reason to tear you down," Jerald advised.

"I'd also suggest you break up with Harper now before she leads you astray and your name gets splashed in the news," Jack suggested.

"I like how you worked that in. Do you mind if I borrow that for Jennie's next questionable boyfriend?" Jerald asked.

"Oh, please do. We dads need to stick together."

"Trust me, this all sounds good until your wives and daughters catch you," I warned them.

"I think I need a beer," Jack said as he got up.

I was surprised when he brought me one. I took it in the spirit it was given and drank it. Both dads seemed happy when my next drink was a soda. I had a good time with the guys for the rest of the afternoon.

◊◊◊

Jack and Bev took Harper and me to dinner. We went to the fancy restaurant Harper had wanted to take me to last night. Both Bev and Harper were happy to see Jack and I were getting along. They were a little shocked when he actually stood up for me a couple of times.

226

Harper and I didn't get to spend as much time together as I wanted, and the beginning of the weekend sucked. Still, overall, I think it turned out well. I felt like I understood Harper better after getting to know her dad a little bit. I think he felt a *lot* better, getting to know me. He'd worried he had another 'Ray' on his hands. It didn't help they'd done a background check on me and uncovered my middle school antics.

He just needed to meet me. It helped I had dated Jennie (well, kind of) and Jerald hadn't needed to shoot me. By the end of the day, he'd taken it upon himself to be the lead recruiter for Notre Dame, his alma mater.

Mom talked to Bev at some point. I was not allowed to spend another night away from home. I expected I would need to explain everything to her. Plus, she wanted to get me to church. I knew better than to fight it, so told everyone goodbye after dinner.

◊◊◊

Monday March 9

When I went to school in the morning, it was nearly a repeat of last Monday: I had an extra bounce in my step; I had a girl whom I loved; my movie obligations were done for now; and best of all, we would play our first baseball game this week. I'd just finished lifting with Wolf when Jeff came in.

"Moose posted the varsity team on his door."

Wolf and I followed Jeff and checked the list.

Varsity – Starters
Tim Foresee – Catcher
Wolf Tam – 1st Base / Right Field
Mike Herndon – 2nd Base / Pitcher
David Dawson – Shortstop / Pitcher
Jake Holcomb – 3rd Base / Center Field
Jim Ball – Right Field / 1st Base

Bill Callaway – Center Field
Jeff Rigger – Left Field

Varsity – Backups
Lou Davis – Catcher
Ed Pine – Center Field
Bryan Callahan – Catcher / Infield / Pitcher
Brock Callahan – 2nd Base / Pitcher
Trevor Millsap – Short Stop
Neil Presley – Outfield
Yuri Antakov – Infield / Outfield
Nick Rake – Shortstop
Wayne Turk – 2nd Base
Ray Quinn – 3rd Base
Bert Nelson – Pitcher / Outfield
Justin Tune – Pitcher / Infield

"Wow!" I exclaimed.

Moose had a roster that included first-year players and freshmen! I was shocked to see who was missing: every senior from last year's team was gone! They'd been involved with steroids and had quit football. One of the conditions they agreed to, if they planned on playing a sport, was that their results had to be opened. If I were to guess, they didn't pass their steroid tests.

"I can't believe Moose would change his mind," Jeff commented.

He clearly meant Moose's rule about first-year players not being allowed to play on the varsity squad.

"I think we got the best ones, though," Wolf added.

"I feel sorry for the JV team. I think we got most of their pitching. Shiggy and Coach Herndon are going to have their work cut out for them to get these guys ready for varsity ball," I said.

Yuri and the Callahan brothers came up to check the JV list.

"The JV list is over there," I said as I pointed to the sheet on the other side of the door.

They all looked at the list, and we kept straight faces as theirs fell because they couldn't find their names.

"What the hell!" Yuri complained. "I thought we played good enough to make the team."

"This sucks!" one of the twins said in agreement.

"Are you guys going to go out for track?" Jeff asked.

They all glared at us. Wolf, normally the comedian of the group, broke and started laughing. He pointed at the varsity sheet. One of the twins got brave and checked the list. Then he got a huge grin on his face.

"We made varsity!" he said and he danced around.

The other two didn't believe him until they looked. The freshmen started to show up. Wolf, Jeff and I left so the trio of new varsity players could have fun with the freshmen who'd made varsity. Wolf and I went to take showers.

◊◊◊

Before we got dressed for practice, Moose met us all in the locker room.

"I imagine some of you are wondering why I changed my policy on first-year players. I had a long talk with the coaching staff and we decided we're seriously lacking in depth. They convinced me we could win some games this year with the help of the freshmen and transfers who were selected.

"I wasn't for it, but I also don't want to lose this year. We'll be fielding a young team with a lot of potential. I plan to work you hard and making you better players and a better team. I'm also making coaching changes. Coach Haskins will be moving up to varsity assistant and Coach Diamond will take over as the JV coach. Coach Haskins brings years of experience to the table and a more aggressive playing style.

"The other addition to the staff is Shigehito Yamamura. Shiggy has an extensive background with both playing and coaching over in Japan. He'll be focusing on helping Coach Herndon with the pitchers, but will also work as our batting instructor.

"Speaking of batting, Range Sports has donated two pitching machines. They've also donated practice uniforms for everyone," Moose informed us.

Sandy Range must have talked to Moose because we each had a duffle bag with 'Lincoln High' and our name and number on the side. I noticed the coaches each had one also. Inside there was everything from cleats to hats. It was funny to watch the guys as they each got their duffle bag and then began to go through it. They were like kids let loose in a candy store. I don't think anything could have wiped the smiles off their faces.

I dug through my bag, put my briefs on, and then inserted the cup into the integrated cup-holder. I liked the feel better than the jockstrap I'd been wearing. I then put on my sliding shorts. They had padding to help prevent bruising and road rash when you slid as you stole a base. I found both a long-sleeve and a short-sleeve t-shirt in the bag. I picked the long-sleeve since it was still a little cool out.

The t-shirt seemed to have a layer of padding. I read the tag. It said the shirt was called 'Impact-Skin.' It was designed to absorb high-velocity baseballs that hit you in the torso. It also was purported to wick perspiration from your body and had a patent-pending airflow-cooling system. I hoped Moose and Coach Haskins hadn't figured that out yet. They would have us digging in and being hit by pitches.

Our shirts had 'Lincoln High' on the front and our last name and number on the back. The practice shirts were blue pullovers with three-quarter-length sleeves. The white pants came with a blue belt that matched the shirt.

230

I found two different gloves. One was a batting glove set, with Velcro to secure the gloves in place. There was also a protective inner glove for fielding. It was a leather glove, designed to be worn on the inside of a fielder's glove. It had special padding on the palm and first finger to help prevent bruises when catching a ball.

I got dressed in my new gear and felt like a million bucks. Looking around, all the guys looked sharp. We were in high spirits when we jogged out to the practice fields. Alan had Duke on his leash. When Duke saw me, he bolted. I took off running to let him chase me. Moose let me take Duke and the guys on a jog around the baseball field to warm up. When we were done, Alan came and got my hound.

We had a good practice. Everyone hustled. The coaches seemed to be well organized and kept us engaged the full time. Moose worked with the starting infield for the first half of practice. I then was sent to Shiggy for batting practice. Finally, I spent time with Coach Herndon, pitching. Practice finished up with Mike and me working with the outfielders and catchers. We worked on the outfielders hitting a cutoff man and Mike and I would then throw home. I think we all felt like practice had gone well.

◊◊◊

After dinner, I was working on my reading assignment for English when a text from Harper to logon to video chat was announced on my phone.

"Hey, baby, what's up?" I asked.

"I wanted to talk to you about last weekend. I feel bad about what all happened."

"Why's that? I'm okay with everything. I thought Jennie was enough of a reward," I assured her.

"Well, I'm not. I talked to Mom on Sunday about you," she said, and then laughed when she saw the look on my face. "Don't worry, it was all good. What I need you to know is, I'm new at having a boyfriend. I know I dated Ray, but he was my best friend first, so it was different. I had Ray wrapped around my little finger, I'm ashamed to say."

I could relate. A certain Tami Glade had had me wrapped around her finger when we were younger.

"I guess what I'm trying to tell you, David, is that I'll make mistakes. With Ray, I would just make plans and he'd do them. I know you aren't Ray. I'll make an effort to talk to you before I make plans for us."

"I take it we'll be doing what you want, though," I teased her.

"I never said you had a choice, 'stupid boy.' I AM the girl in this relationship, after all."

"I admit I was a little bent out of shape Friday," I confessed.

"A little?" she asked and raised her eyebrows.

"Okay, I told your mom on you," I said, getting a snort of derision from her. "You have to realize I've let myself be bossed around by the women in my life for a long time. I've been working hard to stand up for myself. When you told me the plans had been changed, I felt like you were taking advantage of me. To be honest, I would have been fine going to a theater party, but I'd have preferred it if you'd asked me beforehand instead of springing it on me.

"Something else that irritated me was that you left me. I didn't know anyone at the party; well, that's not entirely true, but I hadn't seen anyone I knew when you disappeared. I'm not saying we need to be joined at the hip—I'd hope we wouldn't have to be *that* couple. But I would like to at least have you introduce me to someone before you take off to talk to your friends," I complained.

"See, we did need to talk. I had to use the ladies' room; that was why I took off. If I'd told you, I'll bet you wouldn't have been irritated with me. Was that why you left the party?"

"Yeah, that, and I was feeling claustrophobic with so many people there. I just needed to go gather my thoughts for a while," I said and then sighed. "There's something you need to know about me: if I get mad, and go quiet, leave me alone. I'll need time to figure things out. Once I do, I'm okay. If you push me, I'll say something that can't be unsaid."

"That's good information. Just so you know, when I get mad I'll yell at you. Let me get it out of my system, or I'll hold it against you."

"You and every girl I know," I mumbled.

"What did you say?" she asked, giving me a stern look.

"Nothing, dear," I said as I gave her my innocent face.

"Keep it up, Chuckles, and you'll find out what yelling is. I'm sure Tami was an amateur."

"No, she liked me more than you do," I teased her.

"I'm sure she did, but you have me now, so be good."

"Yes, ma'am."

"Let's get this conversation back on track. We were talking about communication. I understand why you'd be irritated. I didn't tell you about the change in plans and then seemingly left you as soon as I got to the party. Looking back, it would've upset me too. I need to get used to the fact we're a couple. I also want you to know I want that very much. I'll work on it," she assured me.

"I appreciate you talking to me about this. It did bother me at the time."

"Now I need to talk to you about some other things that bother me. I'm not used to being as open with my parents as you are with them. I think my dad was in shock to see his little girl is growing up. I want to ask that in the future you let me take the lead with them," she said.

"I can appreciate where you're coming from. I want you to know I won't lie to them. Your mom can tell if I lie anyway, and I respect her enough not to even try. I know you didn't want her to know we were having sex, but believe me, she knew. I didn't tell her in LA just to rub it in her face. I told her because she asked me a direct question. In the long run, we'll be better off if we're honest."

"You might be right, but I want to be the one to decide what my parents know or don't know. You could have just shut up like you usually do."

"Sorry, she reminds me too much of my mom. I would never think of not answering *her*. I'll try to be better in the future. I like your mom and dad."

"And they like you a little too much," she added.

I just smirked.

"And I definitely want to talk to you about Jennie."

"I was wondering about that. I was surprised when it happened. I thought she hated me," I admitted.

Harper laughed and shook her head.

"No, far from it! Jennie Wesleyan likes you more than a little. She admitted to me that she messed up with you. She begged me to help wake you up on Saturday. I was a little surprised at how far things went. Before you worry, I was there. I know if I'd asked, you wouldn't have had sex with her."

"We need to talk about this. I wasn't planning on having sex with anyone but you," I said.

"I've been thinking about this a lot. I've never dated someone like you. I know you have some friends with benefits. Heck, I was one of them. I enjoyed having no-strings sex with a guy I could trust. I'm sure your friends miss your attention. I'd like it, if you ever do something with them, that I'm there. I would've had a problem with you and Jennie getting together without me in the room. At least, for now, I want you to be just mine. I hope you understand."

"I do, and that's what I want too. Just be aware that when you get up here this weekend, some of my friends might approach you."

"Have they been asking you for sex?" she said with a scowl on her face.

"Don't get mad. Peggy was fine with me being with my friends, since we were just dating. I've had to explain to my friends there's a difference between dating and having a girlfriend."

"I can see why they'd be confused. I promise not to smack them around," she said with a smile. "I did have a good time when we were with Jennie. I might be open to doing more in the future."

"Harper, I assure you we're exclusive unless we talk about it beforehand."

"I know I can trust you. I hope we do some more things together that push my boundaries."

"Are you serious? Because I have a few ideas!" I said, leering at her.

"I'll bet you do," she shot back.

"If you're serious, I have a website you should check out. They have some toys we might want to play with. You can have everything delivered here if you're worried someone might see what you buy. I'd even be willing to pay for them."

"David!" she exclaimed as she went red.

"You know you want to, so don't act all shocked with me."

"Maybe. Can I really have it delivered to your house?"

"I get the mail every day, so we'd be fine. If my mom finds it, I'll just tell her she needs to get her own."

"David!"

"It can't be any worse than when she took me condom shopping," I admitted.

"OH! MY! GOD! I'm logging off before you embarrass me any more. Send me the link," she ordered and then logged off.

I would put money on her sharing the link with her friends at Wesleyan.

Chapter 12 – Barbie and GI Joe

Friday March 13

I was glad today was over. I think every teacher felt they needed to give us a test or quiz. I felt confident I'd done well, but I was just glad the day was done.

Baseball was going well. Moose and Coach Haskins were happy since we were ahead of schedule. Our winter workouts had helped and I felt more confident pitching. I did have some problems with control. Shiggy and Coach Herndon felt I tried to overthrow the ball. I guess they were right because when I backed off I had better command of my pitches. The problem was I was very hittable when my velocity dropped. When I threw hard, I was a little wild, but no one could touch my pitches. Then again, why would they even want to if I handed out walks?

After baseball, Jeff, Cassidy and I had gone to the dojo to practice. I'd cut back to just three times a week for now. Cassidy was confident I could defend myself if needed. The dojo work helped with my balance and flexibility, and both translate nicely into both baseball and football.

When I pulled into our driveway, Harper's car was already here. Duke and I went to the house where I found her seated at the kitchen table with my mom and dad. I think Duke was more excited to see her than I was.

"Down!" Mom gave Duke his command to put all four feet on the floor.

I was surprised when he minded. He was still at the hit-or-miss stage of his training and he seemed to mind Mom and Dad better than he did me. They worked with him more than I did, with the idea of him being a service dog. He thought of me more as a buddy than his master.

I gave Harper a kiss on the cheek.

"We're having dinner with your parents. Go take a shower. After we eat, we'll go out," Harper told me.

I raised my eyebrows. Did she just change our plans again without talking to me? Dad winked at me and I knew my mom had made the change to our plans. I just did as I was told.

When I came back, Angie and Greg were home with Kyle and Mac. Mac saw me and wanted me to pick her up. Kyle was about ten seconds behind her. They were cute since they'd started to say a few words. Duke had learned to settle down when one of them would tell him 'no.' I have to say, Duke was very gentle with them, except for when they got in the way of his tail. He could clear off a coffee table with that thing. Babies had no chance when he walked by and whacked them with it.

I noticed Mac had a Band-Aid on her elbow.

"Mac, what happened?" I asked her.

"Owee," she told me.

She raised it so I could kiss it. Kyle showed me the doll he held. It was a Barbie Doll. I looked over at Greg.

"Just shut up. Mac took his GI Joe," Greg told me.

I knew one little boy who'd get another GI Joe doll. I didn't need my friends seeing him play with a Barbie. I think Greg read my mind.

"Don't bother. He throws a fit if his Barbie disappears."

His grandma came and got him. Mac was content to have me hold her. I checked out Angie because she was now seven months pregnant and starting to really show. I handed Mac to her granddad and led Angie to the living room. She went willingly because I'd given her a foot massage each time I'd seen her over the last couple of weeks as her feet and ankles had swelled. I knew Greg did the same, but she wouldn't turn down a foot massage.

Harper came into the living room to talk to us while I worked on Angie.

"Your mom told me Greg and Angie were coming over for dinner. I hope you're not mad I changed our plans."

"No, I figured it had to be something like that. I actually enjoy seeing my brother and his family," I told her.

"Shut up and get to work," Angie ordered, since I'd stopped rubbing when I talked to Harper.

"Yes, ma'am," I replied, and began again.

Angie had some tender spots that needed to be worked on.

"Do you know where I keep the massage oil?" I asked Harper.

"In the cabinet next to the microwave?"

"Yeah. Could you go get me one of them? I need to really work on Angie," I said.

Harper got up to go get me the massage oil and Duke went to supervise.

"I like her," Angie told me once we were alone.

"I like her, too," I said with a smile.

Then Angie changed the subject.

"I want to hire someone to help me with the nonprofit."

"Do you have the funds to do it?" I asked.

"We have enough money, but I didn't know if I could. Plus, I'm not really good with payroll and all the human resource stuff."

"Do you know who you want to hire?"

"Yes, one of the girls we gave money to wants to help. She's been volunteering, but she could use the extra money."

"You know you don't have to ask me," I assured her.

"As our biggest donor, I want you to be aware of what we're doing. I don't want you to think we're wasting your money."

"Angie, that's why I put you in charge: I know I can trust you. Talk to Kendal and see if they'll do your 'back office.' I know they do it for Adrienne and Tyler. While you're at it, talk to Mom and see if she could use their help for her nonprofit," I said. "How are you and Greg doing financially?"

She gave me a tight smile.

"We're getting by," she assured me.

"Don't bullshit me."

She blushed and looked down as she bit her lip.

"Effective immediately, you're getting a raise. Just tell Kendal how much you need and I'll have her deposit enough in your nonprofit account to cover the increase. I'm sure I need the tax write-off," I told her to keep her from objecting.

Tom and Kendal had worked this out for me. I was able to give money to my brother and his family and have it be a charitable donation. Angie got to help teen mothers. She'd been the first teen mom helped with the charity and knew what a difference it made. She had a real passion for what she was doing.

Harper came back and handed me the oil. I needed the oil so I could do a deep-tissue massage on Angie. When I was done, Angie was a contented woman. Dinner was ready. We had chicken nuggets, apple slices, and salad. Kyle and Mac were very happy.

◊◊◊

At least I had warned Harper about tonight's date. The coaches had gotten together and decided what we needed was to have some good clean fun that did not include drinking. We were going bowling. Coach Hope drew the short straw and had to organize and attend. I think the last time I'd gone bowling was when I was ten. Someone, meaning Alan, had had a birthday party at a bowling alley.

I was surprised Harper was okay with doing this. I figured she would think she was too cool. I mean, I thought *I* was too cool to do this, but I was a dork. We went, got our shoes, and found Coach Hope so he could direct us to the lanes where we were bowling. He told me lane six.

I guess I wasn't surprised to see Jeff and Cassidy as our partners. I was surprised to see we were playing against Pam, Mona, Kim and Sammie. Wolf strolled by with his date, April.

"Jeff, how did you get stuck bowling with David and his women?"

"I know, right? Let everyone know I'm taking one for the team," Jeff shot back.

Wolf just shook his head and found his lane. I was happy to see the whole team had made it. Most of them had brought dates. I was still hungry, so I ordered a basket of fries and a pizza. Mona saw me ordering and had me get everyone drinks, and she wanted jalapeño poppers. When I got back, I found Harper surrounded by the girls and Jeff keeping score. I joined him at the table.

"Do I have anything to worry about?" I asked him.

"Dude, you were the dumbass who left her alone with them. What do you think?"

"Seriously?"

He just shook his head at me and smiled. Crud.

Turned out I was a terrible bowler. The first game I bowled a whopping 79. Harper kicked all our butts and bowled a 167. Even with Harper's help, we lost to the cheerleaders by a wide margin. The second game I only managed a 68. The good news was I had a lot of fun. Harper got everyone to tell her stories about me. She seemed to enjoy that way too much. I filed it away because paybacks are hell.

I barely got any of the food I ordered, so after the third game I talked everyone into going with us to the diner across from the hospital. Jeff and Cassidy had come with her dad, so they rode with us. Mona had driven the cheerleaders. Kim's aunt and uncle owned the place, so she went to the back to talk to them and started sending out food. Jeff and I were happy boys when fried chicken came out on several platters.

Once we'd demolished the chicken, her aunt brought out eight different pie slices. We agreed to pass them around so everyone got a taste. I felt there was a three-way tie for the best pie. I love pecan pie, and they made theirs with an oatmeal crust, which made it even better. The other two pies I liked were a coconut custard pie and one I couldn't believe: it was a pumpkin apple-butter pie with a gingersnap cookie crust. I would order it again for sure.

◊◊◊

Harper and I got home around ten. I grabbed her bag out of her trunk, then stuck my head in the back door to let Mom know we were home and to get Duke. He had sticky stuff on his back. I guessed his little friends had shared with him. We went upstairs and I showed Harper her box of toys she'd ordered. I left her to open it while I took Duke to the shower to get him clean. I didn't need him rolling around and getting it all over the floor.

When we came out, Harper was naked and smiling. There was something about seeing my naked girlfriend smiling that made me happy. Poor Duke got stuffed into his crate.

"Care to get naked?"

I didn't have to be asked twice. While I undressed, she pulled out her toys. When I saw her harness for a strap-on, I stopped.

"What's that?" I asked.

"I thought we might try this out later tonight," she said with an evil grin.

"I hate to do this, but we need to break up."

"Are you telling me you don't want to play with me?"

"Not if you're wearing that, I don't. I'm not playing that game," I said firmly.

"What if we used it on someone else?" she suggested.

That brought me up short. I tried to imagine what she was talking about. It didn't take long for my teenage mind to hit the gutter, and I had some promising ideas. I heard Harper giggle and she pointed at my groin. When Mr. Happy thought we'd be on the receiving end of the strap-on, he'd gone soft. Thinking about other possibilities brought him back to life.

I looked down, then up at my naked girlfriend, and then walked up to her. Harper put down the dildo and harness and decided to use the real thing. I loved to look down and watch her devour me. She alternated between seeing how much she could stuff into her mouth and using her tongue to lick me.

"Dang, Harper! That's so hot!" I exclaimed when she engulfed Mr. Happy.

She lightly dragged her fingernails down my stomach to my knees as she bobbed up and down on my member. It sent shivers all through my body. I couldn't help myself. I grabbed her head and pushed into her face. She grasped the base so I couldn't kill her, but she let me abuse her.

"I'm almost there!" I warned her.

Harper grabbed my backside and pulled me forward. I felt the head bury itself deep into her mouth as I started to release. I felt her swallow as I went over the precipice. My knees unlocked and I staggered back and fell into my recliner so I wouldn't fall over.

"Oh, my God, thank you," I said in appreciation.

She just left me there and went to the bathroom to clean herself up. She came back out, turned her back to me, and bent over. I lined myself up and took her from behind. She was soaking wet. I remembered the condom and pulled out of her, which made her whine.

"What are you doing?" she complained.

"Condom," was my one-word answer.

"You know I'm on the pill, right?" she asked.

"Do you know where this has been?" I shot back.

"Oh, good point, but if you already put it in me, wouldn't I already have your nasty disease?"

"Better safe than sorry."

"Quit talking about it and get to work!" she ordered.

I quickly put on the condom. I'd gotten pretty good at that. I got behind her and got busy. I pounded her through a big orgasm and then pulled out and pushed against her rosebud.

"Are you? Uuuuuhhhh," Harper moaned as I slowly filled her backside.

It took some work, but I finally was able to worm my way in. I took it slow to allow Harper to get used to it. I was surprised when she came from me doing her there. I had expected she wouldn't the first time. All I knew was when she did climax, she didn't do her normal grunting. She actually screamed.

"YEEEESSSSSS!"

It was too much for me. I couldn't hold back as my gut tightened and I came hard for the second time of the evening.

"I feel you pulsing in me," Harper told me as I got off. "Damn that was fun!"

When I finally stopped, I pulled out and went to the restroom to get rid of the condom and to clean up. I found Harper under the covers, curled up. I let Duke out of his crate so he could go outside one last time. I showed him I had a treat so he'd be quick about it. He did his business and came right back in. He even went into his crate without complaining. I gave him his treat and turned out the living room lights.

Harper was sound asleep when I crawled into bed. She seemed to sense me and she rolled over and put her head on my chest, though still asleep. This was what I'd been missing. I fell asleep a happy boy.

◊◊◊

Saturday March 14

I woke up to a buzzing sound. It took me a moment to realize Harper was in bed with me and using one of her new toys. I opened my eyes and she smiled.

"Good, you're up. I like my new toys, but I want the real thing."

"Let me take care of Duke and I'll be right back," I told her.

He would hear us and get quite vocal in the morning if I forgot about him. I didn't need him to rock his crate while I rocked the bedroom. I gave myself a mental head-slap for my terrible play on words. I put on sweats and went to let my pup out. I had his leash so he wouldn't make a jailbreak and think we were going running. He was happy to see me, and when we hit the backyard, he went about his toilette. I took him to the back door of the house and set him free.

When I stepped into the bedroom, Harper tossed me a condom and got on all fours. Mr. Happy was more than ready. I stripped and put the condom on. Harper was on the edge of the bed and waved her cute butt at me.

"I thought we might want to spend some time and talk," I suggested.

"If you plan on being my boyfriend more than a couple of minutes from now, there'd better be some serious lovemaking going on," she warned me.

I smacked her butt, which earned me a glare. She was doing her happy grunts a moment later when I began to do as instructed. Harper must have used her little toy for a while because she was fully aroused. I was trying to keep from getting off too soon by trying to figure out if running or sex was better as a morning cardio when my mom called me on the intercom.

"David, we're going to Granny's for breakfast in thirty minutes," Mom told us.

"I guess we have a timeframe now," I teased Harper.

"Shut up."

I guess someone was close. I was right, she climaxed hard only a few strokes later. I was close, too, so I pulled out and took the condom off, and after a few manual strokes ... I made a mess all over her butt. I admired my handiwork when she came to her senses.

"You're such a bad boy. Now I have your stuff all over me," she complained.

"I guess we'd better go shower."

She made me clean up after myself with the detachable showerhead. We almost didn't make it downstairs in time when I surprised Harper with the different shower head settings and what they could do. She vowed they would get one for the dorm.

◊◊◊

Granny's was packed as usual on a Saturday morning. Dad sent me to the hostess stand to get us a table. Granny was serving coffee and saw me. She came right over.

"I see you brought your whole family. Who's the cute girl?"

I motioned for Harper to come over.

"Harper, this is Granny. She's about to pull a rabbit out of her hat and find us a table for six adults and two high chairs."

"Don't let him bully you," Harper said as she shook Granny's hand.

"He never does, but I think we have something opening up soon. Let me have it taken care of while you two come with me and talk to my guests."

Granny had a good time telling the women I was off the market. Harper did get a few dirty looks, but she took it well. By the time we were done, my family was having coffee and giant cinnamon rolls. I had a big smile when I saw Kyle and Mac working on little pieces of rolls. I imagined Angie and Greg would have their hands full when the sugar highs hit.

We had a nice breakfast as a family. Greg and Angie enjoyed school. Angie told us her due date was in the middle of May and Greg announced it was going to be a boy. That sent Mom into full grandma mode. The university was working to get them a three-bedroom unit. They could get them one for the fall without a problem, but the summer wasn't looking good. Mom told them they would move back in with us.

Dad, Greg and I all looked at each other. There were two additional bedrooms, besides the ones Greg and I grew up in, on the top floor of the house. The only problem was, they were used for storage. We all knew Mom now intended for us to clean them out and get them ready for her grandbabies.

◊◊◊

When we left Granny's, Harper was confused when we didn't head back to my place.

"Where are we going?" she asked.

"One of my friends is in the nuthouse and I plan on springing her."

I had arranged to get Tracy today because she wanted to go to our first baseball game of the season. She'd been getting out on visits to her parents' house about three times a week. Tom thought she might be able to come home soon. I had visited every Tuesday evening I could. Pam had joined me on our visits, so I wasn't surprised when it was commented on that I had a different girl with me.

"How many girlfriends do you have?" Velma asked as we came in.

Velma was in her late twenties and was a veteran who'd had some issues when she came back from the war. I liked her because she was very protective of Tracy.

"Velma, this is Harper, my girlfriend," I said by way of introduction.

We were in the common area and several people turned to listen to our conversation. Tracy was across the room and made her way over to us.

"But Tracy said …"

"Too much," I finished Velma's sentence.

Harper just shook her head. I enjoyed giving Velma a hard time.

"Hey, Velma, did you know that twenty-five percent of women are on some type of mental-illness medication?"

"Oh, good lord, he's been using the Internet again," Tracy almost moaned.

Velma just eyed me.

"It really makes me worried," I told them.

"I know I'm going to regret this, but why are you worried?" Velma asked.

"It means that seventy-five percent are running around untreated!"

Harper was nonplussed that I would make that kind of joke in this setting. She was even more confused when everyone started laughing. I'd found they responded to these kinds of jokes. It showed I wasn't uncomfortable with my surroundings, and by extension with them. One of the nurses had given me my material the last time I was there. They'd heard them all and helped me out with the tamer ones.

"Come on, before he gets started," Tracy said as she grabbed my arm.

When we got to the car, Harper was ready to tear into me.

"What were you thinking?" she began.

"Harper, he was doing a good thing. The elephant in that room is we were just in a mental-health facility which specializes in depression. Most of our guests tiptoe around our reality when they come to visit. My fellow crazies and I appreciate the fact David doesn't shy away from our situation. His stupid jokes put smiles on faces that really need them. We all look forward to when this goof visits," Tracy said in my defense.

I smiled as the light bulb come on for Harper. She wasn't done, though. She was a smart girl and Velma had left enough breadcrumbs for her to figure out that I came to visit Tracy with another girl.

"Who is David bringing to visit you?" Harper asked innocently.

Tracy burst out laughing.

"David, I like this one," she said and then turned her attention to Harper. "I think you know our David has some friends. One of them is my best friend Pam. Velma assumed Pam and David were dating. Velma and I have had a few frank discussions about him."

Harper had met Pam last night at bowling. She gave me a look that said we would have a talk later.

"Oh," Harper said, as she pondered her response, "and Velma wants to jump his bones, too!"

I about drove off the road after I heard her leap in deduction.

"Velma would probably do him in the middle of group therapy," Tracy agreed. "The one thing we miss the most is sex."

"TMI—waayyy too much information," I complained.

"I'm just putting you on notice! I have a need, and you're my friend," Tracy said cheerfully.

"I think we need to talk," Harper told her.

Somehow, they convinced me to drop them off at Tracy's house while I was sent to get ready for my baseball game. When I got home, I found the Callahan triplets waiting for me. I traded cars with my mom so I'd have enough room when Harper came home with us. Duke claimed shotgun.

◊◊◊

We played Lang Academy today. They were a reform school and always had boys coming and going, so they were never great. Lang was normally the first team we played each year as sort of a warm-up for the season. I got to the ballpark in the middle of the JV game. I took Duke to Alan and was impressed when he curled up at Alan's feet.

I went to stretch and get ready. Shiggy wanted me in the batting cage, so I did my normal routine as he watched. I'd play shortstop today and Justin would start as our pitcher. Moose had big plans for this year. I could tell he had everyone more focused than we were last year, playing JV. Shiggy pulled me aside to talk to me.

"David, you need to get a set routine before each game. Do everything the same way so you're prepared to play."

He then took me through his old warm-up process. He made me get Jeff so he could help me. When I explained what we were doing, we had the rest of the team gather around. Shiggy made sure we were stretched out. He explained this would reduce injuries. We then did a quick run to get our blood flowing. He had us do the long toss, which helped further loosen our arms.

That was where our normal routine went out the window.

"Baseball is not a slow or static sport. When playing baseball, the playing actions are centered on power, acceleration, explosiveness, and movement," Shiggy coached.

He had us do runs of ninety feet and back where we did different things; examples would be high knee lifts, lateral side-skips, and 'fast feet.' I recognized similarities to what I'd learned from my speed coach. Shiggy used the warm-up to make us better baseball players. The other coaches came out and took note of what we did. They seemed to approve of the new warm-ups.

He then split us up. The first four batters for today went with him to the batting cages. The pitchers went with Coach Herndon to get ready, and everyone else went with Moose. Shiggy had us visualize our at-bats.

"I want to you to close your eyes and describe what you're doing," Shiggy told us.

He had Bill and Jake in the batting cages. What I liked about Shiggy's coaching was he individualized his approach for each batter. Too many coaches have a cookie-cutter approach. Each guy described their at bat. He did ask me why I had a more open stance than most players. I bat right-handed and my dominant eye is my right eye. I'd found that the more open stance helped me see the ball better.

Shiggy made us talk through and visualize each step at bat, which helped us think it through. I found when it came my turn, I was more focused and able to hit better and with more power. As we would finish, two more players would come over and get ready to bat.

By the time the JV was done with their game, I had a good sweat going, and we took the field to finish warming up. I was focused and ready to play when all hell broke loose.

Lang Academy doesn't have girls. Last year we'd had some issues when Eve had played on JV. Cassidy actually had to take one of their players down. Today's entertainment, I would later find out, had started when they made some comments to Tracy, Pam and Harper. The JV guys heard it and stepped in. I don't know who threw the first punch, but it was soon a full-blown brawl. The mistake Lang made was focusing on just the players; Coach Hope, Cassidy, Brad and Shiggy could all handle themselves. We also found out the coaches from Lang had training in subduing their charges.

Luckily for me, Coach Herndon saw me take off to find out what was going on. All I could see and hear were my girls screaming and people in Lincoln High uniforms fighting. He grabbed me before I could get over the fence to join in. By then the guys from Lang who'd caused the problems were face-down on the ground. My girls ran over to assure me they were okay.

Lang Academy's JV team was loaded onto the bus and sent home. They arranged with Lincoln to use one of our buses to take the varsity home after the game.

I was fired up to win this game. I felt like I did before a football game, which meant I had to dash to the locker room and throw up before we started. When I got back, we took the field, and every guy had his game face on. Last year had been all about fun. Now? We were ready to dominate!

Justin seemed to throw well in warm-ups. Their first guy up was their speedy center fielder. Justin hung a curveball and he slapped it up the middle. On contact, Mike and I exploded out of our stances and made an all-out effort to get to the ball. We'd practiced where if we ever crossed, he would go deep and I would go in front. The reason was that I had a better chance to get and throw out the runner since I was headed towards first base. I snagged the ball just behind second base and came up throwing a rocket to Wolf. I think he caught it out of self-defense.

I ended up handling all three balls in the first inning. Two of them would normally have been base hits if I hadn't been focused and hustled. Justin swatted me on the butt when I came into the dugout.

"Thanks, man," he told me to let me know he appreciated me getting him out of the inning.

I was up third in the first inning. Both Bill and Jake hit the ball right at someone and were out. I came up and Moose signaled for me to take the first pitch. I dug in and watched a fastball catch the outside corner for strike one. I stepped out of the box and visualized hitting the ball over the first baseman's head. I saw the ball well as it came out of the pitcher's hand. It was a hanging curveball, right in the zone. I held my hands back to keep from overswinging and then punched the ball over the first baseman.

Coach Haskins had worked with us to run full speed to first base. He said good things happened when you hustled. A cardinal sin, according to him, was to jog when running the bases. The right fielder hustled to get the ball. I was surprised when no one covered second base. I didn't even look at Moose at first, but instead just rounded first at full speed. The second baseman had gone out to cut off the throw, but the shortstop hadn't paid attention. I think he assumed I would settle for a single. When he finally looked up, it was too late.

"That's the way to steal an extra base," Coach Haskins' gravelly voice boomed from third.

Our dugout was on their feet. Coach Haskins had preached to us the importance of picking up bases. The more pressure we could put on them, the better we would do. I wasn't surprised when Coach Haskins gave me the steal sign. He was making a statement that we would run at every chance. As a pitcher, if I knew the other team would steal, it unnerved me.

Wolf dug in at the plate. He'd hit some tremendous shots in practice. Normally we'd allow him to drive us in with his big bat. The catcher was obviously nervous, and I guessed they'd try to brush Wolf back. At least, that's what I would do. The pitcher looked back at me, then began to throw home. I took off like a shot. The pitcher tried to stop the pitch but ended up throwing it in the dirt.

Coach Haskins had taught us to watch him when we were two-thirds of the way to third. The first part of my run was to keep low and dig to get to maximum speed. Once I was up to speed, I would look for Coach. Wolf did his job and stood tall in the box, which caused the catcher to have to first trap the ball and then look around him to make the throw. Coach Haskins gave me the slide sign, so I knew a throw was coming. I slid into third and popped up. The catcher had thrown the ball on the outside of the base. I was safe.

That is where I 'died.' Wolf hit a golf shot to dead center field, but it came up short. By the third inning, Lang Academy hadn't hit a ball out of the infield. It wasn't that Justin struck them out, it was that the defense behind him had played lights-out. The guys had taken their cues from me and we were determined we wouldn't lose today.

Lang's pitcher had a heck of a game. He'd let a base runner on in each inning, but we were scoreless. Justin led off in the third. I think he surprised them when he laid down a bunt to get on. Bill came up and hit a long sacrifice ball to right field to advance Justin to second. Jake hit a screamer right at the third baseman. He decided to throw out Jake, instead of holding Justin at second. I came up with two out and a runner at third. Shiggy called me back to the dugout, just before I went up.

"Ignore your signs. We think they've picked them up. You're going to get the hold sign for the first pitch. I want you to hit away."

I just nodded and hustled to the batter's box, since the umpire had started to give us dirty looks for holding up his game. I chanted in my head, 'quick hands, quick hands.' Their pitcher looked over at Coach Haskins and grinned when he gave me the hold sign. I let my shoulder slump. I'd learned a thing or two about acting. I tried hard not to smile when a fastball rocketed right down the middle. I concentrated to keep my swing level, extend my arms, snap my wrists, and have good bat speed. As soon as I heard the *ting* of the aluminum bat, I knew I'd gotten all of it.

I ran hard to first base as I'd been taught and then looked up to see the umpire indicate I'd hit a home run. I made sure to keep good speed around the bases and not embarrass the pitcher. Nothing pissed them off more than a home-run trot. Justin waited for me at home. We acted like we did this every day and headed to the dugout after a fist bump.

We ended up winning 3–0. I went two for three with two RBIs, one stolen base, a double and a home run. Justin had faced twenty-five batters over seven innings. He had struck out three and walked one. He'd given up only three hits. I was involved in eleven plays, one of which was a double play. Mike had handled eight plays. Our defense up the middle had been solid all game.

After we had shaken Lang Academy's hands, Moose wanted to talk to us.

"Good game today. Now go blow off some steam, but no drinking. I expect everyone to be ready to practice on Monday," he told us and sent us on our way.

I stepped forward to get everyone's attention. I knew if I didn't say something, there would be a party organized.

"Monical's at 6:30, the arcade afterwards, and parents are welcome."

Someone needed to pay for my big plans.

◊◊◊

Harper had insisted I not take a shower at the school. She liked the way I smelled after I worked out. I liked that she liked it, and Mr. Happy liked that she liked it. We were both very clean and satisfied once Harper was done with us when I showered at home with her assistance.

When we got to Monical's, the place was packed. I was glad I'd had Greg reserve the banquet room. The guys were all eating free appetizers. I noticed his favorite assistant manager had taken care of us. I was also pleased to see someone had told the JV team, because they were all there too, most with their parents.

I started to walk around the room to say hi to all the guys and their dates. I made a point to introduce Harper. She knew most of the JV guys from earlier today. I thanked them for protecting her and the cheerleaders. Mona and the rest of the cheerleaders had singled out the guys who helped them today and gave them each a hug and a kiss. I had to smile when they'd light up like a Christmas tree with huge grins on their faces. It's not every day a freshman gets kissed by a hot varsity cheerleader!

Harper gave me a hip-bump.

"You're not jealous, are you?"

"No," I said, then gathered her in and gave her a kiss. "I'm the luckiest guy in the room."

"You big goof! You keep saying things like that and I'll fall in love with you."

"You already love me," I teased her.

She looked me in the eyes.

"You're right, I do love you."

◊◊◊

Chapter 13 – It Sounds Bad

Friday April 10

Spring had arrived in our sleepy little town. Mom's tulips were in full bloom and the trees were greening up. I was taking in the signs of the change of season when I saw my first robin. It was predicted to be in the low 60s this weekend. I was looking forward to the warmer weather because we had our baseball tournament.

Lincoln High had lost their first game on Wednesday. Our record stood at 7–1. I had started three games and my record was 2–0 with a 1.37 ERA. Justin was also 2–0 with a 2.43 ERA. The surprise was Bryan; working as our closer, he was 2–1. Mike started one game with no decision. Bert and Brock were our middle relievers. Coach Herndon and Shiggy prepared us for tournament play. We had played several simulated games to give our pitching staff more stamina than we had last year at this time.

Even Moose admitted that the Callahan twins were the difference. They'd had varsity experience pitching when they played in New Jersey last year. With their addition, we were now able to feel like we had enough pitching to be competitive in a tournament, where you might play as many as four games in a day.

We had solid pitching, but our defense was winning us games. Working with the players and coaches at State had made a big difference. We were just ahead of the other teams, as far as preparation was concerned. As teams played together, they were catching up. We also steadily got better as a group. I wasn't surprised we were made the number one seed for the upcoming tournament.

◊◊◊

At lunch, Pam wanted to eat with me, alone. She needed to talk about something and seemed nervous. We found a table at the back of the cafeteria so we could have some privacy. When people had a choice, they preferred to sit near the windows, which overlooked the school grounds.

"What's wrong? Did something happen to Tracy?" I asked when we were settled.

"No, no, Tracy's fine. In fact, she's getting better. She told me they might let her out by the end of the week. She still won't be coming back to school, but she'll be home with her family," Pam shared.

"If I ever see Bill Rogers again, he might not survive the encounter."

Pam could tell I was serious. The young man really had done a number on Tracy. I was sure this wasn't the only reason Tracy was depressed, but his abuse was a major factor in how she was doing right now. Dr. Hebert was working to get Tracy's antidepressant medication balanced before she was sent home. They had to be careful because it took a while for it fully to take effect. They wanted her in a controlled environment while they were finding what worked for Tracy. They also wanted to help her recognize her depression for what it was and give her the tools to handle it. No one wanted Tracy to try to hurt herself again.

"I have other girl troubles," Pam said cryptically.

"That doesn't sound good. I sure hope the freshman cheerleaders haven't come up with some plan to corrupt me," I said, smirking at her.

"No, these would be older girls."

"I can deal with Mona and her band of troublemakers," I said more confidently than I felt.

"No, these girls would be even older girls," she said, not looking at me.

I was stumped. If it was Beth, Cindy or Suzanne, I'd be fine. I would just explain to Harper Greg's 'free pass' arrangement. I thought about it for two seconds and remembered Angie got an equal number of passes. Nope,

Harper wasn't getting any free passes. She might just use them.

"Do I even want to know?" I asked.

"Cora," was Pam's one-word answer.

Her sister was an older version of Pam. She was a knockout who was currently decimating the fraternities at State. Cora was a slut, but a picky slut, according to Pam. She only went after the best guys. Her problem was she got bored with them when they couldn't keep up.

"What about Cora? I hope she isn't expecting a repeat of the three of us being together," I worried.

Pam gave me a wicked smile.

"Quit your complaining. I was there, remember? You'd do it again in a heartbeat," Pam said, challenging me to deny it.

I tried to act tough, but knew she was right. I was sure Pam would have used her sister to get into my pants if she thought it would work. She still wasn't completely on board with Harper being my girlfriend, as it meant no random hookups. The girls had started calling Harper directly, and lucky for me, Harper enjoyed the byplay. She had no intention of letting me play with any of them right now. I didn't complain because Harper was more than enough for me, even if I only saw her on weekends.

"I choose not to answer," I said to evade her. "What does Cora want?"

"You know she's pledging a sorority, right?"

I nodded.

"Normally pledge activities are tame. I know you've probably read some Penthouse Letters or been on the Internet and read stories about the wild things sororities get up to," she said.

I wasn't about to deny it. I think every boy my age had read something along those lines. I just shrugged.

"Well, get your dirty thoughts out of your head. Sororities are about sisterhood and making the most out of the college experience."

"We both know Cora is 'experiencing' college. What does all this have to do with me?" I asked.

"Sorry, guess I should just tell you. Cora has been a bad influence on her pledge class," Pam said, and then looked up at me.

"And?" I encouraged her.

She tilted her head down, bit her lower lip, and glanced around. I thought about getting up right then but was too curious to leave without knowing what Cora had cooked up.

Pam leaned forward and made sure I was the only one who could hear her. "She wanted me to have you invite yourself and four of the guys from your baseball team to her sorority for a party Saturday night after your tournament," she said.

"I'm sure the guys would enjoy it. I'm just concerned it's too late a notice. They might have plans for after the games."

"There's more," Pam said, getting my full attention. "Cora told me the theme of the party is 'Fresh Meat.' The pledges plan to hook up with your guys for an anonymous one-night stand. Cora assured the pledges she could find guys they wouldn't run into on campus."

I rocked back into my chair. Pam gave me a confused look when I got out my phone and sent a text. She was even more confused when Tim and Bill came over and joined us.

"We have a dilemma," I told the guys. "Pam's sister is in a sorority, and they want five guys from the team to come over Saturday night after the tournament to have sex with them."

Pam blushed and gave me a dirty look.

"Hey, it's what it boils down to," I defended myself.

"I guess, but the way you described it sounds bad," Pam complained.

"David, are you bullshitting us?" Tim asked.

He had a point. This would make a heck of a joke. Was Cora pulling one over on us? I looked at Pam questioningly; I could imagine the sorority girls would think it would be fun to torment high school boys.

"What do you think? Is Cora just getting us there to punk us?" I asked Pam.

"No. My sister might do something like that, but she was way too excited about the prospect of having no-strings sex with the guys. Now, would the older girls play a trick on you guys and the pledge class? Maybe," she agreed.

"We could get into so much trouble," Bill worried.

Tim and I looked at each other and then gave him a look. Bill slapped his forehead.

"I know, I'm such a wuss, but you both know Moose would never let us play baseball again if we got caught."

"Moose said we'd get kicked off if we got caught drinking or doing drugs. He never said anything about getting laid," Tim reasoned.

"Would Cora make sure there was no booze or drugs at the party?" I asked.

Pam got up and called her sister. That gave us a chance to really talk.

"Part of me says this is a REALLY bad idea. The other part of me says I'll regret it if we don't do it. If I had to decide right now, I'd say we go for it," I shared.

"What about Harper?" Tim said, ruining my bravado.

Both Tim and Bill smiled at me. I pulled my phone out and called her.

"I was packing to come see you," Harper shared with me.

"What would you think about going with me to a sorority sex party Saturday night?" I asked.

Tim and Bill's eyes got very big.

Harper had a lot of questions and I didn't have answers. Pam came back to the table, so I handed the phone to her. She blushed when she found out it was my girlfriend on the line. She did the smart thing and gave her Cora's number.

"I thought you wore the pants in your relationship," Tim teased me.

"Dude, if I went behind her back and went to a sex party without her, she wouldn't be my girlfriend come Sunday," I explained.

"Is this how you manage all your friends?" Bill asked.

"Sneaking around is the quickest way to screw up a relationship. If any of the guys we decide to join us are dating anyone, I would suggest they come clean before they do anything. They still might lose their girlfriend, but I will guarantee they'll be in more trouble if they get caught cheating," I explained.

"David's right. He's always up-front with his friends, and they appreciate it," Pam said, and then realized what she'd indirectly admitted to.

The guys looked at both of us and grinned.

"You two settle down. If I hear anything concerning Pam and me, I'll have Cassidy come and find you," I threatened.

"All you had to do was ask. Making threats wasn't necessary," Tim said.

"I agree, we're good," Bill assured us.

My phone rang. It was Harper.

"I swear, you're such a slut. I have no idea why I put up with you," she started.

"Because I'm *your* slut."

The guys mimed grinding and I gave them a hard look.

"Would you be disappointed if we went and you weren't allowed to partake in any of the girls?" she asked.

"No," I answered without hesitation.

"What if I decided to go off with one of the guys, would you have a problem with it?" she asked.

"Yes."

"If we go, you'd be fine if we were exclusive?"

"Yes. I keep telling you, we're together," I assured her.

"In that case, we'll go. Put Pam back on the phone. I need to know what to wear," Harper ordered me.

I handed the phone to Pam, then turned to the guys and gave them the thumbs-up.

"Seriously, you just talked your girlfriend into going with you to a sex party?" Bill asked in shock.

"We talked about our expectations and agreed to what we would and wouldn't allow for each of us to do. You might want to try talking to your partner sometime. You might be surprised by what they'll say if you give them a chance."

The look they both gave me said they'd never even considered doing something like I'd just done. I was glad Greg had trained me well, or I might have been in trouble with Harper right now.

"So, are we doing this?" Tim asked.

"I say yes," I voted.

"I say no," Bill told us.

"I say yes. Will you have a problem if we do it?" Tim asked Bill.

"You both know my concerns, but we voted and I'll go to the party and make sure nothing gets too out of hand," Bill said.

"Fair enough. Who should the other two be?" I asked.

"Why don't we let Bill decide? That way he'll make sure they're okay with going and know to keep their damn mouths shut afterwards," Tim said, giving me a hard look.

I mentally added a talk with Jeff on my 'to do' list if he were picked. Pam handed me back my phone and we told her we would attend the party. She called her sister who was very excited, if what we heard through the speaker was any indication.

◇◇◇

After practice, we had a players-only team meeting. Tim and I let Bill run it.

"Tomorrow's a big day for the future of Lincoln baseball. We'll be laying the foundation for the rest of the year. I want to remind everyone that we need to show class and sportsmanship. If there are any problems, let the coaches or your captains handle it."

"Like David handled Wolf getting beaned last year," Mike chirped.

Everyone chuckled. I had rushed the mound and knocked the pitcher out.

"I'm serious. If we need to take care of something, we will. If one of us is suspended for a few games, it's just us and not the whole team. If you're hit by a pitch, suck it up, be a man, and take first base. Let David kill them," Bill said with a grin.

I shook my head.

"I need to talk to you about one more thing. Your captains will be picking the MVPs for the tournament. If you're selected, you'll have to be free Saturday evening for your reward. It'll be like Vegas, where what happens Saturday night is never spoken of," Bill said as the room went dead silent.

"There's no way any of us are going cow-tipping, right?" Jim asked.

"No cow-tipping. David arranged the outing," Tim blurted.

I gave him a dirty look. They didn't need to know that.

"Oh, never mind," Jim said, as if my arranging it explained everything.

I sat back and smiled as Tim and Bill fielded questions about what the MVPs could expect. When Tim and Bill were done building the mystery, it sounded like a fun evening. Bill convinced the guys to make a pact. I think it had the same effect as when someone had you sign a waiver which said if you died doing something you couldn't hold them responsible: it just made everyone want to do it more. I let it slip that Tim and Bill were responsible for picking the MVPs. They suddenly had twenty new best friends. For some reason, they both flipped me off.

◊◊◊

When I got home, I found Harper helping my mom and dad get dinner ready. We'd started having dinner with them on Friday nights so my mom could get to know Harper better. Mom was still trying to wrap her mind around Harper possibly replacing Tami for my affections.

"David, what are you up to?" my mom asked me.

I gave Harper a dirty look.

"Don't blame me; your mom asked. Remember when you said we couldn't lie to parents?" she asked and gave me a cheeky smile.

"I think we also agreed we weren't going to share things with the other's parents," I shot back.

"Leave her alone and tell me about the party you're going to," my mom ordered.

"If it's a sex party, like Harper told us, I have some serious concerns if you're inviting teammates," Dad warned me.

"Riddle me this, Dad: if you were my age, and there was a sorority party where you could get laid by college girls, wouldn't you want your friends to invite you?" I asked.

"I'm out," my dad said, conceding he'd want to go.

"I think we may have a talk later," my mom said menacingly.

Dad just shrugged. Mom turned her glare on me.

"Harper agreed to go," I said, throwing her under the bus.

"David!" Harper complained.

"Don't even start. You got me into this mess," I warned her.

"Do I need to ground you two? Better yet, do I need to call Harper's parents?" Mom threatened.

"I love you, Mom," I said as I hugged her.

She pushed me away. I had to give it a shot because sometimes it worked. Okay, let's be honest: it worked once. But it was sort of a ritual now, so I kept trying. I knew it wouldn't work this time because Mom was loving making Harper and me squirm. I understood why she didn't make nice when Greg and his family came in the back door: she wanted to let Angie have some fun at our expense. I was ordered to catch them up with what I'd planned for tomorrow night.

"Oh, you are such a bad boy," Angie said and shook her head.

It didn't help when Greg high-fived me. He was sent to help Dad finish dinner.

"So how should we punish him?" Angie offered.

Harper gave me a weak smile. It was then I realized she, Angie, and Mom were in on this tormenting game together.

"Just put me out of my misery. What do you all want?" I said in surrender.

I wasn't surprised when they each had a list to hand me. Mom wanted me to get the garden ready and several other outdoor tasks, now that it was spring. Angie had a few very inappropriate suggestions. I handed her list to Greg and he smiled when he read it. He agreed to satisfy her needs. Harper wanted me to be her sex slave at some point in time. I went to hand her list to Greg, and she smacked me.

G. Younger

◊◊◊

Chapter 14 – Fresh Meat

Saturday April 11

We had one of the first games today, so Harper got up early to help me get ready. Dad had reserved a pavilion next to the fields. Harper was making five gallons of Gatorade while I cut up oranges and apples for my teammates. Greg and Angie were busy making breakfast.

When Harper was done, Greg helped me carry the Gatorade container to the Jeep. We were meeting at the high school to warm up and get our batting practice in before we took a bus to the park for our game.

"Did you work your way through the list Angie gave me?" I teased him.

"I think you might have to help me with some of it. She's wearing me out."

I knew he wasn't serious. He had confided in me when she was pregnant the last time that her libido had gone up during a certain portion of her pregnancy. I just couldn't remember at what point. If it was now, she really was wearing him out. I did remember him telling me right before Kyle was born it all slowed down. It took a few months after his birth before they were back to normal.

"You know I'm there for you if you need me."

"If you ever did, Angie would be a happy girl. Nancy gave her a full report," he told me, and I groaned.

I put him in a headlock and messed up his hair. We went back in to our women with smiles on our faces.

"This can't be good," Angie warned Harper.

I kissed Angie's cheek and then planted a serious kiss on Harper.

"What are you waiting for, dumbass?" I asked my brother.

Angie was tapping her foot until Greg figured out he needed to follow my lead. We had breakfast and then I left to get ready for the game. Harper was going to come with my parents. As I walked out I saw her sneaking Duke pieces of bacon. She was worse than Kyle and Mac.

◊◊◊

Our first game was against Lang Academy. I wasn't surprised they were the bottom seed. I was surprised when Harper's ex-boyfriend Ray was there. I'd forgotten she'd told me he was sent there after he'd been kicked out of his second boarding school. I knew Harper would be happy to see him. He saw me walking over to their dugout and came out to talk to me.

We were catching up when Harper and my parents showed up. I pointed her out to Ray and he went into the stands to catch up with his best friend. His teammates were blatantly checking her out.

"Careful boys, she's my girlfriend," I said just loud enough they could hear me.

We didn't need a repeat of what happened when they visited us during our first game. I would gladly kick their butts if they hit on Harper.

I went back and fielded some ground balls to finish getting ready for the game. I felt I was where I needed to be mentally. I think Moose felt confident because he had Bert pitch the first game. Last year we trotted Justin out because we didn't know if we'd be playing more than one game. Most teams would play their best pitcher to assure they got to the second round.

It was soon time to get started. Everyone was focused and determined to win today. Bert had worked hard to perfect his two-seam fastball. It was a good pitch because it tended to tail away. Batters routinely topped the pitch and hit grounders. Bert wasn't overpowering, so if he could get them to hit grounders and let us play defense, we had a chance at winning.

Bert normally ran into trouble if his pitches started to get up in the zone. When he did that, it was like watching batting practice. I was happy to see the first three batters he faced all grounded out. We came up to bat with smiles on our faces. Bert was going to have a good outing.

Our only problem was our bats deserted us. Come the bottom of the seventh inning, we were deadlocked at 0–0. Neither team was able to get a runner further than second base. It wasn't like their pitcher was very good. We should have been lighting him up.

I was leading off and had gone 0–3 so far today. I guess I wasn't surprised when Moose pinch-hit Brock Callahan for me. Brock had looked good in batting practice before the game. On the first pitch, Brock hit a screaming line drive right at the third baseman. I groaned, knowing it was a sure out, but was surprised when the ball bounced off his chest. I was sure that would leave a mark.

Moose sent Bryan up next, taking the bat out of Wolf's hands. He stepped in and hit a hard shot right back at the pitcher. The ball brushed the pitcher's hip, which caused it to change direction just enough so their shortstop wasn't able to field the ball cleanly. We now had runners on first and second.

Jim was sent in as the third straight pinch hitter. Their pitcher tried to get Jim to chase a fastball high in the zone. He showed good discipline and held up. The next pitch was a hanging curve. Jim parked it, giving us the win 3–0.

◊◊◊

I guess I should have expected it when Moose benched Jeff, Wolf and me for the second game. The Callahan twins and Jim were inserted into the lineup. Mike pitched a good game, but the defense wasn't as strong without the two of us in the middle of the infield. The good news was our substitutes paid off at the plate. We ended up beating Lakeview 8–6.

I pitched the next game against Washington. We met them in the semifinals last year. They'd forfeited when they ran out of pitchers. I had a good game. I actually struck out Ty three times. My bat also came back to life as I hit two singles and a double. We cruised to a 6–1 victory.

We met St. Joe in the final. I personally thought they should've been the number one seed. They always had a strong baseball team, and they were undefeated this year. Justin shut them down. He wasn't flashy, but still only allowed six hits. We won the tournament with a 12–3 win. Our record stood at 11–1, the best start Lincoln had had in over ten years.

The team gathered around to find out who the MVPs were. The three of us had talked during the day. It was decided the winners had to be single and not freshmen. They also had to be guys who wouldn't embarrass us or talk afterward. Justin was eliminated for what he did to Piper. My buddy Jeff was also taken out of the pool of possible candidates by Bill and Tim. I decided not to fight them on their decision because he was dating Cassidy. The 'no dating rule' took out a lot of the rest of the team.

"It was easy to name the MVPs of the tournament. Both guys came through with clutch hitting and stepped in when we needed pitching. The winners are Brock and Bryan Callahan," Bill announced.

After the brothers had been congratulated, I saw Bill and Tim talking to them. They both had big grins and were nodding as my fellow captains explained what was expected of them tonight.

◊◊◊

Harper was acting nervous when we pulled into the parking lot of the Alpha Chi Omega house. Cora had instructed us to park in the rear, come in through the back door and go down to the basement. We were sitting in my Jeep as she turned to me.

"Am I being a bitch by not letting you spend time with other girls?" she asked.

I almost laughed until I realized she was dead serious. I took a deep breath and looked at the back of the Alpha Chi Omega house. It was a monster of a sorority house that looked like it was built at the turn of the 1900s. You could have moved it to a plantation in the Deep South. I jerked my mind back from wandering and answered her question.

"Harper, you confuse the hell out of me. When I first met you, I was attracted to your spunk and quick wit. I have an affinity for smart, self-assured women. It certainly didn't hurt you have a killer body. Then you go saying something like that. If I said it, you'd look me in the eye and tell me to quit being a wuss and grow a pair. I don't understand why you think you need to change the way you think, just because we're dating."

"Did you just call me a wuss?" Harper asked as she glared at me.

"No, I said you'd call *me* a wuss," I clarified.

"No, I think you're just finding a clever way of calling me a wuss," she shot back.

I started to say something clever and then stopped myself. Harper was a lot like her mom. She could smell bullshit from a mile away. I decided to 'man up, and grow a pair.'

"I guess I did," I said.

"Oh. You know I'm going to kick your butt."

"Have at it, tough girl," I said, unable to hide my amusement.

"All right, I'll quit feeling sorry for you and make you watch as your teammates get laid."

"Fine with me," I said and kissed her.

"I hate it when you kiss me just when I'm getting a good mad on," she huffed, and we got out of the Jeep.

Harper found her way under my arm as she led me in. I knew she wasn't mad, she was just feeling insecure. She'd be back to normal as soon as she got a feel for what was going on. I found it funny that Harper made sure I was looking good tonight. I had planned to wear jeans and a t-shirt with my letterman's jacket. She had me try on several outfits before she was satisfied. I wasn't surprised when she picked out something casual from Dakora. I think she wanted to make the other girls jealous. I was a little surprised when she wore a skirt that barely covered her butt. I wasn't sure what the purpose of her attire was. If it was meant for me, then okay, but I was worried she'd dressed for the college guys who'd be there.

When we got inside, we found we were the first ones there from my group. Cora saw me and smiled. She was talking to several of her sisters, so we went and grabbed a couple of sodas. I was confused at the different clothes the girls were wearing. I asked Harper about it.

"The ones in the jerseys must be the pledges. The girls wearing normal clothes have to be the sorority sisters."

I noticed the ones wearing jerseys seemed to be *just* wearing jerseys. I checked out the pledges and they were all cute. Pam had told me Alpha Chi Omega was noted for having the best-looking women on campus. While I hadn't seen the other twenty-some sororities, I would take it on faith she was right. I sent a text to Tim and Bill, letting them know the ladies were waiting for them. They were in charge of getting Bryan and Brock here.

There were already several guys here and most looked to be college age. They were talking to each other. I shook my head when I realized that it wasn't much different than high school, with girls clustered in one group and the boys in another. Harper and I were people-watching as we waited for the rest of our crew to show up. Five minutes later all my teammates showed up, wearing jeans and baseball jerseys. I guess I missed the memo.

"The poor dumbasses," I mumbled.

"What did you say?" Harper asked.

"Sorry, I was looking at the guys. They reminded me of my mom and dad when she made him wear a matching sweater."

"I know it's cliché, but does it surprise you a bunch of jocks would do something like that?"

"Hey, I resemble that remark."

"Just saying," she said as she squeezed my hand.

Cora came over.

"Are they all here?" she asked me.

"Yeah, this is all of them," I said.

She went back to the girls she was talking to and let them know. One of the older girls got everyone's attention.

"I would like to welcome the men from Lincoln. I hear they won a tournament today," she began.

The sorority sisters started chanting, "Fresh Meat! Fresh Meat!"

"Settle down, ladies. At the request of the Fresh Meat, there will be no alcohol served tonight. Normally we would let you have a few drinks and then have our way with you. Since we don't have alcohol to lower your inhibitions, we'll have to resort to other methods. The first is a 'get to know you.' We'll do a version of speed dating. Men, please get into a circle and face the outside for me," our master of ceremonies directed us.

When the guys were in a circle, she then directed the pledges to make a circle facing in.

"Now, I have a stack of cards. I'll read what the card says and then you follow the directions. The first card says: 'Kiss the person in front of you.'"

This was going to be fun as we watched the wide range of reactions, which was fascinating. Some of the guys blushed and looked like they wanted to bolt. Others got into it. Cora didn't appear to have a partner. She motioned for me to join the circle. Harper saw her gesture.

"I can't believe I'm saying this. Go join your teammates."

"I'm good," I assured her.

"No. I want you to go have fun. Remember our rule: I have to be involved."

I don't think she expected me to pull her along with me. Cora gave us a funny look.

"Do you expect me to kiss both of you?"

"Oh, yeah," I said.

Before Harper could make a run for it, Cora leaned over and kissed her. When she was done, Harper was gasping for breath. I grabbed the back of Cora's neck and kissed her. I then kissed Harper. I thought it wouldn't be fair unless we all kissed each other.

"Time! Ladies, walk around the circle and guess who has the largest package. When you pick your winner, stand behind him."

I looked at Harper and she rolled her eyes. I had to agree, this was crass. I always figured it only mattered if you had enough to get the job done. I'd never received any complaints, so I never bothered to measure myself. From what I'd heard, I was well above average, but I assumed that had to do with my being six-four.

I chuckled when the girls decided one of the college boys had the biggest package. He looked like a bodybuilder. I doubted their selection for two reasons. He was maybe five-ten and he had small hands. I was willing to bet he was average in size. He seemed to puff up with pride.

"Girls, get back into your places and move one person to your right," she ordered, and she waited until everyone was in place. "The card says: 'Guys, using only your teeth, remove your partner's thong.'"

It looked like we weren't at a high school party after all. If this was what happened in college, I couldn't wait to get there.

"Get busy," I ordered Harper.

I was shocked when she turned the girl around and stuck her head under her jersey. I couldn't resist. I got behind Harper and stuck my head under her skirt. I tell you, getting a thong off with just your teeth is work. I was able to get Harper's off first. I was bad, though, because I did use my tongue to separate her sex from her undergarments. Harper was at a disadvantage because I distracted her. When her thong was on the ground, I walked around and knelt before our pledge. Working as a team, we were able to get the offending garment off. Again, I took a few liberties.

We were done first, so we got a chance to watch everyone work to get the girls' panties off.

"Time! If you still have on a thong, please take it off."

At this point several of the girls were flushed. I guess the guys hadn't been working very hard to get their panties off. You could smell the arousal in the room. This had started to be a lot of fun.

"Okay, move one to the right. The next card reads: 'Strip your guy from the waist down.'"

Harper and our new pledge worked to get my shoes and socks off. I thought they took a few liberties getting my slacks and boxers off. I was not happy I was completely exposed. My jacket and silk shirt both only covered to a little below my waist. Mr. Happy and my butt were exposed. My guys had on baseball jerseys that covered their butts. I smirked when their shirts split open to expose their aroused members. I made a quick glance at the bodybuilder and was assured when I saw my estimation was right, but he had nothing to be embarrassed about.

The college boys must have been clued in because they had on extra-long t-shirts or jerseys that covered most everything. I caught Harper checking out every guy she could see. I gave her a hip-check and she looked me in the eye and shrugged.

"Very nice! Ladies, move one to the right. 'Kiss your partner.'"

I pushed Harper in front of me. The pledge gave her a thorough tongue-lashing. I wrapped my arms around both of them, pressing my rapidly rising member into Harper's butt. I leaned over her shoulder and began kissing and nibbling the pledge's neck and earlobe as I ground myself on Harper, which caused a chain reaction. The girls rubbed up against each other as they kissed. I admit my hands ended up cupped on the pledge's little butt.

"Time! I'll give our threesome points for style," our master of ceremonies announced. "Girls, move one to the right. The card reads: 'Pick out sexy underwear for the person across from you.'"

Harper and our pledge went to a box one of the sisters brought out. The two of them seemed to be conspiring over what they were going to make me wear. What they brought back was a blue cotton Speedo. I wasn't sure if I liked them or not, but Harper had a big smile on her face. I looked around and almost choked when Tim appeared in a diaper. If his pledge hadn't rewarded him with a searing kiss for being a good sport, I think he would have left. The girls had most of the guys in tighty-whities, similar to what I was wearing. The Callahan twins had been put into matching boxers.

"Girls, rotate to the next guy. 'Remove your guy's clothing above the waist,'" was our next order.

My new pledge got into slowly taking my jacket and shirt off. Harper collected my clothes and put them on a chair next to the wall. She swatted the pledge's butt when her hands wandered a little south. I was actually grateful to Harper because it wouldn't take much for me to embarrass myself. I already had the beginnings of a serious bulge.

"From the looks of the guys, I think they're ready. Now it's time for some fun. There are privileges that come from pledge ranking. I want the girls to line up in order and

I want the guys to line up. Ladies, your job is to take a guy up to your designated room, have him fill a condom and then bring him back. The rule is neither one of you may touch the other with your hands. Now the first pledge will select her Fresh Meat."

"Should we bow out?" I asked Harper.

"No, I'm actually having fun. Let's play it by ear and see how this goes."

The guys found it funny I wasn't picked until ninth. I didn't complain because the girl seemed to have eyes for Harper. I chuckled when the pledge grabbed Harper's hand and led her to the second floor. I followed along to see what kind of trouble Harper was in. As we walked past a number of rooms, we saw Tim and Bill getting blowjobs. The doors to the rooms were left open, and there were several sisters roaming the halls to make sure everyone followed the rules and was being safe.

The pledge we were with had Harper sit on the edge of the bed and buried her face between Harper's thighs. Harper's eyes got big and I could tell the pledge knew what she was doing. The pledge was on her knees, so I got on mine and wiggled my face until I had access to the pledge's sex. I began giving her slot a tongue-bath. I worked her over good and could hear Harper making happy grunts. I could tell the pledge was ready, so I put my condom on and then slowly buried myself deep within her folds.

Harper was laying back in complete bliss. I slowly moved in and out of the pledge as I checked out the room. I had to chuckle when I noticed my butt poster on the wall. I was trying not to cum too soon as I began to do the pledge in earnest. Harper came hard and wiggled to get away. She complained that she sometimes got too sensitive when she climaxed. The look in her eyes said she wanted me to push her over the edge.

"David, get on your back," Harper ordered.

278

I pulled out of the pledge and lay down so Harper could mount me. I stopped her and put on a new condom. The pledge straddled my head and didn't take long to get her cookie. She tapped out to relax on the bed and watch us.

"Quit holding back," Harper ordered me.

It sounded like Harper wanted to find out what round two had in store. I obliged her. The pledge wasn't too happy when I handed her the used condom. We followed her downstairs and met our hostess.

"Cora and I organized tonight to help the pledges get a safe sexual experience with boys. I was a little worried when she told me you were bringing your girlfriend," she said and turned to Harper. "Are you okay with what we've been doing?"

"When we arrived, I told him he wasn't doing anything tonight, but so far, it's been fun, though different. I can't see doing anything like this on a regular basis, though," Harper answered.

"Some of the pledges want to learn to give a proper blowjob. Would you be willing to allow your boyfriend to be our test subject?"

She looked at me and I kept a neutral expression on my face. I had come and I had experienced the party. I was fine with whatever Harper decided. Was I willing to allow college girls to suck my dick? Hell, yes! If Harper wanted to go back to my place, I would gladly do that, too.

"As long as I'm in the room, you can have him," she said with a glint in her eye.

I wondered what was going through Harper's head as we went and grabbed a couple of bottles of water.

"So, what do you want to do?" Harper asked.

"I'd like to do a bunch of sorority girls, but I'm a teenage boy. I could just as easily go dancing with you. I hear there's a good band at the Thunderbird tonight."

Harper could tell I was giving her a hard time. I wrapped her in my arms and kissed her.

"Baby, I don't need all this when I have you," I said, looking her in the eyes.

"I know. I'm not sure why, but it turns me on seeing you with other women. When I saw you doing the pledge, I had to have you right then. I hope that doesn't make me a slut," she told me.

"You're my slut," I said with a big smile. "As long as we're not playing with other guys."

She gave my shoulder a soft slap.

"You're all the man I need."

Cora walked over to us.

"Rumor has it if I want to do this big guy I have to eat your peach," she told Harper.

Harper blushed. I'd heard rumors about girls at boarding schools. I had never seen Harper show the least bit interest in the same sex before. She hadn't yet gone down on a girl. I didn't really think Harper was into girls, but the thought of it made me hard.

"I think she's shy," I chimed in.

A pixie of a girl came skipping up.

"I was sent to come get you. We're ready."

She stuck her tongue out at Cora and pulled me toward the stairs. Harper followed us to a bedroom on the third floor. As we went to the end of the hall, we saw a few of the college guys having sex with girls other than the pledges. It looked like some of the sisters were horny.

In the room across the hall from the one we were going to, I saw the twins. I stopped Harper and we watched as they double-teamed the girl that we'd been with. They saw me and smiled. Harper giggled when they grinned and reached over the girl and did fist bumps. I don't think anything was going to wipe the smiles off their faces.

The pixie was impatient and grabbed my hand.

"Come on," she said, sounding like she was ten, wanting to hurry us along.

We entered the room to find another pledge and a sister. The sister took charge.

"Welcome, and thanks for allowing us to use your boyfriend like this. I promise we won't break him. I'm Helen, by the way, and this is Jan," she said, pointing to a serious-looking redhead. "You've already met Debbie."

"Nice to meet you. I'm Harper and this is David. I had to convince him to do this," Harper said.

"I bet you did," Helen said.

I don't think she believed Harper for one minute. She got right to work teaching her charges.

"David, could you get comfortable on the floor, and please do me a favor and lose the underwear?" Helen asked.

I dropped my shorts, grabbed a pillow off one of the beds, and propped my head up as I lay down. Helen sat down Indian-style at my waist as Harper and the pledges got comfortable on my other side.

"David, do you like blowjobs?" Helen asked me.

"Yes, very much so."

"Describe the best blowjob you've ever received."

I looked at Harper. She rolled her eyes at me and then nodded.

"I picked up a woman in Miami, on a dare. It turned out one of my friends knew her, and it was a setup. Anyways, the three of us went back to my hotel room."

"I'm sorry, but what were you doing in Miami?" Debbie asked.

"I was there to do a photo shoot. I model when I'm not playing ball. I'd flown in the night before the shoot. I met some executives from Ford Models and three of the models who were going to be in the shoot the next day.

"Anyways, one of the models and the woman I picked up went back to my hotel room. The two women knew each other, and I figured they wanted to talk, so I went and took a shower. When I came out, they were drinking wine and catching up. I was surprised when the woman I picked up decided to give me a blowjob in front of her friend."

"Was it because you were doing it in front of the other girl that made it so good?" Helen asked.

"I guess, but to be honest, this woman just knew how to handle a dick. Sorry, I didn't mean to be crude."

"No, it's fine. What do you mean, though?" Helen asked.

"She was phenomenal. Most girls when they give you pleasure focus on doing what I call 'the bob.' They take three or four inches of your member and simulate sex. Please believe me, it's fantastic. No guy will ever complain, and I promise you, you do it and your guy will get off.

"She took it to the next level. She was able to swallow my whole member and did things with her throat that turned me inside out. She also used her tongue and mouth suction to add to my pleasure. She didn't just focus on my member, she pleasured my balls and teased my body as well."

"David has some good points. He's right, even a bad blowjob is good; at least, according to every guy I've ever met. Let me give you some tips on taking it from average to spectacular for your guy. First of all, set the stage. Most men would prefer a relaxed setting. Light a few candles and play some mood music," Helen coached the girls, and she got up and lit a few scented candles and turned on soft music.

"I would suggest clean sheets for him to lie down on. Slowly undress him. Make sure there'll be no distractions, so turn off his cell and lock the door. You want your man focused on his pleasure.

"Before you get to the main event, explore his whole body. Start slowly. Touch, lick, and kiss your partner, not just the areas that turn him on, but the ones that turn you on as well. This is a hands-on experience. Go ahead and get started."

Helen had just taken a page out of Greg's playbook. I found if you took your time and explored a woman's body and found what turned her on, you were ahead of the game. I about went out of my mind when all four of them worked to arouse me. At one point it felt like a litter of kittens was slowly licking me all over my body. I was ready to jump up and attack somebody when Helen finally called a halt to them getting me turned on. I think my moans gave them all a clue I was ready to go.

"David, did you enjoy what we did?" Helen asked.

"Let me put it this way: if someone doesn't suck me soon, I'm taking over and none of you will be safe."

"I think we have him aroused. Now how can you tell? Let me show you. Besides his member being hard and leaking, notice his balls. Earlier they were hanging loosely between his legs. They're now high against the base of the penis and the scrotum is stretched tightly across them.

"Let's get to the main event. We're going to cover a lot of ground tonight. I'd suggest you focus on two or three of my suggestions and try them on your man. Not everything I'll show you will appeal to your lover. Even if some things don't work now, in time your lovemaking may change, or you may end up with someone who does like what you learn.

"What's good about tonight is we have someone we can ask about what he likes and doesn't like. David, what's the most important thing to you when a girl's giving you oral pleasure?" Helen asked.

I thought about it for a moment.

"Excitement. I would rather have a blowjob from someone inexperienced but enthusiastic, who has no idea what they're doing, as opposed to the best technical performance by someone who showed no interest," I answered.

"David's right. The best lover is completely involved in what she's doing. If you're aroused and show your man you enjoy pleasing him, he'll have a mind-blowing experience. I know I personally love the feeling of power I have over my man as I control his pleasure. Other women feel the intimate act of giving of yourself is fulfilling. Whatever it takes for you to show your man you're as into giving him a blowjob as he is into receiving, it will make the experience for him unbelievable," Helen taught them.

"I'd like to add you should not be afraid to crawl all over your man. I know David enjoyed you kissing and licking him. What really turns him on is when I rub myself up and down his member," Harper almost purred.

"I'm sorry baby, but I need to do you right now," I said, but they all held me back.

"Do you see what she just did? She was creative. Sometimes, sexy talk goes a long way. She also pointed out if you use your whole body to arouse your man, it works very well. I think you get the idea by David's response. I personally like to rub my boobs on a man's chest and then squeeze them together and let him do me that way," Helen said.

She shrieked when I trapped her under me and began kissing her. Enough of this, I was going to do everyone. Wait a second, someone had ahold of my balls! I turned to Harper smirking at me. It was amazing how a little thing like that will make you do what a girl wants. I was a good boy and lay back down.

"I think we need to practice a little bit. Someone needs to take the edge off or I think we'll have to teach this class at another time," Helen said as she got out a condom.

"Why are you putting a condom on him?" Jan asked.

"While giving a blowjob is an alternative to contraception, it's not without risk of disease. If you plan to have fun with guys in college, I'd suggest you have him wear one for any activity where there will be some form of penetration. For oral sex there are flavored condoms like this one," Helen said as she showed it to the girls.

"She's right. You can't tell who has an STD just by looking at them. I try to use one every time I have sex, regardless if they're taking birth control or not," I said.

"Now here's a trick your guys will love."

Helen put the condom on the tip of my member and then used her teeth to unroll it onto me. The whole time she had her eyes locked on mine. When she was done, she dripped lube on the condom and then used her hand to make sure it was coated.

"Start slowly. Get acquainted with his member. If he isn't hard, suck him in your mouth and suck and lick him. The suction will draw blood into his length and help harden him. This is especially useful if he's having a hard time going another round. Sometimes I'm not willing to wait for my man to get hard again," Helen confessed.

"David doesn't seem to have that problem," Harper shared.

"In that case, does someone want to get him off so we can focus on the rest of what I want to show you?"

I looked over at Harper, hoping she'd help me out. Her eyes got big and she put her hand over her mouth as I felt someone grasp Mr. Happy. My head snapped around in time to see Debbie, the little pixie, trying to stuff my member into her mouth. It looked like she was trying to stuff a baseball bat into her face. I had been on edge way too long. I grabbed the back of her head and with a few quick strokes came hard.

"AAAUUUGGHHH!" I moaned.

Poor Debbie had tears in the corners of her eyes.

"Oh, honey," I began, feeling like a complete shit.

"No, I'm okay. I just had never done it before and you took me by surprise," she assured me.

Harper hugged her.

"He gets carried away sometimes. This is why all the women in his life call him 'stupid boy.'"

For some reason, that comment caused smiles all around. I removed the condom, and Helen handed me a tissue to clean up and put the condom in. I think I impressed the girls when I tossed it into the garbage can across the room.

"Now that he's calmed down, it's time for more lessons," Helen started, then took hold of my semi-hard shaft. "Jan, do you want to get him stiff again?"

Jan eagerly took me into her mouth and used her hands, mouth and tongue to explore every inch of my hardening member. When I was hard, she leaned back, and Helen took me in hand again.

"Don't forget his balls. Most men love to have them licked and sucked. Just be careful and treat them gently. Nothing will end a good session like hurting his balls. They're such babies when you do that.

"Now notice around the head of his penis there is a little ridge. Use your tongue to explore this area. Pay special attention to his frenulum. This is the extra skin on the underside of his member where the head meets the shaft. This is an extremely sensitive area. Start out being soft and gentle and then increase the pressure and intensity. Watch how he reacts and gauge what you need to do from that. Who wants to try?"

I was surprised when both pledges and Harper wanted to try me out. They soon had me squirming again. Helen told them this was called edging. It was when you teased a guy by using your tongue to work the underside of the head of his member. I'll give Helen high marks: *I* was learning things from *her*. She continued with the anatomy lesson.

"Take the tip of his penis, or head, into your mouth and make it wet. Harper, get him wet for us," Helen asked, and Harper obliged. "The head will feel smooth and firm. Use everything to stimulate it. You can also use your teeth if you're gentle. I also want you to tongue the slit, called the meatus. This is a little hit-or-miss. Some men enjoy it, others won't."

Each girl got a chance to work the tip of my dick over. They figured out they could easily stimulate my frenulum with their tongues. I really liked the sensation of them sucking the head of my dick while their tongue pleasured me.

"Let's take this to the next level. David told you he enjoyed having your head simply bobbing up and down his shaft. As he shared, this will produce results. What I want to teach you is more advanced skills here. You aren't merely simulating intercourse. You'll find your mouth and hands have a great many more ways to pleasure his penis. Use both to pleasure him," Helen offered, and then let the girls try out their skills on me.

"Good. How are they doing, David?" Helen asked.

"I think with hours and hours of practice they might get there. I'd be willing to work with them on it," I offered.

Harper smacked me on the back of the head.

"Hey, I was just trying to help."

"I'm going to show you a technique which will make it easier to take him deeper into your mouth," Helen taught.

I was all for deeper.

"Stick out your tongue and say 'ah' like you're at the doctor's office," Helen said and then demonstrated.

Helen grasped my manhood, then stuck out her tongue and plunged down. I felt my member enter her throat and her tongue swipe back and forth across my balls. I threw my head back and held my breath. When she slowly pulled off, she was still swiping her tongue back and forth until only the head was in her mouth. Her tongue was sending me into overdrive as she massaged my frenulum.

"Did you see what I did with my tongue? Did you like it, David?" Helen asked.

"More, please!"

"I'll take it that he liked it. Something else you can do is moan or hum around his member while sucking him. The vibration adds to the stimulation. Do different things until you find what he likes. You can try long, hard strokes along the entire shaft with just your tongue or with your mouth, or quick light strokes with your mouth just on the head. Use your imagination, women.

"I would suggest that you use your hands to stroke him while you're giving a blowjob. There are two reasons. The first is self-defense. I think Debbie wished she had a grip on this big guy to slow him down from stuffing his length down her throat. Most guys you can probably handle, but I prefer to decide when something's going to be shoved into my throat," Helen said with a playful grin.

"Use your other hand to tease him. Run our fingernails down his thigh. Play with his balls. Guys are really sensitive right below their sacks. Run your fingernails back and forth under there," she said as she demonstrated. I think the girls understood when I sat straight up.

"Another way to get a big response from your guy is to massage his prostate," Helen started.

"This is something I don't enjoy," I stated.

"Would you allow me to teach them?" Helen asked.

I was ready to say no until I saw the pleading look in Harper's eyes. I just nodded.

"You better use plenty of lube," was my only instruction.

"I find guys protest about this too much. Once you do it to them, they seem to enjoy it. David's right, though, lube is our friend," Helen said, then proceeded to grease up her index finger.

"Insert your lubed finger into his anus. You'll feel a marble-sized bump. This is his prostate. Massage it with your finger. Use your other hand to press against the area between his anus and his balls," Helen said.

She demonstrated what she meant and used her little tongue technique on me. I have an aversion to someone putting anything in there, but every time a woman does this prostate thing to me, look out. I surprised Helen when I suddenly exploded. I didn't feel sorry for her when she choked and started coughing. When she finally stopped, she gave me a dirty look.

"That wasn't nice."

"Then don't stick things up my bum."

"I'm next," Harper said, as she lubed up her finger.

"Hang on," I protested, "once does not mean open season!"

"You promised we could learn," she shot back.

I just rolled my eyes at her. I allowed the other girls to find my prostate, but that was it. Helen took back control of her class.

"The final thing I want to teach you is what to do when he climaxes. You have two choices: you can allow him to do it in your mouth, or you can pull off. If you'd ask a guy, nine out of ten would want you to let them release in your mouth."

"I don't know about that. Sometimes I like to pull out and explode in a girl's face or on her breasts, but I'm a bad boy," I said. Harper leaned over and gave me a kiss.

"Just have his shorts handy and cover him up if he gets ready to shoot," Harper suggested.

"I'll let you decide what you like best, ladies. After he's cum, you can milk your man. Grasp him at the base and squeeze as you push upward. This will get out any leftover. If you want to give him maximum pleasure, look him deep in the eyes and then lick the last few drops off the head of his dick," Helen said and then demonstrated.

Damn! This girl knew what she was doing. She gently cupped my balls with her other hand. Mr. Happy twitched, wondering if we were going again.

"Finally, this is for David. If you want your partner to give you lots of blowjobs, you need to learn to reciprocate."

I turned to look at Harper.

"Take me home, Stud," she ordered.

◊◊◊

Chapter 15 – Spring Break

My phone woke me up; the caller ID said it was Tami.

"Happy Easter!" I heard her and her host family call out.

My clock said it was six-thirty in the morning. I tried to remember if she was five or six hours different. Anyways, it was too damn early for Sunday morning.

"You're all evil. You do realize it's the crack of dawn here?" I complained.

"I know, but you love me anyway. We're off to see historic folk dancing by the Morris Dancers. They assure me it's an English tradition dating back to the fourteen hundreds."

"You poor baby, you want me to come get you?" I offered.

"Oh, shut up. I'm sure it can't be too bad, or my host-siblings wouldn't be excited about going. What are your plans?"

"I get to go to church with both of my grandmothers. Greg and Angie are here, as are Uncle John and Bonnie. I guess it's a good thing you woke me because I promised to go to Granny's and pick up cinnamon rolls for breakfast."

"You totally suck. I want a cinnamon roll now. What are your plans for spring break? Are you doing a shoot for Range Sports again this year?"

"I'm going to Chicago. Bo Harrington has arranged a week with specialized trainers. I plan to stay with Harper and her parents. Adrienne has a couple of photo shoots organized, as does Ford. So, I'll be either working out or working the whole time."

"Does Harper know this? I bet she has plans for the two of you," Tami said.

"She did mention something about the country club tonight, and then I had to free up Friday night and Saturday or I was no longer going to have a girlfriend."

Tami laughed at me.

"I bet you'd have to do more than that for her to give you up."

"Maybe," I admitted.

Harper and I had gotten closer. She seemed to relax after the party at the sorority house. I think she realized that even with temptation all around, I only really wanted her. Our return from the party had turned into one of our epic love-making sessions.

The fallout from the party was interesting. On Monday, before practice, the coaching staff pulled everyone who went to the party into a conference room. I still don't know how they found out. Moose asked what we were thinking. I suspect he thought we would confess to horrible crimes and he would suspend us. The other guys weren't talking, so I did. I told them everything that happened. Well, I kept it PG-13. I confirmed that we had all had sex, but none of us drank or did drugs, and I'd brought my girlfriend. I think the last part rocked the coaches a little bit. I pointed out we hadn't broken any team rules or forced anyone to do anything they didn't want to do. Moose decided there wasn't much he could do. The evil man put the five of us in charge of conditioning the team. By the end of practice, I wished we had let Cassidy have her way with us!

Speaking of baseball, we won both our games last week. We were now 13–1 and pegged as the team to beat in our district. I was now 4–0 with a 0.97 ERA, which triggered my first recruiting letter, from State, for baseball. I had never thought about playing baseball in college.

Tami and I wrapped up our call so she could go see the folk dancers. Even though I teased her, I knew she'd have fun today.

◊◊◊

When I got to Granny's, she was talking to customers. I was sent to the kitchen where they had everything ready for me. I was surprised to find Mom had also ordered food for after church. Granny came back and gave me instructions on how to reheat everything for our lunch.

When I got home, Angie was making coffee and Kyle and Mac were making a racket. Granny had only halfway-cooked the cinnamon rolls, so I put them in the oven to finish up. She had sent along a container of cream cheese frosting to top them with. I put the ham and everything else in the refrigerator. The smell of cinnamon rolls soon had everyone coming into the kitchen.

Mom called Uncle John and Bonnie over the intercom. They had stayed in my apartment. We had cleaned out and painted the two extra bedrooms on the third floor. My grandmothers took both of them. Greg and Angie stayed in his old room, and I shared with Kyle and Mac in the other one. Duke insisted he sleep in his crate in the apartment. He was getting set in his ways.

Angie pulled the rolls out and iced them. She put a huge platter on the kitchen table.

"I slaved over these all morning," she announced.

"Greg, you're a lucky man to have such a talented wife," Aunt Bonnie told him.

I just ignored them. Angie could live in her fantasy world.

◊◊◊

I arrived in the Lincoln Park neighborhood of Chicago just after three that afternoon. I was near the DePaul campus and the sidewalks seemed to be full of college-age kids and young professionals. The street was lined with three- and four-story older buildings, with storefronts on the main floor. There were bars/restaurants with outside seating and all of them seemed packed. If that many people were drinking on a Sunday afternoon, I was afraid of what I would do if I lived here.

It wasn't hard to see why people wanted to live in the city, especially if they were young and single. There was an energy about the area. I was a little sad when I realized I'd passed up a summer of living in Chicago with Tami. I could picture myself sitting at a table on the sidewalk, people-watching. It was so much more inviting than New York where everyone seemed to be on top of each other.

My GPS was telling me to make a turn when I was close to where Harper lived. As I turned there was a large sign announcing a Mass Development. Harper told me her dad owned several blocks and they were gradually removing the old walk-ups and building detached single-family homes. What I saw as I drove down the street were three- and four-story homes built in a style that fit the neighborhood architecture. Harper said they used reclaimed Chicago bricks for the exteriors so her dad's new homes would fit in.

I was given directions to turn off into an alley. I sent Harper a text to let her know I was there. I found a gate was opening and one of the garage doors went up. I pulled into the six-car garage to find a smiling girlfriend. I barely made it out of the Jeep before she had me in an embrace and was kissing me.

"I missed you, too," I said when she finally let me go.

"Come on! I want to show you our new home."

I was surprised to see stairs inside the garage leading to the rooftop. The top of the garage was an outdoor deck, complete with a huge fireplace. It had a terrific view of the downtown skyscrapers. We crossed a bridge into the back of the house's second floor. We came into an entry room, where the back staircase was. Harper had me leave my bags by the stairwell and then led me into the kitchen.

It came right out of a kitchen idea book, something you could only dream of. It was all cream and white, with marble countertops and with touches of dark wood to make the whole room spectacular. The stoves were top-of-the-line commercial models. The refrigerator and dishwashers were hidden in the cabinets to give the room a clean look.

Harper led me through the butler's pantry into a dining room in which you could easily entertain twelve people. I was amazed at the architectural details and the twelve-foot ceilings. You felt like you were in a modernized turn-of-the-century home.

As Harper showed me the rest of the house, I began to understand how wealthy her parents really were. The third floor was her parents' area. They had a master bedroom suite, her mom's office, a sitting area and an exercise room. On the fourth floor there were five bedrooms and a lounge area. Each bedroom had its own bathroom. Harper told me she had a surprise for me. It was Sarah Spence.

"Hey, Good-looking," she said and gave me a hug and kiss on the cheek.

"What're you doing here?" I asked.

"My parents are in the process of moving to Colorado for my dad's newest job. Harper offered to let me come home with her for the week. When she said you were coming, I couldn't refuse. I'm hoping you'll let me tag along on some of your shoots."

"Do you want to meet Adrienne again?" I asked.

She blushed and nodded. Harper smiled and we both looked at her. You could tell she had a surprise for us.

"Adrienne and Kendal will both be staying with us. Mom talked to Kendal to get your schedule and insisted everyone stay here. We have plenty of room."

I should hope so. Harper told me they had eight bedrooms and nine-and-a-half baths. I had yet to see the floor I was staying on. The girls took me back down to the second floor to grab my bags. We then went down to the lower level. I'm not sure if it was technically the basement since it was only halfway underground. On the lower level there were two bedrooms, a laundry room, another exercise room, and a man cave. I could see living down here!

"Get ready for dinner. Mom and Dad will be home soon," Harper told me.

She could see the need in my eyes and gave me a sad smile.

"Remember, I promised my parents no funny stuff under their roof," Harper reminded me.

I growled at her, and she and Sarah scampered out before I could grab one of them. I smiled at myself. We would just need to get creative and find somewhere else to have a little fun.

◊◊◊

We had dinner at the Ridgemoor Country Club on Gunnison Street. Harper teased her dad by saying this was his bar with a very nice backyard. He just gave her a dirty look but didn't deny it. I had been warned they had a strict dress code. Harper made me put on a shirt with a collar instead of the silk t-shirt I had selected to wear under my jacket. The irony was the t-shirt was twice as expensive as the shirt she picked out.

We went to the President's Room, a private dining room that overlooked the tennis courts. We were the first to arrive. I would guess the room was arranged to seat fifty. A buffet was being set up on the back wall. We had some time before the guests arrived, so Harper took Sarah and me on a tour. She told me people from her dad's work were having dinner with us tonight. We went out onto the terrace overlooking the putting greens and ordered drinks. I had a hot tea since it was a little chilly out.

"Harper Mass, where have you been hiding yourself?" I heard a girl say from behind us.

Harper let go of my hand and jerked it into her lap before turning around. If I didn't know better, I would have suspected that Harper was embarrassed to be seen with me. Sarah caught her actions also and gave me a confused look.

"Melisa Higson, how nice to see you," Harper said as she got up and gave a little air-cheek kiss.

Melisa had long black hair and was dressed in a dark sweater and black skirt. She didn't even acknowledge Sarah or me. I could tell this girl was a snob with a capital S.

"Come, I told the girls I thought it was you," Melisa said as she pulled Harper toward their table.

"That was rude," Sarah said after they had left.

I was more than a little pissed-off. If Harper didn't want to be seen with me, I wasn't sure what it meant for us as a couple. I would never have been so rude as to leave my friend and girlfriend to fend for themselves. I sure as hell would have made introductions.

"I need to take a walk," I told Sarah.

"Do you want me to go with you?" she asked.

"Will you be okay if I don't?" I asked. I didn't want to leave her there on her own if she felt uncomfortable.

"No, I'm a big girl. If I get lonely I'll text you," she assured me.

I shook my head and got up and went to the pro shop. I was sure Dad would want me to look around for ideas they could use at his golf and tennis club. One thing I liked was they had a locker room manager. The locker room itself was very old-fashioned, but they had attendants to make sure everything was picked up and there were plenty of towels. Dad had shared with me that the women's locker room constantly needed to be straightened up. I would bet that if they had an attendant, it would stay neater.

I'd had time to calm down, so I went to the President's Room. A guy about our age had Harper's full attention, so I figured she didn't want me to interrupt. I did my usual introduction tour and went around and met everyone. Jack's employees seemed to be nice people. Most of them had brought their families. I made a point not to identify myself as Harper's boyfriend, just a friend visiting for Spring Break.

I was happy to see Ray, Harper's best friend, was there with a date. I was surprised it was a girl.

"Hey buddy, how's it going?" he asked me.

"Good, how about for you?" I asked.

"I've been better. David, this is Gail, a friend of mine. Gail, this is the David I was telling you about."

I decided I really didn't want to know Ray's problems.

"Ray tells me you're a great guy. Did you really do a movie?" Gail asked.

"Yeah, they tell me it'll be released either late fall or early winter. I had a great time doing it."

"Ray's jealous," she shared, to his discomfort.

Ray was into acting and I could see where he would like to do a movie himself. Dinner was announced and I let them go to their seats. Harper and her family led everyone through the buffet line. Bev, Harper's mom, gave me a probing look when I wasn't in line with Harper. I just gave her a blank stare and turned around to leave. Sarah headed me off.

"Don't do something you'll regret. Give Harper a chance to explain," Sarah advised.

All I could do was think of Jenny Wesleyan and how she had treated me. Everything had been fine when it was just Jenny and me, but as soon as people in her circle came around, bad things happened. Was I being oversensitive? I had to admit, until I talked to Harper I would never know. I ended up eating with Sarah, and the guy Harper had been talking to was seated next to her. They seemed to be getting along very well—too well, in my opinion.

When dinner was over, Sarah went up to the main table and told Bev we would wait in the lobby. Harper was still in a deep conversation with her guy friend. Fortunately, Sarah left me to my own thoughts as we waited. Twenty minutes later, Jack, Bev and Harper found us.

"Where were you all night?" Harper asked me.

"I didn't want to interfere with you catching up with your friends."

"You're so thoughtful. I'm lucky to have you," Harper said.

I didn't know how to answer, so I just let her lead me to the car. I was appalled that Harper hadn't even bothered to track either Sarah or me down all night. I would have at the very least checked to make sure my friends were doing okay. Bev noticed my not being happy, and Sarah shook her head. When we got home, I begged off, saying I needed to get some sleep for tomorrow. I left everyone talking in the kitchen.

I went downstairs and called my Uncle John. I explained to him what happened.

"Let me summarize," Uncle John started. "This was the first time you have gone to Harper's home and the first time meeting her friends. You told me how the Wesleyans treated you. Will you let me offer an alternate possibility?"

"If it keeps me from wanting to break up with Harper, I'm all ears."

"What kind of vibe did you get off the girl who approached Harper?"

"My gut reaction was I didn't like her, but ..." I started.

"Stop doubting yourself. One of the things people need to do is pay attention to their gut more. A good example is if you feel you're in danger, you need to pay attention. Too many victims talk themselves out of what their gut warned them about. It's the same with not liking someone, or better yet, liking someone. How many times have you heard someone make excuses why a friendship or relationship won't work? Anyways, enough of me getting on my soapbox. If your gut told you the girl was trouble, doesn't it make sense Harper would try to protect you? Has she ever not introduced you to someone before?"

"Well, no, but what about the guy?" I said.

"You're a real piece of work, you know that?"

"Uncle John, help me out, please," I almost begged.

"Could he have been a friend? Is it beyond the realm of possibility that Harper might have a male friend? Oh wait, wasn't her best friend a guy? Who else do we know where they're best friends and they're a guy and girl? Hmmm ..."

"You weren't here," I protested.

"I'll give you that one. Tell me, David, did it look like they were more than friends?"

I hate my uncle sometimes. If I had to make a quick decision, I would say there was a spark there. Would either of them ever do anything about it? I had no idea.

"So I was the best, most understanding, and perfect boyfriend after all," I joked.

"Whatever gets you to sleep at night," Uncle John shot back.

I decided it was best to hang up on him before I told him my true feelings about his advice.

◊◊◊

Monday April 20

I had a nine o'clock appointment at the Sports Training Institute of Chicago, or STIC. Bo had had to pull some strings to get me in. All the Chicago-based professional sports teams had players who used STIC. They specialized in helping top athletes become even better. I was surprised when my dad showed up right before I had my appointment.

"You keep forgetting you're a minor and you need one of us to sign contracts," Dad reminded me.

I normally had Kendal with me. She had a power of attorney to be able to make decisions on my behalf. Since this involved medical-type matters, either Mom or Dad had final say. Dad and I went in and met the lady in charge of setting everything up.

"Here at STIC we use a Performance Training approach. It's a scientifically based training program which is customized for each athlete. We plan to evaluate you this morning and then design a training program to help you be healthy, lean, and strong, so you're able to perform at the highest level possible for your sport.

"What we plan on doing this morning is identify how we can best help you. I've read your medical chart, and you've been injured several times in the side and back area. Repeated trauma of the kind you've sustained can cause you to have those spots become problem areas in your overall development. We have a therapy which can show immediate improvement. I suspect this will help with your throwing motions for both baseball and football."

"You're right. My sides and back sometimes stiffen up. If you have something that'll help, sign me up."

"I think you'll be impressed with the results. We'll also be looking at your overall health and any medications or supplements you might be taking. Our goal is to make sure everything's in balance, with the goal of making you the best athlete you can be."

Dad stayed for my initial evaluation. I was taken through a variety of tests to assess any flexibility deficits, muscle imbalances, and explore underlying issues which might predispose me to potential injury. They then did an assessment of my body fat and the correlation to any possible hormone issues.

Once the evaluations were done, Dad and I met with Dr. Hollings. He didn't waste any time in getting to what they'd found.

"We've identified some areas of concern. It looks like David's been injured in several areas. The one which concerns us the most is his upper neck. It looks like he has some damage in the C1 and C2 area."

"David had someone try to rip his head off in a football game," Dad explained to the doctor.

"Our test also shows problems with flexibility in your torso and glutes. I would suspect you've been hit several times and been injured in these areas."

I just nodded.

"I'd like to have David see our chiropractor and have him look at David's neck and hips. I would then like one of our therapists start him on fascial stretch therapy. Think of the skin of a sausage. The fascia is the tissue which surrounds your muscles. When you're injured, this tissue becomes constricted and prevents you from performing at your best.

"The stretch therapy will help you in a number of ways," Dr. Hollings said and started ticking off the benefits. "Improve your posture, reduce the risk of injury, improve your strength, improve performance, reduce muscle soreness, decrease stress, and even improve sexual performance."

Dad rolled his eyes at me when I sat up straighter as Dr. Hollings finished saying the last one. It was arranged for me to stay and get the chiropractic treatment and the stretching taken care of. Tomorrow I would meet with two coaches to help me with both baseball and football.

◊◊◊

I was done with the chiropractor and therapist by one that afternoon. I was scheduled to do a shoot for Jade starting at three o'clock. I took Dad to a Chicago hot dog stand and we both got combo Italian beef and sausage sandwiches. We thought we'd died and gone to heaven. Over lunch, I told Dad about the Ridgemoor Country Club. He wanted to see it, so I called Jack and let Dad talk to him. He agreed to call them so Dad could get a tour of their facilities. Dad said that if he did the tour, he could write off his trip as a business expense.

I sent text messages to Sarah and Kendal to let them know when I'd be at the studio Ford had arranged for the shoot. They let me know Kendal would drive Sarah over. Jade had used Sarah in several shoots last summer. I think she was hoping they'd want her again today.

It didn't take me long to figure out that parking was a pain in the you-know-what in Chicago. If I hadn't just come from the suburbs, I would have just taken a cab. I hoped Kendal was smart enough not to try to drive over. I finally double-parked in front of the studio and ran in to find out where I could leave my Jeep. They directed me to a garage six blocks away. It doesn't sound like much, but city blocks are much longer than regular blocks.

Sarah and Kendal were smarter than I was. I saw them get out of their cab when I was still half a block away. Sarah saw me, and they waited for me to catch up. We were early, which surprised the photographer. They sent me in the back to start getting ready. There was a second chair for the female model, who wasn't here yet, so Sarah sat down to talk to me.

"I had a long talk with Harper this morning. I think we misread what happened."

"I talked to my Uncle last night and he told me the same thing. Let me guess: the guy was a good friend and the girl was a bitch and Harper was trying to protect us," I offered.

"That's everything, except Alex ended up hitting on her. She said she was glad you weren't there to kick his butt. She let him down gently, but he now knows she's with you. She was a little pissed you didn't sit with them last night, but she understands.

"On another topic, she's working to find somewhere where the two of you can spend some time together," Sarah said and then laughed when she saw me blush.

"I would never have guessed I could get that reaction out of you."

The photographer and Tiffany, my Ford agent, both came back to find us goofing off.

"The other model is running late," Tiffany told us, being Captain Obvious.

I just smiled. Sarah nudged me.

"Last summer Sarah worked with me for Jade in New York. She could fill in until the other model shows up," I suggested.

Tiffany gave me a dirty look. The photographer was okay with it, once he looked Sarah over. I could tell Tiffany wasn't happy, but her model had put her in a bind. I guessed they thought I wouldn't show up on time, so it wouldn't be a big deal. I didn't want to be doing this shoot into the late night, and so wanted to get things moving.

We had been shooting for over an hour when the other model arrived. I think her seeing Sarah working with me was a wake-up call. To the girl's credit, she didn't get mad, she just went and got ready. She came out and Sarah stepped off set to allow her to take over. The photographer liked Sarah's look for certain shots and Linda's for others. He got permission to use them both, and Jade agreed to pay them both for a full day's work. We even did some shots with just the two of them, and a few with all three of us.

Tiffany was all smiles when we finished at eight that evening. She wanted to reward us by taking us out to dinner. I called Harper and we all went to a converted fire station close to the Loop. They had mashed potatoes done fifty different ways. I tried their blue cheese variety and really liked them. Harper went with chipotle. Neither one of us was a big fan of that. I think she ate most of mine.

Harper and I were back on a strong footing. Once we talked about it, we were both glad we hadn't said anything stupid to the other. We vowed in the future to talk if we had any concerns. It was almost mature. I still had an issue with

Harper taking me to something and then leaving me, but I'd get over it.

◊◊◊

Tuesday April 21

I arranged to be at STIC at seven in the morning so I could get my chiropractor and therapy stretching sessions out of the way.

I met with my baseball trainer first. We were going to work on my pitching today. He had a catcher who turned out to be on the White Sox roster as a backup. He was also here today to get worked on. He'd volunteered to help me this morning. They had me warm up and then they started videoing me. I will give Donnie, the trainer, credit. He didn't comment on my new pitching style.

My volunteer catcher John's only comment was I would be hard to hit. Donnie wanted to see me after I worked out with my football coach so we could go over what he found on the video.

The football coach had me throw all my passes as he videotaped me. Connor then took me into the weight room and had me lift. They wanted me to increase the strength of my back and lats. My assessment had shown my stomach was stronger than my sides and back. They wanted to balance my core, to help prevent injury. They also felt that if I gained muscle, I could better take the hits.

I then went to see Donnie. He showed me all my tells, which were signs of what I was throwing before I threw my pitches. Once I saw them, it became clear to me how it would be easy to hit me if my opponents ever figured them out. I wasn't happy when I saw how bad it was. He then had a long talk with me about my style of pitching. He told me that with my height, I wasn't suited to pitch the way Shiggy had me doing it. I was missing out on power by not using my length to whip the ball. He felt that if we could convert me back to a normal pitching style, I would pick up as much as five miles per hour on my fastball.

Donnie also wanted me to play summer ball. He suggested American Legion baseball. He felt I could be a top prospect if I worked at it. I needed to just play. I think I remember some football coaches telling me the same thing. I wondered when I would have time to do both.

◊◊◊

I met Kendal and Adrienne at the Chicago Yacht Club. We were doing a print ad for a new men's cologne called 'Sea Mist.' The photographer wanted to get shots of the Chicago skyline from the deck of a sailboat. I was excited about going sailing until they had me stand on the bow and we slammed down, causing a spray of Lake Michigan water to soak me—it was really cold. Our photographer thought I looked great as we headed directly into the waves so we could maximize the amount of water the boat would send flying as it cut through the chop.

When my lips turned blue, they finally let me go below decks to warm up. What a mistake that was. I was fine until I couldn't see the horizon anymore. The boat was rocking, and I closed my eyes only for a moment. I had never experienced seasickness before. I thought it was just something made up. How could you get sick from the motion of a boat? It felt like my inner ear was completely off, causing me to be dizzy. I felt my stomach warble a little song of distress, which had me concerned. I decided I might want to get myself to the head before I had an accident.

I think the bathroom was smaller than one you find on an airplane because my shoulders actually touched the walls on each side. The boat swayed in unpredictable directions and I started to feel claustrophobic in my confined space. I felt bile creep up my throat and my mouth suddenly filled with saliva. Neither was a good sign. I began to giggle at the absurdity of it all. Adrienne had talked me into doing higher-paying gigs. If I had stuck with working with Mr. Hill, I would be in a nice warm studio right now. Instead, I was trying to keep from gagging as I went into shock from hypothermia.

I'll remember the next few moments for the rest of my life. I heard our Captain call out, "Coming about!" and the boat suddenly tilted to the side and we slammed into a wave at the same time. I felt like I was on the set of *Star Academy* as our spaceship was rocked. I stumbled as my stomach had finally had enough. I threw up so hard I shot spaghetti out of my nose! That might have been fine, but I was spewing vomit like a bad Monte Python skit. I was hearing the famous phrase the waiter uttered before the customer had exploded.

Somehow, my stomach managed to turn itself inside out and shoot its contents all over the coffin of a bathroom I was trapped in. When I finally stopped long enough to inspect the damage, I started to gag again when I saw a long string of wet mess dangling down from the ceiling. It hung for what seemed like an eternity then snapped free and landed on my cheek.

I staggered out of the small bathroom and the makeup/wardrobe guy started gagging. The captain came down to see what the problem was. I think the smell must have hit him first because his face wrinkled up and he took a step back.

"What the hell!" he exclaimed.

I was pissed when they made me go on deck to literally hose me off. I was sent back down to change and get my makeup fixed. The makeup guy was such a wuss. Every time I belched, he took cover for fear I would hurl on him.

I noticed my two managers were nowhere to be found on this boat ride from hell. I contemplated how they would both die as I shivered in my chair. I had time to come up with some creative ways of ending their miserable lives for getting me into this mess.

The Captain finally convinced me to come back on deck. He explained if I focused on the city's skyline, I would feel better. I almost believed him when they trotted me back out onto the bow and I did my whole Titanic routine. The photographer assured me he had some great shots between my bouts of feeding the fish. After seeing the damage to the head, I was surprised I had anything left.

The crew thought it was the funniest thing they had ever seen! I'd be okay for a while, and then I would start to dry-heave. "Thar she blows!" they would call as I would find more yellow bile somewhere in my depths. I finally had to beg them to take me back in.

When we got back to the dock, I took two steps and fell down. My former managers came running up.

"David, what's wrong?" Kendal asked as she and Adrienne looked at me with worry.

I lifted my arm and crooked my finger to point at them.

"You! You must die!" I croaked out.

The Captain hopped off the boat and shook his head at me.

"He got a little seasick," he offered.

The photographer joined us. He had an evil grin.

"I have some great shots," he said.

I was surprised when everyone wanted to go see the pictures and left me lying on the dock to die.

◊◊◊

"You want to get an order of oysters?" Adrienne asked me.

This had been going on for the past several minutes. Harper and Sarah had joined us for dinner at Ruth's Chris Steak House. All of them had their shoulders shaking as they tried not to laugh aloud. Harper squeezed my hand under that table.

"I always thought it was like sucking down a phlegm ball," Kendal said and shuddered in disgust.

I took a deep breath and must have gone green because even Harper let go of my hand and scooted back.

"I think that one got to him," Sarah said with a touch of worry in her voice.

I actually felt better, but I wouldn't let them know that. I felt Kendal and Adrienne had acted very unprofessionally when they had the photographer send them pictures of me being seasick. They then sent them to Lily who posted them on my Instagram, Facebook and Twitter accounts. Seeing me hanging over the rail of a sailboat with drool hanging from my chin got a lot of likes. My phone sounded like a slot machine as I got all the notifications.

The comment which hurt the most was from Hannah Minacci: '*And you wanted me to go to Prom with you?!?!?*'

Harper wasn't happy when Hannah's comments triggered several women to offer to nurse me back to health and go to Prom with me. I was secretly happy to see Bree, Suzanne and Halle all volunteered. I was surprised when Lisa Felton said she would take one for the team and be my escort.

I showed Hannah Minacci's comment to Adrienne.

"Don't pout. She's now following you on Facebook. I'd say it's a step in the right direction."

"Good point," I cooed.

Harper took my phone away from me so we could order dinner. I got their Cowboy Ribeye and made sure we had sides of mushrooms and creamed spinach. I'm not normally a big spinach guy, but Uncle John told me to order it if I ever went to Ruth's Chris. He was right in his assessment.

The girls watched in wonder as I made short work of the bone-in ribeye. I had to admit, it was huge, but it was cooked to perfection and was one of the best steaks I'd ever had. I reminded them my stomach was more than a little empty. We passed on dessert because I'd ordered a cheesecake and we planned to pick it up on the way home. We were meeting Bev and Jack back at the house for dessert and coffee.

When we arrived at Harper's home, Adrienne took me aside and told me I did a good job today. She said if it had been her, she would never have gone back on deck after getting sick. The company was happy with the photos. It looked like they might use one of the later ones in their ad campaign. Luckily, it wasn't one of the ones with me hanging over the rail.

Chapter 16 – Spring Fashion Show

Wednesday April 22

STIC was the first stop on my itinerary again today. In the morning, I received another fascial stretch therapy session. After just three sessions, I could feel a difference in my mobility and flexibility. I worked with Connor and their speed and flexibility trainer. I had been running 30 to 35 miles a week. They wanted me to cut back on my distance running and focus more on sprints. A plan was set up where I would only run 15 to 20 miles a week by running five miles a day, three to four times a week. The other days I would do speed work.

They did most of the same things my speed coach had taught me last summer. They all agreed I needed to focus on improving my speed. I'd gotten lazy because in high school you really didn't face many really fast guys. They proved their point to me by having one of their clients, a defensive end for the Buffalo Bills, chase me around. Watching this 280-pound gazelle explode off the ball shook me up. If I ever hoped to get to the NFL, I needed to be better in every phase of my game. Speed, strength and mental toughness were just three areas that came to mind.

Granted, I wouldn't be facing anyone of this caliber in high school, but it did make me listen to Connor a lot harder. I made sure I was completely focused and gave my best effort on every drill they had me run. I now understood Ridge's approach when I met him at the USC camp. I at first confused his approach as being self-absorbed and even a little arrogant. I later learned he was so focused on the task at hand that he wasn't worried about getting to know me.

After lunch, I met with Donnie. We worked on making my delivery more uniform to eliminate my tells and improve my pitching technique. He didn't want to do anything drastic since I was still in season. We then went to

311

the batting cage and he used high-speed video to capture every nuance of my swing. I had another modeling gig with Ford, so we made plans to break down my morning workout another day.

◊◊◊

The Chicago-area designers were doing a Spring Fashion Show. They were putting together a catalog for buyers who would be attending. Ford basically had all their models show up at a huge studio. When I walked in, Deb Thomas was acting as a traffic cop.

"Tiffany has your schedule. Go down the hall and to the left and you'll find her," she directed me.

They had a centralized place where you'd get your makeup done. I found Tiffany checking the makeup on a cute redhead.

"Good, you're here. Take your shirt off and get into this chair," she said and pointed.

I sat down and one of the 'artists,' as Ford called their makeup people, started working on me. Tiffany pulled out my schedule.

"I'm going to need you to be fast today. When the designers found out you were here, they almost all wanted you. We were able to bump you up to a premium billing. If you could talk Adrienne into working today we could make a fortune."

I knew Adrienne was meeting with a model she'd worked with in the past who was looking for a change in management. I dialed Adrienne's number and handed it to Tiffany. She about dropped the phone when she realized what I'd done. I could tell they were in an intense discussion. I was mystified when Tiffany took off with my phone. Kendal came in with a big smile a few minutes later.

"What did you do?" she asked me.

"I'm not really sure. Tiffany said if Adrienne would agree to work today we could make some money, so I hooked them up."

"I heard Deb tell your agent to get other models to cover your shoots today. At first, I thought you'd pissed them off. I'd bet Adrienne had a hand in the change of plans," she clued me in.

I shrugged, knowing Adrienne would help me out. Then my stomach growled. I'd picked Chinese for lunch and I was hungry again. Kendal heard it.

"What do you want? I saw a deli and a pizza place as I came in."

"Greg told me I should try a gyro. If they don't have that, I want an Italian sub."

I was done with makeup and was relaxing in a lounge area when Kendal came back. She handed me a gyro and she had a Greek salad. We were eating when Deb Thomas found us.

"You do make it interesting. Adrienne agreed to help us out if she worked with you. When everyone found out, we had a bidding war start. Adrienne told them she was only willing to do one session, and it has to be with David," she said and then handed Kendal the contract.

I was shocked when Kendal started signing without even asking me. I was already under contract with both Adrienne and Ford. I wondered why we had to sign a new one. Once she finished signing, Kendal handed it to me. I flipped through it and two things jumped out at me. The first was the designer: it was Alice Ural. She did stunning custom wedding gowns. The second was the number on the contract. My compensation was a lot more than I would have otherwise made today. According to the contract, my combined fees to Ford and Adrienne were reduced to be the amount I normally paid Adrienne alone. Even after they had both dipped into my pocket, I was ahead by a large margin. I wondered if I would ever make the kind of money Adrienne could command.

Adrienne had agreed to pay Ford for finding the job. I was sure it was so Deb Thomas could say she delivered Adrienne for the shoot. This way they could tell their customers they could deliver the best possible models. I knew Adrienne sometimes missed the work. I think it was part of the reason she had agreed to do the Range shoot with me. I suspect she'd come out of retirement a few times a year for the rest of her life. It was just so much of who she was.

As soon as Adrienne arrived, Deb took the two of us to meet Alice. She looked to be in her late 40s and was slightly overweight. She was wearing a huge diamond ring.

"Thank you for coming out of retirement and consenting to wear my design. It has been a dream of mine to have you model one of my creations," Alice said, fawning over Adrienne. "I have the perfect dress in mind. Come, we need to get you fitted."

I chuckled when Adrienne was whisked off. Two minutes later Alice came rushing back.

"You must be David. I apologize, but I wanted to get them working on her dress right away. Follow me, we need to get you fitted as well," she said as she took my hand and led me to a room with several people measuring Adrienne.

Alice stood me up in front of a trio of mirrors so she could get a view of me from different angles.

"Bring me the Gucci, Prada and Brioni tuxedo jackets."

A harried girl rushed to bring the three jackets. She had me try them on. Alice wasn't happy with any of them. She seemed to be stumped when a distinguished-looking gentleman came up.

"Darling, he would look gorgeous in the Canali suit. It's playful, and with his young looks he could pull it off."

"Which one are you talking about?" she asked.

"Rachel, could you get me the Canali wool jacquard suit with a subtle decorative motif?" he asked the young assistant.

"Do you mean the one from their Festive Formality line?"

"Yes, dear. Bring me the charcoal-gray one."

The girl brought out a jacket which at first glance I thought was made from someone's drapes. It was a dark charcoal gray with a swirling, slightly lighter gray floral design. Alice tilted her head and had me turn around so she could see me in the jacket.

"Yes, this will work. Put him in a white silk shirt and find some colorful cufflinks. Rachel, go down and talk to Robert and see if he has a tie to go with this," she said, deciding. Then she turned to the gentleman. "Carl, get him fitted and ready. We need to hurry to get the photos taken. I know you'll make him look marvelous."

"Of course, Darling. I know exactly what we need to make him shine."

Satisfied that Carl had me in hand, Alice hurried off to make sure Adrienne's fitting was going well. He found the slacks and had me put them on. They needed to take in the waist and hem the cuffs. I was surprised when he didn't use pens or chalk; he just hemmed them with me wearing the pants.

"Try not to move too much or it might come undone," he suggested.

I was getting the jacket fitted when a man came in with an assortment of ties.

"Rachel? Honey, bring me the cufflinks, please!" Carl called.

She had two options, a black onyx or a set with rubies. Carl had me put a different one on each arm.

"Alice, dear! I need your opinion, please!"

Alice looked at both and then the ties. She ended up picking out the ruby cufflinks with a thin dark red tie.

When I was done, I had to admit they knew what they were doing. I would never have thought to wear a suit with a floral pattern on it. I was a little nervous to move too much because they'd made everything a snug fit. I didn't want to pop a seam and delay the shoot.

Carl was like a mother hen. He escorted me to the studio where we were shooting while he checked me for imaginary lint. The studio was a huge room and it was packed with people. It looked like all the designers and models wanted to watch Adrienne in action. It wasn't every day you saw someone with her pedigree work.

I knew when she entered the room by the sound level going down. One of the artists was touching up my makeup, so I didn't see Adrienne until I was brought on set. When I saw her, I froze. She took my breath away. She watched as I put my eyes on her. She smiled at my reaction, and my knees almost buckled when I realized that her smile was just for me. I guess the photographer wasn't a complete amateur because I heard his camera going off in rapid succession as we came together.

On a subconscious level, I knew we had something special—there had to be sixty or seventy people in the room, and the only sound you heard was the camera snapping pictures.

"You are a vision. I wish Tyler was here to see how beautiful you are in that dress."

It was strapless, and tight, with no decorations on the top. A touch of cleavage, to focus the eye on her femininity, gave the dress a sleek, clean line, which only enhanced Adrienne's considerable assets. It clung to her figure as Alice's design continued with this sophisticated look. It wasn't until you got below the knees, where the dress flared out slightly, that there was beadwork and hand-sewn lace. Any bride seeing this dress on Adrienne would simply demand one for herself.

I was surprised when Adrienne closed the distance between us and put me into a lip-lock. It reminded me of when I first met her in Chicago. I knew we would need our makeup fixed after this. I took her in my arms and lifted her up so I could twirl her around. When I set her down and our lips parted, I heard the photographer say: "Look at me."

Sure enough, after a few more shots, our Ford artist pulled us back to makeup to repair the damage we'd done to each other. I was surprised when Adrienne reached over and held my hand while we were getting fixed. I caught her eye and glanced down to ask what was going on.

"When you said that about Tyler, I thought my heart was going to burst. You made me feel like I was the prettiest girl in the room."

"If you could see yourself through my eyes, you'd know it's true. I meant it, you take my breath away."

"You keep it up, and when you turn eighteen, I might decide I like guys," she teased me.

"Don't tease me. I might have to give up Hannah if that happened."

"You have to catch her first, and I think her boyfriend might have something to say about it."

"Details, details. You just need to have a positive mental attitude."

We were soon back on the set. Something I loved about working with Adrienne is that I always learned new things when I worked with her. I think all the other models were hanging on her every word as she continued to teach me the finer points of being a model.

◊◊◊

Adrienne had dinner plans with a few of the models she met today. Kendal had found herself a boy-toy to take her out on the town tonight. He had to be the dumbest guy I'd ever met, but he made up for it in other areas, according to Kendal. I covered my ears when she wanted to go into detail.

It was a good thing I was Harper's boyfriend or I would have been in trouble. What is it about seeing a woman in a wedding gown that makes other women horny? Adrienne had to intervene while I was getting dressed, or I might have been having sex right there. I was sure Ford would look down on their models doing the deed with clients around. Adrienne took my arm and walked me out of the building. She was teasing me because one girl came up right in front of Adrienne and made me an offer I was considering. These older women were not shy.

"I don't think we can leave you alone tonight. I think she was serious about you taking her back to her place and tying her up."

"You know, this might be a nice group activity. What do you say? We use her body for the next ten or twelve hours and add it to our bucket list," I said hopefully.

Adrienne pulled her phone out.

"Hey, I need you to get on the next flight to Chicago. David has me so revved up I'm about to jump him," Adrienne said, obviously talking to Tyler.

We got into my Jeep and I took her to a condo building on the lakefront. On the drive over, I could hear her whispering naughty things to her life partner. With a hefty tip to the doorman, I was allowed to park my Jeep out front. Adrienne wanted me to meet her friends.

I could only stay a few minutes because I'd promised the doorman. Adrienne already had a few of the pictures from today's shoot. They only released ones they knew weren't going to be in the ad campaign but wanted sent out via social media. It helped create some pre-buzz for whatever we were working on. She made sure I had copies and I sent them to Lily and told her to have fun with them.

318

On the way to Harper's house, I got a text to pick up Ray first. I swung by his house, another McMansion. Ray was waiting for me on his front steps.

"Thanks for getting me out of the house. My parents won't let me go anywhere unless they approve of who I'm with," he confessed.

"I take it Harper's in charge tonight."

"When isn't she?"

We both laughed. I pulled up to Harper's house and Ray jumped out to go let her know we were there. As he went in, I was surprised when Bev came out to the Jeep and got in.

"Are you joining us tonight?" I asked, trying not to sound disappointed.

"Don't act so excited."

"Sorry, was I that obvious?"

"No, but you forget who you're dealing with, young man."

I hung my head in mock shame. She wasn't buying it.

"I wanted to talk to you about Ray. Tonight is a test run to start allowing him more freedom. I'm sorry to put this on you, but if he acts up, please call me. We're afraid Harper would never let us know if he was up to anything."

"If she won't tell on him, I don't think it's my place to keep him in line. Harper is funny about things like that," I said.

"If it will make you feel any better, she knows why I'm out here talking to you. She agreed it would be better if you were the responsible one tonight."

Something didn't ring true.

"For some reason my bullshit detector is going off."

"Was it the part where she agreed you were responsible?"

"We both know she doesn't believe that for one minute, even though it's her that has us doing things we shouldn't."

"Oh, do tell."

"Not happening," I said as I shook my head. "She was very clear on what I can and cannot tell you. Do us both a favor and interrogate her. We both know if it was anything really bad, I would step up and tell you regardless of what my girlfriend thinks."

"I know you're a good boy. It's why you're not already dead. Now, back to Ray."

"I'll make you a deal: if I see Ray touch drugs or alcohol, I'll call you immediately. If he's up to something else I don't approve of, I'll talk to your lovely daughter first. If she agrees, I'll call."

"I guess that's the best I'm getting out of you. I expect a full report when you get home."

"Again, your daughter has rules. Talk to her," I said.

Bev went into the house and Harper and Ray came right out. Before I could pull into traffic, the interrogation began.

"What did my mom want?" Harper asked.

"As if you're surprised? Apparently, Ray is on something like double-secret probation. I was instructed to turn him in if he doesn't do everything I tell him."

They looked at each other and then back at me.

"And what do you want from me?" Ray asked, a little worried.

"I figured you could help Harper decide where we're going to dinner. If I have to find parking, you'll be responsible for keeping her company and treating her like the princess she is. You know, hold the door for her and submit to her every whim," I decided.

He looked at me and then smiled.

"So, I'm supposed to do everything she would have me doing anyways," he stated.

"I think he can handle it," Harper added.

"Good, because I didn't want to tattle on him," I said with a big sigh.

320

We had a great time together. Ray was going stir-crazy. He hadn't been out of the house without his mom or dad since he got home. I sat back and let the two friends talk. It was nice to see them reconnecting. I did ask where Sarah was. She had gone to dinner with some of the models she'd worked with today.

Ray and Harper picked out a nice restaurant, the Indian House. I really liked it. They taught me how to eat my meal by tearing off a piece of flatbread called naan and use it like a fork. My favorite dish was Chicken Makhani. It was chicken roasted in a clay pot and then mixed with a tomato-cream sauce. I found I truly liked their vegetarian dishes. The only dish I didn't like was dessert. It was way too sweet.

After dinner, I was tired, so we took Ray home. He made us promise we would take him out again the next evening. When we got back to Harper's, we found her mom and dad waiting for us in the kitchen. Ray had a lot of people willing to help him get his life turned back around. I begged off the family conversation and went to bed.

◊◊◊

Friday April 24

Today was my last day at STIC. Both Connor and Donnie worked together to come up with workouts which would serve me well for both baseball and football. I was happy Bo suggested I come here. Their main focus was on professional athletes. I felt they were helping me lay the foundation for what I needed to do to make it to my ultimate goal.

Donnie wanted me to come back after baseball season to work on my pitching delivery. He felt I had the physical attributes and drive to make it as a high-level pitching prospect. For my fielding and batting, he wanted me to work on my reaction speed. Both he and Connor had several exercises for me to do to help in that regard. What separated the very best from the rest was tracking the ball off the bat.

They were both impressed when I realized the changes needed wouldn't happen overnight. It would take hard work and dedication to reach the highest levels. I knew how to execute a plan. I had been working towards my life goals for a year now. I would need the same focus to get to my final destination: being a starting quarterback in the NFL, or playing Major League Baseball. I figured it never hurt to have a backup plan.

◊◊◊

Adrienne and Kendal both went home. I was done modeling for the week. I finally had a free afternoon I could spend with Harper. I parked my Jeep and came into the kitchen to find Sarah and Ray waiting for me.

"We're going to play tourist today. I want to take you on the *L* and go downtown to the Loop," Harper said.

"I want to go to Berghoff for lunch," Ray told us.

"What do they serve?" Sarah asked.

"It's only the best German restaurant in the city. You can either go to the stand-up sandwich bar or sit in the dining room. If I'm in a rush, I do the stand-up, but I think you need to savor their fantastic food," Ray explained.

We walked to the *L,* or elevated train, stop. I was pleased they planned to show me what the city had to offer. We were in high spirits when the train came. Since it was just after noon, the train was almost empty. It was noisy and you rocked as it made its way to the Loop. I loved it. We stopped at the Adams/Wabash station and only had a block and a half to walk to the Berghoff restaurant.

The Berghoff family started brewing beer in 1887. During prohibition, they switched to making near-beer and soda pop. Ray assured me they had the best root beer in the world. He insisted we all get a glass of it.

Ray was our culinary guide for lunch. He wanted us to try all his favorites. For appetizers, he ordered a Bavarian pretzel, which came with a beer-and-cheddar dip and a couple of different mustards. The huge pretzel came out on a hook and you tore off chunks and dipped it in the different sauces. He also ordered potato pierogis. They came with chive sour cream. As far as I was concerned, Ray was batting a thousand so far.

For lunch, he ordered sandwiches. We had the Reuben, hot corned beef, and bratwurst. Sarah was watching her weight, so she chose their goat cheese salad. I couldn't pick a favorite—they were all good.

After lunch, we walked to Grant Park. We found a stand where they had double-decker bus tours. None of us had ever been on one before, so we decided to try it. Of course, we climbed to the top so we could get a good view of everything. It was a beautiful day and the four of us enjoyed the ride.

After we crossed the river and were headed to Water Tower Place, we decided to jump off when we smelled the caramel corn store. It was a little hole-in-the-wall storefront where they made fresh caramel popcorn. They were marketing geniuses because they had big blowers that push the smell out onto the street. Their ploy worked—it got me to get off the bus to track them down. It was even better than it smelled. Piping-hot caramel popcorn is a must if you ever go to Chicago.

I heard blues music coming out of a bar on a side street. We spent an hour snacking on fried mushrooms and listening to music. As we came out, a horse-drawn carriage was driving by. There was a cute girl driving and I flagged her down. She was a lot of fun as she gave us a tour of the Gold Coast neighborhood.

She let us off near Rush Street. This was where many of the young professionals who work in the Loop come for after-work fun. We were approached by a homeless lady, who had to be close to seventy, who offered to show us her tits for five dollars. I wasn't missing this. She reminded me of the old lady in the Playboy cartoons. I think Ray was scarred for life.

We decided to go back to Harper's and get ready for the evening. She had been in contact with her old friends and they were having a party tonight. I was a little sad our afternoon of exploring was over. I would rate this in the top five of all afternoons I'd ever experienced that didn't include sex.

◊◊◊

When we got back, everyone went to the man cave in the basement. Ray had his tablet out, checking his emails. I don't how we got on the topic, but Sarah blurted out, "Do guys masturbate a lot?"

I thought poor Ray was going to have a stroke.

"If you mean like ten times a day, probably not. How many times do you do it, Ray?" I asked.

"Screw you, David."

"In your dreams, Brother," I teased him.

Harper couldn't stop giggling when she saw Ray go bright red.

"Come on, I'm curious," Sarah pleaded.

"I probably do at least once a day, maybe twice," I told her.

"Sounds about right," Ray confessed.

"How do you do it?" Sarah asked.

"Are you looking for a demonstration?" I asked.

"NO! I mean, I …" she started.

"I think she wants to know what you're thinking about when you do it," Harper helped.

Sarah nodded. I looked at Ray and it was clear from his expression that he wasn't going to satisfy her curiosity.

"Uh, guys are visual, so I normally watch video," I confessed.

Now Harper sat up. She smiled sweetly at Ray. I had seen this particular smile before, and knew Ray was a goner.

"Ray, do you mind if I borrow your tablet for a sec?" she asked innocently.

"Sure," he said, handing it over.

The poor bastard. Harper brought up his browser history and giggled. She motioned Sarah over and suddenly the room was filled with moans. I think Ray was brain-damaged because it took him a full two minutes to figure out that they were watching gay porn. I thought he might have actually busted his tablet when he smacked it out of Harper's hand and it crashed on the floor.

The little minx turned on me.

"David, dear," she began.

I held up my hand.

"I'll show you mine if you show me yours," I offered.

She jumped up and I could hear her running up the stairs. It sounded like a herd of water buffalo. At least I think that was what my mom yelled at me when I ran up and down the stairs. She came back and handed me her laptop.

I checked her browser history and found Chris Pine and Ryan Reynolds as her dream guys. I handed over my iPad and she found my secret: Little Caprice. She was a porn star from Eastern Europe. Even Ray wanted to see who she was.

"I hope this isn't kiddie porn," Sarah warned me.

I just rolled my eyes. I watched for their reaction as the first video started. Ray was the first to figure it out. Then it dawned on the other two.

"She looks just like me," Harper said as she looked up at me.

"Yep, if you're not around, I want to be thinking of only you," I said.

I was almost knocked off the couch when Harper launched herself on me and gave me a sizzling kiss. I had to pull her off me before we broke the house rules.

◊◊◊

I was surprised when Bev and Jack came home at a reasonable hour. They ordered pizza from Lou Malnati's. They got one of each, a thin and a deep-dish pizza. Harper and I made a salad to go with it. I felt like they knocked it out of the park with both styles of pizza. I have to admit, two slices of deep-dish pizza filled even me up!

◊◊◊

"Explain to me again why we're going to a party thrown by a girl you can't stand?" I asked.

"It's because I went to middle school with these people. I like them, for the most part, and I want you to meet them. Shouldn't that be enough?" she challenged me.

"Yes, ma'am. Can I ask one more question?"

"If it's not going to piss me off."

"Is the guy from the banquet going to be there?" I asked.

"Alex? I think he might be," she answered.

"Fair warning, if he hits on you, I might punch him."

"Alex isn't like that. Plus, I can handle myself, David. You'll not be hitting anyone, is that understood?"

"Fair warning," I answered her.

"Men!" Harper complained and went to see what was taking Sarah so long.

We took a cab to Melisa's house. Ray had received a talk from Harper's parents about not drinking. Ray was just happy to be out from under his house arrest. I wasn't worried he was going to be up to no good.

I will admit, Melisa's party was pretty spectacular. Where I was used to kegs and maybe tequila shots, she had a full bar, with bartenders. Where we might have someone's playlist, Melisa had a kick-ass band. I had been to see a few bands at State, and none of them was this good. Where we might have Mona running around with a couple of pitchers of beer, she had actual waitstaff. Finally, we never had a buffet table. The best we ever had were a couple of bags of chips.

If it hadn't been for the songs the band was playing, and the age of the partygoers, I would expect it would be for people in their 40s and older. I must not go out enough, or get invited to the right parties.

"Thank you," I told Harper.

"I thought you might enjoy this. Come on, I want a drink and then you'll meet my friends."

We went to the bar. Sarah and I got sodas, while Ray and Harper ordered Tanqueray and tonics. If Harper was going to let him drink, I wasn't babysitting.

I was happy to find out that besides the upscale treatment, kids at parties are pretty much the same. I really enjoyed meeting Harper's friends and dancing with most of them. Alex approached Harper and they seemed to be getting along okay. I was happy to see he left after a few minutes.

What I wasn't happy about was Ray seemed to disappear. Harper looked like she was looking for him, too. When the song ended, I went to talk to her.

"Have you seen Ray?" she asked me.

"No. Something you have to realize is if Ray doesn't want to stop, you can't make him."

"I know, but he's my best friend. Will you go look for him?"

"Of course, I will," I assured her.

I didn't have to look for him because he came out from the back and headed right for us.

"Ray!" Harper scolded him.

327

It was obvious from his eyes that he'd found drugs. He gave her a weak smile. I figured I had better separate them and steered Ray away from Harper. She at first looked pissed when I stepped between her and her quarry. I didn't think she really wanted to deal with him right now, so she and Sarah went to the bar. I guided Ray to a library that wasn't quite so loud.

"Dude, you're messing up," I told him.

"It was only a joint. I mean seriously, what's the big deal?

"The big deal is you, once again, are putting Harper into a predicament. It's not like you haven't gotten in trouble for this before. Remember where you're going to school?" I reminded him. "Everyone trusted her to keep your nose clean and let you spend the week with us. She could have said 'no' and you would've been stuck at home for break. The big deal is you've taken advantage of your friendship with her."

I hadn't expected Ray to burst into tears.

"I can't help myself. I know there're consequences, but in the moment, I don't care."

I don't know how long Ray and I talked. It had to be over an hour, maybe two. I don't know if our talk helped or not. His problem wasn't casual drug use. I think a large number of teens experiment and use drugs recreationally and turn out just fine. Ray's problem was he couldn't say no to drugs. If left to his own devices, he'd be high 24/7. He was smart enough to recognize the problem, but he found he couldn't stop. Ultimately, Ray had to elect to stop on his own. Unfortunately, I didn't think he was there yet.

◊◊◊

Sarah walked into the room and both Ray and I looked up.

"Are we ready to go?" I asked.

She turned her head and wouldn't look at me. I had never seen Sarah look so nervous. My immediate thought jumped to Harper and Alex. My gut told me if she was really my girlfriend and there was nothing to her relationship with Alex, she would have introduced us Sunday. Sarah saw my jaw set and blocked me from leaving.

"Hang on. She's been drinking and she and Alex have been flirting. Remember, you promised not to get physical tonight," she almost begged me.

At that moment, I knew Harper and I were finished. If Sarah felt it had escalated to the point I was going to punch Alex, then it had gone too far. Ray darted around Sarah.

"I'll take care of this," he assured me.

I went to go around Sarah. I wasn't going to let Ray take care of my business. She wrapped herself around me to stop me. She was all of 110 pounds. I just started walking with her hanging on me. I found Harper and Alex on the dance floor, rocking back and forth to a slow song. His hand was on her butt and groping her. She had a big smile on her face as she looked deep into his eyes. He leaned down to kiss her when Ray arrived.

"Get your hands off her!" Ray shouted.

I wasn't really surprised when the music stopped. Alex and Harper were obviously drunk and looked around, confused. Ray had to physically separate them. Sarah had a death grip on my arm. I looked her in the eye and she let go. There must have been something in my look that scared her. I strode up with the intent to punch Alex when Ray did it for me.

It wasn't a jab to get someone's attention. This was one of those where you see the guy pull one out of left field and it was lights out. It was probably a good thing Ray hit him on the side of the head instead of the face, or something would have been broken. Alex looked like someone hadn't paid the electric bill and the power was shut off. He just dropped and then twitched a couple of times.

"What have you done?" Harper wailed.

"I stopped you before you did something really stupid!" Ray yelled back.

"But ..." she began.

"Don't *but* me. I know you've had a secret crush on Alex since middle school. Tell me why it's only been a crush up to this point?" Ray demanded.

Harper wouldn't look him the eye. It seemed she had a history with Alex.

"Remember Tracy Altman?" Ray prodded.

"I can't believe Alex would have done what she said. She just was trying to get even with him because he wouldn't date her!"

Ray looked her with sadness in his eyes and shook his head.

"Harper, I'll never understand you. You have one of the best guys I know as your boyfriend, and you go and make out with slime like Alex."

That seemed to snap Harper out of it. She looked around and saw everyone staring at her. She then saw me and burst into tears. She ran up to me and buried her head in my chest. I think she expected me to wrap her in my arms and all would be forgiven. Instead, I stepped back and turned around to leave.

"NO! No, wait. I can explain," Harper begged.

Thankfully, Ray came up behind her and wrapped her in his arms. I would let him deal with her. I was in a daze when Sarah led me out to catch a cab. I was surprised when Ray came out and joined us. He gave me a sad look.

"Can I get a ride with you guys? Someone called an ambulance, and I'd rather not be there when they come. There might be some uncomfortable questions," he explained.

We dropped Ray off at his house and then went to Harper's. Bev and Jack were eating leftover cheesecake when we came in. They looked at us curiously when they didn't see their daughter.

"Where's Harper?" Bev asked.

"She broke up with me and is with her new boyfriend Alex," I told them. Her parents just stared at me in disbelief. "I'm going to pack and take off."

"Can you give me a ride back to school?" Sarah asked.

"Sure," I said and went downstairs to pack.

I was followed by Jack and Bev. It seemed I wasn't getting off that easy.

"What exactly happened?" Bev ordered.

I knew I had no reason to pull any punches. I told them about Ray first, and my fears. I think they had come to the same conclusion, but I could tell it hurt to hear their suspicions confirmed. I then told them what I saw and what I suspected about Alex and Harper. I didn't tell them Ray had punched him.

We heard the front door open.

"I'm in no mood to deal with her right now. Please head her off," I asked Bev.

She gave me a tight smile and nodded. She went up and we could hear the two of them arguing. Jack gave me a weak smile.

"It sucks to be your age. So many lessons to learn, and too many have to be learned the hard way. Let me give you a piece of advice. People make mistakes. I think my daughter made a doozy tonight. I understand if you don't want to date her anymore, but you were good friends before this. My wife is a good judge of character and she has nothing but good things to say about you. I had my doubts when I first met you, but I've come to agree with Bev. I'd hate to see Harper lose a good friend."

"Jack, I like Harper a lot. I think it's obvious that's the case, or I wouldn't have asked her to be my girlfriend. I don't have a crystal ball that can predict the future. I can't really see Harper and me ever being more than friends, after tonight. Once the trust is broken, it would be very difficult for me ever to trust her again. I know she was drinking, but she decided to allow his advances, and with me at the same party. We talked before we got there about what would happen if she did allow him to get fresh with her. Yet she did it anyways."

"Son, if you ever need anything, call me. Even if you and Harper are no longer friends," Jack said, and then shook my hand.

I finished packing and then headed upstairs to help Sarah with her bags. Harper met us at the back door. Her eyes were puffy.

"David, I'm so sorry. Can you stay and we work this out tomorrow?" she asked.

"No. We both know we aren't getting past this. Please don't make it worse by trying to force the issue."

"I understand. What are you going to do about Prom?" she asked.

"He's going to take me," Sarah said before I could respond.

I didn't feel like arguing. I think Harper suddenly realized how quickly she could be replaced and ran up the stairs to her room. I decided we needed to leave. Jack walked me out so I could give him the gate and garage-door openers.

◊◊◊

We were on the Dan Ryan Expressway before Sarah or I talked to each other.

"What's this about you being my date for Prom?" I asked.

"I was wondering when you would ask that. I was just at the right place at the right time. I knew you'd probably go stag if I didn't say something."

"You don't think I could've found a date with only a week to go before Prom?" I teased her.

"I have no doubt you could. Heck, Missy's going to kill me when she finds she missed out."

"You do know I'm not ready to date anyone right now."

"David, I'm not stupid. I'd hope we're good enough friends to go and have a good time. Heck, I might even get lucky," she teased me.

"Anytime, anywhere," I shot back, reminding her of the offer I made all the models in New York.

I was surprised she had gotten me to smile. She just winked at me. When we got to Wesleyan, we found the dorms weren't open yet. I was tired and didn't feel like driving home. I took her to the hotel where last year's Formal was held. Sarah insisted on just one room.

I was glad when all she wanted to do was hold me. I needed someone.

◊◊◊

Saturday April 25

I woke to a very naked Sarah holding onto me as if she was afraid I would disappear into the night. Even though I was sure Sarah wouldn't be opposed to a little morning fun, I wasn't ready. I got out of the bed to take my morning shower. I really didn't feel like running. I just wanted to get home and get some unconditional love from my hound and parents.

Mr. Happy, on the other hand, was not happy. I took a quick peek out the bathroom door to take in Sarah's exquisite body. He was making the case you didn't turn down a model who was naked in your bed. As I stepped into the shower and turned the water to cold, I was talking Mr. Happy off the ledge. I explained I had been there, done that, and had the t-shirt. I don't think he bought it for a second.

When I was done with my shower, I came out to see Sarah naked and bent over the sink, brushing her teeth. Okay, Mr. Happy had a very good point. I knew Sarah was teasing me. Somehow the little head took control of the body and stuck his nose in where it didn't belong. Sarah jumped when she felt me pop into her little butt.

I smiled when she had a rubber handy and put it on me. She then guided me to where she wanted me and pushed back. I hadn't had sex all week out of respect of Harper's parents, so it didn't take much convincing for me to give in. I had forgotten Sarah's hidden talent. She used her muscles to massage my member. She giggled when I moaned and climaxed. I simply wasn't able to hold back.

"I sure hope that wasn't all you had in you," Sarah teased me.

"I was trying to be a good boy, but girly, I'm going make love to you until you're unconscious."

She squealed in glee and ran to the bedroom. We ended up keeping the room another night. It had been a long time since I had spent all day in bed with a woman. I highly recommend a marathon sex-session and room service to work out all your frustrations over being dumped. I wish I'd figured this out when Tracy and Eve dumped me. It was so much better than being depressed.

◊◊◊

Chapter 17 – Special Treatment

I opened the door to my apartment to let Duke out. I was surprised when he went towards the back of the garage like he was stalking something. I had a mission, though, so I let him have his fun. Mom bought doughnuts yesterday. She always bought us two each and only two Bavarian Creams. Dad and I had made a game of hiding them because they were our favorites. We both knew we weren't allowed to eat them, because Mom had explained what would happen if we did.

As I walked across the front of the garage towards the back door, I saw a little movement at the edge of my vision. I stepped back away from the corner of the garage and wondered if this was a new game Duke had learned. I wanted a little room if he decided to spring his trap. What I saw made me chuckle. Precious was crouched down, ready to ambush Duke. I was impressed that he was smart enough to circle around and come up behind her. He slowly stalked the unsuspecting cat. I was almost to the back door when he struck.

I give him high marks on his plan, but the execution needed a little work. I had just opened the back door when Duke rushed forward and nipped Precious on the butt. His momentum caused him to roll the now distressed feline. Duke broke for the back door to escape. It was like watching National Geographic when the hunting cat would flail away and make a giant swipe with their paw to bring down their prey. Precious made one of her loud yowls—which sounded like a bobcat—got lucky and sunk her claws into my pup's rump.

Duke sensed his impending doom and sprinted through the back door with the crazed cat stuck to his butt. It was one thing to let the two of them play outside, but to let them inside was a very bad idea. I made it into the kitchen to the sounds of a major fight going on. I guess Precious took offense to being stalked. That was *her* job! It was also apparent Duke was pissed. I had never heard such ferocious growling.

Duke was now big enough to do some serious damage. I didn't want to have to take an injured Precious home to Brit—for some reason, she loved that cat. I grabbed Duke's collar and jerked him off the pinned feline, which gave her a chance to escape. Duke and I looked perplexed as Precious darted deep into the bowels of our home. He started wagging his tail because he was happy he was victorious. I hoped Precious wasn't hiding because I didn't have time for this mess.

"What the hell just happened?" Mom asked, and from her tone it was clear she wasn't happy.

Mom was not in the mood for half a story. I explained my hero's exploits in detail.

"So, you're telling me the Callahan cat from hell is loose in my house?"

"We should probably go find her?" I suggested helpfully.

Mom glared at me, so I gave Duke the command to 'get the kitty.' It turned out either Duke was a terrible hunter, or Precious was the Queen of Hide-'N-Seek. We came downstairs to confront a pissed-off cat owner.

"What did you do to my baby?" Brit demanded.

"He and his hound chased her into my house," Mom told her.

"Well, if she was scared, you won't find her anytime soon. I'll come by after school and get her when she comes out."

"Sit down and have a doughnut," Mom offered as she put a plate out with my Bavarian Cream on it.

◊◊◊

This week was jam-packed with school activities. Wednesday was our last home baseball game and Friday kicked off the State Baseball Tournament. We had already locked in a slot, and the final home game would help decide our seeding. Then Saturday was Prom.

The word on the school grapevine was that ticket sales for Prom weren't very good. The senior ass-hats had made this their big final party of the year, and frankly not many people wanted to join them in the festivities. Since ticket sales were so poor, our Prom had been switched from the Country Club to the gym.

If I'd known, I wouldn't have bought tickets. I guess if I knew Harper would flake out on me, I wouldn't have bought them, either. On Sunday, Sarah and I had locked horns. I refused to go to Wesleyan's Formal this year. She finally relented when I explained I had no desire to run into Harper so soon after our breakup. Even though I wasn't devastated, I didn't need to see her there with Alex. My best guess was she wouldn't take Alex, but why tempt fate? There was a high probability I might punch him if I saw him again.

The upcoming dance was the talk of our lunch tables. I quietly sat back and listened as I tried to figure out what was in today's lunch. The sign said it was beef stroganoff. I always thought the dish was supposed to have a creamy sauce with sour cream in it and egg noodles. This tasted like they'd used canned turkey gravy and it looked like there were leftover spaghetti noodles mixed in. I was pretty sure it wasn't even beef. I wasn't eating this. I got up to go see if they had any sack lunches left.

"Where are you going?" Wolf asked.

"I'm getting something else."

He smiled and grabbed my plate. I swear, he would eat anything. I went up and found the sack lunches were gone. I sweet-talked the lunch ladies into making me a Rueben. It was what they were having. When I came back to the table, no one was happy with me.

"How come you get special treatment?" Gina complained.

"Yeah, what's the deal?" Alan asked.

I just glared at them. Pam and Mona were eyeballing my sandwich. If I engaged in conversation, the girls would end up talking me out of it. I just stuffed a big bite in my mouth and grinned at them. Pam and Mona made Gina and Jeff move so they could sit on each side of me. Wolf about lost his hand when he reached across to snatch some chips. Pam smiled at me, leaned close, sucked my earlobe into her mouth, and nipped me. The momentary distraction gave Mona time to steal half my sandwich. When I went to grab it back, Pam got the other half.

"Guys, no fair!" I complained.

"If you learned to share, you wouldn't have these problems," Wolf advised me.

"Shut up, I gave you my lunch already," I said as he grabbed more chips. I was still hungry, so I would have to go back up and see what I could get. "Who all wants something else to eat?"

It seemed everyone did. I made Mona and Pam go with me to see if we could get sandwiches for everyone at our table. I explained to the lunch ladies that the girls had eaten my sandwich and everyone wanted something else to eat. Good looks and charm didn't work this time. I paid one of the lunch ladies for a big loaf of rye bread, a couple pounds of Swiss cheese, sliced ham, mustard and individual bags of chips. She even threw in paper plates. For what I paid, I could have ordered everyone pizza and had it delivered. I think the lunch ladies made a profit on me.

"That's more like it," Alan said.

Pam made me a sandwich. I wasn't taking a chance this horde of locusts wouldn't eat it all before I got to eat.

While everyone ate their sandwiches, Gina quizzed me about Prom.

"Are you and Harper renting a limo this year?"

"Harper and I broke up over Spring Break."

"Oh please, don't tell me we're going to have to find you a last-minute date again," Cassidy moaned.

Last year had been a disaster. Ford had set me up with a faux girlfriend for publicity. Between her dad, who tried to pimp her out, and her being a raving bitch, it had been a disaster. I ended up at Prom stag. I smiled when I remembered what had happened after Prom. If it worked out even half as good, I would have a night to remember.

"Settle down, I have a date lined up," I assured them.

They all turned and looked at Pam. She gave a nervous laugh and waved her hands.

"It's not me."

"So, what did you do to Harper to make her dump you?" Alan asked.

"Alan, don't distract him or we'll never get the story out of him," Gina warned.

"Can we have the leftovers?" a freshman from another table asked.

I looked around and everyone who wanted a sandwich had gotten one, so I let the freshmen take the rest. Lunch must have really sucked for them to be brave enough to come and ask for food. Then again, they were growing boys.

"You guys would love Chicago. We should plan a day when the Cubs are in town and go to a game," I told them.

"Where all did you go?" Jeff asked.

Gina threw her hands up in the air when she realized Jeff, Alan and I were playing our misdirection game. We always did this if we didn't want to talk about something. Gina got out of her chair next to Mike and came and sat in my lap. I looked at her boyfriend and he just shrugged. She grabbed my face so I would look right in her eyes.

"You can tell us all about Chicago after I get a few facts," she said. I just nodded.

"Who are you going to Prom with?"

"Sarah."

She took a deep breath to keep from yelling at me. I made the mistake of smirking. She suddenly had my ears in her grip, which made me much more forthcoming.

"She goes to school at Wesleyan and stayed at Harper's house over break. I met her last year when I went to Modeling Camp during the summer. She and I worked together last week. When Harper broke up with me, Sarah volunteered to be my date. We're just friends."

"What kind of friends?" Gina asked.

"None-of-your-business kind of friends," I informed her.

"If we could arrange an alternative to Prom, would you be interested?"

"Are any of you going to Prom?" I asked.

"If we had something else to do, I wouldn't mind skipping it. My brother and his friends are being dicks," Cassidy told me.

It seemed everyone felt the same way.

"For grins, what all do we need to do to put our own dance on?" I asked.

Gina started ticking the list off on her fingers.

"Location, band, decorations, chaperones, tickets. I'm sure we'll need other stuff like drinks and food."

"I'll call my dad and see if he can get me a deal on the Country Club. Who knows a band?" I asked.

"Cora's roommate is dating a DJ. Maybe I could talk him into doing it," Pam offered.

"I could make the tickets," Alan offered.

"I could ask my dad to be a chaperone," Mike suggested.

"Let's make some calls and everyone meet me before baseball practice. Are you sure you guys want to do this?" I asked.

Everyone seemed to want to if we could.

◊◊◊

I made Gina go with me to an empty room and called my dad. He went and found the banquet manager. We told them what we wanted to do. The Prom Committee had put a deposit on the room, which would have gone towards the event at the Country Club. Since they canceled last minute, the Country Club planned to keep the deposit. The banquet manager was willing to apply the funds to our event. I guess they had pissed him off. Since my dad was an employee, they would give us his discount. Between the two, it would cover about half the cost for the room, setup, and teardown.

He gave us an idea of different services they offered, food- and beverage-wise, and ballpark costs for the different options. All we had to do was confirm no later than tomorrow morning and give them a firm count by Thursday evening.

◊◊◊

I was shocked when about forty people showed up before baseball. I guess people disliked Brad and his buddies as much as I did. I was even more shocked when members of the Prom Committee showed up. I addressed them first.

"Dan, Alicia, I hope we're not stepping on your toes," I said.

"Not really. Tommy Cox and Brad Hope have taken over the planning for the event. We have some decorations, if you guys want them. We'd rather go to your party," Dan said, which shocked me.

341

"Before we do this, we haven't antagonized them lately. Do we want to risk them being jerks the rest of the school year?" I asked.

"They wouldn't sell me a ticket to Prom because they said I didn't fit in," Yuri told us.

For the next five minutes, we heard similar stories. If I'd known they were bullying the kids, I would have confronted them. The more I heard, the more I wanted to pound one Tommy Cox. It seemed when they let him come back to school after Christmas break, he'd been busy behind the scenes.

I put Gina and Cassidy in charge, and they recruited Mike. He had no choice since he was Gina's boyfriend. Dan and Alicia agreed to help, which made everything easier. They had already worked to plan Prom, so they knew what all needed to be done. Pam and Mona also volunteered. When Yuri saw who was on the committee— hot single girls—he joined also. I talked Alan and Lily into helping since they could get the word out either through our sports database or my Twitter account.

◊◊◊

When we were done, Jeff and I went to my house to get Duke. Jeff went in the back door first and started laughing. I came in to find Duke and Precious in his crate. The cat must have come out of hiding sometime during the morning and Mom found her at lunchtime. Duke and Precious were both looking at us, wanting to get out. I wasn't about to open that door without some sort of protection. I'd had Precious claw and bite me way too many times. Then I remembered I had Jeff with me.

"Grab an extra leash and put it on Brit's cat. I'll go make us sandwiches. Oh, and close the mudroom door in case the kitty gets out. Mom doesn't want her running loose in the house."

I just had gotten started making us sandwiches when all hell broke loose. I heard a loud yowl from Precious and a scream from Jeff. Duke added to the racket by barking. I heard a couple of thuds.

"Son of a! OH MY GOD! OH MY effing GOD! HELP!" Jeff screamed.

I felt bad, but I couldn't help laughing. I pulled the door open an inch to see what was going on. Jeff was hunched over with Precious attached to the center of his back. It looked like both of his hands were bleeding. Duke was all the way in the back of his crate. Whatever vibe the cat was giving off seemed to have him scared.

I eased into the mudroom and picked up a leash. I snapped it into Precious's collar and handed it to Jeff.

"There you go," I said, trying to keep a straight face.

"Screw you, Dawson! Get this cat off me!"

"Are you sure? It might hurt," I said reasonably.

"As sure as I'm going to kick your ass if you don't!"

Some people have no sense of humor. I pulled out my cell phone and snapped a picture. Precious hissed at me; this made it a keeper. I about shit when she launched herself off Jeff's back at me. I guess she recognized me as someone who antagonized her. I snatched her out of the air by the scruff of her neck. I made Duke get out of the crate and stuffed the cat from hell in. I was amused to see the hair on Duke's back was up. He was wary of all the hissing going on.

I took Jeff into the kitchen and cleaned him up. I made him take his shirt off and made a face.

"How bad is it?" Jeff asked.

"I don't think you need stitches," I said.

"You do know I'm going to have my girlfriend kick your butt," Jeff threatened.

"Hey, Buddy, no need for that."

"I think I'll have her do it right after practice, so everyone will see you cry like a little girl."

343

"How about I just cry? There's no need for Cassidy to get involved."

"Nope, she hasn't kicked anyone's butt in a while. She's been giving me funny looks. I think this'll kill two birds with one stone. You get what's coming to you, and she gets to vent her frustrations," Jeff said.

"If you need some ideas to help Cassidy relieve some stress, I'm your guy," I teased him.

"Shut the hell up. I'm trying to be mad at you," he said as a little smile crept onto his face.

◊◊◊

After practice, everyone seemed to be hanging around. I then saw a bunch of people following Jeff and Cassidy to the baseball field. The little shit had told on me. I looked for an escape route and found my teammates had blocked my exit. I gave them a look.

"Nice," I hissed at them.

Cassidy stomped up and was pissed. This didn't look good.

"I hear you made my boyfriend bleed. You do know I believe in an eye for an eye. I think you need to bleed," Cassidy proclaimed.

"Hang on; I didn't do anything to Jeff. I actually helped him."

Cassidy turned to Jeff. It sounded like he hadn't told her the whole story.

"You knew that cat was evil," he started.

"Whoa, you've heard plenty of stories about the cat from hell."

Cassidy was trying to decide what to do. I thought I might be able to head things off before she chose to hurt me.

"I'm a lover, not a fighter," I told her and waggled my eyebrows.

What's the point in being a movie star-slash-model if you can't get a girl to keep from kicking your butt by flirting with her? Cassidy grabbed my thumb.

"Pitching hand! Pitching hand!" I said as I went to my knees.

"Give me your other hand," she ordered.

I'm no dummy, so I held it out for her so she could get it in the same hold as she released my right hand. Once she had me on my knees, she leaned down and kissed me. She turned to Jeff.

"Happy?" she asked.

"He didn't cry," Jeff complained.

I stuck my tongue out at him and everyone laughed. Cassidy set me free and explained if I ever let Jeff get hurt again, she'd be back. I was careful not to make any remarks about my best friend being a wuss. I would save that for when he and I were playing Call of Duty. I'd probably have to off him. I know it's not right to kill a teammate, but sometimes you just have to do what you have to do. I was sure Alan would agree. He might even help me kill Jeff six or seven times. 'Friendly fire' sometimes happened.

◊◊◊

Unbelievable! I have never seen a cat suck up to anyone as much as Precious did when Brit came home with me from baseball practice. You have never heard such pitiful meowing as when she saw her mistress come through the back door.

"How did you get the leash on her?" Brock asked, leaning in so only his brother and I could hear.

"I had Jeff let her cling to his back," I told them as if I were parting with some pearl of wisdom.

Bryan looked at Brock and began to chuckle.

"Think again, little brother. I'm not getting anywhere near Precious after the day she's had. She'd tear me to shreds," Brock said and started to back up.

I looked up in time to see Brit open the crate. I swear the cat's eyes glowed red as she stared me down. Even Duke was smart enough to find something else to do at that moment. I about kicked Bryan's ass as he used me as a human shield. Precious had the big tough brothers fearing for their lives.

"Come to mama, baby," Brit said as she picked up her cat.

As she walked out the back door, Precious hissed and swatted at me.

"That's right, protect mama from the bad man," Brit cooed.

I was looking for my protection. He was peeking around the side of the house behind me. I guess he figured if I got maimed, he'd have a head start.

The triplets had just gotten home and I got a big grin on my face when I heard a muffled squeal and then, "Get her off me." I hoped it was Bryan who got to play with Brit's kitty. The whole human-shield thing irritated me. Maybe I could get him to play Call of Duty with Jeff, Alan and me later. A little 'friendly fire' would do him some good.

◊◊◊

Tuesday April 28

When I got to school, I was looking for some people. My plan for killing Jeff and Bryan had been an epic fail. Jeff was a very smart guy, so I should have figured he knew what I was going to do. I hadn't counted on Bryan and Brock turning on me also. I was okay with it until Alan set up as a sniper and camped my spawn locations. Those are where you come back to life after you die in the game. It's considered very poor gaming etiquette to camp (wait) for an opponent to come back to life. They're defenseless as they're reborn, and you can kill them over and over again. You can only listen to 'Oops, my bad,' 'Sorry' and 'I

346

thought you were on the other team' so many times. Many games have rules about killing your own teammates that include apologies. Then Alan put together a video clip of me getting wasted in the most entertaining ways. It might have been funny if it was someone else. I did die spectacularly several times.

I got even, though. I logged off. I received more than one inappropriate text calling my manhood into question. I called Ty Wilson, my friend at Washington High, and got his logon. He had played with us several times. They let him join their team for the next game. When we all spawned to start the game, I hosed them all down with my machine gun. I think Ty was in for a rude awakening the next time he logged on to play.

I came storming up to everyone and out of the corner of my eye saw Cassidy talking to Gina. They were lucky she was there.

"You guys suck," I said as my way of saying good morning.

"Bite me, Dawson. You let the cat from hell attack me," Jeff said, still whining about playing with Precious.

"How did you get Ty to kill us all? Did you go whining to him about how unfair we were being?" Alan asked, mimicking my voice.

He made me sound a little shrill. Surely, I hadn't sounded that bad. I wasn't about to tell them Ty gave me his logon. I figured Ty needed to find out the hard way. He'd killed me more than once on purpose. Maybe I started it, but he should have been the bigger man and chalked it up as a learning experience.

"I have a question," Bryan said. "Why in the world did you give Cassidy your other thumb? Couldn't she just have snapped them both off?"

"Ah, you have much to learn," I said, gathering the guys around. I didn't need Cassidy overhearing me. "There were two reasons, well maybe three, as to why I did it. The first was she did have my pitching hand and it was a little uncomfortable. The second was Cassidy is nothing if she isn't honorable, so I knew if I made the offer she would accept it and not take advantage. The third is she's my friend and her dad told her not to hurt me. Finally, Cassidy knows exactly how much pressure I can take before I'm really hurt."

"That was like five reasons," Alan offered helpfully.

"Plus, if David had wanted to get away he could have. Shiggy taught him how to counter that move," Jeff shared.

"Yeah, that works so well," I said as I rolled my eyes. It might work once out of every ten times. The other nine would result in a dislocated thumb. No way would I want that to happen.

The bell rang. I ran over, scooped Cassidy up, and put her on my shoulder. She didn't even squeak. She stole my baseball cap and put it on as I walked into the school.

"What are you doing?" Gina asked.

"She defeated me in combat yesterday. I'm carrying her to her locker as her reward."

Cassidy was doing a royal wave to her subjects as they parted to let us through. All was fun and games until her dad saw us and made me put her down. I was pissed when she scampered off with my baseball cap.

◊◊◊

At lunch, we confirmed that our Alternate Prom was a go. Stacy Clute, Alan's girlfriend, had come up with the name and artwork. Someone had the ingenious plan of doing a hog roast, and the Country Club would provide age-appropriate beverages and side dishes so we could have a sit-down dinner.

We got food from Alicia, the girl who was on the original Prom committee. Her dad owned a hog farm. He agreed to sell us a hog at his price, and he had everything we needed to do a hog roast. Alicia's uncle said he would do the actual cooking of the pig. We just had to provide the beer.

"We've already sold forty tickets and none of you have bought any yet," Alicia told the lunch crew.

It turned out the price for tickets was less than what I'd paid for my Prom tickets. I noticed the tickets specifically said there was no dress code.

"What's this about?" I asked.

"One of the biggest complaints about Prom is people have to get dressed up. Buying a dress is expensive," Stacy said.

"What if they want to get dressed up?" I asked.

"I hope most people do, but for the ones who can't afford it, or don't want to, we want to include them," Gina said.

"I have a question," Mike said. "What if a couple from another school wants to come?"

"I'd say that if we have room, after everyone who wants to go from Lincoln, then it would be fine," Wolf gave his opinion.

"Who wants to come?" I asked.

"I talked to Ty Wilson from Washington. Their prom may get canceled because of what happened."

At their Spring Fling dance, a carload of teens was injured when the driver lost control and it flipped. They'd all been drinking at the dance, and the school board was concerned about their potential liability. It looked like their prom might be canceled this year.

I sat back and let them debate the pros and cons of allowing Washington to share in our dance. I knew before they even began what the answer would be. It all comes down to small-town values. We look out for each other, and the kids from Washington were in need. Gina said the ballroom at the Country Club would seat 300. It was decided to give half the tickets to Washington to sell.

I was just glad I didn't have to organize this. We were lucky to have Dan and Alicia helping. They'd worked on the Prom Committee from the first of the year and knew almost everything we needed and where to get it. What I was happy to see was the confidence everyone seemed to have. Alan, Jeff and Mike had really stepped up. I know for a fact that my best friends Alan and Jeff could not have pulled this off a year ago.

Uncle John had encouraged me to delegate to help build other leaders, and this was a demonstration of what he was talking about. They no longer needed me to hold their hands. They could take projects on and see them to fruition. Uncle John had explained to me that I could only do so much on my own. When I learned to delegate, and through that responsibility helped others grow—well, that's when I could really impact things.

As I sat there, reflecting on what my friends were accomplishing made me realize I had more work to do. This summer we needed to get ready for football next year. My goal was to be a three-time State Champion. Schools would be gunning for us this year, and we'd have to work even harder to meet the challenge. I knew we needed a plan, and also that we needed to get everyone's buy-in, including the coaching staff. I assumed Tim and I would still be captains. Jim would be a senior. I thought he could take Bill's spot as the third captain. I needed to get the three of us together and schedule some time with the coaching staff.

Chapter 18 – Baseball Ends

The baseball coaches had met yesterday and decided I would pitch today and Justin would start in the first game for the State Championship Tournament. If we won, we would play again on Saturday. The good news was the State Tournament was being played at State University. It would be almost like a home game for us.

Tonight, we faced our conference rivals, Eastside. We were pretty sure there wouldn't be any carryover from the hostility during football. There had been a little tussle during basketball this year, but nothing got out of hand. If things got chippie, I could always uncork a fastball into someone's back. I had learned that even with our high-impact shirts, it hurt. It sure would discourage me.

Tonight was senior night, so Bill, Trevor and Lou would be honored. All the parents had also been invited, so we had a nice crowd as I walked down to the bullpen to warm up. Adding to the festive atmosphere, the boosters had set up a hospitality tent and were selling $1 hot dogs. These were the big ones, so you felt you were getting your money's worth.

All the proceeds were going to the Booster Club. They were raising money to buy a couple of JUGS Football Passing Machines. State had two they wanted replaced. Coaches Hope and Diamond had checked them out and found they were in good shape. Mrs. Sullivan had bought them out of her pocket, but the Booster Club insisted on raising some money to help defray her cost.

I made a point to give money to Pam and Mona so if someone wanted a hot dog and didn't have the cash, they could get a couple. I was thinking in terms of our JV team or little kids. I about decided it was time to have a talk with them when I saw them paying for Eastside to get some food. Then I remembered baseball pants weren't designed for carrying a wallet. Plus, the goal was to pay for some equipment, which would help our team.

Personally, I stayed away from eating any hot dogs before the game. I'd found I tended to have a nervous stomach when I was pitching. I was very sure I did not want to throw up in the bullpen. It was going to be a little tense tonight. If we won, we could possibly get the number-one seed in the tournament. The other thing that had me nervous was Tim wasn't catching me tonight. Lou was our backup catcher and a senior. Moose made the call that the seniors would start their last game.

Shiggy called a halt to my loosening up in the bullpen and we all went out and did our pregame drills. I found a good sweat helped me with my pregame jitters, and the new warm-ups helped the whole team get ready. We had made a name for ourselves by scoring on our opponents early. Shiggy seemed to have a knack for getting us focused.

When I got back to the bullpen, I could feel tonight was going to be a good game. I had a good snap on the ball and my pitches all seemed to be working. Moose finally waved me in so I could throw a few off the mound to finish my warm-up.

It was a perfect night for baseball, except for all the mayflies. Each spring we'd be invaded by swarms of the insects. They had a remarkably short life-span, literally only one day as adults. Over the next week or so we'd get a new batch each day. They seemed to congregate near lakes, and Lake of the Woods was only two blocks from the ball field. Seeing the mayflies told me the water was warming up and we could soon try out our jet water board. I couldn't wait to go play with it.

I was finished warming up and had the ball in my glove to start the game. I heard my name called from the stands. I looked around to see who'd yelled my name and saw Tracy's smiling face as she waved at me. I tipped my hat to her and then focused on the first batter.

Since this was Eastside's last game, their coach had decided to play several of his JV players today. I didn't recognize the first batter from the information Alan provided me. I could only assume this was one of those guys. Based on that, I decided to throw him breaking balls. The poor kid had no idea what to do when I threw him a curve, split-finger fastball, and finally a slider.

Everything was going well until their third batter topped a split-finger fastball and essentially did a textbook bunt down the third base line. When Jake saw he wasn't going to throw the guy out, he allowed the ball to roll to see if it would go foul. The Eastside runner decided to try for an extra base. Mike alerted Jake and he easily gunned him down to get us out of the inning.

You know you're having a good first inning when the opposing team has to trot out three pitchers. We batted around twice and were up 13–0 after the first inning. Moose pulled me from the game at that point to save me for the State Tournament. After Eastside batted in the fifth inning, the game was called via the mercy rule. It stated if you were up by ten or more after four innings, you gave the team that was behind a last chance to bat again. In our case, that was the top of the fifth. You then called the game if the leading team was up by ten runs or more. We ended up winning 18–4.

◊◊◊

After the game, I was accosted be a very happy Tracy. I was pleased to see my friend was out of the clinic. What I didn't know was whether she just out on a day pass, or if she was out for good.

"Are you surprised to see me?" she asked.

"I didn't know you'd be here tonight. What's the story?" I asked.

"Dr. Hebert said I was well enough to come home. So you, my friend, are taking me out tonight," she informed me.

"What makes you think that?" I asked.

She just smiled at me. She knew I'd take her out if she asked. Pam came up and hugged her best friend. They went off to talk while I found my family. Duke was being all bouncy, so Mom made me take him out on the field and play Frisbee. I talked Jeff and Mike into playing with us. Duke loved keep-away, and these two were willing to chase him.

We heard a loud whistle and Duke's ears perked up. Dad gave him the hand command to come and he took off like a shot. Dad told me Duke needed to respond to commands regardless of what was going on. I was actually proud that my boy had stopped playing and responded to Dad's command.

Mom and Dad took Duke home. I loaded up the Callahan triplets and went home to take a shower and change. I told Mom on the intercom that I was taking Tracy out to a late dinner. She reminded me it was a school night. When I picked up Tracy, she wanted to go to Monical's. It would be the first place I would've picked if I had been away for a while.

Being that it was a Wednesday night, they weren't busy. Several people who were at the game were there and congratulated me. Tracy just shook her head as almost everyone talked to me.

"Is it me, or are you becoming more popular?" she teased me after we were seated.

"Hey, it is what it is," I joked with her.

"Next it'll be because you're famous and so good-looking that no one can help themselves."

"Tracy, Tracy, Tracy, we both know that *is* the case now," I said, shaking my head.

"I think I was released just in time. Someone needs to take you down a notch or two."

"If anyone could—and I'm not saying it's possible—it would be you," I assured her.

She smiled and then got more serious.

"I sometimes wish I hadn't been crazy, before. I miss you," she told me.

I found myself a little choked up. You can't help but wonder 'what if?' when you're with your first love. Fortunately, I remembered the hurt and heartache I'd gone through after our breakup. It hadn't helped that I was recovering from the avalanche and it was right in the middle of my mom's cancer treatment. I'd worked my way out of all the negative feelings I had for Tracy back then, but I would never willingly allow myself to fall into that trap again.

"I know, but I think right now we both need friends," I said.

"I can tell something's wrong with you. What is it?" she asked.

"You're almost as bad as Tami," I said, giving her high praise. "I put myself out there again and it didn't work out."

"I'm sorry to hear that. Do you want to talk about it?"

"Tracy, do you really want to hear all the gory details of me breaking up with another girl?" I asked.

"No, not really. I have enough crap to deal with. I don't need to deal with yours, too."

"Fair enough. Let's just say I'm not sure if getting serious is in my foreseeable future."

"I disagree. You're a romantic at heart. You crave having someone special in your life," Tracy said, getting too serious.

I couldn't look her in the eye, because she'd hit too close to home. She reached across the table and squeezed my hand. I looked up and she was smiling at me.

"Does this mean you're free to have some fun?" she asked me.

I shook my head at her.

"I think it's too soon," I told her.

"I call bullshit. I think it's *exactly* what you need," she said, as she ran her foot up my calf.

"I call bullshit right back at you! You're just horny."

She giggled and didn't deny it. I was about ninety percent sure we'd be naked within the next hour, but a guy has to play like he's hard to get. Doesn't he?

◊◊◊

Did I ever call it? Tracy waited until we were in the Jeep on the ride to her house before she made her move. I about wrecked when she casually reached over and cupped my package. I was ordered to go to my apartment. She had me exposed by the time we got home. She was ready to mount me in the driveway, but I talked her into waiting until we got inside.

There had never been a question as to whether we were good in the sack. Tracy knows my body too well for it not to be rewarding with her. She's also no shrinking violet. She was always up for new and fun things. I got nervous when she found Harper's strap-on. I calmed down when she wanted to invite Pam over.

This was one of the best sessions we'd ever had. Tracy got me off four times before she let me off the mat. She was right: this was *exactly* what I needed. I now had fantasies about Pam being double-teamed by both of us. I looked forward to making my dreams come true.

It was a good thing I didn't fall asleep afterward. Tracy had to get home. I was sure her parents were keeping a close eye on her.

◊◊◊

356

Friday May 1

Do you remember the phrase, 'I'm glad I'm not *that* guy'? Today I was glad I wasn't Mike. We were up 1–0 and Richwood had a runner at second with two outs for their final at bat. Their pinch hitter hit an easy grounder to Mike and he whiffed. The ball went under his glove. I've played next to Mike for two years and I'd never seen him miss a ground ball like that, even in practice.

The runner at second was off like a shot and easily scored when the ball was finally returned to the infield. The next batter came up and hit a line shot at Mike, who wasn't there. He had broken to the second-base bag, thinking Bert would try and pick off the runner. If Mike had stood still the ball would have hit him the chest, at the very least. Instead, the ball split our outfielders and rolled to the fence, allowing the guy on first to score and win the game.

I could tell Mike was about to cry. He felt like he'd let his team down. I walked up to him and gave him a hug.

"If you cry, I'm going to kick your butt," I told him.

He gave me a shove.

"Dick!"

"Wuss!" I shot back.

I know, it made us sound like we were in middle school, but it made him smirk. I leaned down so I could whisper to him.

"Guess who no longer has to worry about team rules and can get drunk tonight?" I asked.

He got a big grin on his face and we started dancing around. The rest of the team was confused because we looked like we were celebrating when we just lost in the first round of the State Tournament.

"What the hell are you two up to?" Wolf almost growled.

"David said we could get drunk tonight," Mike explained.

"Hell! Yes!" Wolf exclaimed. "Where's the party?"

"I have no idea, call Mona. She'll know where one is," Sammie suggested.

Moose came out and wanted to know what was up.

"What are you bunch of idiots so happy about?!" he demanded.

"Uh, David said ..." Mike started.

"That we should celebrate making it to State for the first time in nine years," I supplied.

"Yeah, right."

I don't think Moose believed us, but we didn't need him mad at us. We still had two years of baseball to play for him, plus he was one of my football coaches. The guys were nodding as though I'd just pronounced the gospel truth that I was a virgin. I needed to give these boys acting lessons.

"Jim, you're in charge of David. Tim, you make sure the rest of the team stays out of trouble," Moose ordered.

"Why me? I want to have fun, not watch him all night," Jim moaned.

"Good point," Moose said. "Jeff, you and Cassidy have to watch him too."

I had a big stupid grin on my face that caused the team to laugh at the hound-dog looks Jeff and Jim gave me. I rubbed my hands together. We were going to have so much fun.

◊◊◊

We made it home by four o'clock. Lincoln had drawn the early game and Moose made the executive decision that the team didn't need to go back to school. Mona didn't know of any parties but was able to get Brit to volunteer to have one at the Callahans' house. I knew my apartment would end up getting used, so I was busy packing away anything of value that might get broken.

I heard my downstairs door open and was surprised to see Brit and Precious. She put the cat from hell down and

Precious walked over and lay down by Duke. He opened one eye to see what was going on and went back to sleep. She was a different cat when Brit was around.

"Why isn't she hissing at me?" I asked.

"Because I'm here. Bryan and Brock were mean to her when she was a kitten. She doesn't trust men."

I wish she hadn't told me that. I had little tolerance of anyone who would abuse an animal, and by Precious's reactions, they must have been hard on her. Then again, Precious was mean to everyone. I wondered if she was just evil.

"I hate to ask, but why is she in my apartment?"

"I was hoping you'd let her stay here while we have the party," Brit said hopefully.

"No way, she'll turn into something evil as soon as you leave, and Duke and I will be trying to find her secret hiding place all night."

"Put her in the crate," Brit suggested.

"I'm not falling for that one. *You* put her in the crate," I said, then realized I had just agreed to keep Duke's nemesis for the night.

"Mona said you had to come and help set up," she told me as she put her cat behind bars.

◊◊◊

Mom came home as Bryan and I hauled the Callahans' couch into our garage. Mom looked at us and squinted. I think she tried to read our minds. Bryan broke under her scrutiny.

"David said it was okay," he blurted.

Mom turned her look to me. I just stared at her. Mom decided to go to the Callahans' to see what was going on. Bryan got a panicked look.

"Take a deep breath. It's only my mom," I assured him.

"Dude, it's your mom!"

"She's going to talk to your sister and Mona. We're just the help. Mom will want to talk to the people in charge."

He didn't seem assured, for some reason. I just shrugged and we went back to find Mom talking to all the girls.

"When I was in college, we made a killer garbage-can punch," Mom said, and then gave them the directions on how to make it.

"No alcohol?" Mona asked.

"We put Everclear in it, but …"—Mom paused for dramatic effect—"there will be none in this punch. You're all underage."

"This is going to be the worst party ever," Bryan moaned after my mom went home.

"Don't worry, I'll get rid of my mom and dad," I assured him.

I called Dad.

"Dad, Buddy …" I started.

"What did you do?"

"Nothing, I was hoping you could take Mom out for dinner tonight and maybe dancing afterwards."

"Really, why would I want to do that?" he asked.

"Wow, if you need to ask, I don't know what to say."

He wasn't buying it.

"Come clean, or I'll have your mom get it out of you," he said.

"The Callahans are having a party."

"And?"

"Mom told them no booze."

"So, you want me to take your mother out so she doesn't drop in and bust the party," he deduced.

"I hadn't thought of that, but this could be a side benefit to you spending quality time with the woman who bore you two wonderful boys."

"I don't know. I know how much your mother enjoys her opportunities to make you uncomfortable."

"I'll pay."

"Now we're talking. There's a little bed-and-breakfast over in Crystal Oaks I've wanted to go to."

"You're the best, Dad," I said and hung up.

Mona kissed me on the cheek.

"Nicely done. I need $400."

I gave her a confused look.

"You need to pay for the beer and Everclear," she told me, as if I was mentally challenged.

"And I'm buying because …?"

"It was your idea. Just be happy the Callahans volunteered their house," she said as she held out her hand.

Between Mona and my dad, tonight was going to cost me some serious money. I gave up and handed her the cash. I'd been to several parties Mona was a part of and had never paid to get in. I hoped this covered my party entry fee for a while.

◊◊◊

Bryan and Brock broke out the grill and made hot dogs and hamburgers for everyone who helped set up. Duke had assisted, so he was eating the leftovers. The alcohol finally arrived. They had a couple of sleeves of plastic shot glasses, cases of beer, gallon jugs of orange juice, Jagermeister, Red Bull and Everclear. The beer was warm, so Brock went to get ice. I went to our house and found our large coolers. I also brought over my five-gallon Igloo water dispenser I used for Gatorade. The girls wanted it to make the punch in.

When Brock came back, we loaded the coolers with beer and then dumped ice on them. Mona got the hose, put water in the coolers, and then added salt. She explained they would get the beer colder faster than just dumping ice on top.

Mona then made the punch. She dumped in half a bag of ice and then added equal parts orange juice and Kool-Aid Tropical Punch. Mona added a bottle of Everclear to the mix. I designated myself the taste-tester. It was actually very good. I found punch at parties wasn't very consistent, taste-wise. With this batch, you couldn't taste the alcohol. People would have to be careful or we'd end up with some very drunk party animals.

Mona then went and made pitchers of 8-Balls. This was a 4-to-1 ratio of Red Bull and Jagermeister. She added ice to keep it cold. She gave me a shot to try. I needed to stay far away from Mona tonight or she was going to get me wasted. I had lost my tolerance to alcohol over the past two years and could feel a pleasant buzz coming on after what I'd already drunk. I went into the backyard and ate another hamburger to slow my buzz.

I was relaxing with my hound at my feet when a police officer came out back.

"Hey, Billy, grab a burger and beer and take a load off," I said.

"Sorry, I'm on duty, so no beer," Billy Delaney told me.

Billy and I knew each other through my brother and because he worked security at most of our games. He was a good guy. I wasn't surprised to see him tonight, but it was earlier than I expected. Brit made him up a plate and found him a Coke.

We talked baseball while he ate. He hadn't heard we'd lost today. I told him he should arrest Mike for his bonehead plays. Then he got around to telling why he was here.

"Word gets around, and it looks like there might be a party here tonight with underage drinking."

I looked around and then leaned into him so only he could hear.

"I think it might have already started. You want me to point out the offenders?" I asked him.

"Not really. It's too much paperwork and a waste of time. I'll leave you alone if you work with me."

"Just name it," I told him.

"No drinking and driving, no peeing in the neighbor's bushes, and the music has to be off by one a.m.," he said, counting off with his fingers.

"Can we pee in our own bushes?" I teased him.

"If you do, I'll be back," he said in his best Terminator voice.

"Yes, sir."

"Okay, be safe and have fun," he told me as he left.

Mona and the Callahan triplets all heard him.

"You are now officially in charge of the police at all my parties," Mona said.

The triplets all nodded in agreement.

◊◊◊

I was kicked back, drinking a beer with Jeff, Alan, Mike, Jim and Tim. We were talking about guy stuff when Lily came out with an extra beer. Since there were no seats, she sat on my lap and handed me a new one.

"Thanks," I told her.

She turned in my lap and gave me a serious kiss.

"What was that for?" I asked.

"You owe me pay for doing your website and social media," she teased me.

"I might have to give you a raise."

She wiggled her butt.

"I think you are."

"You're such a slut," Gina said as she sat on Mike's lap.

"Where's my beer?" Mike asked.

"Get your own," Gina told him.

"I think you need to work on her training," Jeff said.

"Don't you start, I know things about you," she threatened.

Jeff and I both looked at Alan. He just shrugged. We all knew he couldn't keep a secret. It only stood to reason that while Gina and Alan were dating, she had wormed some embarrassing stories about Jeff and me out of him. I took her threat seriously and stayed out of it. Tim had no such worries.

"Mike, did you see how David did it? He had a pretty girl bring him a beer and then kiss him like she wanted to have sex with him right here, and she isn't even dating him," Tim said, firing a shot across his bow.

"Shut up," was Mike's snappy comeback.

While all this was going on, Lily had reached behind her and adjusted Mr. Happy. She was wearing a skirt. I slid a hand down and was surprised to find a bare butt. Lily leaned forward to put her beer on the ground. When she did that, she managed to lodge my member between her butt cheeks. I was confused, but Mr. Happy was not.

She leaned back and ground her butt against my rising member. The debate of what made a good girlfriend was swirling around us.

"What are you doing?" I hissed in her ear.

She gave her butt a little wiggle as an answer. I was getting hard in a hurry. I couldn't believe how bad Lily was being. She was always the quiet one. I guess I shouldn't have been surprised she had a kinky side because our first time together I was blindfolded. Her little movements were driving me crazy. I slid my hands onto her stomach and kissed the back of her neck.

"Get a room," Gina said, cutting through the conversation.

I became aware of everyone staring at us. Lily picked that moment to squeeze her butt cheeks along my length, which caused me to let out a little moan.

"See, I told you, you need to train her," Jeff said.

Everyone laughed when Mike flipped him off and Gina turned red. Lily hopped up and grabbed my hand to lead me to my apartment. Jim and Jeff got up. I was confused when they started to follow us. I gave them a hard look.

"Moose said we're supposed to watch you," Jim said with a straight face.

I guess I had a look on my face, because Jeff snapped a picture, to the joy of everyone. I ignored them and let Lily coax me away from my tormentors.

◊◊◊

Duke led us into the apartment and there was big hiss when he hit the top of the stairs. I about ran over Lily as she froze. If you've never heard a bobcat get its hackles up, it can be a little frightening.

"What the hell is that?" she asked.

"Brit's cat," I told her.

"That's no ordinary cat."

"They think she's half bobcat," I said.

"Is it loose?"

"No, the cat's in Duke's crate."

Being assured, she went up the stairs.

"That is the biggest cat I've ever seen," she commented, as the demon spawn locked eyes with me. "Boy, it doesn't like you."

"Nope, let's leave her alone. The last thing I want is for Precious to decide on a jailbreak."

"Precious?" Lily asked.

"I know, right?"

We went into my room.

"Where were we?" I asked as Lily came into my arms.

I realized as I kissed her it had been almost two years to the day since my journey had begun. It was at my party where she'd almost died, and from that I was sent to live with Uncle John for the summer. Since then Lily and I had become good friends. She helped me with all my social media stuff. I had never chased her sexually because we were just friends.

I normally wanted to have a little more than friendship before I slept with a girl, but Lily was different. If she really needed me to scratch her itch, I was more than happy to do it. I had taken her virginity, after all. The last time we'd had sex, she'd teased me to no end while I was blindfolded by Beth during my birthday-week festivities. I wanted to make tonight special for Lily.

We both stripped and I went to the living room. I kept my massage oils in one of the kitchen cabinets. I found one that smelled like lilacs.

"What are you doing?" she asked.

"I'm going to give you a massage."

I took my time and worked my little waif's body into submission. Lily was really horny, so I helped her get off twice before I concentrated on giving her a massage. I was disappointed when she fell asleep on me. Mr. Happy was drooling in anticipation. I threw on shorts and a t-shirt and went back to the party. I found Mona serving shots in the Callahans' kitchen. She looked at me and her eyes got big.

"Oh, shit," she moaned.

I grabbed her behind the neck and kissed her. If she had any doubt about what I wanted, it disappeared at that moment. I think she realized I might take her right there on the table, so she pushed me towards the bathroom. We were lucky it was empty. I dropped my shorts, then grasped her neck again and guided Mona to Mr. Happy. She didn't hesitate in taking me deep into her mouth.

I leaned back against the sink as Mona gave me her best effort. I rewarded her by trying to drown her. I had been on edge for too long to last. Mona got up, spit into the sink, and then rinsed her mouth out. I found a condom in my shorts and put it on.

"Strip," I told Mona.

She did as directed. I picked her up, put her on the edge of the sink, and then returned the favor. Suddenly there was pounding on the door. Mona told them to get lost as she grasped my hair in both her fists. I sucked hard on her lower lips and ran my tongue up and down her slit. Mona grunted in pleasure.

"Ooohfff, Oh hell, Oh Yes, OH SHIT! OH YES!" she wailed as she came.

I helped her off the sink. I had to steady her as her knees threatened to give out. I kissed her and played with her firm breasts. When she was stable, I turned her around and bent her over the sink.

"I'm going to screw you senseless," I warned her.

I slowly pushed into her folds as I grabbed her hips.

"I love this butt," I hissed as I began to do her.

"Oh yes, oh yes," she began to chant.

I reached around and massaged her button as I took her from behind. She felt so good as I pounded her. Mona was just the right amount of slutty. If she had her way, we would be exclusive. Because of that, I tried not to hook up with her very much. When we did, though, it was spectacular. My hips were a blur as I pressed as deeply as I could. Mona had stopped her chant and her head hung down as she absorbed my relentless pounding.

She threw her head back and her chest, neck, and face went flush. I smacked her butt, leaving a large handprint. It was the added sensation she needed to explode all over my member. I could feel my balls boil up and empty themselves.

We both started to giggle when we were done.

"What the hell was that all about?" she asked me.

"I needed to cum. Thank you," I said.

"If you need help again, let me know. I had fun," she told me as we got dressed.

"Well, I could go a couple more rounds," I said.

"Not with me you're not. My kitty is going to be sore for days after that."

"Sorry."

"No, I needed it more than I realized. I just want to recover before we do it again."

We came out of the bathroom and did the walk of shame. Mona's friends grabbed her to get the details. Gina came up to me and took me into the living room to dance. Now that my head was clear, I had a good time. Lily made an appearance before we had to turn off the music and danced with me. We kissed some as we slow-danced, but we both knew the moment had passed. We were back to just being friends.

When the party ended, we had enough designated drivers to get everyone home. I helped Brit, Bryan and Brock clean up. Tim, Jeff, Gina and Mike all stayed, too.

"Where's Cassidy?" I asked Jeff.

He looked sad.

"I think after tomorrow night she's going to break up with me."

"Anything I can do?" I asked.

"No, but thanks for asking."

Being a guy, that was all we needed to say to each other.

◊◊◊

Chapter 19 – Alternate Prom

Duke and I had walked out my back door to run when he darted into the backyard to do his business. I heard the low rumble of him growling, so I decided to go investigate. I found Precious guarding something, something furry.

Oh Dear Lord, she caught one of Duke's squirrels.

You have to understand, there's a sacred bond between dog and squirrel. It's the squirrel's job to torment the dog by bouncing around and then running up trees. The squirrel then twitches its tail and chirps at the dog, heckling it from above. It's the dog's job to kill the little bastards. Duke explained this to me on more than one occasion, as he seemed to chase every one he saw. He was very serious about taking one of them out.

Duke was totally frustrated to see Precious had taken his job away from him. How could a cat catch a squirrel and he couldn't? I was worried we might have to move. The shame of it all! He danced around to indicate I should take the squirrel away from Precious and give it to him. I grabbed him by the collar, took him to the house, and pushed him through the back door. I had started to go to Brit's house so she could deal with her cat when Duke decided to wake the neighborhood with his barking. This was a sure recipe for disaster, as it would wake my parents. I figured the damage was already done, so I hurried over to Brit's and pounded on their back door. Bryan answered.

"Get your sister. Her damned cat has caught a squirrel."

"Why don't you take the little guy away from Precious?" he said with a smirk.

"The same reason you won't: the damned cat is evil."

He went and got Brit. She was in a shorty nightgown and I just stared at her long legs. Her large breasts were swinging free, and I forgot why I was there. I may have even forgotten my name for a moment. Bryan smacked me and told her the problem. I watched in amazement as she walked over to our backyard without a care in the world. I had a bad feeling Precious wasn't going to give up her prize so easily. I liked Brit, except for her taste in pets, so I was worried she might get hurt.

"You want me to get you some garden gloves?"

I was on the receiving end of 'the look' every teenage girl seems to have mastered. I decided standing at the edge of the garage was probably a safe distance. Duke was still losing his shit, and I was torn between quieting him down and the possibility of missing Precious make a believer out of Brit. I heard Mom yelling at Duke to 'Shut the &%@^# up!' Brit had just bent down and her shorty nightgown no longer covered her boy-short underwear when I heard the back door open. My mind locked. At least that was what I would use as my excuse later. Brit had an outstanding butt!

"Don't let …!" died on my lips as Duke crashed out the back door.

Five things seemed to happen at the same time. Duke crashed into Brit, trying to get to the squirrel. Precious saw her mistress about to fall on her, so she jumped to the side. The stunned squirrel looked for an escape route and jumped into the gaping neck of Brit's nightie. Brit let out a scream that could have awakened the dead. My mom charged out to see what was going on. I think she was more pissed than Brit was, if that was even possible.

"Classic!" Brock exclaimed as he caught the action on his phone.

"Did you get that?" I asked.

"Oh, yeah!" Brock confirmed.

Brit rolled around on the ground, which caused the squirrel to get excited. She screamed and Duke barked like crazy because he couldn't see where the squirrel had gone. The neighbor on our other side stuck her head out her back door, so I gave her a little wave. Mom came up and whacked me on the back of the head.

"Go help her," she said with more than a little menace in her voice.

I figured I should get my mutt under control, so I did a loud whistle and then gave him the 'come' command. Hey, it worked for Dad. Duke ignored me until Mom stomped her foot.

"You get over here right now!" she ordered, which had Duke come and sit next to her.

I would have to learn that trick.

Brit finally got smart and ripped her nightie off. This caused me to have another brain cramp as I admired her gorgeous breasts. The only flaw was there was a squirrel stuck between them. Brit did the only logical thing: she jerked the fuzzy rat from between her breasts and flung him as far away from her as she could. Unfortunately, for Mom, he landed on Mom's head.

The stress was too much for Duke. He made a mighty leap and tried to remove the squirrel from Mom's hair. The squirrel, seeing its demise just moments away, made a jump I still can't believe! It landed on Bryan's leg, scampered up his back, and soared to safety onto the garage roof. I'd bet I would never see that particular squirrel ever again.

Brit finally came to her senses and realized she was in only her panties. She tried to hide her magnificent breasts while she ran for her house. Duke circled the garage in hopes that the squirrel might fall down to him. Precious casually headed home, now that the fun and games were over. I was going to see if the boys could send me the video when my mom grabbed my ear and marched me into the house.

Dad came downstairs to find me backed up to the wall as Mom waved her finger in my face and explained how Duke and I would move to my uncle's farm for the summer. When Mom finally calmed down enough, Dad asked what had happened. When Mom explained it to him, he broke out laughing. You could tell it was the last thing he wanted to do, but he couldn't help himself. I soon found out Dad was to go to live with Duke and me at Uncle John's farm, too. I didn't look forward to a summer putting in fence posts.

◊◊◊

After I got back from my run, I was looking for something to do away from the house. Then I got a text from Greg.

Jet Water Board!

Hell, yes!

I went and found Dad hiding in the garage and told him our plan. He was scared to go into the house to get a swimsuit. I convinced him we could buy him one on the way. I went upstairs, put on a swimsuit, and got my GoCam so I could video us having fun. I also sent Lily a text to let everyone know what we were going to do. Her tweet arrived a few minutes later.

I hooked up the trailer for the Jet Ski, and Dad and I were soon headed to State to pick up Greg. When we had Greg in the Jeep, we went to the sporting goods store. The water was still cold, so we got some wet-suit tops. Dad bought a swimsuit and wore it out of the store. We were soon at our favorite beach.

It took Greg and me a few minutes to figure out how everything hooked together. You could tell how much we wanted to use our new toys when Dad was forced to get out the instructions. It was good they had big pictures, or I think my brother would have been lost. Both Greg and I were pissed when Dad called first dibs. It was decided I would show Dad what to do and Greg was put in charge of driving the Jet Ski. I put the GoCam on Dad's head and showed him how to use the controls for the jet water board.

He was seated on the edge of the dock when he fired it up. When he felt comfortable, he stood up from the dock and began to float over the water. He had a blast as he hovered next to the dock. I told him to lean forward, which caused him to start to move, and he began to get the hang of it. Greg did his job of following him around. The hose from the Jet Ski to the jet water board was only forty feet long. Dad took a turn around the lake, then came back, got to the edge of the dock, and sat down. He never got wet.

I took the GoCam off of him and grabbed my phone so I could upload the video. While I did that, Greg took his turn. I wished I'd left the video running because Greg was in the water more than he was hovering above it. I finally got it uploaded to my Dropbox account and sent Lily a text to let her know it was there. I'd gotten her some video editing software. She liked playing with videos and she'd make it look like it was professionally done, if she had the time. I expected this would just be a quick upload to my YouTube page and then she would tweet it out.

People started to show up when it was my turn. I figured I needed to show off. I gently hovered out deep enough to ensure I wouldn't crash into the bottom of the lake if something went wrong, and then switched to the back jet. I let the nose of the board dip and skimmed the top of the water. Then I tipped the nose up and went almost straight up. I tucked tightly and put it into a spin. I hadn't tucked tight enough and went flying into the water as I was ripped off the board by the centrifugal force generated from the tight corkscrew action.

Of course, I had to try it again, and again, and again, until I got it right. When I finally came back in, Dad had a line wanting to go next. Mike was the lucky candidate. I have to say he had some moves I was going to have to try.

Pam put us all to shame. I had no idea she had skateboard skills she'd brought with her from California. She could make the jet water board dance. I made sure I had the GoCam recording as I was operating the trailing Jet Ski. It wasn't anything pervy; the video was shot as a service to young men everywhere. Who wouldn't want to see a California surfer girl in a bikini doing sick tricks on a jet water board? When we got back, I traded with Dad and it was now Cassidy's turn.

While she went, I uploaded the video of Pam. I sent it to Sandy Range. Ten minutes later, I got a call from Sandy.

"Two things," she started, without saying hi. "The first is Devin is green with envy. The second is, please have the girl in the video sign a contract and release. We want to use her to make an ad. We also need to know who shot the video."

"Yours truly," I told her.

"I love you. It makes it so much easier with you being the videographer. Now get to work. I need everything signed today," she said and then hung up.

I found Pam while she talked to Mike and Wolf.

"You want to make some money?" I asked her.

"Don't trust him," Wolf warned.

"I heard you fell for that line," Mike said to Wolf.

"Yeah, and now I'm his handyman and gardener."

I showed them the video and told Pam what Sandy offered. She called her parents so they could sign the contract. They showed up just before Kendal.

"David, what have you been up to?" Kendal accused me.

"Making you money," I shot back in our familiar banter.

"I want to see the video," Cal, Pam's dad, said.

I showed it to everyone. He quickly signed the contract and went to get into line for his turn. His wife wasn't happy when he came back soaking wet with a smile permanently plastered on his face. He made me promise to tell him the next time we were going to use our new toy. I had a sneaking suspicion that in his mind he'd already spent the check from Pam's video on his own jet water board.

◊◊◊

One the way home, I got a text from Angie to let me know my date for tonight was at my house. Angie and Greg planned to spend the night. Mom had agreed to watch the kids for them so they could go out. When we got home, Mom was now talking to us, much to Dad's relief. I looked around for Sarah but didn't see her. Angie found me.

"She's in your apartment."

Maybe she wanted to fool around before the dance. I hurried out the back door, with Duke trailing me. He bounded up the stairs to my apartment ahead of me. I came to the top of the stairs and froze. Sitting in my recliner was Harper. Duke didn't hesitate to say hi. Of course; he liked everyone. I edged up the last step and we looked at each other. She smiled at me as I walked into my bedroom and went to take a shower.

I needed to get the lake water off me and also needed a moment to think. What did I really think of Harper? Why was she here? I thought I'd made it clear I wasn't the sharing type. The only way I was ever going to figure this out was to go out and face her. I still cared for her enough to do that.

I put on sweats and walked back into the living room. I put water on to boil because I wanted some tea to warm up with.

"Want a cup of tea?" I asked her.

"Yes, that would be nice."

She waited me out as I cleaned up the kitchen while the water boiled. I opened a box of loose-leaf rooibos tea. It was a nutty herbal tea made from the South African red bush plant. The leaves were sometimes referred to as 'red tea.' I liked it because it was different and caffeine-free. The trick to making it was to bring the water to a boil and then steep the tea for five to six minutes. If you went much longer, it became bitter.

"Are you hungry? Would you like a snack with tea?" I asked.

"If it wouldn't be too much trouble."

When I was in England, we had either cakes or what they called biscuits. I would call them cookies. I had a bag of Oreo cookies because every once in a while, I craved them. I think my mom got into my stash more than I did. I checked and she'd left me half a bag. She was pretty good about replacing them if she ate them all.

I tried to keep busy because I couldn't seem to come up with what I wanted to say to Harper. I finally was done preparing the snack and tea. I turned the coffee table into a dining table and then brought over the china teapot and cookies. Harper smirked when she saw our snack. I had seen her attack chocolate, so I knew she'd like what I brought. I poured us each a cup of tea.

Harper sampled the tea and seemed to like it.

"I wanted to come visit you to give you a chance to reconsider breaking up with me," Harper began.

I looked up to see if she was messing with me, but her face was unreadable. Could she be serious with this approach? I had to give her credit for not telling me how sorry she was. I would have shut her down and kicked her out if she'd pulled that. I wondered if Tami had coached her. Harper wasn't rushing me. She allowed me to consider what she was telling me.

How did I feel about Harper? I'd made an effort to seek her out and ask her to be my girlfriend. The last girl I had done that with was Nancy. I normally went with the flow and let girls come to me. Harper was different. She'd intrigued me from the moment I met her. I knew she had a boyfriend, and yet had hit on her shamelessly. For Harper, I had broken one of Dawson's Rules: thou shall not be with girls who are with other guys.

"I thought *you* broke up with *me* when you decided to spend time with Alex instead of me," I said.

My comment seemed to piss her off and she took a moment to collect herself.

"Alex was a mistake."

The light bulb came on, and it made me a little sad.

"Let me tell you a story; you tell me when I get it wrong. Alex has always run with only the best people. He always seemed somehow unattainable when you were growing up," I said, then paused to see if I was on track. "There were times when you'd find yourself alone with Alex. You found he was charming and seemed so different than he was when he was with his group. Alex is from generational wealth. His father is either a lawyer or banker."

"Investment banker," Harper supplied.

"His mother does charity work. Your family's money is relatively new, only going back to your grandfather. Your mother's in politics and your father's in construction and investments. You'd never be a fit, but you and Alex were attracted to each other."

Harper looked away from me. I waited. I poured us both another cup of tea. She finally looked at me before I continued.

"Alex is a fool. He has no idea what you're made of. You have an inner strength which could have stood up to the pressure and eventually had you accepted. He was too weak to see it in you."

She looked me in the eye.

"No, I was the fool. Let me tell *you* a story."

She gave me a look that seemed to delve into my soul.

"You're one of the few special ones. You transcend social status. I've watched you grow into being more confident in yourself. You once said to Tami she would never think you were good enough. You're comfortable talking to the least of us and the mightiest among us. Even

Tami knows you're good enough. Every girl at Wesleyan was envious when they heard we were dating, Jennie Wesleyan most of all.

"You're not normal, in a good way. I've watched you walk into a room and every head will turn. It's not because you're attractive. It's because you give off a vibe of confidence and authority. What amazes me is you don't even notice. If Alex had whatever it is you have, he'd be strutting around like the cock of the walk. I guess what I'm saying is you'll never have to worry about fitting in. You described my inner fears and insecurities perfectly. I have a feeling the more I'm around you, the less I'll worry about them.

"You're right, Alex played me. He's not near the man you are, or will become. I'd forgotten what Jennie Wesleyan did to you. Only you would understand Alex and his thinking. I had a blind spot for him. With years of growing up, working to find the right guy, Alex was always put up as the ideal mate. What I didn't realize was I had the right guy, and I let him get away."

She seemed to go deep into thought. My tea was forgotten as I stared at a spot on the wall. Always before, my emotions overwhelmed me. Everything was either black or white. Harper flirted with another guy; she had to go. Tami took her relationship with Trevor to the next level; Tami had to go. I know I talked a lot about trying to stay friends, but deep down I knew it was over. Why didn't I feel that way with Harper now?

Was I, God forbid, growing up? Or could it be I was just so numb I no longer cared?

It seemed like trust was my biggest hurdle—with *every* girl. When the trust was broken, it was the beginning of the end for me. Could any girl ever live up to my high ideal? Wouldn't there always be a time when something would be said or done to break our trust?

Trust was a two-way street. I needed to talk to Harper about my dirty little secret.

"Before we go any further, I need to tell you about myself. I'm not like other guys. My uncle tells me I'm an Alpha Male. I'm not sure I completely believe him, or if it just helps justify how I'm wired. Let me give you an example to help explain it. Answer me two questions. While you were my girlfriend, how many girls do you think I slept with, without your knowledge? Next, since we broke up, how many girls would you guess I slept with?"

She cocked her head. She was with me when I was given blowjobs by three sorority sisters and she watched as I had sex with one.

"I never once thought you were sleeping around on me."

"Correct."

"Since the breakup, I would guess one at the most."

I shook my head.

"Four."

I let it sink in.

"Harper, I was trading fidelity for affection. When I was happiest, I had three very special friends. I loved them all, and they knew I was with all of them. My only rule was they had to be faithful to me. I really tried to be just with you. I'm not sure I'm ready to make that kind of commitment, at my age. I know someday I will, but I can't see it being anytime soon.

"I'd love to date you. I may even love you. What I can't handle, though, is if you plan on dating other guys. I told you I would kick Alex's ass, and I meant it."

"Is this part of your being an Alpha Male?" she asked.

"That, and leadership stuff, and a few other things. Basically, you're supposed to be my sex slave, while I can do whatever the hell I want," I said with a straight face.

"What does your mom think about your plan to have a harem of sex slaves?"

"She's okay with it. She went through it all before with my brother."

"Oh, really? So what would the whole sex-slave thing entail?"

"Let me think. Let's say we were in line for a movie. No, that wouldn't work; you're with me, and we would never need to wait in line. But for argument's sake, let's assume they were idiots and didn't know who I was. I might see a pretty girl and get aroused. I would expect you to go fetch the girl and we have a hot threesome."

"That's all?" she asked.

"Oh, Oh! An alternative would be you go down on me while we wait in line," I said with a big grin.

"So I'd be in charge of finding you other women and giving you blowjobs on demand?" she asked as she crossed her arms over her chest.

I didn't like her body language.

"If you were a good little sex slave, there'd be rewards."

She leaned forward in her chair.

"What kind of rewards?"

"I'd allow you to give me blowjobs and find me hot women," I said with a firm nod of my head.

She burst out laughing and tackled me. I found myself pinned to the couch as she kissed me.

"I suppose you want to reward me right now?" she asked.

"Yes, I think we could start your training right now."

"You're not happy with how I give blowjobs?" Harper asked in disbelief.

"Practice, practice, practice," I encouraged her.

She raised her eyebrows and I pointed to the bulge in my sweats. I made Mr. Happy twitch, which made her giggle. I had a dancing snake in my pants. Harper made me spread my legs as she went to her knees in front of me. She grasped the waistband of my sweats and pulled them down enough so they hooked under my balls. She grasped me at the base and waved my member around.

She used her tongue to bathe my shaft to get it wet. She then flicked her tongue back and forth around the crown. Harper took about a third of my length into her mouth and sucked. I let out a little groan. She began to bob up and down my member as she used her right hand to stroke me. Her actions were to get me off, not to make this last.

I was wise to Harper's plans. I was much more compliant once I had gotten off. I expected we'd have our real talk once she had me in the mood to do whatever she wanted. Women had done this for ages. Greg confessed to me this was the reason Angie wore the pants in their household. He said he knew she wanted something when they had special sex. He just wished she wanted more things. I never asked what he meant by 'special.'

Harper knew me well enough to know when I was going to go over the edge. I think it was the way I moaned and tried to grasp her head so I could take control. Both of those actions might have given her a clue. She shocked me when she slammed down and took me to the root. I think my eyes rolled up in the back of my head as I unloaded. Harper kept me buried in her throat until I finally stopped. I slumped back and closed my eyes. I felt a little dizzy.

She waited until I opened my eyes and smiled at her.

"We need to talk," were her first words to me.

I just nodded.

"First of all, I really hope you know you're full of shit about public blowjobs and me fetching you women."

"A guy can dream, can't he?" I asked.

"I'm not on board for anything like that. If you keep leading me astray, as my momma says, I might eventually be up for some of that stuff."

"Harper, what I was trying to tell you is I find myself enjoying wilder things. I'm not going to lie to you about anything. I was feeling sorry for myself when we started dating. What I missed from having my friends around was the tenderness of a loving relationship. I see what my brother has now that he's married. I also see him struggle at times. Not because he doesn't love Angie, but because he was used to dating different girls.

"The difference between Greg and me is he was a serial dater. He went out with one girl at a time for four to eight weeks. I, on the other hand, can't give a girl up once I bond with her."

"What happened with you and Tami?" she asked.

I stopped and thought for a moment. I came to the discovery it was okay to talk about it with Harper.

"Tami held a special place in my heart," I began.

"You said 'held'?" Harper inquired.

I bit my lower lip.

"I guess I did," I said, and wondered what it meant for us when she came back in a few weeks. "Anyway, we were best friends since first grade. You never saw one of us without the other. Everyone assumed we would live happily ever after."

"What happened?"

I felt my chest tighten as I remembered the slow disintegration of our friendship.

"When we were younger, I wasn't nearly as confident as I am now. Tami helped me grow up. I think we thought it was normal for her basically to run my life because someday we were going to marry and have kids. However, I was holding her back. As a matter of fact, we were holding each other back. We were making decisions about our lives based on what was best for the other, rather than what was best for each of us," I said and then paused.

"Tami wants to be a doctor. I have no doubt she'll be one of the best. When she went to Wesleyan, it was the first time we were separated. No, I take that back. My being sent to my uncle's farm was the first time we were separated.

With me out of the picture, she had the courage to go to Wesleyan."

I got up and paced around. What really caused us to drift apart?

"People much older and wiser than us have had difficulties holding together long-distance relationships. I guess it's not a surprise we weren't able to make it work. Two things finally did us in. The first was Tami's need to be involved in all phases of my life. It wasn't working. She couldn't pull it off from long distance.

"The second was she needed to experience life. I couldn't handle her dating other guys. I had to pull away, or I was going to kill someone. You have no idea how close I came to flying over to the UK and ending Simon's miserable life."

Our eyes locked.

"Harper, you need to know this is the one thing which is nonnegotiable with me. I will not share you with other guys if you expect me to be around."

"And yet you have no problem sleeping around?" Harper said.

"I've come to grips with it. I'm not ashamed of who I am. I know in my heart, once I find the woman who's going to be my one-and-only, the mother of our children, my soul mate, I will never stray. I don't see it happening anytime soon. My best guess would be when I settle down after college."

"So, what happens when Tami comes back?"

Here was what had alarmed Harper. I gave my head a little shake.

"I have no idea. I'm not even sure we'll be friends. I'm sure it'll never be what it was; at least, not now. Tami and I need to lead our own lives."

"So, there's no chance you'll dump me and she'll swoop in and take you off the market?"

I chuckled to myself. Not even in my wildest fantasy did I see it happening like that. I would always love Tami. What was that stupid saying? If you loved something, you needed to set it free. If it was meant to be, it would come back to you. I felt my heart break all over again at the memory of setting Tami free. I was afraid I would never get over her. I felt a tear leak out of the corner of my eye and come to rest on my cheek.

Harper reached over and brushed it off. She wrapped me in her arms. She knew where things stood. I didn't need to confirm her fears. What was it they say about the best-laid plans? God takes one look at them and then laughs. They also said God won't give you more than you can handle. I hoped they were right.

◊◊◊

Sarah showed up and found Harper just holding me. She gave us a curious look.

"Are you still taking me to the dance?" she asked.

I held out my arms and she joined us on the couch. I gave her a kiss.

"I needed to fix things with David," Harper explained.

"Are you two …?"

"Friends," Harper furnished.

Sarah was a questioner. I needed to slow her down before she had a meltdown. I pulled her to me and gave her a kiss with some serious heat.

"Better?" I asked when we finally stopped kissing.

"Yes, much," she agreed, and then turned to Harper. "What are your plans?"

"I'm going back to school. I needed to clear the air with David."

"What does 'friends' mean?" Sarah asked.

I reach over and pulled Harper into a kiss similar to the one I'd just given Sarah. Sarah smiled when I finally let Harper go.

384

"I see," was all she said.

I pulled them both close to me and we talked about other stuff.

◊◊◊

We walked into the ballroom at the Dunn's Country Club and the place went quiet. Sarah was wearing a Vera Wang black cocktail dress that looked like it was made for her. I had a little smile on my face when I saw my friends with their mouths open as they stared at the vision I had on my arm. They had all met Sarah before, but she'd been in jeans and a sweatshirt. This was Sarah in full model mode, with evening makeup and her hair pulled up so you got the full view of her elegant neck.

I was in my Tommy Hilfiger tuxedo, which made the perfect backdrop for Sarah's entrance. She walked in with her head held high, using her 'runway strut' as she held onto my arm. She had mastered the model's expression of the thousand-yard stare. She knew all eyes were on her. Then she giggled, and I think every guy in the place fell in love with her at that moment. She was no longer the unattainable beauty. She was now a sexy teenage girl who didn't take herself too seriously.

Sarah looked at me and I smiled.

"Now that was an entrance, my lady," I assured her.

"Introduce me to everyone," she commanded.

She had seen me work a room at Wesleyan. She went up a couple of points in my estimation by suggesting we make the rounds. I was eager to see my friends from Washington. As we walked around, it was apparent people had taken the lax dress code seriously. There were guys in everything from jeans and t-shirts to tuxedos. Everyone had a smile on their face and seemed to be having a good time.

Mike and Gina had saved us seats. Ty and Isaac joined us with their dates. I hadn't seen Bill, Trevor, or Lou.

Come to think of it, Mona, Kim and Sammie were 'missing in action,' also. I asked Mike about it.

"They all went to Prom since the guys are seniors. Rumor has it Bill will be Prom King. He said once they're done they'll come over here and join us."

I turned my attention to my Washington friends.

"So Ty, what are you going to do now that Isaac and the rest of your team are graduating?" I asked.

"I'm trying to talk my parents into moving here."

I looked at him and he was serious. My mind raced with the possibilities. I had been a little worried we wouldn't be able to make up the offense Bill was taking with him to USC. I sure hoped he wasn't kidding.

"If you need us to help you pack, let me know," I told him.

"Washington's fans would kill him if he left," Isaac complained.

I waved him off.

"They'd get to see him play when we play you guys," Mike said.

I think this was the first Ty's date had heard of his plans. They went off to talk, so we turned our attention to Isaac.

"Where are you going to college?" Mike asked Isaac.

Isaac was one of the better quarterbacks we had faced last year. The only one I would rate better was the kid who had a scholarship to East Carolina for college.

"I'm going to State as a preferred walk-on. They told me I had a roster spot and would be able to practice with the team. If I show them what I can do, they said they'd work to get me a scholarship," Isaac said.

"When are you going?" I asked.

"Not until fall. I need to work to make spending money, so I decided to skip summer school. I'm close enough to go lift and work with the team during off-season workouts. Everyone seems to be very nice and I can't wait to get started," Isaac said.

It was announced the buffet was now open. The country club had a system where they only sent one or two tables at a time. I was glad because it made it much easier. They had ended up cooking three hogs to feed this group. Sarah had never been to a pig roast. She was impressed at how tender the meat was. I had her take some crackling to get the full experience. Sarah was appalled by the side-dish choices. It wasn't model food! There were a variety of rolls, baked beans, mac and cheese, coleslaw, and baked potatoes. I assured her we would dance off the calories.

After dinner, the DJ started, and I pulled Sarah onto the dance floor. I knew she could dance from when we'd hit the nightclubs in New York last summer. I still couldn't believe they'd let us in since we were all underage; but when you walk up with five models in provocative outfits, bouncers find a way to allow you entrance. This was especially true when we would come back for a second or third time. They knew we weren't drinking alcohol and the girls would all dance with guys at the club. We could have all gotten blitzed from all the drinks single men sent to our table. We made a point to give them away to cute girls. This was a win-win for me: I got to dance with Sarah and the rest of the models *and* with all the other girls we attracted with free drinks.

I was glad to see Jeff and Alan join us on the dance floor. They both had learned their lesson about not wanting to dance. We soon had the dance floor full. Everyone wanted to dance with Sarah, which gave me a chance to dance with all my friends. Every once in a while, I would go rescue her when she looked like she needed a break.

After one of the DJ's breaks, I looked for a new dance partner and spotted the Callahan triplets sitting together. Bryan and Brock had Brit bracketed, and it was obvious by her scowl they had scared off potential dance partners.

"Which one is your date, or is it both of them?" I asked.

Brit's head snapped around and Bryan and Brock blushed. I don't think they realized it looked like they'd brought their sister to Prom. I held out my hand and Brit took it. She saw my eyes were on her breasts so she punched me in the chest. I just smiled at her as we walked onto the dance floor.

"When are your brothers going to let you start dating?" I asked, and pulled her in close since it was a slow song.

"Those idiots have no say as to when I can date. If they keep it up, I might have to do something drastic."

"Do you need any suggestions?" I offered.

"I can handle those two."

I believed her. I made a point of rubbing up against her chest. She blushed but didn't push me away. Once I got her on the dance floor, I don't think she ever left. I was proud of Yuri for cutting in on me when the song ended.

Bill showed up with our missing friends; as expected, he'd won Prom King. He told us one of the ass-hats was having a post-Prom party and we were all invited.

Overall, the Alternate Prom was a success. I had expected some problems when we invited Washington, but for the most part it went well. Of course, you can't have over three hundred teens and not have some nonsense. The good news was that nothing escalated and the police were never called.

◊◊◊

Sarah and I made a quick stop at home to change into jeans and polo shirts. I swear I hadn't planned to match her, but we both picked Jade clothes that happened to match. I remember seeing pictures of my grandparents from the seventies when they wore matching sweat suits. I burst out laughing when she appeared wearing the same outfit as me. I wasn't laughing when she told me I couldn't go change.

I stuck my head into the kitchen and told Mom we were off to a party and wouldn't be home until late. She wanted to take blackmail pictures, but I hustled Sarah out before Mom could collect her evidence.

The party was located at a farm quite a ways out of town. I hoped people decided to spend the night if they were drinking, since a long stretch of the journey was through the woods on a narrow dirt road. When we finally arrived, Cassidy and Jeff were waiting for us.

"Evening, Good-looking," Cassidy said as she hugged me.

I looked at Jeff and he showed me they'd been drinking, which put Cassidy in a flirty mood.

"How you doing, Sexy?" I asked her.

"Jeff, David thinks I'm sexy."

"Come on before you and David do something you'll regret tomorrow," Jeff said as he hugged her.

"Yeah, come on before you do something," Sarah said, tugging me towards the party.

Jeff and Cassidy followed us in to get a beer. We had just gotten our first when Tommy Cox came into the room. He was obviously drunk and had a nasty sneer on his face.

"Dawson, I'm gonna kick your ass!" he said as he started towards me.

Cassidy, my little ninja, put him in a chokehold. Tommy was out in seconds. I had to chuckle when no one even checked on him. More than one person seemed to 'accidentally' spill their beer on his supine body. Tommy came around and found he had a very wet crotch.

"Dang it, I pissed myself," he slurred.

Tommy took off for the restroom. Everyone enjoyed Lincoln's least favorite student getting a little payback.

I was happy to see Pam and Tracy show up. Tracy seemed happy, which made me smile. I hoped she was on the mend. Pam was put in charge of music and I pulled

Sarah out to dance with me. I wasn't sharing her anymore tonight.

As the night wore on, people started to get drunk. I only had two beers, but Sarah was feeling no pain. She sent me to get her another beer. I went to the kitchen where Tommy was seated in a chair, almost out of it. Pam and Tracy followed me in. As I filled Sarah's cup, I heard Pam and Tracy yelp as Tommy grabbed them each around the waist and sat them on his knees.

"Dawson, you're so stupid. You have two of the best-looking girls in school with the hots for you and you ignore them. I'm going to show them what a real man is," Tommy said.

"Let go of me!" Tracy said as she tried to struggle loose.

Tommy had a firm grip on them as I tried to figure out the best way to get them free. I thought about just punching him, but he wasn't hurting the girls, yet.

"You think you're all that! What say you, ladies? You ready to learn what a real man is all about?" Tommy asked.

I think it would have been more impressive if he hadn't suddenly projectile vomited on both girls. It looked like a fire hydrant was suddenly opened and he sprayed their jeans down. What is it about corn? Does it ever digest? There was no holding them now. The look of horror on the girls' faces was priceless. If you ever want to get a crowd to step back, puke.

Poor Tommy had no idea what hit him. It was like the girls came to the same conclusion at the same moment: they were going to mess him up. There was a whirlwind of slaps and punches. Tommy did the only sensible thing he'd done all night and tried to cover up. He stood up, which was a mistake. Pam and Tracy were both cheerleaders. They could both kick so their toes ended up above their heads. I'm not sure who kicked him in the nuts, but it sure had an effect!

Tommy slumped down and started to eject the rest of the beer from his gut. I watched in horror as Tracy pulled out her key chain. I remember yelling '*NO!*' but she was not to be dissuaded. She sprayed Tommy with her pepper spray.

Tommy rolled around on the floor and tried to decide which body part he needed to protect, his face or his nuts. Pam and Tracy were not backing off. Pam tried to kick him in the nuts, and Tracy would spray him every time he pulled his hands away from his face.

As soon as the pepper spray began to drift through the kitchen, people exited the house as fast as they could. I have no idea why, but I probably saved Tommy's life. I scooped up his two attackers and hauled them out the back door. Tommy was a jerk, and if you asked almost anyone, he deserved everything the girls dished out. I was afraid it would end up going too far and Pam and Tracy would get into trouble.

None of the three of us was happy when we made it out of the pepper-spray bomb area. They were both beating on me to let them go and allow them to finish him off. I now had Tommy's puke on my jeans, too.

"Enough!" I finally said.

"I hate that S.O.B.!" Pam screamed.

Tracy actually growled at me.

Brad Hope came storming up with a couple of his ass-hat buddies. Brad and I had forged an uneasy truce over the last year, but we still didn't like each other.

"You're not treating our friend like that!" Brad yelled at the girls.

I pulled them behind me and faced Brad. I dropped down into my stance.

"DAVID, NO!" Cassidy screamed.

She ran up to separate her brother and me. I had a deep desire to kick his ass. Ever since he'd moved here, he'd been a pain in my butt. I owed him payback for far more than I could list. I'd always tried to take the high road and do the right thing, but Brad and his bunch of ass-hats had gotten on my last nerve. I was not in a very forgiving mood at the moment. My only problem was Cassidy. I owed her, and I couldn't turn my back on my obligation for what she'd done. She had gotten me and the rest of us in shape. She never gave up on us. She was there every day to make us better.

"Stay out of this!" Brad yelled at his sister as he slapped her.

There was stunned silence. You could see Cassidy's heart break. Her big brother had just slapped her. I hated to see the innocence robbed from my friend. I looked at Cassidy as she turned to me. She gave me a little head-nod. She wasn't going to protect her big brother from his idiocy.

Brad assumed a fighting stance and bounced on his toes. Cassidy had taught me not to hesitate, and if I ever did fight, to end it quickly.

Brad was about to make some stupid taunt when I moved, using the front kick Cassidy had taught me. I reached out with my lead foot and hooked his front calf, causing him to stumble towards me. I continued in one fluid motion and kicked up, catching his chin with the side of my foot. When I kicked a speed bag, it sounded like a gun had gone off. When I kicked Brad, I felt something give as my foot connected with his head and I pulled back, not finishing the move. Brad dropped like a rock.

Brad's buddies decided it was time to leave. Cassidy and I knew Brad was hurt. I ran over and checked to make sure I hadn't just killed him. I thanked God he was still breathing.

Nothing clears out a teen party faster than the prospect of the police and ambulances showing up. I had firsthand knowledge from when Lily needed help. I just hoped I wasn't in as much trouble as last time.

G. Younger

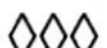

Chapter 20 – Babies

Sunday May 3

I woke up in the same cell I'd occupied almost two years ago. I wasn't happy to be still in my jeans with puke on them. I was told Brad had a dislocated jaw. They had fixed him up and his dad was able to take him home last night. He was lucky it wasn't broken. He would have had some serious issues if that were the case.

Tommy had been treated by the paramedics at the scene. They flushed his eyes. He was lucky Pam hadn't caught him flush in the nuts or he wouldn't ever have children. His balls would just be sore for a few days.

Officer Billy Delaney came and pulled me out of my cell.

"You have a visitor," he told me and took me to an interrogation room.

I was surprised when Coach Hope was waiting for me. I sat down across from him and waited until Billy left the room before talking.

"How's Brad?" I asked.

"He's hungover and complaining about his jaw hurting. I need to know what happened last night. Cassidy won't talk to me and Brad claims he doesn't remember."

I told him about Tommy and breaking up the fight between him, Pam and Tracy. I explained how Brad and three of his buddies looked for a little payback for what happened to Tommy. I admitted to wanting to kick Brad's butt, but Cassidy had stopped me.

"So why didn't you listen to Cassidy?" he asked.

"Brad slapped her."

"Excuse me?" Coach said with a look that told me I was very close to crossing a line.

"Brad told Cassidy to keep out of it and he slapped her. I'm afraid she may not forgive him anytime soon. She took it pretty hard that her big brother would hit her."

"Then what happened?"

"Cassidy let me know she wasn't going to interfere. Brad dropped into a fighting stance and I acted first. I hooked his lead leg to take him off balance and followed up with a front kick to his chin. I felt something give and Brad was out before he hit the ground. I then made sure I hadn't really hurt him."

I waited for Coach to say something.

"I'm not happy with you, but I understand why you did what you did. Frankly, I'm surprised this hasn't happened sooner. I thought you and Brad would come to blows during two-a-days last fall. I think I should also be thankful it was you and not someone else he got in a fight with. If it had been me in your situation, I would have hurt him."

With that, Coach Hope got up and abruptly left. Billy came in after several minutes.

"You're free to go. Brad Hope isn't pressing charges, and we have no desire to mess with this if no one was seriously hurt. Do me a favor and don't make us arrest you again. You're one of the guys I like, and I hate having to do it."

"I'll seriously try. Thanks, Billy."

I came out front to find my dad waiting for me. He gave me a hug and I looked around. I didn't see Mom. Dad saw my worry.

"Your mom is at home taking care of everything."

"What do you mean?" I asked.

"It was either let everyone come to the police station, or have them all wait for you at the house."

◊◊◊

As Dad and I walked into the kitchen, Mom came up and checked me over to make sure I was okay.

"David Allen Dawson, you will not get into any more fights. Is that clear?" Mom said while giving me a hard look.

"Yes, ma'am."

She then took me into her arms and gave me a fierce hug.

"You did good, kid," she whispered in my ear.

She then turned and disappeared into the crowd in our kitchen. Sarah, Pam and Tracy all grabbed me and put me into a group hug. They all seemed to be talking at the same time. I just let it roll over me because I couldn't follow what they were all saying. The funny thing was they all stopped at the same exact time and looked at me expectantly. Thank goodness, Angie was there to translate *teen girl* for me.

"Kiss them, 'stupid boy,'" she ordered.

This I could do. It seemed to make them all happy and they let me go to my apartment to shower and change clothes. I came back and talked to all my friends. Hanging back were Jeff and Cassidy. When I saw Cassidy, I broke off my conversation with Wolf, Jim and Tim, went right to her and gathered her into my arms.

Cassidy broke down and cried in my arms. She would have collapsed if I hadn't been holding her. Jeff gave me a grateful, pleading look, which told me he wasn't sure what to do. I picked her up and took her to the office so we could have some privacy. I wasn't surprised when my mom followed me in and kept everyone else out. I sat down in a big comfy chair with Cassidy wrapped around me. I gently rocked her and stroked her hair. Mom looked on with worry and compassion.

Cassidy finally stopped crying and then looked at me, embarrassed.

"I'm sorry. I shouldn't have done that."

"I think you needed to get it out. I'm always here for you, Baby," I assured her.

"He hit me. My own brother hit me," Cassidy moaned.

"I think David hit him back," Mom said.

Cassidy gave me a dirty look, which had me more than a little concerned.

"Why did you pull your kick?" she accused me.

"Because he's your brother, and someday you'll be glad I didn't kill him," I said with a lopsided grin.

"David, I thought I taught you better than that. Brad is no novice. He could have seriously hurt you. If he wasn't so lax in his training, he could have easily countered your move. If you'd gone full-out, he wouldn't have had a chance. I appreciate you didn't hurt him any worse than you did, but don't ever hold back again. If you're forced to fight, protect yourself," Cassidy lectured me.

I did the one move I knew Cassidy couldn't defend against: I kissed her. I had meant to let her know I cared for her and loved her as a friend. She grabbed the back of my head and took our kiss to the next level. I will forever be grateful Mom was there and cleared her throat, or I would have ruined my friendship with Jeff. Cassidy also seemed to snap out of it, and we both had sheepish looks like we'd been caught doing something we weren't supposed to.

Cassidy hopped off my lap and Mom kicked me out so they could talk. Cassidy needed to work through being hit by her big brother. I was glad Mom stepped in because this was beyond my experience. I couldn't imagine hitting a family member, or a woman for that matter. It just wasn't something that would be tolerated in my family.

◊◊◊

Monday May 11

Finals week! Just the whisper of that phrase caused the brightest of students to tremble. I sat at our lunch table and watched everyone lose their minds. I had never seen such stage fright since I was twelve and had to pee off the back of my uncle's fishing boat while everyone watched. This was ridiculous. We'd all survived finals before. I didn't

397

understand why everyone was suddenly freaked out. Being a man of action, I needed to solve this.

"You're all a bunch of wimps," I politely suggested.

Throwing hard garlic bread was not a polite response to my offer of help. I had to give it to the lunch ladies: they somehow had turned garlic bread into inedible chunks of stinky rock.

"Shut up, freak," Mike said.

"David can't help it he'll get straight A's," Gina said. "He's the star quarterback."

My former friends all seemed to agree with her messed-up logic. I tried to be helpful again.

"As Bill Shakespeare said, 'I must be cruel, only to be kind.' I think he meant you bunch of dumbasses are much ado about nothing. If I have to kick your asses to get your heads on straight, then that's what I'll do. They are only tests of your knowledge. I watched most of you show up and at least pay partial attention to the droning of our teachers."

Where did they find these garlic missiles? Damn, that hurt. I decided a little tough love was needed. I had about thirty garlic rocks scattered around me. It was time this bunch found out what a varsity pitcher could do. I clocked Wolf in the back of the head and in rapid succession Jim, Jeff, Alan, Tim and Cassidy all got a little payback. Rewind! Did I say Cassidy? Shiiiiiiiiit!

Everyone froze as Cassidy realized she now had garlic butter in her hair. She slowly turned to see me jump out of my chair. Everything went like the *Matrix* in super-slow motion. Cassidy screamed to get me, and everyone seemed to have a roll in their hand. Not just my table, either. I mentally made a list of freshmen who would die later today. I did my best to dodge them. I was doing pretty well until I decided to chuck one at Mike. That was when Coach Hope entered the lunchroom.

"Dawson!"

You have never seen such a room full of little angels innocently smiling at my predicament. I glared at them all and turned to Coach Hope.

"Sir, why is it always the guy who retaliates who's the one who gets punished?" I complained.

Everyone started laughing, and Coach led me out into the hall. You could feel the mood change. Everyone seemed to have shifted their focus to having a little fun, which caused them to relax. There were actual smiles around the lunchroom as I was marched out. Coach looked me up and down. He could see garlic butter all over me. He just gave me a dirty look.

"Go shower and change your clothes. You stink," he said as he walked away.

◊◊◊

Today the only final I had was in PE, which was Ballroom Dancing. Our PE teacher wanted to see each of us show her thirty seconds of each dance we'd learned this year. She allowed us to pick our partner to do the dances with. I was a little irritated when all the girls wanted me to be their partner. The guys thought it was funny.

Then the guys went, with me dancing last, of course. I didn't think it was fair the other guys all did theirs at the same time. I don't think we were being graded very hard. Our PE teacher seemed to be happy that there were guys in the class.

When it was my turn, I smiled when Dana joined me. She'd been my partner for the talent show last year and she was one of the best dancers at Lincoln High. Our PE teacher decided to have some fun. She had a tape that flowed from one type of music to another. She started the music and called out what dance she wanted to see. We went through all the ballroom dances and then there was a pause. The music changed to stuff from this century, and Dana and I just went for it.

I was twerking Dana when everyone joined us, even our PE teacher. We spent the last fifteen minutes just having fun. She announced that everyone received an 'A.' I hoped all my finals went that easily.

◊◊◊

As I walked to my next class, I received a text from Angie.

'Need your help now!'

'In school' I sent back.

'Baby!'

I tried to call Mom, Dad and Greg. Every attempt went to voicemail. Alan was in my next class.

"I think Angie's having her baby. Let my teachers know where I went," I said as I ran for the parking lot.

I made it to Greg and Angie's apartment in record time. When I got there, I didn't care where I parked and just pulled in behind a couple of cars. I sprinted to their apartment and found the door locked. I pounded on the door and there was no answer. I had a key, so I used it. I found Angie slumped over in the bathroom, holding her stomach as she had a contraction. There was a puddle of something on the floor. It looked like her water broke.

"What's wrong?" I asked her.

"Help me up. I'm having this baby."

She had trouble standing as another contraction hit her. Something was wrong. The contractions were coming too close together. I picked her up and rushed her to the Jeep.

"No, I'll mess up your seat," she whined.

"You want to have your baby at home?" I asked her.

She still could throw a punch to my arm. I took that punch as a 'no' to my question. The hospital was only six blocks away. I pulled up at the emergency room entrance and ran in.

"I need help!"

A nurse looked at me over the reception desk.

"What's wrong?"

"Angie, she's having her baby and I think something's wrong. I need help," I repeated.

She rushed out with me and checked Angie as she had another contraction. I got really scared when the nurse waved over some paramedics who were coming out the automatic doors. She said something that had them scurrying to get her out of the Jeep and onto a gurney. I was even more scared when they sprinted into the ER with her. I tried to run in with her, but they blocked me from going into the back.

When I went to move my Jeep, I found blood on Angie's seat. I tried everyone again and Mom answered.

"Mom, something's wrong with Angie and the baby," I blurted out.

"What happened?" she asked me.

I told her about the text messages and trying to get ahold of everyone. I then told her about finding the blood in the Jeep. A doctor came out while I was talking to Mom.

"We've stabilized your wife. She lost some blood, which caused her blood pressure to drop. We want to take her to surgery and do a Caesarian," he informed me.

"Did you hear that?" I asked Mom.

"Tell them to go ahead."

I just nodded. They needed me to sign a form. I didn't even think about being too young, I just signed the release form.

Greg, Mom and Dad all showed up about the same time. Luckily, Mom had filled them in as to what was going on. Greg had been taking a final and had turned off his phone. Dad forgot his at home. I hadn't even thought about just calling the country club. Mom's excuse was she'd sold a farm and had been in a bad cell area.

I became an uncle thirty minutes later. Nathan Edward Dawson was born at 4:35 p.m. He and Angie were doing fine. I missed the birth because I was put in charge of picking up Mac and Kyle at daycare. Greg had called ahead so there weren't any problems with me picking up my niece and nephew.

They were bouncing off the walls when they saw Unca David was there to pick them up. When we got to their apartment, Mac informed me they wanted a snack. I found Angie had tangerines so I peeled them each one and removed the seeds.

While I had them occupied with their snacks, I went to the bathroom and cleaned up the mess.

I will admit that I might not be the best uncle: I fed them toaster waffles and pudding for dinner. They didn't seem to like any of my other suggestions. After dinner, we played for a while, then I got some blankets and we snuggled up in front of the couch and watched *Finding Nemo*.

Greg found us all asleep. I woke up when he picked up Mac to take her to bed. I picked up Kyle and tagged along. We put them in their beds and then he joined me in the living room. When the door was closed, he pulled me into a tight hug. I could tell he was emotional.

"Angie told me what you did. She said she felt dizzy and knew something wasn't right when the contractions started to come too quickly. Thank you for coming and getting her. The doctor told me the placenta tore from the wall of her uterus, causing some bleeding. I guess it's normal to have some, but this was more serious. I hate to think what might have happened."

"Do you have pictures?" I asked, trying to get his mind on what was important—his wife and new baby.

He wiped his eyes and got his phone out. I fell in love with the little guy at first sight. I could see the pride Greg had for his second son.

◊◊◊

I stopped at a drugstore and got boxes of bubble-gum cigars with blue wrappers that announced that it was 'A Boy.' I planned to hand them out at school tomorrow. I walked into the kitchen and gave a box to Dad and one to Mom. They could take them to work.

I then grabbed a bucket and rag to go clean my Jeep. Duke came out and helped me. I think his job was to make sure no squirrels invaded his territory. When I was done, I forwarded little Nathan's picture to everyone and posted it on my social media pages.

◊◊◊

Tuesday May 12

I had one of my worst days in a long time. I'd obviously left my brain at home today. It'd been a little over a week since I pissed off Coach Hope by knocking his son out. He was our substitute teacher for Coach Stevens. The lesson plan was to review for our Geometry final. He'd drawn a trapezoid on the board with three angles identified and told us to find 'X', the measure of the fourth angle.

I, in my infinite wisdom, had decided it would better to study for my English Lit exam, which was next period. Everyone furiously worked out the answer. I think all teachers have a sixth sense as to who was paying attention and who wasn't. Normally I'd be one of those who did listen. I think I may have counted on Coach Hope ignoring me. Wrong.

"David, you seem to be done. Come up to the board and show us how you found 'X.'" Coach Hope challenged.

If he planned to embarrass me in front of the class, I would at least try and take a stab at the answer. I glanced over at Pam's sheet, and she had '24' circled. Pam was a 'C' student, so I wasn't confident she was right. Then I was inspired.

"Sir, could you repeat the question?" I asked.

"Please find X."

I looked at the trapezoid. Angle A was 87°, angle B was 94°, and angle C was 98°. Angle X was unknown.

I knew 24 wasn't the right answer. I'd have to get Pam into her study group before our test on Thursday. I felt my classmates' eyes drill into my back. I decided to go with my inspired idea. I walked up the board and circled 'X' and stepped back.

Coach looked at me, at the board, then at me again. He then looked back at the board and blinked.

"And?" he prodded.

"You said to find X. It's right there," I answered.

I guess he no longer had a sense of humor since he sent me to the office. I had to explain to the vice-principal why I was there. She at least found the humor in what I'd said. She agreed that technically I was right and sent me to my English Lit final.

◊◊◊

After school, I took Cassidy's spot and ran *sixty minutes of hell* so she could study for finals. We had a small turnout since it was finals week, but we decided to go ahead and hold the workout. I know I always was more focused after I'd exercised.

When I got home, I found my trusty hound was full of energy. Since I still had my workout clothes on, I took Duke for a run. He'd started to get big and Dad had told me he was about 80% grown. He was currently being a teenager and acted like a total goof half the time. I had gotten him a retractable leash so he could have some freedom while we ran. His stamina had gotten much better. We did a quick mile run to bleed off some of his built-up energy.

I took him up to my apartment and showered. Dad told me over the intercom that dinner was almost ready. Duke and I went to the kitchen to find Peggy Pratt helping my dad cook. It reminded me of when we dated. I wondered what was going on.

It was amazing how we fell right back into our old patterns. Mom arrived just as we sat down to eat. She gave me a curious look and I just shrugged. I had no idea why Peggy was here. Ever since she started dating Mitch we had been friendly, but I'd taken a step back to give them their space. She seemed happy, so I left it alone, even though I couldn't really stand the guy. It wasn't anything specific, just something about him rubbed me the wrong way. I had never delved into it very much because it felt a lot like jealousy. To be honest, that was part of it; but, just because you think people are out to get you, doesn't mean it isn't so.

After dinner Peggy, Duke and I went to my apartment. I planned to study. Peggy had other plans. She sat down on the couch next to me and then pulled me into a kiss. I was so shocked I let her kiss me. I'm ashamed to admit to being an active participant since Peggy had always been one of my favorite people to kiss. The thought of Mitch kept flashing in the back of my mind. I was about to stop her when she started to cry.

A guy's first reaction was always to try and fix something. Tami had pounded into me it might be better to let my first reaction pass. She explained I was a 'stupid boy' and should let women decide what to do. Tami had said something about girls being smarter than boys when it came to stuff like this. I fell back on what any Dawson would do in this situation: I shut up and just comforted her. Peggy would tell me her story when she was ready.

"David, are you my friend?"

"Of course, I am."

"No, I want you to think about your answer before you say you are."

I didn't know what she was getting at, but it was something big. My first thought was her parents were getting a divorce. Peggy had moved in with us for a week when things had gotten bad last fall. I wasn't sure what we would do if she needed to move in again. Greg and Angie planned to come home for the summer and the extra bedrooms would be taken. I didn't see her living with me as a good option, especially if she were dating Mitch. I didn't think he would appreciate her sharing my bed, even if nothing happened. The bottom line was if she needed help, I would be there for her.

"There's nothing to think about. You and I were friends before we dated. Once we did, I knew we'd be friends for life. I'm here for you," I assured her.

"I want to believe you because I need a friend right now."

I waited her out as she stared at me. I wasn't sure what she was looking for, or what I should have done. Peggy buried her face in my chest and began to sob. I started to think this had nothing to do with her parents. I started to plan the demise of Mitch.

Peggy pulled her face away from my chest, and the look on her face made my heart break.

"I'm pregnant," she whispered.

My first instinct was to jump up and go track down Mitch. The only problem with my plan was that Peggy needed me. We didn't say anything for a long time. I just held her and let her cry it out.

Of course, the whole time I seethed about him not respecting her wishes. Peggy wanted to be a virgin on her wedding night. I admit to having had a short-lived pang about being a gentleman and respecting her wishes, but thankfully, it was momentary. I couldn't see Mitch forcing her to do anything. Peggy was stronger than that. If I found out he'd forced her, he wouldn't survive the week without grievous bodily harm.

Peggy must have been exhausted because she fell asleep in my arms. I was able to get her to let go of me so I could study. I still had finals. History was tomorrow and Suzanne had given me passages to reread. She had taken the class and remembered the kinds of things I'd be tested on. I wanted them fresh in my mind for tomorrow.

After two hours, her eyes fluttered open and she looked confused until she saw me.

"How long was I asleep?" she asked with that husky rasp you sometimes get when you just wake up.

I went to the refrigerator and found a bottle of water. She took a big swig and sat up.

"A couple of hours. You needed it."

"I really do need a good night's sleep. You mind if I stay here?" she asked.

"I don't mind, but you better tell your mom where you are. I don't need her hunting me down."

"You'd be fine with my mom. For some reason she likes you. Now my dad ...." She left unsaid that he wasn't my biggest fan.

She called her mom and I could tell the conversation was tense. When she was done, she gave me a weak smile.

"Mitch has been looking for me. I blocked his calls," she said. "I'm going to go take a bath. Can I use one of your t-shirts?"

"You've never asked before. Why would tonight be any different?" I said, reminding her of all the t-shirts she'd taken in the past.

"It was different, then," she said, obviously flustered.

"I know, but you're my friend. All my friends seem to take t-shirts. Why should you be any different?"

"Okay. I was just checking," she told me and headed to the bedroom.

I grabbed Duke's leash. I didn't need him taking off. I went out to let him do his business and then went to find Mom and Dad. I told them what I knew and asked for any advice they could give me.

407

"All you can do is be there for her right now. She needs someone she can count on," Dad began, and then he asked the big question. "If she asks, what advice are you going to give her?"

Surprisingly, our family had never talked about the pros and cons of abortion.

"I'm not sure I could advise her. If it was a perfect world, I'd side with having the baby. I'm not one of those who tries to split hairs. I think it's obvious a baby's alive at conception. I also believe one size does not fit all. Peggy's of an age where having a baby could really affect her life."

"You didn't seem too worried about Angie," Mom said, to play devil's advocate.

"Angie had a support system: Greg, who'd stand up and give her baby a father; you and Dad; and me. I knew if it came down to it, we'd raise the baby as our own. Peggy doesn't have the same assurances."

"Would you be willing to help?" Dad asked.

I laughed.

"As much as a friend can. I won't be there for the important things, though. Peggy will need to decide how she handles it with her family and Mitch. It's not my place to take over."

Mom got up and gave me a hug.

"I think my little boy's growing up. You can help, but you can't live her life. Ultimately, Peggy must decide what's right for her. She's lucky to have you as a friend."

◊◊◊

Chapter 21 – Family Night

Wednesday May 13

Peggy kissed me awake.

"Morning," I said.

"Can we talk?" she asked.

My clock read six o'clock. I really didn't have an excuse not to, so I nodded.

"First of all, I wanted to thank you for never pressuring me to go all the way. I can't really blame Mitch, because I allowed him to take my virginity. I knew after it happened it was a mistake. There's no greater evidence than what's growing in my belly."

"Have you told him?" I asked.

"You're the only person who knows."

"Are you two going out?"

"I plan on breaking it off. I've come to realize Mitch is not Mr. Forever—at least, not for me. I won't let myself be trapped into marrying him," Peggy confessed, and then got a playful look as she nudged my ribs. "If you were older, I might try and trap you."

"Try a *lot* older," I suggested.

"I hear you. Having a baby right now was not in the plans," she said, and then looked off into space.

"Do you know what you're going to do?"

"I may have to get an abortion. My scholarship is for running cross-country. If I can't do it because I'm pregnant, I won't have the money to go to school."

"Can your parents help?"

"Not if I'm in Arizona and they're here."

"No, I meant financially?"

"Maybe, but I don't want to count on it. Dad's been a little flaky over the past year. Turning up pregnant might send him over the edge."

"If you decide to have the baby, you know I can help you with money for school, housing, and daycare, through

Angie's charity. Mitch would also have responsibilities for helping financially. I know his family can afford to help."

"Thanks. Knowing you're there to help takes a lot of pressure off me," she said as she hugged me. "I need to get home before my mom and dad kill me. I have a couple of finals today that I might want to study for."

She got dressed and left. I had planned on going back to sleep, but some furry-butt was awake and demanded to be let out of his crate.

◊◊◊

As I walked up to the school, Mitch came marching towards me. He had bad news radiating from him. He must have figured out Peggy was with me last night, so I put my hands up to slow him down.

"We just talked," I told him.

Mitch took a swing at me. He had terrible technique and I easily ducked his punch. I sidestepped him and backed up towards the school. He made another run at me.

"Mitch, you're just going to get hurt," I said, trying one more time to reason with him.

I easily dodged him again. We were now drawing a crowd. I kept my hands up to fend him off. I knew there were cameras recording everything. I didn't want to get suspended for fighting because of the school's zero-tolerance rules. I wanted the record to show I kept backing off.

Peggy came running out and stood in front of me.

"Mitch, stop this right now!" she yelled at him.

"I know what you did! I drove by his house last night and again early this morning!" he yelled at us.

This got everyone's attention. He looked like he planned to hit her, but he finally got control of himself and walked away. Peggy went with him to try and talk to him. He got in his car and drove away, leaving her crying in the parking lot. Pam went to go get her. I figured it was better if we weren't seen together, after Mitch's declaration.

◊◊◊

At lunch, Pam found me in the lunch line, as I tried to figure out why I wasn't bringing my own lunch. They had some foul-smelling greens which had been boiled to within an inch of their life. In the next trough was Spam loaf. Their meatloaf was bad enough, but to make it with Spam? The third trough was empty. It must have been better than the first two because it was gone. I guessed it was peanut butter and apples again. I walked down the line and picked up several apples.

I shuddered when Pam got the loaf option. The girl must have a death wish. She guided me to a table where we could have some privacy.

"Are you really going to eat that?" I asked.

"Why, do you want to trade?" she asked as she took a bite.

She made a face and then stole one of my apple slices. There was no use fighting her over it. I just chopped up another apple and gave it to her.

"How's Tracy doing?" I asked, feeling guilty that I hadn't been to visit her.

"Much better now that they have her medication fixed. You should go to her house for dinner some evening. She misses you."

"Maybe once finals are over. I miss her mom's cooking, and Tracy."

The conversation slowed down and we ate our apples. Pam finally decided to tell me why we were eating lunch together.

"Are you dating Peggy again?"

"No, we're just friends."

"Why did she spend the night with you last night?"

"She has some problems in her personal life and needed someone to talk to."

"Okay, I guess. What's going on with you and Harper?"

I had a feeling this was going somewhere I wasn't going to like.

"She's no longer my girlfriend, but we're still friends."

"What about the girl you took to Prom?"

"Sarah and I are friends. Did you want to ask about Mona?"

She blushed and looked at me for an answer.

"Friends. Is there a point to all this?" I asked.

"Tracy wanted to be absolutely clear you were not in a relationship with anyone," Pam explained.

"I'm almost scared to ask this, but why?"

"Because Mike is dating Gina, Jeff is with Cassidy, Wolf is seeing April, Jim is going out with Piper. That leaves just you and Tim who are currently acceptable to all the girls and are not dating anyone."

"Does Tim need to be part of this conversation?" I asked, being a smartass.

"Please," Pam said.

I sent him a text. He came over and sat down.

"What's up, slut? I hear you're poaching girls who have boyfriends now," Tim teased me.

"Tell Gina I'm coming after her next."

"I think Jeff's more worried you'll be after Cassidy."

"Do I look like I have a death wish?" I asked Tim.

Pam cleared her throat.

"I think we're in trouble again," I informed Tim.

We both looked at Pam.

"You're both invited to Tracy's lake house this weekend."

"This sounds like fun. Tracy has a boat. We could go water skiing," I told Tim.

"You could bring your new toy," Tim said.

412

"Good call. My brother can't come and hog all the fun, since he has the new baby."

"So you guys'll come?" Pam asked.

We both nodded.

"Oh, and you can't tell anyone about it," Pam added.

We had visions of water sports all weekend. We even planned to bring our fishing poles. Tim agreed we should keep our trip quiet because it meant more time on the jet water board for each of us.

◊◊◊

After school, Cassidy and I rolled out a wrestling mat so we could spar. We had just gotten ready to have a little fun when Mitch came storming in.

"What did you do to Peggy?" he huffed.

"I listened to her."

"That couldn't have been all. She broke up with me."

"I'm sorry to hear that," I said.

I must not have sounded sincere, because he wanted to punch me again.

"Before you get your ass kicked, why don't you watch Cassidy and me spar for a minute and then decide if you're man enough," I warned him.

Cassidy must have been intent on what Mitch and I were saying and wasn't paying attention because she about shit when I tossed her on her ass. My little ninja recovered and we went at it furiously for a minute. I then turned to see Mitch try to sucker-punch me. I ducked, and Cassidy snatched his fist out of the air and used his momentum to toss him with serious intent. I jumped on him and with my knees pinned his shoulders to the ground. Mitch's eyes went wide when he figured out I could hold him in place and turn his face into a punching bag.

"Please," he begged.

"Are you going to do right by her?" I asked.

"You know?"

"I know," I confirmed.

His face scrunched up and he began to cry. My desire to kick his butt left me. I let Mitch up and he ran from the gym. Cassidy gave me a funny look.

"I can never get them to cry just by talking to them."

I smiled at her.

"The student becomes the teacher," I teased her.

I admit it, I had tears in my eyes two seconds later. She concluded her method was easier.

◊◊◊

Friday May 15

Today was a half day. We would get our test scores and then be free for the summer. I was happy to report I'd gotten straight A's again. The class rankings showed Jeff had edged Alan out of the top spot. Gina was fourth and I was fifth. Mike was now in the seventh spot. If I didn't take AP (Advanced Placement) classes, I would slip in the class rankings next year.

Coach Hope had sent me a message to meet him in his office right after school about this summer. When I arrived, I was directed to the conference room. I found the coaching and training staff along with Tim, Jim and Alan.

"I'm sure we're all on the same page as far as wanting to win our second State Championship," Coach said to our nodding heads.

"I want to avoid a repeat of last year's fiasco where we had, in essence, two separate teams. I think in a large part it was due to not working out as a team. I've made arrangements to have the facilities here open all summer. The school is going to pay the coaches and trainers to be here to supervise your activities. I asked the training staff to join us to talk to you about strength and conditioning."

With that, Coach turned the meeting over to Jill.

"I was asked by Coach Hope to come up with strength and conditioning programs for everyone. Coach Stevens and the strength coach at State have helped design a program for each position's needs. I've also talked to Bo Harrington, David's quarterback coach, and he's helped me quite a bit.

"My plan is to use Monday and Tuesday to get the varsity started. The rest of the week will be for the JV and the freshmen coming in," Jill said and then sat down.

Coach Diamond stood up and went to the front.

"We're going to change the offense. David talked to the coaching staff at Kentucky and they had some interesting ideas. What it boils down to is the triple option, run from the shotgun."

"How are we supposed to defend against that?" Tim asked.

"Exactly! This offense will take time to learn, but with these new tools I think we can pick it up quickly. Speaking of which, Alan, show them what we have."

Alan turned on the big-screen TV and it showed what was on his tablet.

"David asked a few of us to either create or find software for football. We ended up finding a product I think you'll all like. The playbook can be searched by specific play or you can look at it by formation," Alan told us as he opened the *Playbook* portion of the software.

Alan opened a basic 'I' formation and then selected the play 'Dive.' On the screen it showed a typical playbook representation of the blocking assignments and where the runner was supposed to go. On the right there were boxes with different defensive formations. Alan switched from the current display of a four-three defense—four linemen and three linebackers—to a five-two formation. Now it showed how the play should be run against that defensive alignment.

"As you can see, the playbook is dynamic. The hard part was getting it set up. Luckily, I had a lot of help from the audiovisual geek squad here at Lincoln, and the

University of Kentucky guys let me upload a lot of their plays. Now for the fun part," Alan said.

He pointed to boxes with video icons under the play. He clicked on the first one. It was an animated version of the play, with Coach Diamond using a mouse to point to each player and explaining what their responsibilities were. The next button showed our team running the play in a game.

The final thing he showed us was you could flip the play from 'Dive Right' to 'Dive Left' with just a click of the button.

Alan then backed out of the *Playbook* section and pulled up *Scouting Report*. Our opponents for next year were listed. He clicked on our archrival Eastside and smiled.

"We were able to get every team in the conference to exchange game films from last year, all except Eastside. For them, we had to contact their opponents. Under each team, there are options. You can look at game film of them on offense or defense," Alan said as he showed a play on offense when they played us.

"You can also see their playbook. I won't waste your time now, because it's the same as ours. Another section is *Situation*," he told us, and then clicked on 'Red Zone Defense.' "The key to making all this work is putting in down, distance, time left, our formation and several other factors. You can use this to figure out what's the most likely defense they'll be in."

Alan clicked on one of the defenses and then played the coaching video. It was Alan's voice telling us what defense they were in and showing us what our keys were to identify it. I could see this helping us prepare for games.

"The final section I want to show is the *Game Manager*. You select your opponent, down, distance, and yard line. It'll give you the best three running plays and the best three passing plays to run against your opponent."

The coaching staff and Alan all had smiles on their faces as the three of us sat in stunned silence. I had no idea they'd been working so hard behind the scenes.

"We'll be giving you online access to the new offense on Monday," Coach Diamond told us. "I would hope you'd use the software to learn the plays before the season starts. If you'd happen to get together and practice them on your own time, that would be great."

Coach Hope assigned us each a coach to be our main contact. Jim was given Coach Stevens and Tim was paired with Moose. I would work with Coach Diamond. Then Coach Hope gave us some great news.

"I have one last announcement: Ty Wilson, from Washington, is transferring in. His parents just bought a house and he'll be joining us in a few weeks. I hope you guys will welcome him and get him up to speed."

We would have some serious depth at running back with Bert, Ed, Jake, Mike and now Ty. I wondered if Coach Diamond would move one of them to Bill's old position so we could get a majority of them on the field at the same time. I was almost positive Jeff would lock down the other wideout slot and Wolf would play tight end. This meant we had five running backs to fill three open skill positions. At the very least, we would be fresh late in the game.

◊◊◊

After I was done with the coaches, I went to State and helped Greg and Angie pack and move back home. Greg was really out of shape. Going up and down the three stories at our place just about killed him. We arranged it so Nate was put into my old room. Kyle and Mac were put into one of the rooms across the hall. The remaining third-floor bedroom was made into a playroom. Mom had bought bunk beds with safety rails for Kyle and Mac.

By the end of the day, I was ready to kill my sister-in-law. She was doing a lot of pointing and complaining. I realized she'd just had a baby, but being bossy only goes so far. I started to regret not going out tonight.

Tonight, there was a big graduation bash for the seniors. Cassidy had suggested I skip it because Brad and Tommy were going to be there, not to mention Mitch. I was fine with that since we had a family night. Dad grilled steaks and I was able to play uncle with my niece and nephews.

More Books by G. Younger

Sell Anything On Craigslist!

Jeremy Tucker thought he lived in the most boring town in the world. This town held its residents in the palm of its hand, and it knew everything about everyone that lived there—the good, the bad, every sin, every secret. This quiet little town was about to change, and all because he put an ad on craigslist. Some would say he was a genius, while others would accuse him of being the Devil himself. Read his story and you decide.

www.gyounger.com/sell-anything-on-craigslist/

Excerpt:

I used to think our little town, tucked away in the mountains of West Virginia and buried in the backwoods, was the most boring spot on the planet. This was the place where nothing exciting happened and nothing was ever going to change. The place felt like it was a movie set from the 1950s. Each morning, as the sun began to peek over the ridge of the valley, you would hear the old milk truck shuddering down the back alley as he made his delivery just like it had been done for over 75 years. People liked tradition, and change was not easily welcomed.

As the sun would reach the crest of the ridge, people would be up and about, which was irritating for the teens in our town. My Grandma Tucker always said, '*Be thankful for another day, you never know when it might be your last, so don't miss a second of it,* which was usually followed with, *Get your butt out of bed!'* People were early risers, and by the time I was out of the house the old women would be sitting on their front porches, slowly rocking with a steaming cup of coffee clutched in their hands, watching everything that happened.

419

Our little town was great for kids because we were allowed to run wild. No one worried about someone snatching a child like they did in the big cities. In our little town, everyone knew each other and kept an eye out. While we were allowed our freedom, there was a price. If you did anything wrong, it beat you home, and there was a butt-whupping waiting for you. My granny was an *expert* with a hickory switch...

Our little town had a rhythm. Mondays were back to work or school; Tuesday was laundry day; Wednesday evening was church; Thursday was for doing the grocery shopping at the Shop 'N Save, the only grocery store in town; Friday was for football; Saturday you did your chores; and Sunday was for church and family.

This little town held us in the palm of its hand, and it knew everything about us; the good, the bad, every sin, every secret, and everything was known about each and every resident. Most people were from here. You could trace family trees back many generations to the Founders. Only a few ever left, and if they did, you never saw them again. My secret desire was to be one of the few. I wanted to be a writer, and to do that I needed to experience life outside our little town.

Our quiet little town was about to change, and all because I put an ad on Craigslist.

While normal folk cut their grass, or made out at the overpass, my imagination was taking flight. Some would say I was a genius, while others would accuse me of being the Devil himself. What they all agreed upon was that I was justified in what I'd done.

www.gyounger.com/sell-anything-on-craigslist/

◊◊◊

Stupid Boy Series

For updates on the series follow the link below.

Stupid Boy is a series of books about a small Midwestern town filled with cute girls, Friday-night football games, and life lessons that stir up some major drama and fun.

To everyone who knows him, David Dawson is your stereotypical nerd, the good kid who has a great family life and good friends. A cute girl, way out of his league—according to his friends—leads him astray. His sudden shift to hanging out with the wrong crowd sends him spiraling into teenage depression and upsets his best friends. It all comes to a sudden end when a girl at a party he throws almost dies.

It is his crucible. Crucible is a great word. It means to go through a severe test. For David, it means he must take responsibility for his actions. He is sent to his uncle's farm for the summer to get his life back on track. What he doesn't know is his uncle John has a degree in child psychology. With a combination of hard work and long talks, he begins to pull his life back together. When he returns from his exile, he's changed. He is no longer the slightly pudgy-looking nerd due to a growth spurt and hard work on the farm. His best friend, Tami Glade, isn't quite sure what to make of her 'stupid boy.' Before he was sent to the farm, she'd screamed at him out of frustration that she never wanted to see him again.

David has changed. He is suddenly popular, way too handsome for his own good, and going out for football. The changes aren't just physical. He seems more confident and focused. He even has Life Goals. Tami isn't quite sure what to make of the new David. Her 'stupid boy' of a best friend has been transformed into a hunk. The problem is, he doesn't realize it, and she isn't sure if they should be just friends, or more.

www.gyounger.com/a-stupid-boy-story-series/

◊◊◊

Notes from Author

Thank you for reading *Sophomore Year Spring*. I hope you enjoyed this book. If you have a moment to post a review to let others know about the story, I would greatly appreciate it! I love hearing from fans.

Want to know when I release new books? Here are some ways to stay updated:
- Check out my webpage at Books2Read.com: Author's Page
- Visit my website at www.GYounger.com

Thank you again and I hope we meet again between the pages of another book.
- Greg

CPSIA information can be obtained
at www.ICGtesting.com
Printed in the USA
FSHW011944091118
53700FS